PENGUIN BOOKS

THIS PLACE IS
STILL BEAUTIFUL

PENGUIN BOOKS

UK | USA | Canada | Ireland | Australia
India | New Zealand | South Africa

Penguin Books is part of the Penguin Random House group of companies
whose addresses can be found at global.penguinrandomhouse.com.

www.penguin.co.uk
www.puffin.co.uk
www.ladybird.co.uk

Penguin
Random House
UK

First published in the USA by Balzer + Bray, an imprint of HarperCollins,
and in Great Britain by Penguin Random House Children's, 2022

001

Text design by Jessie Gang
Printed and bound in Great Britain by Clays Ltd, Elcograf S.p.A.

The authorized representative in the EEA is Penguin Random House Ireland,
Morrison Chambers, 32 Nassau Street, Dublin D02 YH68

A CIP catalogue record for this book is available from the British Library

ISBN: 978–0–241–53261–4

All correspondence to:
Penguin Books, Penguin Random House Children's
One Embassy Gardens, 8 Viaduct Gardens, London SW11 7BW

THIS PLACE IS STILL BEAUTIFUL

XIXI TIAN

PENGUIN BOOKS

To my parents, for every sacrifice;
and to Chris, for every beautiful day.

One

The predicted rain on the first day of summer never comes, meaning I can count on two things: my mother spending most of the morning in the garden, and Thom Froggett coming by the Sprinkle Shoppe for a double scoop of Rocky Road in a waffle cone.

My mother is endlessly good at gardening, which is why she spends an unreasonable amount of her free time furiously deadheading her prize-winning golden roses in the backyard. My sister, Margaret, is endlessly good at school, which is why she charged through high school as valedictorian and class president, signed up for a double major in economics and political science with a minor in gender studies at NYU, and is now spending the summer before her sophomore year at a fancy summer internship with a McBain-type consulting firm in Manhattan.

I, on the other hand, am a B student, a second-chair flautist who sometimes still goes right when I should be going left in the drill set for marching band, and I suppose, above average at applying eyeliner with one swipe using the rearview mirror of my car in the mornings.

One thing I am better at than both Mama and Margaret is scooping ice cream (mainly because they're lactose intolerant, so they never eat ice cream), and thus, I have a summer job at the Sprinkle Shoppe. I am determined to use my unremarkable talent to do something remarkable: catch the attention of a certain Thom Froggett, soccer star and hazel-eyed underwear model look-alike.

Thom and I have been in each other's lives peripherally since elementary school because his last name and mine (Flanagan) are close to each other in the alphabet, although always with a certain Justin Frick right in between. So from grades one to eight, we were almost together when we lined up every day. Except instead of chatting up Thom, I endured a slow transition of first-grade Justin flicking spitballs into my hair to eighth-grade Justin trying to convince me to be his girlfriend.

On the other side, Thom was always blissfully oblivious, except for when the barrier of Justin was removed. The few days a year that Justin stayed home sick were the greatest days of my young life. Sadly, waiting for spongy chicken nuggets and plastic, stab-able bags of chocolate milk in the hot lunch line was not the ideal backdrop for a grand romance, and the young love of my formative years went unrequited.

In high school, we didn't have lunch lines anymore and we were in different classes, so we were separated by more than the unfortunately placed Justin Frick. Puberty hit Thom like a freight train, and basically overnight, he shot up a foot in height and learned how to style his dark blond hair so that it swooped gently over his forehead with the blessed curve of an angel's wing.

He got a girlfriend at the end of freshman year. And that was that, until they broke up this past January of our junior year, as I found out approximately four days later from my best friend, Violet (whose particular prowesses are Filipino home cooking and finding out about people's personal lives when social media doesn't give them away).

Violet had told me her plan after school as we shouldered our backpacks and headed out the door. "This is it," she said. "Your chance."

"The way you've delivered this news is a little creepy," I told her, wincing against the sharp midwestern wind as we climbed the hill toward the parking lot. "Like I've been stalking him my entire life."

She shrugs unrepentantly.

"I just think that it seems crass to jump on this right after his breakup."

"You snooze, you lose. That boy is going to go faster than hotcakes. You don't want to still be formulating your plan when Cheerleader Number Two catches his eye."

"They have names, Violet. Besides, I don't want to be a rebound."

"Worrying about being a rebound is an abstract concern right now. It's like worrying about whether you'll like the weather in Georgia enough to go to college there before you've even applied to any schools. You deal with that problem later."

"Fair point," I acknowledged.

We stuffed our snow-dusted selves into Violet's tiny Honda Civic and cranked up the heat before continuing our plot.

"Look, here's what you should do," she said. I should not have been surprised that Violet already had a plan.

Essentially, it was to work at the Sprinkle Shoppe, because Violet and Thom *did* have a class together, and he mentioned to her once that he went there for ice cream on summer afternoons, like it was his job, and ordered the same thing, right after his daily run, because it was on his way home. "He loves ice cream," Violet said triumphantly, as if she had just invented a new element for the periodic table.

I paused and thought about it. "Vi, this is a supremely stupid plan."

"No, it's not!"

"Yeah, it is."

"Well," she said, turning toward me defensively, "feel free to contribute. Do you have a better idea?"

I didn't.

"Just apply when the time comes," she instructed bossily.

On my first day at the job, the Sprinkle Shoppe greets me with a blast of cold air when I push the door open. The little silver bell over the door tinkles.

Aside from just providing me a paycheck and an opportunity to stake out Thom, I like the place. The building is small and brick in downtown, with an old-timey vibe. The name is in big curving letters, slightly chipped white paint, on a wooden sign that hangs beneath the sharp angle of the eaves in front. I like the heavy silver handle of the door and the cabinets, the checkered black-and-white floor, and the scalloped trim that overhangs the serving counter. It reminds me of one of those wholesome fifties hangouts, where teenage boys in letterman jackets would take girls out on ice cream dates and ask them to go steady.

Audrey is already behind the counter in her apron. Audrey is one of those cheerleaders who Violet was concerned about. She has wavy hair the color of rust and these long golden eyelashes resting on the lightest dusting of freckles, like sprinkles on top of an ice cream cone. Incredibly pretty, except right now she's scowling at me.

"You're late," she says.

I check my phone. "No, I'm not."

"Two minutes by my watch."

I think about saying something rude, like *I'm sure the Sprinkle Shoppe was totally inundated in those one hundred and twenty seconds of time that I wasn't here*, but I decide it's not worth the effort. I have to be around her all summer, after all. "Sorry."

"Whatever."

Audrey has worked here the last four months. For the Sprinkle Shoppe, that's practically forever, because most people just work the short summer months when business ramps up. It's just my luck that she and I have the same shifts, so she gets to tell me what to do.

"You," she says, jabbing an ice cream scoop in my direction like a dictator, "are going to scoop the ice cream. *I'll* handle the payments."

No arguments here. Math was never my strong suit.

She hands me the silver scoop. It looks pretty self-explanatory, but then the first customer who comes in asks for a scoop of mint chocolate chip and a scoop of regular chocolate. I don't get as full a scoop of ice cream as I need to for the mint chocolate chip, and I don't pack the scoop of regular chocolate tight enough onto the first, so it tumbles to the ground with a soft splat. This is apparently harder than it looks, and I also apparently oversold my scooping skills.

Audrey has to clean it up. She rolls her eyes so many times in the next two hours that I'm afraid she's just going to start looking at me with her eyeballs already fixed toward the ceiling to save time. But by the tenth customer, I've pretty much gotten the hang of it.

I feel almost like a natural when the door swings open.

It's him. Just like Violet promised.

At that moment, I silently thank her for having so much foresight. She's wise after all. I owe her a gallon of free cookies 'n cream.

Thom is in his running clothes. My eyes automatically move to the hard outline of his calves as he strides toward the counter, shaking his hair, darkened with sweat, out of his eyes. I think about my next move. I think about taking his order. I think about doing literally anything other than stand here like a buffoon.

Audrey sweeps past me and seizes the ice cream scoop right out of my fingers. I'm so startled I don't put up any resistance.

"Hi, Thom," she says, smiling with all her dimples. Scooping ice cream isn't too menial for her when it's Thom's order she's taking. It occurs to me that other people—namely, Audrey—might be using the same plan and might be better at it than me.

I've lost my chance. I can't undermine Audrey's authority, so I slink away. She motions sharply for me to move to the register. Like Violet said, you snooze, you lose.

"Would you like the usual?" I hear her say.

"You know it. Thanks." His voice is friendly. I strain to hear any hint of flirtation like a thirsty person strains for the last drop of water in a canteen. I don't think he's looked in my direction, even though I'm right here.

I watch Audrey pile two perfectly round scoops of Rocky Road into a waffle cone as if she's competing in the Olympics of ice cream service. She deserves the gold.

Thom takes the ice cream gingerly and moves down the line until he's at the register. Right in front of me. I snap to attention.

"Hi," he says, all tanned skin and white teeth. Even though he's coming off a run, he smells good, a magical combination of musk and apples. Can sweat smell good?

My heart tumbles down into my gut and is lost. What does one say in response to hi?

"It's been a while since the junior high lunch line, huh?"

"Yeah," I say, surprising myself. "I barely know what to do without Justin Frick in between us."

I make him laugh. It feels really good.

"You're working here, are you?"

"Yep. Needed a summer job."

"Well, you should know that I come here every day."

I resist the urge to say, *So I've heard*. Because that would be extra creepy, and even I have some sense of self-preservation. "Okay, should that be a problem for me?"

"I hope not." He's grinning. We're flirting. This is unbelievable! From the other side of me, Audrey is glaring daggers at me, but I can't be stopped.

By now there's another customer behind him who's already gotten ice cream. I remember that I'm supposed to be ringing him up. I look down at the cash register in amazement, because I realize at that moment that I have absolutely no idea how to use this archaic-looking machine. I'm afraid if I push something wrong, it'll just break.

Helplessly, I glance back up at Thom. "I'm sorry," I say. "This is my first day, so I have no idea what I'm doing."

"No problem," he says. "I have cash, and I know how much this costs." He hands over three crumpled dollars and two quarters.

I take it. "I trust that you're not pulling a fast one and giving yourself a discount, because I really don't know how much two scoops costs."

"I'm not," he says as he turns to go. "But for the record, it actually costs three dollars and thirty cents. You can keep the change, though." He winks at me, and I die a thousand deaths internally.

Nothing Audrey does can ruin my summer now.

"Just admit it. I'm a genius," Violet crows as I open the door to let her in a few days later.

"It wasn't a bad idea," I admit as she blows past me.

Violet has come over every afternoon in the summer since we were kids. This year, since I've finally been pushed toward a job, we've had to scale back our daily rendezvous, because afternoon is prime ice cream shop boom time in the summer, and I'm scheduled for Mondays, Wednesdays, and Fridays. "Which means Tuesdays and Thursdays without Thom," I say, sighing.

"Sure," Violet says. "Some friend you are. I hook you up with the jock of your childhood dreams, and you don't even so much as bat an eyelid when you ditch your BFF three times a week. Are you going to be the person who completely flakes on everyone when you and Thom start dating?"

I roll my eyes.

"Don't give me that attitude!"

I escort Violet into the kitchen, swing open the freezer, and plop a sweet, sweet full tub of cookies 'n cream on the countertop triumphantly. "Courtesy of the Sprinkle Shoppe. Is that enough of a thank you?"

Violet's eyes practically bug out of her head, and her lips split into a wide grin. "It's a start."

My mother slides open the screen door to the backyard and ducks inside. She's wearing a wide-brimmed hat and grimy yellow gloves that she sheds and tosses onto the deck behind her.

"Hi, Violet," Mama says, spotting us.

"Hi, Auntie," Violet replies, waving.

"Oh, before you leave, I have things for your mama. Don't let me forget."

Violet and I have been friends for so long that it's pretty

9

normal for Mama to send her home with a cut of new roses or a container of fresh stir-fry for dinner. And Violet's mom is the same when I am there. We're like extended family.

We take our bowls of ice cream, heaped high because it's summer and because nobody's around to watch our gluttony, onto the deck. I love feeling the warmth of the stained wood under my bare feet, channeling the heat of the summer sun. I curl my toes. The ice cream is sugary and cooling. Everything feels so good.

"Your mom's roses are really taking off, huh?" Violet says.

"Early summer is the best time." Mama is almost religious about her flowers. Margaret told me she started growing them after our father left, when I was too young to remember. Since then, she's become virtually professional. She spends a good part of the warm summer months outside, inspecting, pruning, mulching, watering, and fertilizing the soil with the perfect blend of compost material to achieve ideal acidity.

Actually, one of the things I like best about our house is the backyard full of roses. The golden ones are at peak bloom in June, and they really are magnificent.

We admire the Garden of Eden for a while. Then we scrape the final liquidy residue from the inside of our bowls and step back onto the cool linoleum of our kitchen floor and drop the bowls into the sink.

The real reason that Violet comes over in the afternoons is so we can watch our favorite baking competition show on Food Network, and my house is super quiet, whereas her house is jam-packed with her younger siblings scurrying around. It's been our tradition for years and will probably continue until we go to college or Food Network finally cancels the show.

It's the show that first got me into baking. We watch, and I usually jot down the interesting ideas for me to try and re-create on my own. Violet can always count on a new batch of something sweet every week.

"I can't believe this idiot is trying to make a napoleon," Violet groans. "Does anybody actually watch the show before they go on it? Judges *hate* it when you make a napoleon. So unoriginal. You might as well whip out a package of Toll House cookies and bake those instead."

"Don't be a hater. There are plenty of interesting things you can do with a napoleon."

"Please don't make that this week," she says. "Make the lady's dessert. The peach cobbler. Looks to die for. And goes great with ice cream."

I shove her playfully. "I'm not taking orders at this time."

"You don't *have* to. Just putting it out there in the universe, in case a certain someone wants to continue showing her gratitude for her brilliant best friend, hooking her up with the boy of her dreams."

"I'll see what I can do," I say. "Besides, don't you think you're jumping the gun a bit? Thom and I have had something like two conversations."

"You're going to be together before we even hit July," she predicts.

"How are you so confident?"

"Well, first, because I know things. And second, jeez, are you really going to play dumb? You're gorgeous. There's no way he hasn't noticed."

"I'm not!" I'd kill for Violet's perfect long curls, which shine in a mass of glossy black down her back. We've had countless sleepovers, and I know she wakes up like that. Plus, she has perfect arched eyebrows that don't require any shaping.

"Yeah, you are. It's why the Sprinkle Shoppe hired you the minute you walked in, and why I would never be able to get a job there. You realize they only hire attractive people, right?"

Violet's self-deprecating bluntness makes me uncomfortable. I know she isn't trying to fish for compliments or make me feel bad. It's just how she is.

Violet, who was the first person to march up to me in third grade when she moved here from New Jersey and declare friendship when everybody else ignored me. Who steadfastly insisted on bringing kare-kare and pork adobo to school in her lunch box even though the other kids called it smelly and weird. Who probably knew from the minute she was born that she was going to grow up to be an environmental scientist and date and marry her boyfriend, Abaeze Adebayo, easygoing and soft-spoken, basically the opposite of Violet in every way.

It's one of the things I love the most about her, because she's always honest with me.

And it makes me wish I were like her. To just know what I want and be able to say exactly what I'm thinking.

If I were like that, I'd tell her that I'm not so sure about Thom liking me one day, because there's nothing particularly special about me, the girl who's the second best at everything.

Instead, I just laugh and say she should start preparing for plan B in case I botch this one.

She says, "Don't you worry, Annalie Flanagan. I'm always ready with plan B."

The manager gives me a call the morning of my Wednesday afternoon shift the next week, swearing about Audrey not being able to make it and asking me if I can hold down the fort myself.

"Of course," I exclaim. My voice comes out higher and squeakier than I mean it to, because hello, nothing seems better than having the entire shop to myself when Thom comes by. My excitement betrays me.

"Are you sure?" He sounds skeptical, and I can imagine his face. "This is, what, your fourth or fifth full shift?"

"I can definitely handle it," I say confidently. Because really, how hard can it be? I've mastered scooping, and I've even mastered the cash register. And I feel like those two things are pretty much the sum total of the job. It's not like we're doing brain surgery here.

"You have my number if anything goes wrong."

"What could go wrong?" I ask, right before everything goes wrong.

I show up for my shift, after spending two hours deciding what to wear and how to do my makeup. I didn't want to look too dolled up, like I was trying super hard. But I did want to add a little oomph to my normal look. I watched probably four YouTube makeup tutorial videos. I tried on three separate outfits. I redid my eyeliner twice. I thought about putting on subtle falsies, and then decided they were too obvious. I braided my hair, and then undid it because it looked too cutesy.

It ends up not mattering at all because there's a line of people out the door, including the entire softball team, and my hair is sticking to the back of my neck from sweat as I rush to scoop ice cream and check people out at the same time.

I'm running between scooping ice cream and running the dirty scoops under the faucet. The cones are getting low, and I have to dash to the back to get another bag of them. A family comes in with little kids, who are screaming with impatience. I'm so warm. I'm afraid that my makeup is entirely sliding off my face.

After what feels like an eternity, the softball team finally gets all the way through the line. The family sticks around, but most of the shop empties out. Luckily, there's not a lot of seating. There are a couple of tiny round tables crowded by rickety old chairs, but in general, the idea is to encourage people to get their ice cream and then get out.

I'm trying to wipe my sweat and double-check my face in my iPhone camera on selfie mode when Thom walks in. Three o'clock, on the dot. As usual, he's sweaty (which makes me feel better about myself), in his running clothes, and just about the hottest thing I've seen this side of the sun. He catches my eye behind the counter and melts into a slow grin. I melt right along with it.

"I guess you're starting to become part of my daily routine, A," he says.

Nobody calls me A. And I kind of hate it when people give me nicknames that I didn't come up with. Sometimes people want to call me Anna for short. I'm definitely not an Anna. Nor am I an "Ann" or an "Ally" or a "Lia." But Thom calling me A sounds so sweet.

"Just like old times," I say, smiling. "Double scoop of Rocky Road?"

"You got it, babe."

I like "babe" even better.

Stop grinning like an idiot, I scold myself, but I'm immune to my internal sober voice of reason.

"Where's Audrey?" he asks.

"She's out, and the manager couldn't get anyone else to sub in. But I've been okay so far. Busy day, though."

"How come I've never seen you work at the Sprinkle Shoppe before?"

"This is my first summer."

"I can see that. What made you decide to take a job here?"

Well, I can't give him the truth there. It's somewhere between Desperationville and Stalkertown. I shrug. "Needed something to do, and this seemed like a pretty low-key summer job."

"I'm glad you did."

I feel my face redden. I'm grateful it's hidden under a layer of full-coverage foundation, although it may have partially melted off already.

The scoop slides into the bucket of Rocky Road effortlessly—too effortlessly—just as the person in line behind Thom pipes up, "Hey, why is it so hot in here?"

Thom frowns. "It *is* really warm in here today."

And then it dawns on me, slowly, that the hum of the air-conditioning unit on the side of the window is gone. Instead, all I hear, as if the entire store is straining to listen, is silence.

"Um," I say. "I think the air-conditioning might be broken." I look down at the buckets of ice cream in pastel colors lined up behind the glass, and some of them are starting to get a bit . . . sludgy. "Oh shit, oh shit, oh shit."

One of the women who has a kid in tow throws me a dirty look, but I don't have time for that. I check the thermostat on the chiller that holds the tubs of ice cream for serving. It's at eight degrees Fahrenheit, which is normal. I breathe a sigh of relief. At least the ice cream isn't all going to melt into liquid in a couple of minutes. But then I run over to the window unit, the only air conditioner in this single-room brick bungalow. As I feared, it's not blowing any air. I try flicking the switch. Nothing happens. And the forecast today said it was supposed to hit ninety outside. No wonder it feels like hell itself in here.

"What's the verdict?" Thom calls over.

"It's broken. Totally broken."

He jogs over and checks it out himself. "Well, it's plugged in. Don't know what to tell you. Looks like the thing is busted. It looks pretty old."

I swear again. "Sorry, Thom."

"You should say sorry to that mom over there who looks like she's going to call the cops on you for your language." I glance over in the direction he's pointing. He's right. She's scandalized, as if I swanned up to her three-year-old and started showing him porn on my phone. I ignore her. I'm sure the Sprinkle Shoppe will miss having her as a patron. But. Bigger fish to fry at the moment.

The manager let me have the shift to myself once, and I've already screwed it up. I'm trying to think of what to do, and I'm coming up empty except to call him and confess my sins.

So I do.

He picks up after one ring, like he was waiting by his phone, expecting me to screw up. I put it on speaker, not because I want Thom to hear my humiliation, but because I'm desperately trying to hustle people out of the shop at the same time. "Jesus, Annalie. You had literally one job."

"Please don't fire me!" I say. "I didn't touch anything. It's not like I broke it myself."

"We'll see how bad the damage is. I'll call the repairman in to come fix it later." I hear him audibly exhale in a crackle, like he was expecting something bad to happen just because I was on the job.

I'm so embarrassed. Even more embarrassed to be yelled at in front of Thom, who must think I'm useless.

"Hey," Thom says, leaning over my phone, his eyes flashing with anger. "Don't be a jerk. She couldn't have known that the AC would break. Maybe *you* should be better about maintenance."

I can't stop a small smile from growing on my face. I'm definitely going to be fired now, but also . . . it was totally worth it to see Thom so mad on my behalf. His brow is furrowed, and he's frowning.

"Who's that?" comes from the voice on the phone.

"A valued customer," Thom says firmly.

"Whatever. Calm down. Just put the tubs in the freezer, clean up, and try not to mess anything else up when you close the store. I'm not going to fire you, Annalie."

"Thank you," I say meekly.

"Don't thank me. Thank the fact that there aren't enough people on payroll right now to cover your absence." He hangs up.

"Well." I look over at Thom with a sheepish grin. "That went well. Thanks for defending me."

"I'm at your service," he says, and I'm melting again. "Let's finish up."

We head back behind the counter and start slapping lids on all the open tubs. I lift them out of the trough. Heavier than I thought. Thom helps pull open the freezers in the back, which are luckily still running and blast icy-cold clouds in my face as we take turns shoving the endless flavors onto the shelf.

After we're done, it's just the two of us. My heart starts speeding up, and not because I just lifted twenty tubs of ice cream into the freezer.

"So, it sort of looks like your afternoon schedule has freed up." He's nonchalant. I'm not. Is he asking me if I'm free? He's smiling from his feet to his eyes. The boy really can lay on the charm.

"Yeah, it looks like it," I say carefully, trying not to be too eager. I want to act relaxed and cool. Instead, I feel like I have actually transformed into an awkward beaver. What are people supposed to do with their hands?

"Want to hang out at the park for a while? It's a beautiful day."

Do I?! Yes! Yes! Yes!

"Let's do it," I say, breezy as can be.

We walk out of the Sprinkle Shoppe together, I put up a Closed sign, and lock the door. I'm so light, I might as well be flying.

It's hard for me to imagine a more perfect afternoon than this. Thom and I settle on a park bench in view of younger kids playing baseball. His leg is four inches away from mine. Even though he's already gone on his run, he smells good, so wildly good. Not like gross boy gym, more like musky man supermodel. I wrap the scent around myself like a blanket under the sun. I just want to inhale him.

I try not to get distracted.

Close up, his hair is a dark blond with a slight curl at the ends. It looks a bit like a mop—a beautiful mop—and the light glinting on it makes it light up. He has smile lines that bracket his mouth. He has the kind of eyelashes that make girls jealous and make boys irritated because they catch all manner of dust and rainwater. His eyes are a shifting hazel, the color of spring puddles. The bridge of his nose is a little red from the sun. I think that in these few moments, I've completely memorized every aspect of his face.

"Well, I've finally gotten you somewhere away from the ice

cream shop. I was trying to figure out how to do that."

"I guess I should thank the AC for breaking at just the right time," I tease. I can't believe I'm making him smile.

"And that Audrey wasn't there."

"Right. Can't wait to see her again and get chewed out separately."

"Is she mean to you?"

"Oh," I say, surprised. "Not really. I mean, she's not the friendliest." Even though I don't like Audrey and she *is* especially dismissive of me, I still feel weird talking about it. I wonder for a minute if Thom is just trying to get more information about her. Maybe this is a fishing expedition to learn more about her.

"She's like that to everybody. Don't take it personally. And I think she hates me a little bit because I don't pay her as much attention as she would like. But let's stop talking about her. I want to hear about you."

I flush for the millionth time and fumble for anything to say about myself. "There's not much to know."

He leans in. "I think there's plenty to know. It's been years since we've been close to each other in the lunch line, after all."

"I can't believe you remember that."

"Well, I do. You're a hard person to forget. You've just been dodging me all this time since then."

Me? Dodging him? "I definitely haven't been dodging you."

"I was so glad to see you at the Sprinkle Shoppe last week. I've just been trying to come up with an excuse to strike up a conversation with you."

I'm speechless. "Are you always this good at your conversation striking?"

His laugh is the most delicious sound in the whole world. "I'm glad you think so."

"I know it's hard without Justin Frick in between us."

"Yes, that. I guess we'll just have to get used to it. I think we can manage. So what are your plans this summer?"

"I don't have much planned," I admit. "Working this job. And then trying to figure out what I want to do with my life, since it's time to start applying to colleges in a few months. You?"

"Me too on the college thing."

"Where do you think you'll want to go?" I have this brief, intense fantasy of us going to the same college. Holding hands on the first day and facing the scary world of adulthood together. Maybe we'll end up dating in college. Maybe he'll propose to me senior year and then we'll be one of those couples that were high school sweethearts everyone *aww*s at.

"Probably wherever I end up getting a good soccer scholarship. My dad went to Duke, so he's pretty into me going there."

"Do you want to go to Duke?"

"It's fine, I guess." He shrugs, as if he hasn't really given it much thought. "I've been there a bunch of times with my dad for games and stuff."

It's clear that Thom has known forever where he would go. I'm kind of jealous. Margaret was the same way. She knew, probably from when she was seven years old, that she was going to go to New York City, either Columbia or NYU. "I'm moving to New York, and I'm never coming back to this back-water," she announced in high school to Mama. To her credit, she followed through on it. She won't even come back this summer.

Me, on the other hand . . . I have always thought it would be great to see somewhere new. And yet. Some part of me finds it hard to say goodbye to this place. Margaret might not have been able to, but I see the beauty in where we live. I love the warm-weather sunsets, the golden stretches of corn in late summer that go so far that they seem to touch the edge of the horizon. I don't know how you could go out on a crisp winter night and not love the soft, deep silence that coats a small town after a heavy snow. I would miss being somewhere I know every corner of. There's magic in those things too.

"Where do you think you'll want to go?" Thom asks.

"I don't know." For a second, the fear of the future completely overwhelms me, but then Thom pats my hand. My heart flutters, and I'm back in the present.

"You'll figure it out," he says, confident. This close to me, I can see his light brown freckles against his tan skin. I want to get even closer.

My phone rings. It's Mama. A flash of annoyance. Why is she calling me now? I want to ignore it, but I have this thing where I can't reject phone calls, because I'm convinced it's an emergency and something terrible has happened.

Of course, it's usually just that she wants to know what to make for dinner, or something equally unimportant.

"Sorry, it's my mom," I say to Thom, and I answer the phone. "Hello?"

"Jingling," Mama says. Her voice is quiet and muffled.

I'm immediately alert.

"Mama, what's wrong?" I say urgently.

"Can you come home?" she says softly in Chinese. My mother is normally upset in only one direction: angry. The only time I've ever heard her cry was when Margaret left for college. She didn't even cry when Dad left. I'm alarmed to hear her voice wobbling on the other end of the line.

"What's wrong?" I repeat again, louder.

"Bad men came to our house."

My insides crawl with panic. "Call the police. I'm coming home."

"Police won't help. They're already gone, Jingling. Come home now." She hangs up.

My ears are ringing. I don't know what's happened, but I know that it's bad.

I turn to Thom. "I have to go home right now."

He looks really concerned, and we exchange phone numbers just in case I need anything. I'm so stressed that I don't even have it in me to be excited that Thom now has my number. "Can you call me so I know you're okay?" he says as I start walking to my car.

"Yeah, of course," I say, but it comes out without thinking. He's the farthest thing from my mind. All of a sudden, this day has completely changed.

The entire drive home feels like a never-ending dream. It's a miracle I don't run any traffic lights or get into an accident. But then again, I'm so used to the roads in this town that I could probably drive home with my eyes closed.

My mind is racing the whole time. Did someone break in? Is Mama hurt? Did anything get stolen? Even though my family isn't rich, Mama likes to keep some valuables at home. I know she keeps a hidden lockbox of gold jewelry in her bedroom. Twenty-four-carat gold. Real gold, she used to say, all heirloom jewelry from her mother in China. She took it out once to show my sister and me. She said she was keeping it for when we get married. She doesn't trust putting it at the bank. She wants it where she can see it. I can't imagine how she'll feel if somebody stole that.

We'll be able to find it, I tell myself. We'll file a police report, and surely, they'll be able to catch the guys who did it. This town is small, and people talk. It's not even sundown. Somebody must have come in broad daylight. Somebody will have seen.

I turn the corner on our street in slow motion. The house comes into view. It's a small Craftsman, the same one that we've lived in since I was a baby. I know every inch of it.

I know the parts of the front railing that have white paint chipped off, leaving the wood exposed.

I know the panel of vinyl siding that has fallen off, which we've never bothered to replace.

I know how the drainage pipe on the side of the house is slightly askew.

I would be able to identify anything different about it in a heartbeat. But I don't have to look very close to see what happened.

Our house faces west, which was not Mama's preferred direction, but my dad had talked her into it. This tidbit surfaces to me, because I'm starting to believe that west might not have been auspicious after all, just like Mama believed: the afternoon sun shines bright on the front, like a spotlight, revealing everything.

The white garage door is marred with an ugly spray of bright red paint. At first, it just looks like scribbles of random graffiti, but then I read what it says.

CHINKS.

Initially, it doesn't even register, like it's a word in a foreign language, or one that I've never read before. I read it again and again. I think it must be a mistake. Or a misspelling. Or maybe they meant something else.

My second thought, stupidly, is that I forgot until just now that I am Chinese.

The inside of my throat grows hot. My fingers are numb as I pull up onto the driveway, trying to shield the garage with my car. If it was a burglary, I'd know what to do. But I sit there for a minute, frozen. I keep staring at it, as if I've misread or I can divine another meaning if I just reread it enough times.

The word rings through my head, drowning out all other thoughts. I can't interpret it. I can only listen to it endlessly in the prison of my skull.

I should call the police, but I don't know if I even can get the words out of my mouth. I have to go inside and find Mama. But I can't get out of the car.

So I do the only thing that swims through my confusion and pain. Hands shaking, I call my sister. And when she picks up, I start to cry.

Two

I watch the shadows move slowly across the stucco ceiling until they fade into morning gray. My body isn't cooperating. I doze off for an hour or so before my alarm starts beeping. I must've had a sweet dream from my past, because at first I think I'm back home, waking up in Rajiv Agarwal's basement. But then I remember I'm in a college twin bed, eight hundred miles away in New York City.

The crush of sadness from this memory threatens to ruin my first day of work. I shake it off and cross my tiny ten-by-ten box of a dorm room to turn off the alarm. It's six thirty. I have two hours before I have to be at orientation.

Unlike my sister, Annalie, I love the morning. I love how quiet and solitary it feels. I can be alone with my thoughts before the day clutters everything up. There is so much possibility. It's the nights that feel desperate and sad.

The morning is especially good in New York, where people go to work later than in the Midwest. Six thirty is practically the middle of the night. I love the bustle of the city, but the relative stillness of the morning is nice, and I can actually breathe.

I open the blinds to let in the weak light. My window faces an air shaft, so it's not much of a view, but that weak light is what keeps the philodendron, Poppy, in my room alive. The plant was a gift from Mama when I moved to NYU for college; the name came from Annalie. The idea of naming a plant seemed pointless to me (and why a girl?), but now I can't think of her as anything else. Poppy is looking a bit morose, so I dump the leftover contents of my water bottle into her pot.

I take my things and go down the silent hall to the bathroom. The other benefit of getting up early: I get the bathroom all to myself. It almost doesn't feel like it's communal, and I can just pretend I live in a huge mansion with a bunch of shower stalls.

Staying in the dorms for the summer on reduced rent isn't ideal. I know a lot of the other interns at the firm will be staying in sleek apartments downtown. Maybe they'll even host parties. But it just doesn't make sense for me. The pay for the internship is excellent. More money than I've ever seen in a paycheck in my life. But rent in New York is outrageous, and I have to save what I earn for tuition next year. It's amazing how earning the most money I could imagine as a nineteen-year-old could still make me feel poor in the city of dreams.

With Mama as a seamstress, she can't pitch in at all. If it were up to her, I would have accepted a cheaper school that offered more scholarships, closer to home. When it comes up in conversation, her mouth clamps into a thin line and her eyes glitter. I know she feels guilty that she can't give me any money for school. The Chinese way, she used to say. You work as hard as you can so you can pay for your kids to go to Ivy League schools.

Unfortunately, my father, who she counted on to help her make this happen, bailed when I was five and Annalie three. I remember he was talkative and loved to sing. He would pick me up by the waist and run around the yard. When I was a kid, it felt like I was miles above the ground, weightless, free.

He had copper hair and light eyes. I don't know why he left. Just that he did, and Mama didn't even try to look for him. She has never told us why.

I know my mother would like to pay for school, but she can't, and so she is always saying, Jinghua, you should go to school closer to home. Jinghua, your sister misses you. When she says these things, I feel heavy with the weight of her expectation. I can't go home, though. Not when I've finally escaped the desolation of the rural Midwest.

It's not that I hated my hometown. More so that I felt like I was slowly suffocating. People there seemed okay with staying put, never pushing the envelope, and just getting married and having babies. Generation after generation. No interest in trying new things, absorbing new ideas. Homogenous is the best way to describe it. There, I was trapped in a small world with small hopes.

When I arrived in New York, it was like a door opened into an entirely different universe. I might as well have arrived on Mars. Suddenly, I could walk anywhere, get any kind of food imaginable, and no matter what time it was, I could find people. People who looked all kinds of ways; people who looked like me. If I went to Times Square at three in the morning, I could stand with my eyes closed in the middle, bathed in artificial light and drenched in sound. Even though Annalie and I had both been baptized in the Catholic Church, I was not really one for religion. But being in the crush of people, thinking about all the ways they interconnected, felt spiritual for me.

I linger in the shower for an extra bit of time and let the steam soak up my sleepiness. The hot water from the shower feels especially good this morning. I pad silently down back to my room in my towel, yawning.

Last night, I ironed my nicer suit of the two I own and laid out a light gray blouse. Everything is itchy when I put it on, but I'm hopeful that I only have to wear a suit on the first day. I decide that it wouldn't be amiss to swipe on some red lipstick. Something berry-colored, so it's not too conspicuous. I don't want to look like I'm there to flirt. I curl the ends of my hair and inspect my appearance in the mirror one last time. I look ready for an internship. I look very serious. Mama tells me to smile more, but I hate showing my teeth.

The genes between my parents did not shake out quite evenly. My sister came out with lighter hair that eventually darkened to a smooth tea brown, pale skin, round cheeks, and prized big, double-lidded eyes. She has soft features and a wide smile, and she could never be mistaken for full-blooded Chinese, like I am regularly.

I have dark hair, monolids that make it a hundred times harder not to overdo it on eye makeup, and Asiatic features. My skin is the color of sand. I am thinner and more angular than my sister. There's not much of my father in me at all, at least that I can tell from pictures. A slightly wider nose than my mother's.

A widow's peak that I've tried to cover up unsuccessfully with bangs on multiple occasions.

People label her pretty. People label me exotic.

Even though Mama doesn't have an official favorite, I always thought she liked Annalie better. Annalie, warmer and friendlier, quick to set people at ease. Less confrontational. She and Mama rarely fought, but then, Annalie mostly caved on everything Mama wanted. When I go home, I find myself wondering whether, if my father had stuck around, he would have preferred me.

A useless question, as it'll never be answered.

I didn't come to New York City to get away from Rajiv. Even when we were together, I found my hometown to be a place where I was encased in solitude. I wasn't popular like Annalie. I couldn't fold myself into a group of friends and forget what had happened. I spent a lot of time at home or in the library.

So when I applied to college, I thought of all the fullest, most populated places I could go. New York. Los Angeles. San Francisco. Anywhere far away from the flat, sleepy quiet of home. I came to NYU expecting to drown out the deafening silence around me.

And it mostly worked. It's hard to feel alone here.

Except I found out that being lonely is different than being alone. Loneliness, it turns out, isn't quite as easy to escape.

Now nighttime, when I'm back in my dorm room after the first day, the same sense of quiet threatens to engulf me. I turn on the TV in my room and let it play some meaningless show in

31

the background to fill the dead space.

I check my Instagram. No notifications. When I scroll down my feed, a bunch of people from high school show up, posting pictures of their newly found Greek life friends or of themselves with dangling red Solo cups in hand. I don't look up Rajiv's profile. I couldn't bear to unfollow, but I muted him. Now I have to go check his page deliberately if I want to see what he's doing.

Don't do it, I tell myself. *Don't.* I haven't checked for an entire year, but tonight, I'm feeling vulnerable. I think about how happy and warm I felt when I woke up and before the sourness of reality.

I search his name and tap it on my phone screen.

There's a picture with his parents proudly dropping him off at college. A picture with a group of friends lounging in the dining hall.

I'm not surprised he would be quick to make friends.

There are rows and rows of photos. He always posted more than me. But the one that catches my eye is from only a few weeks ago. His arm around a pretty girl with long dark hair, dimples, and green eyes. He is smiling, his white teeth gleaming in his perfect grin, and he looks relaxed. The sight of it feels like a stab to the gut with a rusty knife.

How far back would I have to scroll to find a picture of us? Or maybe I could keep scrolling and never find one. Maybe he deleted them all.

I did this to myself. I don't get to be upset.

I sit on my bed for a couple more minutes, trying to recover, before I decide, no, screw this, thanks. I change into a white formfitting tee, distressed pale-wash jeans, and shiny neon-yellow flats, and I head out the door to immerse myself in the city.

On a clear morning like this one, you can see all across the city, the buildings like staggered gray and black spikes out of the ground. The building I work in is all glass, very sleek as it juts into the sky. The front lobby is white marble. I sign in.

The elevator panel has ten doors. It's the kind where you punch in your floor in the one keypad in front, and an elevator programmed to take you directly to your floor pops open. When I first interviewed, I stood at the elevators for several minutes trying to find the button to call an elevator. The security guard had to come help me. I felt like an idiot, but the guard just laughed and said everyone had that problem. I hate anything that makes me seem like a country bumpkin. I forced a close-lipped smile, but I was so embarrassed.

Now, I type in *44*. The elevator on the far left opens up, and I step in.

When I reach my floor, the door dings softly and slides open. I go to the right, and the lobby of the office is behind glass doors.

The lobby features a panoramic window. It's an incredible view. And it reminds me, again, of how far I've come. The Margaret of two years ago couldn't even have dreamed a dream this grand.

I go straight to my office, which I'm grateful to have as a

summer intern because I'm battling a bruising hangover from the night before, when I stayed out later than I should've to avoid my empty room.

I go to the office kitchen in the morning to fill up a big reusable bottle of water and lock myself in my office, lowering the shades. I work right through lunch and eat at my desk, building an analytical model on projected new customers resulting from various proposed marketing plans for a suitcase company. I skip the networking activity, because I don't think I can civilly interact with anyone speaking out loud.

By afternoon, the backlighting on the computer screen makes my head hurt, so I take a breather.

I break out a notebook and start brainstorming ideas for Environmental Law Society.

During the school year, my calendar is locked up with activities in all the organizations I help out with, and then my schoolwork the rest of the time. I have to admit, my schedule hasn't been the most conducive to my social life. But I feel like I'm making a difference, and that matters to me. I can get over the occasional disappointing lonely night.

My cell phone rings. I get, like, a million spam calls a day, so I reach over to turn off the ringer. Then I notice that the caller is my sister.

My sister never calls me. I think the last time we talked on the phone was six months ago. Instinctively, I know something is wrong.

* * *

Six and a half hours later, I'm driving home at night in a rental car from Chicago back to my hometown downstate.

It's a bit jarring, how fast you can travel seven hundred miles and be in a completely different location. While in New York, home seemed terribly far, but I've made touchdown in less time than it takes to watch *Titanic* from beginning to end.

I haven't been back since Christmas, which seems like a lifetime away. It's nighttime now, so I can't see much out the window. There's not much to see, though. I know without looking that the land is pancake flat, covered in an early green blanket of corn or soybean shoots. As I get closer, I see the eerie synchronized flash of red lights from the wind farm that stretches for miles. In between the flashes, there is nothing but dark.

I arrive at our house, and I'm not sure what to expect. Annalie told me what happened, but she was fairly hysterical on the phone, so I couldn't get too many details out of her. I'm not sure if the vandalism will have already been cleaned off.

Annalie's car is still parked out in front of the garage, so from the road, nothing is really visible. I pull up along the curb and turn off the engine. The house is quiet, but there's a small dim flicker of light coming through one of the windows, which tells me people are home.

Up until now, I've been going through the mechanical motions of figuring out how to get home, and then what things I might still have to take care of in New York. There was no time to think about anything.

But now I am here. I do not feel ready.

I get out and walk up the driveway. My heart is pounding out of my chest so loud, I'd swear the neighbors can hear it. I peer around the side of her car.

It's still there in bright red letters. All caps. Unmistakable. Although my sister already told me about it, seeing it is different.

There's a small paint splatter on the top corner of the "C" where the word begins. I can't look away.

Before, I could only hear my heartbeat, now I can only hear silence. Silence for miles around. I have been punched in the gut with a bowling ball. I feel a pain so deep that there's no way to tell where it begins and where it ends.

Then, rage so white-hot that it supernovas out and swallows the universe.

Three

ANNALIE

Mama and I are sitting quietly in the living room when my sister comes home, bringing a hurricane with her.

Mama didn't have much to say when I came inside, hours ago, bawling. She just kept shaking her head and saying, *"Evil, evil, evil"* in Chinese. She hadn't called the police. But the thing that stood out to me more was that she hadn't cooked anything for dinner. Mama is a consummate provider of food, and she always has dinner on the table by the time I get home.

At that moment, what I really wanted was my sister to come home and deal with this, and to have a bowl of hot beef noodle soup. We had to eat. I couldn't bear the idea of ordering anything and having the delivery guy see our garage.

I went through our refrigerator and pantry. I found some leftover rice, frozen peas, eggs, and Chinese sweet sausage. I couldn't do much, but I scrambled the eggs until they were fluffy, and threw in the rest to make a simple egg fried rice. We ate quickly, barely tasting anything. I left the dirty dishes and pans in the sink, and Mama didn't even make me wash them. We ended up turning on the TV and watching reruns of old sitcoms.

That's how Margaret finds us, covered in blankets on the couch, despite the fact that it's summer and it isn't even cold.

I forgot that Margaret still had a key to the house. She comes in with an enormous suitcase behind her, as if she's moving back in. Seeing her again after so many months is bizarre. She stands shrouded in shadow in the doorway, and I just stare at her.

"What are you doing?" she demands loudly, piercing the self-imposed silence Mama and I have adopted. Her voice in real life is lower than I remember. If I thought Margaret was going to come home and give us the loving comfort we need, I was wrong. Margaret is still Margaret.

Mama gets up first. "You came home," she says, and gives Margaret a hug.

Margaret's entire body is coiled tight like a wound spring. "What have you done so far? What do I need to do?" she says before Mama even lets go.

There's a pause.

"We were waiting for you," Mama says.

Hurricane Margaret's eyes bug out, and she breathes fire. "You've waited this long to call the cops?"

"What's the rush?" I say finally. "The vandals are already gone."

She mutters under her breath. "Okay, we're going to call them right now. We're going to file a police report. We're going to take pictures. We're going to figure out who did this. Then we're going to make sure the DA brings charges."

Her whirlwind of activity throws me for a loop. I hadn't even thought of figuring out who did it. I was thinking more along the lines of who we needed to call to get the paint scrubbed off the garage door or installing a security cam. *It's not a theft*, I thought—or I don't know what I thought—but it didn't seem like there was anything to get back, so what was the point? "Who did it?" I hear myself say. "Probably some racist idiots. I'm sure they're long gone. Seems like a random crime."

"Use your head, Annalie," she snaps. "They know we're Chinese. So they must be people who are local, who are familiar with us. What if they come back and attack us? I can't believe you guys just sat around and didn't call the police immediately."

"Margaret!" I shout. "It's almost midnight. Can we just regroup and not jump to conclusions *right now*?"

She ignores me, already tapping away on her phone. The light of her screen illuminates her face. Her furrowed brow tightens. She hasn't even come any farther into the house than the front hall; her suitcase is still leaning against the front door. But less than thirty seconds later, she's found the nonemergency number of the police department and is on the line with a dispatcher. "Yes, my name is Margaret Flanagan." She explains what happened in crisp, precise terms. Clinical. She doesn't waver at all. "We want to file a report right now. Please send someone immediately," she says firmly before hanging up.

She has been traveling for the last five hours at least. Knowing her, she probably didn't even stop for dinner and cowed her bladder into not forcing her to break at a rest stop. I'm a little impressed at how sharp-eyed and in charge she is, since she must be exhausted. I am tired, and I haven't even moved off the couch in six consecutive episodes of *How I Met Your Mother*. This is why

Margaret is going to make a fantastic lawyer. But right now, it feels like she's counsel for the opposing side, and Mama and I are in the hot seat for her cross-examination. This isn't what I was looking for when I called her.

She's already peppering Mama with questions about insurance and how to submit a claim to take care of this. "We can maybe set up a GoFundMe if we need to." She turns to me. "Do you think any of the neighbors saw? Any witnesses?"

I shrug. "I don't know. Nobody has come over."

"Did you do anything to the scene?"

"Jesus, did it sound like I was in a state of mind where it would occur to me to poke around there?" I say, irritated.

She sighs. She's clearly disappointed with my attitude. "Can you move your car and turn on the porch light?"

"Right now?"

"Yes, right now. The police are coming. They're going to need to examine the scene. Your car is in the way."

I actually don't want to go outside ever again. The idea of baring the graffiti to the entire neighborhood and lighting it up is embarrassing and shameful to me. I put the car in front deliberately. But Margaret is right. I get my keys and go out onto the driveway. I try not to look at the garage when I pull my car onto the curb next to Margaret's.

A police car pulls in just as I'm locking my car. Margaret comes outside.

A single cop emerges from the car. He's white and on the shorter side. "Hi, is this the Flanagan residence?"

Margaret blows past me as if I'm not here, even though she

doesn't live here anymore and has only been home for about ten minutes. "Yes. I'm Margaret. I placed the call."

The police officer looks at me, squinting. "And you?"

"I'm her sister." He keeps looking. "Annalie," I add.

"Right," he says, jotting it down. His eyes flick back and forth between the two of us. "You guys don't look anything alike." Margaret rolls her eyes. I'm too scared to ever roll my eyes at a cop—hello, they have guns—but internally, I also am groaning. This is always the first thing everyone says to us. Margaret looks like Mama's daughter, and I look like, question mark? With the absence of Dad, I'm just the overhang in this family.

The cop ambles over to the garage and glances at it. "So this is the damage, huh?"

"Yes," Margaret says, her voice tight.

"Can you tell me when you discovered it?"

Margaret gestures to me.

I feel like I'm being called on in class involuntarily. "My mother called me at"—I check my phone—"just after four. She was very upset. I came home immediately and saw it on the garage door." I can't even say the word.

"Where's your mother?"

"Inside," I say.

"Can she come out and give a statement?"

"She—she's very upset," I repeat. I don't want Mama to be exposed to any more of this.

"I understand that," he says patiently. His name tag gleams in the streetlamp. Officer Kramer. "But if she's a witness, we'd like her to make a statement."

"I don't think—" I start.

"I'll go get her," Margaret interrupts me.

"Margaret!" I hiss, but it's at her back because she's already turned to go inside. Officer Kramer is not talking to me. He's just writing things down in his notebook. I stand awkwardly a few feet away from him, still trying to look at everything but the garage.

A minute later, Margaret guides Mama out the front door.

Mama's shoulders are hunched over. She's shrinking into herself. Officer Kramer introduces himself to her, and she gives a feeble nod. He asks for her legal name.

"Xuefeng Wang," she says.

"Shweh-fung Wang?" he repeats, the syllables too bloated in his mouth.

His pronunciation makes me flinch. It's not like he's trying to be disrespectful, but hearing Americans try to say Chinese words has always made me feel a little uncomfortable. The way it makes Chinese sound rough and stupid. Mama has always gone by Jenny, but she never changed her legal name.

He asks her questions about what she was doing, what she saw, when it happened, and on and on. She gives her answers haltingly. She was at home, working. She'd stepped outside to get the mail. She didn't hear anything. A few times, she looks to Margaret and says something in Chinese, and Margaret translates to him. Mama's English is normally pretty competent, but in this situation, she seems to have lost her bearings and is grasping for vocabulary. She sounds totally defeated.

I'm appalled that Margaret is letting this interrogation happen.

I go over to her and put my arm around her shoulders. "That's enough," I say.

"Annalie," Margaret says sharply. "Don't get in the way."

"I can do," Mama says gently to me. "I can."

I glance between her and Margaret. Mama nods at me. "Fine," I say. "But I'm going to do the translating."

Margaret clenches her jaw as though she doesn't trust me—she probably doesn't—but backs off.

It feels like hours later when Officer Kramer is done. He thanks us all politely for cooperating and expresses his sympathies for the situation. Mama goes back inside. I wish I could go with her.

"What's next?" Margaret asks.

"We'll take the information and assess what we have. We may come back and ask more questions. If we have any leads, we'll follow them. And we'll go from there."

"You're going to figure out who did it, though?"

"We'll try. There have been some recent incidents in town of property being defaced by graffiti. Downtown mostly, though. Haven't seen anything in a residential area." He sounds apologetic, as if he's trying to let us down gently. "It may be hard to get any leads without security camera footage. These things are difficult to track down after the fact."

"Defacing property?" Margaret asks, incredulous.

"Yes."

"Officer," she says slowly. "This is a hate crime. You have to find out who did this."

Officer Kramer shifts uncomfortably on his feet. "Well.

43

That's an intent question for the prosecutor if we find the culprit. I can't comment on how this would go in a courtroom."

She snorts derisively. Laughs, actually laughs, at him. She truly has no fear. I have to admire her. "Intent? Are you seeing what I'm seeing? Did you *read* it?" She pauses and jabs her finger at the garage. "It says, 'CHINKS.'" I wince when she says the word. "Do you see us?" she continues relentlessly. "What do you think that means? What exactly has *not* been established about the perpetrator's intent? What if this person comes back and attacks our house again? Attacks *us*?" Her face is animated. Her eyes gleam.

"Ma'am, I understand that this is a very distressing situation. But it is extremely unlikely that whoever did this will be back, given that it's been over eight hours. We find that these things do not tend to be repeat crimes. But if you feel that you are in danger or if anyone returns, please call us. Otherwise, we'll be in touch." He turns to go. "It's late. I would recommend you all get some sleep and then call someone to clean off the paint tomorrow morning."

Margaret opens her mouth as if to argue more, but then stops herself. I can almost see her deciding internally that it's not worth it. She lets him get into his car and turn on the engine.

I go over to her. We stand side by side and watch the police car drive away, leaving our neighborhood quiet again. The only thing that fills the space between us is the sound of crickets.

"Let's go to bed," I say finally. "Like he said, we can find someone to clean it off tomorrow."

"Clean it off?"

"Yeah."

"Why would we clean it off? What if the cops want to come back to do more investigation? We shouldn't touch the crime scene."

I'm stunned. She is literally deranged. "They already did the police report. They interviewed us. There's nothing left to do."

"We should keep it up," she insists. "People should be *ashamed* that they let this happen in our neighborhood. How racist can this town be?" She shakes her head. She's acting as if our neighbors encouraged and facilitated this crime. "We need to let people see what happened."

I feel the panic rising within me. She can't be serious. "I don't want to leave it up." It's hideous and insulting. She should want to get rid of it ASAP. She says she wants to keep it up to shame the town, but it just feels to me like we're the ones being shamed. "Why do you want to punish us by marking *our home* with a massive racial slur? No way, Margaret. No fucking way. Take some goddamn pictures and call it a day. I never want to see this again."

"Let's talk about it in the morning."

I know my sister. I know this is her way of winning the fight in the end. She deflects, and then she seizes victory later when your defenses are down. But I'm not backing off. I'm not going to proudly wear a scarlet letter of someone else's making. "We are *not* leaving this up, okay?"

She is staring intently at the garage.

"Okay?"

She sighs and relents. For the first time tonight, she looks tired. "We will find someone to clean it off." I note that this is not a direct answer, as it leaves out the *when* part. Another very Margaret trick. Still, I file this away as a win.

And with that, we don't have anything left to say to each other. The day, and Officer Kramer, have drained away all our words. All that remains is a kind of rawness that hurts with every touch.

We silently file inside. Double-lock the doors. Mama has already gone to her room, but I can see the light underneath her door.

Margaret takes her giant suitcase upstairs into her old bedroom, which has been untouched since she moved out. It's as if she never left. I don't know how long she plans to stay.

In fact, when I crawl into bed and lay exhausted under the covers, I realize I didn't even say hello or ask how she was doing or say she was missed.

We've barely spoken at all.

When I wake up the next morning, still clouded with sleep, two thoughts enter my mind:

One, Thom gave me his number.

I'm incredibly excited for two seconds, and then the feeling immediately evaporates.

Two, someone vandalized our garage with a racial slur.

What a roller coaster of emotions before I've even had my coffee.

I hear someone banging around downstairs, and I remember, oh right. My sister is home now.

I'm dreading talking to her, but I also don't want her to start charging through her to-do list (which she's definitely already created) without another chance to curb her worst impulses. After all, this is the girl who consistently humiliated me my freshman and sophomore years with her need to be the mouthpiece for every perceived social injustice in high school.

I was relieved when she graduated, because for the first time, I didn't have to answer for whatever she was doing. I could just be *me*.

I'm sure this latest thing is simply reinforcing her mental narrative about how our town is filled with racism.

I slip into the kitchen in my pajamas, and she's already fully dressed, ready to head out.

"Where are you going?" I demand.

"Wow, not even a good morning?" she replies. She slings her purse over her shoulder. "Some kind of welcome I get here. You were the one who asked me come home and deal with this, after all."

So Margaret, taking advantage of any moment of emotional weakness. "Yeah, I called you, because I was freaking out," I say incredulously. "Are you going to hold it against me?"

She sighs. "Can we not fight? I've tracked down a cleaner who can come in an hour. Here's the number if you need to follow up." She hands me a slip of paper. "You have a credit card, right? Or you can grab Mama's?"

We both glance over in the direction of her bedroom down the hall. The door is still closed.

"Yeah," I say. I pocket the phone number, surprised but still suspicious. "Why can't you stay for them to come over, though?"

"I'm going to the police station," she says innocently. "For follow-up."

"The police station," I repeat. "And not anywhere else?"

"Damn, Annalie. Do you want to put an ankle monitor on me? Turn on the iPhone tracking function?"

"I would if I could," I mutter. "Please, can you give us a second to digest what we want to do next before you dive into your master plan?"

"What? I said we could wash it off. That's what you wanted."

I don't trust her. I don't trust her as far as I can throw her. "Okay. And then you're heading back to New York?"

"I didn't book a return flight yet." She inspects her phone. "I have to go."

She heads toward the door.

I follow behind her like an anxious shadow. "Don't do anything that I wouldn't! Remember that time you made a huge deal about people wearing qipaos to prom and complained to the principal about cultural appropriation like a giant, embarrassing narc? People still don't let me live that down. Please don't do that."

"Complain to the principal?" she says wryly over her shoulder.

"No, make a huge deal! Nobody wants that except you! Don't make me regret calling you!" I call out after her.

The door slams shut, leaving me inside with a knot of dread.

I tell Violet to meet me at our favorite hangout, Bakersfield Bakery.

It's admittedly a ridiculous name, but the guy who owns it is, like, eighty, and his last name is Bakersfield. The bakery has been a fixture downtown since it opened almost sixty years ago. It's set up like a French patisserie. The front is all glass, and when it's sunny outside, it lights up the entire bakery. There's just enough seating along the edges to have a nice tart or almond croissant, if you come on a day where it's not too crowded. Most importantly, the desserts there are to die for. And I really need dessert today.

The drive there is bright and cheery. The early summer sun feels like a saturated Instagram filter against the scenery. The trees lining the streets are especially green; the houses especially quaint. As I pull into the downtown area, everything looks like a postcard of a small town. I feel a sense of comfort, a blanket of peace, the farther I get away from home.

This is not a place where bad things happen.

Violet's not here yet; fifteen minutes late is her MO. I'm too jittery to stand outside and wait, so I go in without her.

Normally, Bakersfield is the only person who works at the bakery, so no matter how busy it gets, all the customers have to wait on him, and the line sometimes goes out the door. People stand in line, though, because it's completely worth it. Worth it, even though he's basically a stock grumpy-old-man character come to life. He's slightly nicer to me and Violet because we're always around, and because, I assume, at least 10 percent of his business must come from us, based on how much we consume on a yearly basis.

But today, for the first time ever, there's someone new behind the counter. I peer around the people in front of me to get a better look. Bakersfield retreats toward the back, and the guy manning the front snaps, "Yeah, I know! I've *got it*, okay?" He turns toward me.

He's very tall and broad-shouldered with short, neat brown hair and square, thick-rimmed black glasses, probably a little older than me. And judging from his accent, very British. He kind of looks like an accountant, if that accountant were built like a rugby player. I'm not sure what a British guy is doing in a small town in the Midwest manning the front of a local bakery, but he's frowning at me as if he's just caught my hand in a cookie jar.

For a second, I stare at him.

"Yes? Can I help you?" he says impatiently. Clearly, Bakersfield has decided to staff in accordance with his standard personality preference, which is: as un-customer-friendly as possible.

"Sorry. Still deciding."

"Right, well. Not to be rude, but people waiting and all, you know. There are only so many options." He gestures behind me.

I don't know who peed in his Cheerios, but I'm already having a bad enough day without this. "Funny, the rudeness seems to be coming through anyway."

He glares at me.

"I'll have a lemon tart." I eye his shirt, which is name-tag-less. "What's your name?"

"Daniel," he says, short and clipped. "You want to speak to the manager about me? Good luck." He rings me up and practically shoves the plate at me. I hear Bakersfield shout something from the back. Daniel grumbles and disappears behind the door.

I take my plate, annoyed, and settle into a seat in front.

Violet appears minutes later. She's wearing Daisy Dukes, an off-the-shoulder frilly top, and red heart-shaped sunglasses. She's the only person I know who can wear heart-shaped sunglasses and not look like a twelve-year-old.

"What's the emergency?" she asks after she gets a chocolate croissant from Bakersfield.

"Ugh," I say. "Bakersfield hired some new guy."

"What new guy? Bakersfield hires people?"

"He's in the back now. He's British."

"Ooh. Wish I could've seen him. Was he cute?"

"Nope. He was an ass. And not in a grouchy, adorable-old-man way."

"Okay, well, anyway. I'm getting dizzy with your array of men." She bites into her croissant. "What's the deal with the emergency meeting? Is it Thom? I haven't heard from you since yesterday morning, when you texted me pictures of your five different potential outfits before going into work."

That seems like a lifetime ago. "No. Actually it doesn't have anything to do with that."

"Oh?"

Violet and I have been friends since first grade. We talk every day. But even though I know I can tell her anything, this feels raw in a way that I am nervous to say out loud. If I tell her, then it really happened. If I tell her, then it's real.

"Someone vandalized our house yesterday," I say quietly.

Violet gasps. "Are you serious? Are you okay? What did they do?"

I wave my hand. "I'm fine, everybody is fine. Margaret came home, and she's taking care of it. I mean, obviously she's Margaret-ing out about it all over the place, but it's good. We already got cleaners, and it's all gone." I'm unable to tell her exactly what they did, so I just pull out my phone and show her a picture from last night. Even though the lighting is bad, you can see what is there.

Violet covers her mouth. "Oh my god," she says. "That is horrific." She looks at me. "I'm so sorry."

It's Violet's reaction that really knocks me down. I was fine. I was really okay. Her depth of horror reminds me of my own distress when I saw it. I start tearing up again. "It's fine," I say shakily.

"That is so not fine, Annalie." Her voice is deadly serious.

"I really just don't want to look at it or talk about it anymore. But I had to tell somebody." I'm wiping my eyes with my sleeve. "Jeez, can you give me a tissue?"

She fishes through her purse and hands me a packet. Gratefully, I dab at my face. "Do you know who did it?" she asks, after I attempt to compose myself.

"No idea. Margaret already filed a police report, though. She's probably following up with them as we speak."

"It's despicable." She shakes her head. "It's really hard to believe that somebody could do that. Do you think the police will figure it out?"

I shrug. "I feel like it'll be hard because there weren't any witnesses. The cop who showed up didn't seem that optimistic."

"Why would somebody do that to you? You guys have lived there forever."

"I know. That's why I think it must be someone random. It's not like we just moved in. Margaret thinks otherwise, but you know her. She always jumps to conclusions."

Violet is wide-eyed. She knows Margaret, of course. "I don't know. Maybe she's right. This town isn't, like, the most woke. I mean that one guy in my AP US History class still thinks the Civil War was about states' rights. In Illinois. *The Land of Lincoln.*"

"Margaret's not right. She shows up and decides she can take the whole thing over herself." I stab at my tart viciously with my fork. "At least she doesn't have much to do now. She'll probably book her ticket and be gone by the end of the week. I forgot how exhausting it is to have her around. Being an only child is kind of nice."

"You're telling me. I have to watch Rose *again* this week," she says. "But cut your sister some slack. She's got a point. This isn't some run-of-the-mill microaggression. Someone spray-painted a racial slur *on your house.* That's a hate crime."

I put my head in my hands, groaning. "Can we please not talk about it? I don't want to talk about it anymore."

Violet shoots me a sympathetic look. "Sure. I'm sorry."

Four

MARGARET

I step outside, my throat warm with annoyance over Annalie's whining.

Everything has to be about her and her feelings all the time. You'd think if anything could shake off her blinders to see something more important than high school popularity, it would be this situation, but she seems to have moved on already. If it were up to her, she'd bury this without even going to the police.

In the light of day, the vandalism looks even worse, starker red against the white garage door. Like a scar. I would have expected neighbors to have noticed it by now, but so far, everything is quiet. We live on a small cul-de-sac, so nobody accidentally comes through. The traffic volume here is virtually nil. Still, shouldn't somebody have seen it and come by to see if we were okay?

The exploding star of anger inside me from last night has simmered down to a dull burn, but looking at the word makes it flare up again. I pull out my phone to take pictures from every angle and get close-ups as well as wide shots. Every click makes me madder, as if each copy saved of the graffiti is being tattooed on my body as a marker of shame.

When I'm done, I'm huffing and puffing like I just ran a marathon. I'm not a crier. I haven't cried since Rajiv and I broke up.

But looking at the pictures on my phone and at the garage, I do want to cry.

To settle myself, I close my eyes and breathe. I won't be able to talk to anybody if I'm a mess. The air is fresh and clean here and smells like plants instead of urine and garbage. I can hear birds of the non-pigeon variety. That is one thing I miss when I'm in the city.

Gradually, I calm down. When I open my eyes, I feel much better.

Annalie is right about the paint having to go, though. Last night, I thought it would be best to leave it up to make a point, but emotionally, it's too much for me. I can't see it every time I come out of the house. My insides will sear to a crisp.

The world is full of ugliness. I know that. It doesn't mean I want to decorate my front door with it.

By nine thirty, I'm already on my way to the newspaper's office.

The *Gazette* is in an old brown brick building downtown. It has a small parking lot across the street, two-thirds of which is reserved for employees. The parking lot is almost empty. The day is ripening up to be a ferociously hot one.

I step inside the front door. There's one bored-looking security guy who mans the front desk. He looks at me lazily and calls upstairs to confirm that they're waiting for me. He waves me over to the elevator.

The elevator takes me to the third floor, and I step out into the *Gazette*'s newsroom. It's sticky in here, immediately apparent that there's either no air-conditioning or no functioning air-conditioning. The windows are open, with fans propped up against the screens to circulate the outside air in. I'm not convinced it's working with the temperature outside being what it is.

The newsroom has an open floor plan, with desks squashed up against each other in uneven lines. Each desk has a computer monitor and a mess of wires. About half the desks are otherwise empty. Bad times for the print journalism business. The other half are scattered with papers and pictures. It's slightly musty.

There are only three people who are in. A woman, who is inside the only enclosed office there. The walls are glass, and she's busy jabbering away on the phone. Another is a guy who is not facing me. He has a man bun and has an entire spread of photos on his screen. The third looks the youngest and has short hair. He sees me enter and immediately comes over to greet me. "Hi, Ms. Flanagan?" he says, sticking out his hand.

I shake it. "You can call me Margaret," I say.

"Great. I'm Joel."

"You're the one I talked to on the phone."

"That's me. Want to come over here so we can chat?" He gestures to a corner by the window. "Sorry, I'd offer a better space, but this is the best we can do right now. Not very glamorous."

"I'm not here for glamorous." I march over to the corner and sit down.

"I'll be right back." He grabs his laptop, balances it on his thighs, and looks up at me. "Okay, tell me what happened," he says.

So I tell him. From beginning to end.

He's typing the entire time. His face is sympathetic, but not overly expressive.

"I have pictures," I say. "I can send them to you. And we've already filed a police report, so you can check on that too."

"Thank you." He finishes typing. "That's really helpful. I hope that we'll be able to help you here. This is a terrible thing that's been done."

His tone is gentle. The gentleness gets me going all over again, and I blink rapidly. No crying, I remind myself.

"This is going to be a hard one. I'm sure you know."

"Yes. That's why I came here."

"We're going to run this sometime in the next couple of days, after we do some follow-up investigation."

"That's great," I say.

"Whatever happens," he tells me firmly, "at least it will bring awareness. This kind of thing is unacceptable in our town."

Unacceptable.

It's funny to me how he says "this kind of thing" instead of "prejudice" or "racism." It's as if it's too shocking or unbelievable that racism or prejudice could exist in a town like ours, where the slogan is *Where People Come to Stay*.

As I walk out of the *Gazette*, I know that I've done something I can't go back from. The paper is going to run this story, and our family will be associated with it. But some things are too important to shy away from.

I think about all the times when boys at the bus stop would pull the corners of their eyes and sing racist ditties at me until I learned that crying only made the bullies try harder. The times when I smiled at old ladies at the grocery store, only for them to mutter slurs under their breath that would wipe my smile clean off. The times when people would speak super slowly to my mother, as if she wasn't smart enough to understand them just because she had an accent.

I think about all the other Asian families who stay quiet, the mothers who tell us that we only need to put our heads down and work hard to succeed in this country, the bitterness of that lie. Our community. They always tell us that we're the good ones, the ones who don't complain, the model minority. We smile as they walk all over us.

Right then, I decide that I can't go back to New York for the rest of the summer. I need to see this to the end.

No matter what my family thinks, this time I won't let us be silent.

It takes me about four and a half hours of calling around to every downtown law firm to get a job for the summer. People are usually amazed at how quickly and easily I can get things done, but the reality is, people generally underestimate the power of just being assertive and persistent. You never know if someone will say yes if you don't ask.

I have a pretty impressive résumé, so that helped. I end up with three offers, two of which are unpaid, and one that pays $10.50 an hour. I take the paid one.

It's nothing like I was getting in New York, but on the other hand, I can stop paying for housing. The good thing about living in a dorm is that NYU lets me get out of the lease agreement scot-free, because people always need housing in New York in the summer, and they can lease it back out at the same high rate, no sweat. I pay for someone to pack up my remaining things and ship them here.

Based on the firm's website, it covers family law, real estate, and general civil litigation. One of the partners there interviewed me on the phone for about five minutes before offering me the job, telling me I can start tomorrow. I, of course, will mainly be filing paperwork and proofreading contracts and briefs, but I've done worse for $10.50 an hour.

The firm is located next to the old courthouse where Abraham Lincoln used to practice law. Like the rest of Illinois, our town has a feverish Lincoln obsession, which means every item Lincoln ever touched or any ground upon which his feet stood is revered and marked with a plaque. The firm is right in the old Lincoln district, across the street from one of the many Lincoln statues that litter the downtown area.

I show up on the first day channeling my best Amal Clooney. Pressed black pants, a white blouse, and pale blush pumps. I break out my best black leather tote. I'm aiming for professional but contemporary.

The building is nothing like the consulting firm in New York. It's in a fire-red brick building, with white doors and white window trim, crowded against the sidewalk. It has a sloped, brown-shingled roof. It's only two floors. There's a small wooden sign that hangs to the left of the front door that reads in clear white block letters: *Fisher, Johnson & Associates, PC.*

I pull open the front door and step inside. They've retained the building's original detailing. Warm chestnut wood floors. The walls are robin's-egg blue, with intricate crown molding along the edges of the ceiling in white. The doors inside are white to match the outside. The foyer has a single dark brown desk where the receptionist sits, typing away, and a seating area with excellent dark blue couches. The building is sectioned off, so all I can see from the front door is the hallway and a set of wooden stairs that disappear into the second level.

The receptionist looks up at me. She's middle-aged and thin, with a head that threatens to be swallowed by a cloud of curly brown hair. "Hello, can I help you?"

"I'm Margaret Flanagan. I just got hired as an intern. Today is my first day?"

"Right," she says. "We're expecting you. Sorry, have to start with the boring stuff." She hands me a stack of employment forms. "Can you fill these out?"

Thirty minutes later, I return them. "Thanks. Let me get Mr. Fisher. He'll introduce you to everybody and show you to your desk."

Jack Fisher, who I spoke with on the phone, is a tall, portly guy with gray hair and gray eyes. He kind of looks like exactly the kind of person I expected to be the head of a law firm, one of those people who overenunciates and also talks really loudly. Way more loudly than is necessary based on his proximity to the listener. He's wearing a dark green polo top and khaki pants. "Nice to meet you in person, Margaret. Meg? Maggie?" he booms, towering over me.

"Just Margaret," I assure him.

"Great. You can call me Jack." He sticks out his large hand, and I shake it. I feel like a child next to him. "We're having a very busy summer, which means it's lucky you called. As you can tell from looking around, we don't have a ton of space, but we have a fair number of people. Let's go meet them before you settle down."

He glances at my outfit. "By the way, we're a casual firm, especially in the summer. You can dress down if you want to." He sounds a little wary, as if he's trying really hard not to comment on my clothes because he doesn't want to sound sexist or inappropriate. "I only wear suits for courtroom appearances." He winks in that genial way that old white guys love to do.

Fisher, Johnson & Associates has six partners, two associates, and a paralegal and a receptionist. Each person has their own office. The partners are situated upstairs. Downstairs, there are offices for each of the associates and the paralegal, as well as a kitchen area and the foyer.

We meet the other lawyers. Most of them look fairly jovial and interchangeable. Of the partners, five are men and one is a woman. All the men are white and the woman is Latina. Johnson, of Fisher, Johnson & Associates, is out for the day. "He has a hearing," Fisher says. "In a child custody case. Very sad."

The woman partner, a certain Jessica D. Morales, is this very imposing-looking woman with rectangular glasses perched on her nose and shoulder-length dark brown hair with a shock of white at the temple that has to be intentional. Her desk is piled high with papers. She tells me she has ten assignments for me

61

already and that she likes my shoes, and I decide that she's my new role model.

On our way down the stairs, Fisher says, "Our paralegal is out on maternity leave, so lucky for you, there will be lots to do around here, more substantive things than a summer intern would normally get."

We turn the corner toward the back of the building. "So there's good news and bad news. The good news is that you get an office with a desk. It's a pretty nice office, if I do say so myself, being the person who did all the interior design." He flashes a smile at me. "The bad news is, you're our second intern this summer, so the two of you will have to share."

Before I have a chance to react to that bit of information, we arrive at the designated office.

There are two desks. And right there, sitting at the occupied one, is Rajiv.

"Rajiv, meet—"

"Hi, Margaret," he says. He is wearing a plaid button-down shirt, rolled up to the elbows, and dark wash jeans. His hair is different from what I remember. It's short on the sides, but longer on top. The top is teased up with a little wave in it. He has a diamond stud in each ear. He looks really *cool*. And except for a small jump in his eyebrows, he looks completely unruffled.

I, on the other hand, am suddenly sweating from every pore.

"Uh, hi?" I say artfully.

"Oh, you two know each other?" asks Fisher. He's glancing between me and Rajiv, and I wonder if he can feel the tension between us, because I'm thinking I might either spontaneously combust or run out screaming.

"Umm," I say.

"We went to high school together. Old friends," he volunteers gracefully, sidestepping the truth.

Fisher claps his hands together, looking very much like he wants to exit the room immediately. "Excellent. That should make it super easy for you to share an office then. I'll leave you two to it." He turns to me. "There's your desk. You can log in and get your in-box set up, and the partners will be in touch. Glad to have you aboard, Margaret."

He scurries out.

Leaving Rajiv and me in the room by ourselves.

I'm still standing shell-shocked in the doorway, and he's staring at me from the other side of the room. I can't meet his eyes.

The last time I saw him in person? Exactly twelve months and three weeks ago, at our high school graduation.

I should be over him. I should not have any issues talking to him like a normal human being, like somebody who means nothing to me. But I can't. Having him this close to me is devastating. It feels like he's cracked open my rib cage and my insides are heaving in open air.

I thought I'd probably go through the rest of my life never having to see him again, but here he is, trapped in a room with me for two months.

This is a disaster.

"Do you want to take that other desk?" he asks coldly after a minute of me being frozen to the spot.

His voice shakes me out of my paralysis. "Yeah." I make a beeline to my chair, head down. I wonder briefly if it's too late to quit and take one of the nonpaying jobs or if I can make it through this entire summer without interacting with Rajiv in any way.

Our desks are arranged so that they're side by side and facing the door. Mine is closest to the window. If I never look over to my left, I can just pretend that he isn't there. I fake type at my computer to make it seem like I'm working on something, which I'm fully aware is the most pathetic exercise of all time. There's a clock over the door, and I swear that time is moving at half speed.

After an incalculably long pause, Rajiv finally speaks up again. "So this is unexpected."

I make a little murmur of agreement, not even real words.

"What brings you to Fisher, Johnson? I thought you were going to be in New York all summer."

I'm surprised. How would he know what I was up to? Then I realize that just because I muted his updates on Instagram doesn't mean he did the same thing. Which then makes me realize that he's been keeping up with my whereabouts. Intentionally? Just in passing because Instagram's algorithm recognized that we were once people who were irreplaceable to each other? I can't keep my mind from speculating in an infinite number of directions.

"Change of plans," I manage to say at last. If this were nineteen months ago, Rajiv would've been the first person I called after the vandalism. He would've put his arms around me, and I would've felt like there was no safer corner in the entire known universe. But instead, we're sitting at separate desks, stiff as boards, and I say nothing to him about it. How strange it is, to be in the aftermath of once having been a person's everything. I clench my hands into fists, startled that for the second time in two days, I'm on the verge of tears.

His face—when I dare take a peek—is impassive. This is unlike the Rajiv I knew, whose emotions always played near the surface.

He doesn't ask further. He doesn't ask about my mom, and I don't ask about his parents. I don't ask about school or how his summer is going. I don't ask if he has met someone new, or if he has forgiven me yet. I don't ask for his forgiveness. I don't know if I have forgiven myself.

I don't ask if his heart is breaking the way mine is all over again.

I don't want to know the answers to any of these questions.

Five

ANNALIE

Thom texts me that afternoon:

> hi A. hope everything is okay. you really ran out on me
> yesterday. anyway, soccer team is playing exhibition game
> against the cross-town team this afternoon. you should
> come. and not just because i'm trying to fill the stands so
> we look more popular. 😉

A semblance of normalcy from Thom. I'd almost forgotten that I saw him only yesterday. I'm happy that I'm still on his mind.

Me: I'll be there!

I don't say anything about the vandalism. What is there to say? It feels icky, and I'm still queasy when I think about it. But I try not to think about it now that it's gone from our garage. I try not to think about whatever Margaret might be out there doing either. In a few days, she'll be gone, and things will be back to normal.

Our high school soccer field has pretty old bleachers. The wooden kind that creak and make you concerned they'll collapse under you if too many people are on them, which would be a really sad way to go.

Luckily, our soccer team isn't particularly good, except for Thom, and doesn't attract much of an audience. Today, the bleachers are only about a third full. Not particularly surprising, since it's only a summer exhibition game. If Thom hadn't invited me, I never would have shown up either.

Violet stands next to me with Abaeze. Most boyfriends would've been super annoyed to be dragged to morally support their girlfriend's attempt to morally support her best friend. But Abaeze has always been the most laid-back person I've ever known. It ultimately makes sense, because only somebody that chill could handle Violet, who's basically got the personality of a hummingbird.

I like Abaeze. He's an amazing artist who's virtually certain to get a college scholarship for his painting, and he's really good to Violet. I can't imagine them without each other. After this week, though, he's going off to Nigeria for the summer to spend time with his extended family. She'll be stuck with her three siblings and me. If it's stressing her out at all, she doesn't show it.

In the bleachers of this soccer game, it doesn't escape my notice that the three of us stand out from the mostly white crowd, such that there's no way Thom will be able to miss us. Margaret would probably have some social science theory as to how we all found each other in a sea of salt, but to me, they're just the coolest people I happen to know, no wild conspiracy theory.

Thom is a forward and probably the only reason the team doesn't end up dead last in the rankings every year. Scouts come to games just to watch him.

His dad, who used to play collegiate soccer, has since settled into being a small-town insurance agent and an older version of his son. He's still got a thick, full head of silvery brown hair, though. He's in the stands, as usual, watching with intense concentration. For a brief flash, I can see what Thom is going to look like in thirty years.

Then Thom shows up on the field, grinning like a superstar. I shade my eyes to get a better look. He's lean and fit. His hair glints in the sun. He turns his head as he runs on, scanning the crowd. When he spots me, he smiles extra big, and I swear my heart skips a beat.

"I don't know why you thought we had to be here," Violet says, pulling out her phone to text. "Won't we just be cock-blocking you after the game?"

"What are you talking about? After the game?"

"He's obviously going to come find you."

"Maybe not." I don't want to get my hopes up. "Maybe he just wanted to get more people to come."

"None of us were born yesterday. He sent you a winky face. He's going to come find you. He was looking for you in the stands."

My body warms from head to toe with pleasure and for a minute I forget about everything else. "We'll see. Anyway, of course you guys had to come. I couldn't show up here by myself. It would be super desperate and obvious."

"You don't have to try so hard. He's already in love with you. I can tell."

I ignore her. Abaeze smiles at me and shrugs.

"How do you deal with her?" I ask, exasperated.

"I listen to her," he tells me. "She's usually right."

"Good answer," Violet says without looking up from her phone.

"Guess that's how you guys have lasted so long," I say, while Violet huffs in response off to the side.

Thom ends up scoring two goals, the only person on the team to score during the game. It's not enough. His team's defense is terrible, and the other side gets three goals, the last one with eighty-nine minutes on the clock.

The teams file past each other and shake hands. I'm watching Thom the entire time, waiting to see where he goes after it's over. He goes to his dad, who immediately starts having an animated conversation with him. His dad is all hand gestures, and Thom is nodding, nodding, nodding. He doesn't look my way. I try not to feel disappointed, unsuccessfully.

"See?" I say to Violet. "He's not remotely interested. He probably didn't even notice that I was here."

"Mm-hmm. I'm not convinced. Let's see what happens."

"Come on." I tug at her sleeve. "Let's just go. I'm not going to wait around like a sad puppy."

"If you say so."

We head out together to the parking lot. I'm prickly with embarrassment at ever getting my hopes up. It was a silly idea. Was he baiting me? Just being friendly? Did I read too much into the text? How could I think somebody like Thom would ever be interested in somebody like me? I'm so out of his league.

By the time I say goodbye to Violet and Abaeze, I've already beat myself up so badly I might as well have transformed into a giant self-servicing punching bag.

But just as I start my car, I get another text from Thom.

why'd you run out on me? i got tied up with my dad before i could get to you. sorry the game was kind of a disappointment. wanted to thank you for showing up. how about i take you out for ice cream sometime?

Bubbles, bubbles, bubbles from typing. I watch them with bated breath.

not ice cream. haha. you probably get enough of that. i'll think of something.

Bubbles, bubbles.

what do you say?

Pause.

He ends with three smileys in a row. No way to mistake the meaning of that.

I think I'm done with surprises for the summer, but then the next one comes rolling in quickly after. Margaret quit her internship in New York and took a new one in town. She's staying for the rest of the summer.

She announces this as a statement over dinner. No input required. Mama frowns slightly. "Is this good idea?" she asks. "For your future?"

"I told them what happened," Margaret replies bluntly. "They invited me back next summer." Mama just nods.

Margaret looks at me, as if daring me to contradict her. I

don't, of course. When have I ever contradicted her, on anything?

I want to say that we're happy to have her here, to spend more time together as a family. But the truth is, I don't know if I am. I just know that it makes our summer more . . . complicated. Things have never been easy with Margaret around.

Case in point, the fact that we have to make conversation with one another now. Something that we've gotten out of practice doing since she's been gone.

Margaret got increasingly itchier to leave senior year. She seemed to walk around with a constant desire to pick arguments with anyone in her vicinity. I tried not to get underfoot. She and Mama fought over everything, from her college applications to the brand of orange juice we'd stock in the fridge. I was relieved when she finally moved to New York.

Now that she's back, she's as prickly and untouchable as ever, and for the hundredth time, I wonder why my initial instinct when the incident happened was to call her.

She comes downstairs one morning in a peplum blouse with polka dots and a swishy navy pencil skirt with a fishtail cut, looking like she's about to give her opening statement before the International Court of Justice. I'm sitting at the counter in my loose boxer shorts and printed tee, with one knee drawn up to my chest. "Not sitting like a lady," Mama would say if she saw me, which luckily, she doesn't. She left breakfast on the table and went out early.

I'm spooning savory steamed egg custard into my mouth. It's a perennial breakfast favorite, drizzled with soy sauce and a fragrant dash of sesame oil. "There's one for you," I say, mouth half-full, pointing to the bowl Mama left next to the stove. "Shouldn't you already be at work? It's half past nine."

She grunts, which doesn't answer the question, and heads unswerving to the coffee maker.

We settle into an awkward silence, pierced only by the sounds of coffee grinds against the bag, the crinkle of the paper strainer, and the clunking made by the coffee maker as it struggles to life.

"So," I say, as she pours herself a strong cup, no sugar or cream (which to me, tastes like tar), "how were your first two days at the firm?"

"Fine."

"Are you doing interesting things?"

"Kind of."

I feel like I'm talking to a brick wall. An intense brick wall. I've always gotten the impression that Margaret finds me annoying, although she's never come out and said it. A vision flashes before me of myself as a twittering yellow canary chirping around the head of a sleeping bear.

Seems pretty accurate.

I try again. "Do you like the people you're working with?" This actually gets her to look at me, so it's progress.

"Yes, mostly." Her mouth twists. "They have another intern this summer. It's Rajiv."

Oh, shit.

Rajiv and Margaret were together for nearly all of high school. It was a secret at home that they were dating. A secret because we all knew Mama's unspoken opinions. First, that dating in high school was a distraction and waste of time. And second, that she would never approve of her daughters dating any shades of brown. My friends, sure. She liked Abaeze and Violet. But she had double standards about her own children. It made me uncomfortable, and it made Margaret angry. I expected Margaret to tell Mama about her boyfriend eventually, despite all this—making Mama mad was one thing she never shied away from anyway—but for some reason, she never did.

I always liked Rajiv. He was nice to me. Nicer than Margaret 90 percent of the time. And thoughtful. When I had questions about electives, I would go to him, not my sister.

Margaret never asked me to lie for her, but I knew not to tell. Until one night, when I accidentally let it slip over dinner. I immediately knew it was a mistake, but I couldn't take it back. Margaret and Rajiv broke up soon after that, but I don't know what went down. We haven't spoken about it since, and I can't help but feel she resents me for blowing her cover.

"That's, um, unlucky," I say.

She snorts. "Yeah, unlucky is one way to put it. More like the universe is playing a cosmic joke on me."

"What are you going to do?"

"Well, I've made it two days without saying much to him, so if we keep it up, maybe I can make it through the summer," she says wryly.

"Yikes. Maybe it'll be better if you guys can just talk to each other like normal?" I wince. It sounds stupid coming out, but she doesn't seem to notice.

"I don't think he wants to talk to me, Annalie."

I want to ask her what happened, but she already looks so broken that I'm afraid she'll just shatter if I do.

Margaret dumps her cup in the sink. "Okay, well, I'm going to head out." I notice she hasn't had a bite of breakfast. She shoulders her tote. As she reaches the entrance to the hallway, she pauses and turns back. "Hey, Annalie?"

"Yeah?"

She looks conflicted, like she's trying to decide whether she should say something. After a moment, her face smooths. "Nothing. I'll see you later."

Audrey has been especially impatient around me since I had to shut down the store during the air-conditioning incident. My job has essentially been reduced to me doing things while Audrey stands over my shoulder, pointing out any deviation from the standard process. *You didn't fill the scoop enough. The double scoop is $3.30, not $3.50. The waffle cone is more expensive than a regular cone. People can't ask for half scoops, Annalie.*

I would ask her to piss up a creek, except I'm pretty sure the manager has put her up to it, even if she's taken on the role with a lot more relish than is necessary.

After half an hour of excruciating micromanaging, I finally speak up. "Do you think this is a little excessive?"

"This is not my idea," she huffs. "I just want to make sure that you don't burn down the store."

"Good thing I'm not working with fire," I say, dry as a bone.

"I'm responsible for whatever you do here today, so I'm trying to make sure *I* don't get in trouble for *you* messing up."

I sigh. "Okay, if you think you have to."

"I think I have to," she says crisply. "By the way, you should try not to get distracted when Thom comes in."

"What are you talking about?"

"Oh, give it up. I can see the way you lose all peripheral vision when he shows up in the afternoons. Also, I can put two and two together. I can figure out when everything went downhill and how it aligns with what time Thom comes in every day. Don't look at me like that. Even you can't think I'm that dumb."

My face is flaming. I wonder how noticeable it is. Answer: probably super noticeable. "Don't be ridiculous," I say in the most unconvincing voice possible. There goes my career as an actress. "I have no idea what you're talking about."

"Sure. I totally believe you." She rolls her eyes and looks down at her phone, finally bored of watching me like a hawk.

She backs off for a minute, and I move on to serving a family of three, all of whom are extremely indecisive about what flavor they want. I just finish checking them out when Audrey lets out an audible gasp. "Oh my god," she says.

I'm expecting her to chastise me for inappropriately man-handling the evidently decades-old cash register by pushing the buttons too hard. "What?" I snap.

Her demeanor does a total one-eighty. "I just heard about your family. You never said anything. I'm sorry. That really sucks." I've never seen her sound anything less than completely put out by my presence.

I stare at her. "What are you talking about?"

Her brows furrow. "Your house. It's on the front page of today's paper."

It's like the room has plunged fifty degrees in two seconds.

"What are you talking about?" I demand.

"People are posting about it. Have you really not seen?"

My heart is pounding. How could it be in the paper? I'm 99 percent sure none of our neighbors know. We filed a police report. But we haven't heard anything, and surely the paper wouldn't have published without at least attempting to reach out to us for comments.

And then it dawns on me. Of course. Margaret.

No wonder she was sneaking around the morning after.

I pull out my phone, which I haven't checked since this morning. Sure enough, I have texts from Violet and Thom, and other people from school. Violet's says: *uhhh did you know you're in the paper today?* I don't even look at Thom's. People are sending around links to the story on Twitter and Facebook.

Local Family's Garage Spray-Painted with Racial Slur. Beneath the headline, a picture of our garage door with the word sprayed across it.

> *Vandals targeted a local Chinese family with a racial slur on Monday, the police department has confirmed. The vandalism has been recorded as criminal damage to property for the time being, although an investigation is ongoing. The residents of the house, which include Xuefeng Wang and her daughters Margaret and Annalie Flanagan, are shocked by the incident. "It*

really goes to show that racism in this community is alive and well," Margaret told the Gazette.

I get hotter and hotter as I'm reading until I can't read any further. Margaret went to the paper. She didn't say anything to me, and I'm willing to bet she didn't say anything to Mama either.

Audrey is gaping at me, eyes wide.

This is exactly what I *didn't* want to happen. This, people gawking at me with a mixture of pity and scandal, the continuous apologies, which I'm sure people are messaging me about. I am different now, apart. And it's not because of the vandalism, but because Margaret chose to make us victims. Margaret decided to mark us, and I feel more different than I've ever felt before. I hate it.

Audrey's expression repulses me. My stomach roils. "I have to go," I tell her.

Her hands flutter in surprise. "Right now?"

A customer at the counter clears his threat. "Excuse me. Is anyone going to take my order?"

"You should probably handle that," I say. I remove my apron and hang it on the door.

"Are you taking a break? When are you coming back?" she shouts after me. But I'm already out the door.

Six

MARGARET

When I come home, Annalie is waiting at the dinner table, and she's fuming. Mama is cooking in the background, turned away from me so I can't see her face.

Everything erupts in a matter of seconds. Annalie slams down a copy of the *Gazette* in front of me. "Look at this."

Our story is on the front page. They finally printed it. The headline screams in all caps.

"Care to explain how your quotes ended up in the paper?"

Mama whips around and stares at me.

"I provided them," I say quietly.

Annalie is angrier than I've seen her in a long time. Her nostrils flare. "Right. Behind our backs. You didn't even tell us after the fact. I had to find out from Audrey Pacer at the Sprinkle Shoppe. Fucking Audrey Pacer! Oh, and social media. I found out from them before my own sister."

I set my tote on the ground carefully, softly against the kitchen wall. I didn't tell Annalie and Mama because I knew that until the *Gazette* printed the story, they might call the newspaper and insist that it get pulled. "I'm sorry I didn't tell you."

"Our names are in here, by the way. Thanks for including them, again without telling us. God, I can't believe you."

Maybe it's the fact that I've proofread five briefs in a row nonstop today, and edited hundreds of footnotes into the proper format according to the legal style guide, or the three days of silent oppressiveness in a room with my ex-boyfriend, who hates me and who is trapped with me until the end of the summer. Or the fact that I'm looking at the photo of our garage and the brazen red lettering along the front, printed in the *Gazette* now for everyone to see. A familiar balloon of rage reinflates itself in my chest.

"Why are you yelling at me? Our garage got vandalized by racists, and your initial reaction is that you're mad I talked about it? How fucked up is that?" I shout at her.

Mama's eyes flick back and forth between me and Annalie. She walks over to the dinner table and picks up the newspaper. Her fingers tighten on the pages. "What is this?" she asks. I can't bear to look at her, but I don't need to because Annalie is louder.

"You can't just show up on our front door after moving out a year ago and pretend like you're suddenly the head of this family, like you can just make decisions for all of us," Annalie says. "You don't even live here. And you're just going to leave at the end of the summer, but we're still going to have to live here, and we're still going to deal with the bullshit you've exposed us to in front of the entire town."

I laugh derisively. "*You're* the one who called me to come take care of this, because you knew you couldn't do it. So don't act like I totally overstepped my bounds. This is what you wanted."

"It's *not*. This is our lives, not some chance for you to prove your social justice warrior cred."

Her words pierce me so sharply that I'm struck speechless.

"You're always doing stuff like this," she rants. "And now you're coming back because here's your chance to be in the spotlight again."

"It's not about that! You think it's cool to be called a racial slur? You're on the side of the racists?"

"So some people sprayed some stupid shit on our garage door. Who cares?"

"Do you really believe that?" I ask her, trembling. "You really think it's not that big of a deal?"

"It is a big deal!" she shouts. "But you're making it all about you. What about us? What about what we wanted to do? You know what I want to do? Stop making ourselves the focal point of this whole thing. I can be anti-racist and still not want to be the face of your movement. But you didn't give me any say." She swallows. "Do you have any idea what it was like to go to high school with you and constantly hear people making fun of how you're always dumping on the smallest things?"

Even though I've been in college for a year now, hearing that makes me freeze. It's not like I didn't know, but I hate how it feels like an open wound. "Sorry that it was so hard for you. You really had it rough," I sneer at her.

Mama drops the paper and it falls with a flutter. "Enough! Girls, stop shouting," she snaps. She steps in between me and Annalie as though protecting us from each other. "And don't use the bad words." She turns to me, her expression laden with disappointment. "You didn't say you gave an interview. You should have told us. You should let us decide."

Her disapproval hurts. It always has.

"Neither of you are taking this seriously," I say.

The two of them are standing together now on the other side of the table, staring me down as if I'm the one who has done something unforgivable to them, even with the picture on the front page splayed out between us. We've fallen back into our old pattern of Mama and Annalie against me, and I can't win.

I shake my head. "I don't understand you two. It's like you want to be bullied."

"Try to understand us, Jinghua," she says firmly. "Not everything is a fight."

"But some things should be!" I insist.

"Don't yell at me. You never listen." She is harsh and final.

"Mama!" I'm so furious I can't lower my voice. "People attacked our house because we are Chinese! Don't you want to do something about it?"

She adds more water to the simmering pot, shaking her head. "There will always be bad people," she says. "You have to accept it. Bad things happen to Chinese people all the time in this country. What does complaining do?"

Her passivity incenses me. How can she say that? How can she be such a doormat? My mother has *never* spoken up when people treat her poorly, not once. Not when I was six in first grade and a boy asked me right in front of her if her name was "Ching Chong." Can't she see that she's fitting into every stereotype about being demure and timid? Why does she want to be that for her daughters? I refuse to be quiet.

"I don't choose to accept it," I say staunchly. "I won't, even if the two of you do."

It's childish, but I leave to go upstairs so I can have the last word, even if it means missing out on dinner.

Nobody stops me.

I don't sleep well that weekend. I show up to the office on Monday, and I swear the bags under my eyes have become the defining feature of my face. Rajiv is already there. He usually is. He likes to come early and get settled.

We usually don't say hello. I sit at my desk and prepare to commence a fourth day of silence.

I haven't been able to stop thinking about whether I should've done things differently with the news article. On one hand, I hurt my family. I caught them by surprise. I knew that would happen before I went to the *Gazette*. But I truly didn't expect that they would be so volcanically angry.

On the other hand, I still believe that if I had said something before, they would've prevented me from going or kept the article from running. Would that have been so bad? Round and round my mind circles.

Annalie should know why I did what I did. She knows what it means to be called a Chink. *Or*, a small, nasty voice inside my head says, *maybe she doesn't because she's not the one who looks Chinese.*

I put in my earplugs and boot up my desktop, resigning myself to a miserable morning. Just as I crank up the volume on my music, I get a tap on my shoulder.

"Hi," Rajiv says. He holds out a cup of hot coffee. With both hands. Like a peace offering.

I just gape at him.

He puts it down on my desk. "It's for you. Black, no sugar. If that's still how you take your coffee, from what I remember."

"Thanks," I say, amazed at hearing his voice but also at the fact that he still remembers my coffee preferences.

He rubs the back of his neck and twists his mouth like it's hard for him to figure out what to say. "I read about what happened to your house."

"In the paper?"

"Someone texted me about it. The online article is making the rounds."

"Right."

A loaded pause.

"Look, that sounds like it was really shitty. I was sorry to see it. Hope you're doing okay." He gestures at the coffee. "Thought it was the least I could do."

"Thanks," I say again. I'm not sure if I've recovered from the shock of him talking to me.

"Is that why you came back here for the summer?"

"Yeah."

"I see. So it didn't have to do with me," he says quietly, almost to himself. My face must give me away, because he gives a short, sharp laugh. "Okay, that was a little narcissistic of me. Of course you had a different reason."

I don't tell him that I intentionally blocked all his updates.

"No, I did not come back here specifically to torment you. I'm not a stalker," I say, and I earn a small smile from him. "In case you hadn't noticed, I also thought it was pretty crappy of the universe to have landed me in the same office as the one person who's the least interested in seeing me again."

"I'm not the least interested in ever seeing you again," he says slowly. I can't read his expression.

I resist the urge to say, *Could've fooled me*. It probably would have sounded bitter.

"Ah, sorry," he says after I don't respond. "I've made this awkward again. Can we start over? I have to say, after three days of cold-shouldering each other, I'm not sure it's sustainable to do it all summer. Let's just not." He holds out his hand.

"What do you want me to do with that?"

"Shake?" He sighs. "You're exactly as I remember."

"I'm going to ignore that." I take his hand, and we shake. His warm fingers send sparks up my veins. I didn't even know I could feel like that anymore. I thought all the nerve endings in my skin had died. *Not allowed*, I tell myself firmly. Against the rules of friendly handshaking. My body still isn't used to Rajiv's touch being something strictly platonic.

I'm realizing, though, that I also don't know what it looks like to be strictly platonic with him. Once upon a time, we were friends, but that was a long, long time ago. Then again, I'm not sure that "friends" is what we're aiming for either. Amicable coworkers? Sounds tragic.

"You did that interview with the paper by yourself, didn't you?"

I nod.

"I knew it. The only quotes were from you, even though the article mentioned your mom and sister." He leans against the edge of his desk. "That was brave."

I meet his eyes. "You think so?"

"Yes. You all must have been so upset."

"My mom and sister definitely wouldn't agree." I take a sip of the coffee. It's strong and piping hot. Invigorating.

"Why?"

"I didn't tell them I was doing an interview."

"Ah." He smirks. "Very Margaret."

"Are you taking their side?"

He holds up his hands. "Whoa, I'm not taking any sides. I'm just saying it's nothing less than what I would expect of you."

"I didn't want the police to write it off as some minor property crime. I thought the media would be the best way to make them pay more attention to it. Do you think it was the right thing to do?" I press. I don't know why I'm asking. He can't absolve me. But Rajiv is honest and would never tell me something just because I wanted to hear it.

He rubs his chin, considering for a while. "Margaret," he says slowly. "If you're asking for my opinion, then yes, I think you did the right thing."

I sigh. "If only you could convince my family of that."

"Well, you can't expect everyone to see things your way all the time."

"I guess," I say unwillingly.

He sits in his chair and puts an acceptable amount of space

between the two of us again. "So are you staying for the summer to keep the family together and take care of everybody?"

"No. At this point, I'm sure they'd rather me go back to New York and leave them alone." I take a deep breath. "I'm here to make sure we find out who did it."

He laughs and turns back to his computer. "Spoken like a true lawyer. Sounds like this is the right profession for you."

I know it doesn't mean we're friends or even that he wants to be friends at any point, but his approval means the world to me. I'm surprised, after all this time, at just how much.

Seven

Mrs. Maples, a widow who lives across the street, comes over the day after the article is published and brings us a massive tray of eggplant parmesan and express her support for my family. It's really sweet of her, but honestly, like Audrey, mainly just makes me uncomfortable. We don't talk to any of our neighbors, other than to wave if they're doing yardwork, so having her on my doorstep feels particularly out of place.

"You don't even look Chinese," she says to me when she hands over the tray. Like the time someone said to Margaret at the grocery store that her English was "so good," or the time my fourth-grade teacher told Mama during a parent-teacher conference that he loved fortune cookies. Things that made me cringe.

I'm just glad that Margaret wasn't the one who was around to answer the door for Mrs. Maples. Her comment annoys me, but I bite my tongue and thank her. She means well. What am I supposed to do? Yell at an old lady for being unintentionally racist? It's not like she was out there spray-painting a racial slur on our door. But I know Margaret wouldn't have been as magnanimous about it. She'd be preaching to Mrs. Maples about microaggressions and telling me to stop being such a wuss.

I don't go back to the Sprinkle Shoppe. The manager calls me a couple of times and then finally leaves a voice mail telling me I'm fired, which is actually quite funny to me, because it seems pretty obvious that I've quit.

I keep seeing Audrey's somber, sympathetic expression in my head. Although I disliked Audrey and her perpetual stink eye, getting her pity face was infinitely worse. I can't stomach that. Even if it means I look extra fragile for quitting over my alleged trauma.

The thing that's most infuriating is that Margaret never apologizes. Not after I blew up at her on the first day, and not any day after. Every successive meal we have together, I keep expecting her to say she's sorry—at least for hurting our feelings, if not for going to the paper—but it never comes. I guess it's too much to assume she would. If there's one thing Margaret hates doing the most, it's admitting fault.

"Why are you letting her get away with this?" I ask Mama when we're by ourselves one night, washing dishes together. "She's ruining everything. And she won't even say sorry."

"Your sister . . . she sees things differently than us," she says, her face pained.

"I don't want her around," I reply brutally. "I wish she would go back to New York."

"Don't say that! She's your sister."

"Doesn't really feel like we are related."

Mama pauses as she hands me a clean plate. "You have always been very different," she says.

Her comment causes me to sink a little. I know the many ways in which we are different. There's a bookcase dedicated to awards Margaret received through her life. Nothing like that for me. Margaret may be a pain in the butt, but Mama also brags about her all the time. To friends, to strangers. I can't remember a time where she did that for me. Even though I know she gets along with me better.

"Not a bad thing," she says. "I like that you are not the same. Boring when sisters are exactly the same."

"Who is your favorite, though?" I say teasingly.

"I don't have favorite," she replies. "You're both my favorite." But she smiles and squeezes my shoulder. "It will be okay. Margaret will do what she needs. We will survive."

"Why can't you tell her not to do this stuff?"

"You think Margaret listen to me?" she says indignantly. "She never listen to me."

"So I am the best?"

She slides a glance over. "You are best at listening to me."

"Okay, favorite. I won't tell Margaret."

I make her laugh.

People from school message me about the article, all expressing sympathy. In some ways, it's nice that people care, but after a while, it starts to feel obnoxious having to reply over and over and then find something profound and not awkward to say about it.

The truth is, I don't know what I feel, whether it's angry or sad or some combination of the two. I guess the closest I can get is: unsettled.

It's not something I know how to share with people I casually pass in the halls. Yet so many of them feel the need to reach out and share some comfort with language that's entirely inadequate for the situation. What can you say? How many different ways can you say it's awful? What does it mean to hear the word *sorry* so many times from people who aren't apologizing for themselves?

Thom texts me too. I don't know how to respond, so I eventually I write him back, *It's okay.* It's *not* okay, but what am I supposed to say to a boy who I've only started seeing? I'm not ready to share my deepest, darkest thoughts with him. I don't want to scare him away.

I wish I knew what types of messages Margaret is receiving, but we're not talking. I know it's unfair to be madder at her than at whoever vandalized our garage, but it's easier to concentrate my anger at her. She's identifiable. She's here. And she keeps acting super smug about how the entire community is talking about our garage.

I can't stand to be around her, but I'm totally trapped at home.

It's Violet who ultimately gives me the idea for something else to do.

"Margaret is organizing a listening session to talk about race relations," I tell her while we're watching our baking competition show one afternoon. "Here. In this town. How many non-white people are there even here? I have to get out of this house."

"Why don't you get another job?" she says.

"I feel like it's kind of late. People picked up summer shifts a couple of weeks ago."

"Why don't you try applying to Bakersfield? It's always busy, and the bakery never has help."

"Well, he's clearly hired somebody this summer."

"Which means he's hiring," she presses. "You're a great baker. The banana cream pie you made last week almost made my mom cry."

Her suggestion falls like a thunderbolt. I spend so much time tinkering with recipes, but I never thought about baking for money. I only do it for family and friends, and because I like it. But why can't I get a job at Bakersfield? I can't make some of the complicated things in the display case, for sure. But I can whip up a chocolate buttercream cake that knocks your socks off, bake the hell out of a French apple tart. I know how to do all the basics, and I'm pretty good at improvising off what I see on TV.

I only got the job at the ice cream shop to be around Thom. The idea of a job that I might actually like is sort of exciting.

"I feel like all your ideas coincidentally provide a pretty serious fringe benefit to you," I say with a smile.

"What does it matter, if the idea is a good one?" she replies innocently. "Am I motivated by the possibility of free pastries? Sure. But that's just a distant secondary consideration."

"Always putting me first."

"Exactly."

That's how I end up at Bakersfield Bakery bright and early in the morning when it opens, wearing my best I'm-not-a-teenage-hooligan outfit and asking Old Man Bakersfield to give me a job.

He peers at me, brows furrowed. "I'm sorry, what?"

"I'd like to apply for a job here," I repeat.

"There are no openings here," he says after a disbelieving pause.

Violet would tell me to be more assertive. She'd have me make my case. I resist all my internal impulses to thank him and slink away.

"But I know you're taking people," I point out.

"I don't know what you're talking about. I work alone." He's firm and insistent, even though I know he's lying, because I saw a new cashier. He glares at me, daring me to contradict him.

"I'd do anything," I say finally. "Come in and prep in the morning. Sweep the floors. Clean the windows. Take customers. I can help bake. I can bake anything!"

"Help bake?" He looks me up and down. "What do you know about baking?"

"I'm a decent baker."

"What's your name again?"

Positive development. "Annalie."

"Right. You and that short Asian girl come in here a lot."

I flinch a little. "Her name is Violet," I correct him.

He hesitates, but then shakes his head. "I'm sorry. I just don't need any help. Aren't there other places you can go get a job?"

"I want to work here." I leave out the part about quitting slash being fired from the Sprinkle Shoppe. Probably would not bode well for my chances of getting hired. "You don't even have to pay me that much." *Great negotiating skills, Annalie.* Desperate times call for desperate measures.

He sighs. "Are you ever going to leave me alone?"

"No."

He audibly grumbles. There are already people standing in front of the display case, trying to pick out what they want for breakfast. "All right. Fine," he says.

"Really?" I'm amazed at my luck, stunned that I've actually convinced him to say yes.

"Eight dollars an hour, no more. This first week will be a trial run. If it's not working, or if it becomes unprofitable, I'm letting you go."

"Completely got it."

"Get back here. There's an extra apron behind the double doors. It's one of mine, so it might be big, but it'll do."

"Wait, right now?" I'm taken aback, unprepared.

"I thought you said you wanted a job," he barks.

"I do!"

"Then yes, right now."

I scramble back to join him. Luckily, I wore comfortable shoes today. I thought about wearing high heels but decided it wouldn't be sensible for interviewing at a bakery.

"Behind the double doors is the kitchen. If you swing a left immediately after you go in, there's an office where I do and keep all the paperwork. You don't need to be in there at all. It's taken care of. On the right is the bathroom. You know how to make puff pastry?"

I nod, glad that I'm not starting from scratch.

"There's equipment in the kitchen. Flour, sugar, and salt are stocked along the shelves, bulk butter in the fridge. I want you to make enough puff pastry dough for twenty sheets and put them in the fridge so they'll be ready for tomorrow morning. We'll see how they come out in the oven tomorrow. Don't mess it up."

With that, he turns to the customers and leaves me to my task.

I tentatively push through the double doors. It opens to a spacious silver world. The room is long and narrow, extending deep. There are two islands back-to-back in the middle, one stainless steel, one wood. The edges of the kitchen are ringed with stainless-steel counters and well-stocked shelves. There's a big commercial refrigerator along one side and an enormous apron sink. The floor is black-and-white-checked tile. There are big windows in the back that peer out into a fenced back lot and let in a strong wash of natural light. The kitchen smells deliciously like butter and sugar. This is the kitchen of my dreams.

The wooden counter already has a dusting of flour from this morning. I wonder what time Bakersfield has to come in to get all the pastries ready for the day when the bakery opens at eight. Probably something like four a.m.

I poke around to gather all the ingredients, feeling nervous. I know how to do this, but I've never baked as part of an audition before. There's an enclosed wooden pantry with all kinds of extracts: peppermint, almond, vanilla. A coffee maker in the corner with a grinder, stacked neatly with different types of coffee beans. Industrial bags of all-purpose flour line one shelf. A very large, nice KitchenAid mixer sits on the stainless-steel island.

Okay, I tell myself. *Don't mess it up.* The adrenaline rushes through my veins. This is my chance to show that I really know what I'm doing. It's fine. *I can mix puff pastry dough in my sleep*, I tell myself. But I've never made this much at once.

I'm elbow deep in flour, kneading the first batch of dough on the counter, when somebody who isn't the old man emerges from the office. "Excuse me," says an alarmed voice. "What are you doing in here?"

I turn around, and it's Daniel. I wonder if he's some hallucination of mine, since Bakersfield hasn't mentioned him, and Daniel seems to only be around to yell at me.

"Haven't I seen you before?" he says. His eyes narrow. "Oh, right. The rude girl from last week. Now you've broken into the kitchen."

"Excuse me? I should ask you what you're doing back here."

"Well, I'm Owen Bakersfield's grandson, so that's what I'm doing here. Back to my question, though."

The grandson! This throws me for a loop. "You're related?"

"Typically, being one's grandson makes you related, yes. And you?"

I don't know what I expected out of Bakersfield's personal

life, but British grandson was not on my bingo card. I kind of thought he was just a loner with no kids.

Daniel is staring at me like I'm an idiot, and I realize he's waiting for an answer. I look down at my hands, covered in flour. "I'm, um, making puff pastry."

"Right. I was asking a bit more of a general question."

I blush. "Sorry, I just got hired. Like thirty minutes ago."

"I didn't know he was hiring."

"He wasn't. I sort of talked him into it."

He raises an eyebrow. "Because you're a professional baker?"

"Uhh, not exactly. I do know how to bake, though."

"Mm-hmm," he says, sounding aggressively unconvinced. He looks over skeptically, and I'm suddenly acutely aware of the flour smudge on my chin that I can feel, my hair tossed up unceremoniously. I'm sweaty, and from the reflective surface across the counter, my eye makeup is smearing. I feel like he's assessing me, and I'm coming up short.

"How long are you staying with your grandpa?" I ask.

"The summer," he says, sounding extremely displeased. "I'm helping my grandad with the books. He's good for the cooking, not so much with the numbers."

"I've never seen you around before."

"That's because I've never been here before. Family situation is complicated. I'm from London."

I nod seriously. "I sort of got that," I say, trying to make a joke.

It falls flat. He frowns. "You couldn't really know, though. Not all British people are from London."

Awkward silence. "And you're going back in the fall?"

"I'm going to be a first-year at Columbia, actually. In New York." He says it like Columbi-ER, with an extra *r* tacked on at the end.

"My sister goes to NYU," I offer.

"Mm," he says noncommittally, like nothing could interest him less than bumping into anyone who could be related to me while he is in New York.

Bakersfield pokes his head back in the kitchen. "Oh, Daniel. This is Annika. She's going to be working here, assuming she's any good at baking. Annika, Daniel."

"Annalie," I say. "It's actually Annalie."

"Right. Isn't that what I said?" Bakersfield says. He turns to Daniel. "Anyway, stop distracting her. I didn't hire her just to keep you company." I can't help but feel mildly elated at Bakersfield's annoyance being directed at someone else.

"Of course not," Daniel says grumpily, and stalks past his grandfather without another word.

"Back to baking," Bakersfield says to me. "Impress me."

"Yes, sir."

Thom has been trying to get me to hang out, but I just haven't been in the mood. I know I'll have to respond to him soon, though.

It's still strange to me that Margaret can go out there and preach about what happened so publicly. I know other reporters have come knocking for follow-ups, but everything has channeled through her. I hate it, but I also couldn't do what she does, so in some ways, I'm glad.

Thom's persistence is both thrilling and strange, because during all of last year, when I would've died for a smile from him, I couldn't get so much as a glance in my direction. But I vow that I'm not going to let Margaret ruin yet another thing for me, not when everything is finally going right.

Me: sry for being MIA.

Him: thats okay. im just glad to hear from you. was afraid you were giving up on me. 😉

Me: nope. not yet.

Him: haha OUCH. sounds like im on a short leash. anyway i miss you. still want to accept my offer of taking you out?

Me: soo old school. like you wanna go on a date?

Him: . . . depends. is your answer going to be yes or no?

Me: hard to say without knowing what the plan is. i reserve my right to say no if it's something really dangerous or something really boring.

Him: playing it safe, huh?

Me: i just want to know what im getting myself into.

Him: lol, okay fair. well the idea is to go to the coffee club downtown. we can get coffee, but then later, some of my teammates and i are in a band and we're gonna play live.

Me: i could go for that.

Him: yeah?

Me: def. ☺

Him: sweet. i'll see you then.

The Coffee Club is right off the center of downtown, a block away from Bakersfield Bakery. Across the street is a circular park with fountains that light up at night. It's probably one of the prettiest places in town, surrounded by all the historical buildings, and a notorious spot for teenage make-outs. I try not to fantasize about anything of that nature as I walk by.

I'm wearing a little black dress with some gladiator sandals to keep it from being *too* dressy. I want to look casual, like I didn't try too hard. I smack my lips together nervously, checking my lipstick in my reflection in my cell phone screen one last time before I push open the doors.

The outside of the Coffee Club is deceivingly modest. It's a narrow storefront with drab lettering on the glass exterior. The inside, though, is quite deep. It opens all the way back, sort of like Bakersfield Bakery if the dividing wall and doors weren't separating the customer-facing part of the store from the enormous kitchen in the back.

I scan around for what feels like an eternity. I hate being the first person to arrive anywhere and having to stand alone while waiting for the other people to show up. The wait always induces anxiety. Even though it's not rational, it always makes me afraid that I'm being ditched. It's why I usually err on the side of being late. Today I keep it to five minutes after the appointed time. Not enough to be rude, just enough to be fashionably careless.

At first I don't see him, but he emerges from the back, grinning.

He is so good-looking I'm already blushing from head to toe.

"Hi," he says. He's wearing a striped shirt and red pants. He's definitely wearing cologne. On any other guy, it would be too heavy, but everything is perfect on Thom.

"Hello." I sound shy. I am shy. I haven't gone on a real first date in, ever? I would never admit that out loud.

"Fancy seeing you here." He leans in close so his mouth is practically brushing my ears. "You look amazing, by the way." I can feel his breath against my temples. I almost faint.

"Thanks."

"I was in the back, getting some equipment ready."

"Are you setting up?"

"Not yet," he says. "In half an hour. Enough time for us to get some coffee. My treat, obviously." He ushers me to the line. "What do you want?"

I'm extra indecisive, but I end up getting a sugary caramel coffee confection with double the height in whipped cream on top. Thom gets an Americano. We settle on a pair of couches by the window.

"My afternoon run isn't the same without you," he says.

"Sorry," I say, teasing.

"Why'd you quit?"

I shrug. I don't want to talk about it.

"Was it Audrey?"

It was, sort of, but not really. "No. It wasn't her."

"Did you break the air-conditioning for good?"

That makes me laugh. I completely forgot about that day. It seems so long ago, even though it was barely a week in the past. "I just want you to know that I quit. I did not get fired."

"Right. You quit before he could fire you." He's smiling, so the words come out as a gentle needling.

"Don't let anyone tell you otherwise."

"I thought you were fabulous at scooping ice cream. Probably the best they had," he says. "Plus, you were the cutest girl there."

It's my cue to turn into a tomato again. "I bet you say that to all the girls."

He shakes his head, his eyes never dropping from mine. "Just you."

We chat about school and soccer, and how he's going to camp later this summer. I learn more about the band, which is called Accidental Audio, and apparently performs semi-regularly in the area. They practice three times a week at Thom's house, where his family has a soundproofed room. There are five of them, all on the soccer team together. Thom plays bass, and he makes an embarrassing "slappin' da bass" joke from that movie *I Love You, Man*, and he gets the inflection so exact that I almost crack a rib from laughing.

I love hearing about all this. All this information about him that used to be so inaccessible and is now being freely shared, just by my asking. He used to seem so unattainable, but now, here he is, sitting across from me like he's been here my whole life and we haven't skipped a beat since the only distance between us was Justin Frick.

He leaves me after forty minutes—"Couldn't not give you an extra ten minutes," he says—to help the rest of the band set up. I loiter on the edge of the "stage" they've cleared out in the back, sipping the remnants of my cold coffee and watching them plug things in and test the mikes. I've seen the other guys around school before, but we've never talked.

One of them, Jeremy, was in my geometry class. Sat in the back, only spoke when called on. I don't think he's looked in my direction twice, but he comes over to say hi along with the other guys: Mike, Brayden, and Cameron, who the guys refer to as "Jones," his last name. They're all fit and gorgeous, with amazing tans and crisp smiles. They are all white.

"Nice to meet you, Anna," Mike, the lead singer, says.

My name isn't Anna, but I hate correcting people. "You too," I say. The other guys seem nice but distant. Thom said they were really excited to meet me, but obviously he was just saying that. This is sort of an obligatory thing for them. I try not to be hurt by it. They're probably all focusing on the performance.

By the time they're doing warm-ups, the Coffee Club is about three-quarters full, with people filtering in. A lot of them are people I recognize from high school. I wave at Alexa, who used to live on my block when I was younger, but moved to a different neighborhood in sixth grade. Although we aren't close anymore, she's always been friendly at school. Other people on the soccer team. Cheerleaders. The entire dance squad is here. And I spot Audrey, who sees me before I can avert my face. To my relief, she doesn't come over, but she does look momentarily surprised to see me here.

Actually, she's not the only one. A bunch of people are staring at me, maybe because this isn't really my scene, and I never would've shown up to watch Accidental Audio if it weren't for Thom. Not that I don't like live music, but these events are for the popular crowd, and I don't belong.

Still, I'm uncomfortably reminded that being here with Thom at the Coffee Club—and I guess at school if we get that far—allows me to blend in, in a way that I don't when I'm with Violet and Abaeze. When I'm with Thom, I look like just another white girl. For some reason, this makes me feel guilty.

There's nobody in the crowd to hang out with, but I try to be brave. I've been invited. I stand a little off to the side, so I have a clear view of Thom and Mike, but not right in front. Too intimidating.

The good thing about being at a concert is that nobody is really paying attention to me. People's eyes are glued to the stage, especially once the music starts. Accidental Audio's repertoire is probably what I'd describe as pop rock. It's really loud for a coffee shop, and it isn't helping that I'm standing just to the right of a huge speaker. But the crowd is super into it, and a lot of people seem to know the lyrics.

I just stand and sway while I watch them jam out onstage. Mike has a pretty decent voice. I'm impressed at how good they are for a high school band. Thom's fingers grip the neck of the instrument and his fingers fly back and forth across the strings. Mike holds the microphone in both hands and sings right into it, his mouth inches away.

Thom takes the mike and describes the next song. Everyone in the audience is listening raptly, and then cheering when he names it. The boys onstage grin. Their confidence radiates across the space. I'm convinced part of what makes the music good is their presence. They're shouting for the audience to join in or clap, and periodically, they point their mics toward the crowd and ask us to sing certain lines. They're standing above us like gods.

I am tiny in the audience below them. The girls around me are screaming, and one of them shouts, "You're so hot!" I'm totally dwarfed by the outpouring of affection coming from the crowd. I'm an ordinary speck, lost and almost invisible against Accidental Audio's overwhelming light.

Then Thom spots me among the masses, through the mess of his hair, and grins right at me, and I feel like a glowing goddess. Found at last.

After the show, Thom tells me to stick around as the band packs up. I ask if I can help, and he laughs and tells me to relax. I can't just stand there or I'll feel like a creepy groupie. So I hang around the coffee shop, helping the staff pick up random garbage that's been dropped on the ground.

The boys load everything into their trunks and come back out to chat for a couple of minutes. Mike is wearing a soccer jersey with *Thom* on the front. It says *The Frog* on the back and the big number emblazoned on it is *69*. It's not a soccer jersey from our school, though. I don't recognize the colors or the team.

"Why are you wearing Thom's shirt?" I ask.

All the guys snicker.

"It's an inside joke," Thom tells me. "We all went to the same soccer camp out of state last summer—we're actually going back in a couple of weeks. I got assigned this shirt, and obviously, Mike, being the mature person he is, loved the fact that my number was sixty-nine."

"It wasn't an accident," Mike says. "We had sign-up sheets for shirt numbers, and Thom left early that day, so I picked his. Whoops. Thought you'd love it!" He elbows Thom gleefully. I'm suddenly embarrassed, flushing red. Was that supposed to be a hint or was it just a joke? Does Thom really like to sixty-nine? I start thinking about the mechanics of it, which only serve to make me more flustered. I start to wonder how many girls Thom has slept with, and if he expects me to have slept with guys before.

"I think it was a hazing activity, since it was my first year," Thom says.

"I got an extra for myself," Mike says. "As a souvenir."

Thom sighs with exasperation and whispers conspiratorially to me. "Again, like I said, really mature. Anyway, what'd you think of the show?"

"It was amazing!" I gush. "You all sounded so good. You should go on a TV competition, like *The X Factor* or something."

They all give me kind of a pained look, and I realize I've said something super clumsy. Going on a TV show for singing is not cool. It's embarrassing. A cool person would not have said that.

There's an awkward silence for maybe several eons.

"I'm glad you liked it," Jones offers finally, delivering me from my humiliation.

"I think we should leave Thom to his date," Mike says, which could've been meant as a kind gesture, but also sounds like he's trying to pawn me off. "Thanks for coming to the show. It was nice to meet you, Anna!" They all file out the back as quick as they can, leaving me and Thom.

"Sorry," he says after they disappear.

"For what?"

"My friends are kind of dumb sometimes. They mean well. They think you're great."

I don't actually believe that they do, but it's a nice thing to say and takes a bit of the sting out of it. I get it. I'm not the type of person Thom normally dates. I'm shy and I don't have that many friends, and I'm not witty. I don't make the right jokes at the right times. Sometimes when I'm around people I'm trying to impress, I feel like all the words inside me are jumbled up, and I want to say things but I'm constantly thinking about how it's going to come out all wrong. Plus, I'm hyperaware of my body and hands. I'm basically a walking awkward turtle around popular kids.

I wish I could just own it, like Margaret does. She wasn't popular, but she never cared. Instead, I let it eat me up inside until I'm convinced everyone is thinking about it just as much as I am, which logically, I know can't be true.

"Come on," Thom says, putting his arm around my shoulders and guiding me out of the now-empty café. It's nighttime outside, and tonight, the sky is shockingly clear. "I'm really glad you came."

"Me too," I say.

"Everybody is gone now. You don't have to lie to me and tell me we were amazing. What did you really think?"

"I *really* thought you were great. I can't believe I haven't heard you guys play before."

He beams, pleased. "I hope that changes. You should come to more gigs."

"I definitely will," I promise.

"Good," he says. "Because I really like you."

His eyes crinkle as he grins. The bad parts of the day suddenly vanish and I want to live in this moment forever.

Eight

MARGARET

There are things that I can never talk about.

One, my father.

Who he was or where he might be. Or even what he looked like. In my house, there are no photos of him. It didn't bother me so much when I was younger, because I didn't realize it was strange. Part of growing up, I think, is realizing that not everything your family does is normal or acceptable.

Only later did it dawn on me that it was weird that Mama got rid of all his photos. I have some vague sense of what he looked like from my memories, but I don't know if those memories are reliable or some mental trick my brain came up with to fill an unnatural hole. The thing is, it's not like I don't know the identity of my father. I know who he is, and I have his name. I remember just enough of him to know what I'm missing.

Two, why Rajiv and I fell apart.

It still stings when he comes up in conversation between me and Mama.

"Rajiv and I are working together," I tell her at some point after the first week.

"Oh," she says blankly. "At law firm?"

"Yes."

She pats my hand. "Good to stay in touch with your high school friends."

It's like a slap. We weren't just friends. I nod, unable to contradict her, even now. She doesn't bat an eyelid at the thought of us working together. She isn't worried at all. I think that makes it worse.

When I go into work now and we greet each other in the mornings, I watch his eyes. I wait for him to bring it up, how badly I betrayed him. Why he never called or texted me back after the night it all ended. He never does. I wonder all the time whether it's because he's gotten over it, or he's decided that he simply can't bear to speak of it, like me.

I keep these things buried deep down. Although I think I am very different from Mama, in some ways we are the same. My family keeps its secrets. We all have things we don't say.

Fisher, Johnson does an annual charitable activity together in the summer. It's supposed to be a chance to give back to the community with the added bonus for the interns of getting to know the lawyers better. This year, it's volunteering at a local soup kitchen.

We all gather in the morning in our best nonwork clothes to walk over. The soup kitchen is about a fifteen-minute walk from the firm. The sidewalk is pretty narrow, so everybody clusters with their closest colleagues to chat. Of course, it leaves Rajiv and me trailing at the end of the group, looking at each other.

"Shall we?" he says. He's wearing a shallow white V-neck tee with jeans. The disagreeable part of my brain notices that the pants make his butt look incredible. I immediately turn to look everywhere but there.

We walk behind everyone. We've gotten better at breaking the silence the last few days, but we still haven't found quite the right rhythm.

"The article about your family is all anyone is talking about," he says. "Among people who know us, anyway."

I know. I don't use social media much, but I've been checking in. People have been messaging me too. I don't respond. There's nothing much I have to say to anybody here anymore. It's all mostly been condolences, except for one. "Did you see Sean Reynolds's post?"

Rajiv winces. "Yeah. He was always a douche, though. I would ignore it."

Sean was our year in high school and one of the co-chairs of the debate team. He had a lot of opinions about everything and hated it when anyone disagreed with him. His grandfather had been the mayor of our town. His dad was on the city council. He always had this attitude of owning the entire place no matter where he went. We clashed a lot in high school when he lost out on class president to me. He was still on the student board, and we never agreed on anything.

He shared the newspaper article but wrote a long post about how the article was unfairly painting the community with a broad brush, and how I was making it look like the entire town was racist. *It's understandable that Margaret is upset, but it's not an excuse to play the race card, and her comments alienate potential allies,* he wrote. *Such a response to an isolated, unfortunate incident divides us rather than unites us.*

While a lot of people commented in support of me, there were plenty of people who had liked and shared his post as well. I tried not to hold a personal vendetta against all those people.

"I can't believe he actually said *I* played the race card." I shake my head. "Apparently I'm the one in the wrong even though someone wrote a racial slur on *my* door. I have this theory that only low-key racist people use the term 'race card.' Obviously Sean had to make this incident all about him, as per usual."

"You shouldn't let him bother you," Rajiv says. "He clearly hasn't changed."

"The thing is, a lot of people agree with him! They think me talking publicly about racism is more offensive than an actual hate crime. People would rather I just kept my mouth shut and looked sad. Then they could white knight in and express sympathy without feeling uncomfortable. I'm not in the business of keeping people from feeling uncomfortable."

"I can see New York did not mellow you out."

I glance at him sharply.

"Relax," he says with a smile. "I'm just kidding. I agree with you. You shouldn't give anybody a pass. But you're not going to convince Sean. He's just in it to stir up trouble. You know he'll never learn to see anything from anyone else's perspective." He shrugs. "Why even try with people like that? If all you did was cry to the reporter, he would've said you were overreacting."

I grumble. "When did you become so enlightened?"

"I was always enlightened. You just rarely listened to me."

"Ha. Ha."

"Anyway, how are you liking New York?"

"I love it," I say. It's true. "It's everything I imagined living in a city could be like."

"Sounds like it was a good choice," he says agreeably.

"The best. You can't imagine. You never run out of things to do. And everything you could possibly want is within reach. Like, I can get a freshly made breakfast sandwich by walking five hundred feet. I can order pizza at three in the morning. I can have the greatest Thai food at any hour. I can go to the best museums in the world by taking the subway five stops. And it's so diverse. Nobody will ever look at you weird because nobody looks alike and there will always be somebody weirder on the next corner." I'm gushing, but I can't stop myself. Talking about it actually reminds me how much I miss being there.

We arrive at the soup kitchen. Rajiv and I immediately get assigned to unloading boxes of donations onto the back shelves, probably because we're young and can keep bending over without messing up our backs. Different cans of vegetables and soups have to get organized in their sections.

Rajiv slices open a cardboard box loaded full with cans. "I'll hand them to you, and you put them on the shelf?"

"Sure."

He picks up a can and hands it to me. "Tomato soup."

I take it and scan the labels on the shelves until I find the right spot. I stand on my tiptoes to slide it into place.

"You know, I've never been to New York," he says. "I have

a cousin in New Jersey, but that's about as close as I've ever gotten."

"You should go visit."

"Maybe. I don't really have anybody to stay with or see."

Awkwardness descends. It's easy to forget that we're no longer anything to each other, which means it makes no sense for us to visit each other.

"Chicken noodle." He hands over another can. Our fingers touch on the exchange. I blush and turn away. "Unless you want to hang out."

"Oh." Did I just hear that right?

"It was just a suggestion," he says mildly, clearly misunderstanding my hesitance.

"I didn't know you would want to. I didn't think we were friends."

"Okay," he says. "Not as friends. But I'd need a tour guide. I don't know anything about the city."

I can't help but smile. Why is he being so nice? The tension between us eases. "As a tour guide. I can do that. Are you going to pay me? I don't offer my services for free."

"If you have a reasonable price."

"I'll have to think about it."

"Get back to me," he says, grinning. "Creamed corn. Catch."
He tosses me a can, and I catch it.

"Don't throw things," I scold. "You know I'm terrible at hand-eye coordination. I'm going to drop it and then we'll get in trouble."

"Didn't pick up a sport in college?"

"Definitely not." I wrinkle my nose. Sports was one thing I could never do, especially after my aborted attempt at tennis. "I think it's pretty hard to pick up something new in college."

"Not necessarily," Rajiv says. "I started something new."

"What?"

"Breaking." He smiles sheepishly.

I think I've misheard him. "Come again?"

"I started breaking, you know, dance."

"What got you into that?"

He stretches his back and gives me a can of green beans. "Our school has this thing, before school starts for freshmen, where all these clubs set up booths on the main quad, handing out flyers and trying to get people to sign up. The people at the breaking booth were cool, and I wanted to try something new."

"Wow. I'm impressed."

"Why? You thought I was too nerdy for that?" he teases.

Definitely not. Rajiv was never part of the popular crowd in high school, but he had this easygoing attitude that made people like him, even if they weren't his friends, per se. He never seemed awkward or uncomfortable. He always seemed at ease, no matter where he was. Nobody would ever have called him a nerd.

He's especially un-nerdy now. He's so relaxed in his casual clothes. His jeans hang off his hips perfectly. The light glints off the studs in his ears. His long, floppy hair is a revelation, and I wish he had it when I still had the ability to run my hands through it. Being around him makes me calmer, less anxious.

"You weren't ever a nerd," I say dryly, laughing at the term.

"But it sounds like college is working out well for you." Rajiv decided to stay in-state and go to the University of Illinois, studying history, with the intention of going to law school like me. So maybe we would have broken up after we went our separate ways in college anyway.

"I like it. It's just far enough away that I can come up with excuses not to come home when my mom wants, but close enough that I can when I want to."

"It would be nice to come home for Thanksgiving," I admit. Tickets home from New York are always stupid expensive and completely not worth it given the winter holiday is three weeks after. Thanksgiving was lonelier than I thought it would've been, especially with a lot of students emptying out that week.

"I bet it's hard on your mom for you to be so far away." He sounds genuinely sympathetic, which is surprising to me, given that he knows what Mama thinks of him.

"She and Annalie seem to be doing fine without me. Anyway, let's stop talking about our parents," I say lightly. It stirs up painful memories. "Are you going to show me some of your newfound dance skills?"

He laughs. "I didn't think you were into breaking."

"I'm not, as a general rule, but I'm definitely interested in watching *you* do it."

"You just want to make fun of me."

"No! It just seems really out of character for you."

"Well," he says, smiling slowly, "a lot of things can happen in a year." It's a reminder that we've lost so much time with each other. And yet, the way he says it makes me hopeful instead of sad.

We end up unpacking and organizing about twenty-five boxes of cans. The soup kitchen people ultimately swap Rajiv and me up front to serve portions during the lunch hour.

While working the lunch shift, Jessica and I chat about her being the only woman partner at the firm and how she ended up getting there. She went to law school in Chicago and decided to come back home to raise a family. Her credentials are super impressive. I am in awe.

At the end of the day, she tells me she's happy to have me around for the summer, and if I ever want a letter of recommendation for law school, she's more than willing to provide it.

I see Rajiv spending the day with Johnson, the other founder of the firm.

He's a stocky man, smaller and younger than Fisher, with a shock of red hair that hasn't yet been touched by silver. The two of them seem to be getting along royally.

Rajiv looks so unlike everyone who works here, with his pierced ears and flamboyant hair. He looks like a rock star. I'm kind of amazed that a generally stodgy place hired him, but on the other hand, they'd be foolish not to. He's perfect for the job. Plus, he's charismatic enough that he can have a conversation with just about anyone. I can imagine him sitting on the other side of a mahogany desk, patiently talking through a case with his client. It's funny that we're so different and yet ended up on the same career track.

Once upon a time, we made a good team.

* * *

We met freshman year in high school.

We went to different junior high schools that fed into one big high school in town. We were in the same World History class. At the beginning of second semester, the teacher put us in groups of three for a group project. We were told that the point was to teach us how to be "collaborative," like in the "real world." We were told that we would all get the same grade, so it was really important to work together.

Here's the thing: it was all a total sham. Group projects suck. What always happens is one person who cares about their grade does all the work, and the rest of the group coasts off that work. I hated them.

We didn't get to pick our groups. My group was me, a guy named Todd, and Rajiv. The project was to do a detailed profile of an assigned country; its geography, food, culture, history, etc. We had to write a paper on each topic. Our country was Mauritania.

I wasn't friends with anyone in World History. I was the girl who raised my hand for every question and never looked away from the teacher for the entire class. Therefore, I had only the faintest impression of both Todd and Rajiv.

Todd was pale, smirky, and in class maybe 60 percent of the time. The classic dude-I'd-have-to-do-all-the-work-for.

Rajiv was a quiet guy who tended to sit near the back of the room, but not all the way in the back. He would show up on time, chatted with the people around him, but didn't seem to be cliquey or best friends with anybody. He was a blur in my mind.

A blip on my radar. Seemed like somebody I could count on to do his part and not screw everything up.

We went into the corner. I told them in no uncertain terms that we were going to get an A on the project, and that if they didn't care about what grade they got, then they should at least have the courtesy not to ruin mine.

Rajiv had a whisper of a smile on his face.

"Are you making fun of me?" I demanded.

He shook his head. "Definitely not."

I started divvying up the work, explaining how we were going to divide and conquer.

Todd snorted.

"Excuse me. Do you have a problem?"

He rolled his eyes at me. "Yeah, I do."

"What's that?"

"You can't just decide who's going to do work."

"Why not? Somebody has to."

"Yeah, well, I don't take orders from a girl."

I could feel my ears flush hot. "I'm sorry, are you five? Are you afraid I have cooties?"

"You don't get to be the leader of this group. Girls can't be leaders." He said this matter-of-factly, not even as a jab. You could tell he legitimately believed it. "I mean, there's a reason we don't have any women presidents."

I think it was the closest I ever got to inciting violence in a class, because I might've seriously thrown a punch at him if Rajiv hadn't stepped in. He grabbed my hand, which would've been a wild breach of my personal bubble, except that I was in so much shock and rage that I was in no position to stop him. "Okay, okay, let's all take a step back. Margaret, I think your plan sounds great. Todd, shut the fuck up, and do what you're told so we can get an A."

Spoiler alert: Todd didn't. Rajiv and I ended up doing it all between the two of us.

But sometime between his first smile and telling Todd to shut the fuck up, I fell for him.

"What's it like to be back home for the summer?" Rajiv asks me over some fish tacos. We started eating lunch together after the soup kitchen event. Usually, we walk to one of the restaurants close by since we're downtown, and we sit at the picnic tables in the park down the block. As an unspoken rule, we don't talk about the past. It comes so easily, if someone had asked me a month ago whether this was possible, I never would've believed it.

"Honestly? Probably the same as when I lived here before. Lots of tension. Everybody avoids talking to each other. Super fun."

He laughs.

"And what made you get a job back here for the summer? I always thought you wanted to go out west to California. Good opportunity."

"I applied to some stuff. I don't know. Maybe next summer. It just wasn't the right time," he says vaguely, looking away. "You didn't intend on leaving New York either."

So home was not his first choice. I've known Rajiv long

enough to know when there's something he doesn't want to talk about. Before, I could always get it out of him. But now, I don't know if it's really my place to do that.

"I guess it was just meant to be that we'd both be here," he says finally. Not flirtatiously, but in seriousness. "My horoscope—"

"Oh, come on." I have to laugh.

"Too many coincidences."

"You're so superstitious."

"Agree to disagree. Our horoscopes always said we'd be a bad match," he teases.

This reference to our old life isn't lost on me. "Well, in that case, I can't argue with you there."

We lapse into silence for a bit after that. I'm thinking about how weird it is to be sitting here with my ex-boyfriend, who I was convinced I'd never see again in my entire life, joking about our old relationship like friends.

"Any news on the case? Anything I can do to help?" he says as we throw out our napkins and paper containers.

"No news," I say. "It really sucks. It's like they took all the information and then went into a black hole. I don't know if I'll ever get any updates or what."

"Hmm. Maybe give it another week. I assume they have to interview the neighbors and stuff."

"I mean, the bare minimum," I say dryly. "But who knows? Nobody really seems to care about it that much. Nobody got hurt."

"Do you think it was just a random crime?" he asks.

I've thought about it a lot. "No," I say slowly. "I don't. I think it's somebody who at least kind of knows us."

We look at each other quietly, not wanting to think too hard about it, before going back inside.

My suit is itchy. It's a tweed, light tan fabric, two-piece, with embellished pockets and a rounded neckline. It looks summery but feels like the jaws of heated death. I'm wearing white patent-leather pumps that taper to a sharp point in front and are squeezing my toes into one giant toe.

I keep looking over at Rajiv, who is also wearing a suit. A plain navy one. I've never seen him wear a suit before. It's good on him, I admit. So good, I'm not sure if the suit is improving him or he's improving the suit.

We're sitting in a courtroom, watching a trial. We've been in here for an hour already after lunch, after sitting through three hours in the morning. One of the lawyers at the firm is handling it. We're only interns, of course, so we're not allowed to sit at the table with counsel. Instead, we're in the audience with everyone else.

It's a pretty impressive state courthouse. The building was constructed in the early 1800s when the town was founded. It's been beautifully restored to its original splendor. The walls and floors are clean white marble, with light gray veins running through. The ceiling is inlaid with a delicate gold trim. The bench, where the judge is and where the witnesses sit when they're called up, and the pews are all polished chestnut.

It's a breach of contract and fraud case between two companies, and we're representing the defendant. Opposing counsel is doing a direct examination.

We grabbed lunch at the Subway around the corner with Richard, the lead counsel, and mostly chatted about his career and his thoughts about how the trial was going so far. Richard has an elegant southern accent that makes everything he says in an opening statement seem believable, and all the questions he asks witnesses sound reasonable and friendly. It's funny how something as simple as an accent or the pitch of your voice, or even how you move your arms, can have an impact on your success as a trial lawyer. It's a surprisingly theatrical role. The part of lawyering I've mainly experienced so far is the paper-pushing part, so this is much more interesting.

You're not allowed to be typing on your computer in the courtroom, so Rajiv and I are diligently taking notes. Or at least, I am diligently taking notes on my yellow legal pad. Rajiv is scribbling something every five minutes or so. My notes look like a neatly typewritten outline. I lean over to glance at Rajiv's notes. They're barely legible. He's always had terrible handwriting. When I'd miss class and he'd lend me his notes, they were less than useless. I couldn't read them and they didn't seem to capture the actual important parts. But then he'd still get as good—or better—a score as I would on the exam.

Rajiv writes something down on a page, tears it quietly out of his notebook, and passes it to me.

I squint at what he's written. I look at him and shake my head. He cocks an eyebrow. I write back on the paper: *Please write using recognizable letters. This is chicken scratch.*

He's suppressing a smile, as am I. He writes more deliberately this time and passes the note to me. I feel like we're in high school, but our phones are off and in our bags. No texting allowed in the courtroom. *Are you really making a list of questions you're going to ask Richard afterward?*

He's been spying on my notes. I make a face at him.

This is supposed to be a learning exercise, RAJIV. I dot the period with extra conviction so the pen makes a soft thud on the notepad.

You and your lists, he writes. *This was supposed to be fun.*

What's wrong with lists? I write furiously. *They keep you organized. Don't knock it until you've tried it.*

At this point, he has given up all pretense of passing the paper back and forth. He's scooted next to me so the paper is between us, and we're both leaning over it. He has it on his notepad, which isn't a loss because he probably wasn't taking real notes anyway.

Ohhh, Margaret. You've made me try so many times. Never stuck. His navy-clad leg is pressed up against mine. His shoulder pushes against my shoulder.

Stop distracting me from the trial. I mean it in more ways than one. I feel abnormally warm where his body is touching mine, and it's making it doubly hard to focus.

Fine, he scribbles. *Don't want to disrupt this educational experience.* He sits back against the pew. Probably for the best. His writing is getting increasingly messier with each exchange. But he doesn't move over, so the two of us are still joined at the side. I sneak a peek at him, and he doesn't seem disturbed in any way.

I can't tell if he's deliberately trying to unsettle me.

For what reason, though? It's not like he's into me anymore. Right? I think of the girl on his Instagram—a whole new life that I couldn't know. He had months to try to get me back, and he didn't reach out. Not once. He's friendly enough now, but he surely isn't going to pretend like everything is the same as it was before. We haven't resolved any of the problems that broke us apart. And when he first saw me this summer, he acted like he wanted me to get run over by a combine harvester. There was definitely no grand master plan in place then. Which means if his intentions toward me have changed, they did so solely due to my accidental proximity. There's nothing less sexy than that. I don't want to be won only because I happened to be close by, the most accessible option.

After about ten minutes, Rajiv bends over the paper again. *HEY*, he writes.

Why are you yelling? (On paper.)

I JUST THOUGHT IT WOULD BE EASIER FOR YOU TO READ MY HANDWRITING IF I WROTE IT IN ALL CAPS.

How thoughtful. You're terrible at playing the quiet game.

I AM BEING VERY QUIET.

From a literal perspective, I guess.

I'M A VERY LITERAL PERSON.

Now I am the one trying hard not to laugh. *Richard is going to notice us and we're going to get in trouble.*

IN CASE YOU HAVEN'T NOTICED, RICHARD IS

A LITTLE PREOCCUPIED RIGHT NOW. TRYING TO KEEP OUR CLIENT FROM BEING CONVICTED OF FRAUD.

It's not a criminal trial. Our client can't get convicted of anything. The jury will find for either the plaintiff or defendant.

KNOW-IT-ALL.

You're going to make me crack up. Stop it.

ARE YOU SURE? YOU LOOK SUPER SERIOUS.

I have to cover my face and grip the wooden lip of the pew to keep my body from shaking with laughter.

SO DISRESPECTFUL, he adds.

You're always getting me in trouble, I accuse him, my writing getting wilder.

IT'S NOT MY FAULT YOU ALWAYS WANT TO JOIN IN.

It's true. I am generally a rule follower, unless I believe that rule is morally wrong, but Rajiv enjoys pushing the envelope on benign rules that make no sense to him. Like not wearing loudly patterned socks that are distracting or not eating a banana whole because it looks too sexual. All things he thought were stupid in high school.

And he'd make the rule breaking look so fun, like when he and others decided to organize a freshman skip day for the first time in school history. Seniors normally skipped a day, no harm, no foul, but it wasn't acceptable for any other classes to do it.

As student body president, I disapproved, but as Rajiv's girl-friend, I couldn't resist the temptation of ditching to go to Six Flags for the day.

We all got detention.

The entire freshman class had to sit in the auditorium—the only place large enough to hold all of us—in silence for forty-five minutes after school the next day.

He was always my Achilles' heel.

He's writing on the paper again. *I'm helping out with Taste of Asia this weekend. Do you want to come check it out? With me?*

Taste of Asia is a food fair with all the local Asian restaurants in town.

I notice that he didn't write this part in all caps. I wonder if he wrote it instead of asking after we got out of the courtroom because it's less awkward to write than to say aloud.

I really want to say yes. I do. But I'm sure what saying yes would mean. This would go way above and beyond the clear relationship boundaries we've established so far. We've been careful to only talk about safe topics at work. What we've been doing at school, what movies we've seen. No hanging out after.

I don't respond right away, so he starts writing again. *Free tickets since I'm involved. How can you turn that down?*

He watches me carefully. And he's right—I can't turn him down, although the comped entrance fee is not the hard part to resist.

Okay, I write crisply. I try not to attribute any significance to the low swoop of excitement in my stomach as he breaks out into a grin. *There's nothing here,* I tell myself. Even the horoscopes say so.

*　*　*

We emerge from the courthouse just after five. I shield my eyes against the glare of the sunlight, blinking to adjust from the dark interior to the bright outdoors. Richard is inside chatting with opposing counsel. They were law school classmates. It's funny how quickly people can go from dramatic accusations against the other side to laughing, backslapping buddies.

Rajiv and I stand on the front steps.

"What'd you think?" he asks.

"It was interesting. I'm glad we got to go."

"How long is your list of questions?" He smirks.

"Twenty-seven," I admit grudgingly. "Would've been more if you hadn't gotten me off track in the middle."

"You can thank me later."

An older woman who I recognize as being on the jury comes out of the courthouse and pauses on the steps by us. "Hi," she says, tapping my shoulder. "I saw you drop this on the way out." It's a silk scarf that I had tied around the handle of my handbag. It must have come unknotted and slipped onto the ground.

I take it, grateful. "Thanks."

"You're welcome, sweetie," she says. "By the way, where are you from? The two of you, I mean."

"We're from here," I say firmly. "This town. Illinois."

She smiles. "Oh, but before that."

I instantly feel the prickling sensation of annoyance. "We were born here," I tell her.

"Your parents, then."

"My dad is Irish American."

Rajiv is looking at me and wisely deciding to stay out of it. I know what the woman is trying to get at, but I refuse to give it to her. It's become a bit of a game for me at this point, to see, despite my extreme lack of cooperation, how persistent people will be to get to the ultimate question they have: Why aren't you white?

Her eyes widen. "Were you adopted?" she asks.

"No."

"Are you Korean?" she tries again. I roll my eyes at Rajiv very visibly. She seems taken aback by my shortness with her.

"No. I'm half-Chinese. He's Indian. Thanks for playing." I grab Rajiv's arm, and we march toward the parking lot without looking back.

"She's staring at us," he whispers to me as I drag him away.

"I don't care." I'm not sure where we're going, as I don't want to stand aimlessly in the parking lot under the gaze of the woman, so I haul him to my car. I get in. He takes my cue and slides into the passenger seat.

We sit there for a minute, not saying anything. "Um," Rajiv says. "Since we're already in your car, should we, like, drive around the courthouse for a couple of laps? I think it's going to be weird if we just sit here, not moving." He cranes his neck and glances back at the courthouse doors. "She's talking to someone and looking toward us. Probably telling them that you're a rude little Oriental."

I have to laugh. "Okay." I turn the key in the ignition, and the engine purrs to life. I pull out of the parking lot and onto the street. It feels off to be driving Rajiv. He is six months older than me, so in high school, we got used to him being the one who drove us around. I try to not feel nervous about him judging my driving.

I'm on my second lap and trying to decide how many times I should circle the courthouse when Rajiv's phone rings. My phone is still off in my bag. I should check it and make sure Mama hasn't called.

He stares at his screen for a few beats. "Do you mind?" he asks politely. "It's my mom."

"Sure," I say. I resist the urge to tell him not to tell her that he's with me, but presumably, he's smart enough not to without my help.

"Hi, Ma," he says.

Vandana Agarwal is a short, wide woman, but she might as well have been seven feet tall, as she always feels like the most important person in any room.

She and I only ever spoke in passing. She rarely smiled. Not that it was necessarily a bad thing. After all, my mother smiled at Rajiv plenty, but she had very little good to say behind his back.

I can hear her low voice on the other side of the line, but not enough to make out what she's actually saying.

"I'm coming out of the trial," he says. "Driving home now." Minor lie. "Yeah, I can pick that up on the way home. Okay, I love you. Bye." He ends the call.

The last time I saw his mother was at high school graduation. She was standing with Rajiv's father, a distinguished tall man in a gray suit. He's an anesthesiologist at the main hospital in town. Mrs. Agarwal was wearing a bright pink dress embroidered with flowers. We had a graduating class of just over a hundred people; it was hard to avoid anybody's family, but especially hard for us to miss each other given that we were two of maybe eight Asian families.

We crossed paths as everyone was gathering after the ceremony, taking pictures with friends, memorializing the milestone. Rajiv couldn't make eye contact with me, but his mother did. She turned around as we were passing awkwardly and looked right at me. I saw a flicker of sympathy flash over her face, and then I couldn't see anymore. She was obscured by another chattering group passing in between us. And that was it. We never spoke after Rajiv and I broke up, and I haven't seen her since.

"Well, I should go," he says, not looking up. The mood in the car has noticeably dampened. I wonder what his mom said to him on the phone. Maybe nothing. Just the presence of our mothers is frankly enough to dredge up the bad memories. "I'll see you this weekend for Taste of Asia, then?"

"Sure. Is your mom going to be there?" I blurt out, unable to stop myself.

He looks at me funny, and I can't tell whether he's upset or surprised. "No," he says after a moment. "She won't be there."

I pull over and watch him get out of the car, his jaw clenched as he walks away.

I suppose I'll never know what he told his mother, after we were over. The difference between me and Rajiv, regardless of what our parents felt: despite everything, he always put us first, and when it counted, I didn't. Then before I knew it, I'd lost him. I will never be able to overcome that. The guilt burns.

Nine

ANNALIE

There's nothing quite like the joy of being told by Thom Frog-gett that he likes me. The memory is like a hit that I can't give up. It runs through my head over and over again, and every time it ignites my pleasure center like a Christmas tree lighting up all at once.

The only thing that slightly deflates my pure, undiluted happiness is Violet pestering me about whether we're together now.

We never really talked about it, so I don't know.

Violet doesn't understand why I can't just ask him.

But how do people go about asking these types of things? How do I even raise that if it doesn't come up naturally? It sounds so old-fashioned to ask if he wants to be my boyfriend. I might as well ask him if he'd want to "go steady." I can imagine him laughing at me. I don't want to be the desperate girl. I want to be effortless, casual. I can be casual.

Besides, Thom and I are texting back and forth intermittently throughout the day. I keep it light and flirty. I don't push things. Isn't this enough? Eventually it will be presumed that we're together, and I can be patient.

Anyway, we haven't even kissed yet, although we're planning another date.

It's good that I have something to look forward to, because the first week at the bakery is rough. I thought I got hired because I made something halfway decent with the puff pastry, but Bakersfield quickly knocks me down a peg.

"Too tough," he says of my first batch of scones. "You over-mixed the dough. And the texture is wrong. You didn't cream the butter and sugar exactly right, so it came out all dense. Dump it out. Try again."

And those are the nice comments. He limits my time alone in the kitchen in the beginning, and his watchful eye is overbearing. "What if you break something?" he asks. "Those KitchenAids are worth more than your life."

"So if there were a fire, you'd save the equipment instead of me?" I say in an attempt to lighten the mood.

"Yes," he says without even a pause. "And don't be fresh."

I continue going back to scrubbing down the stainless steel until I can see my pores in the reflection.

The only time I feel slightly less bad about myself is on the few occasions Daniel has the misfortune of coming back into the kitchen.

He pops in while I'm there with Bakersfield and says, "When you're done in here, I need you to come to the office. I can't figure out where the expense records are."

"They're in the second drawer from the top in the file cabinet," Bakersfield snaps. "I thought I told you already."

"They're not there," Daniel insists.

"You're not looking hard enough."

Daniel raises a hand to his forehead like he's hoping for some divine intervention to preserve his patience. "Just come in here when you're done."

"You were supposed to be making things easier for me," Bakersfield mumbles.

"Yeah, well, I wouldn't have to be organizing your cabinets if your accountant hadn't fired you, which for the record, I didn't even know was possible. I thought termination only happens the other way around."

I cough to hide a snort.

Bakersfield swivels and glares back and forth between me and Daniel. I look down at the counter and start flouring it more aggressively, like it's the most interesting thing in the world. "No respect! From either of you. I thought at least Europeans were supposed to be polite."

"You'd be disabused of that notion if you ever visited. I'll be in the office," Daniel retorts. "Come by or not. It's your business, not mine."

The door shuts.

"What are you smirking about?" Bakersfield barks at me. "You think this is funny?"

I hold my hands up, offended. "I didn't say anything!"

"If you have to make these scones a *third* time, I'll teach you who does the firing around here."

It's a blessed day when Bakersfield finally lets me be alone in the kitchen without breathing down my neck after a week and a half. I guess I passed the initial test, and I'm still employed. I'm only allowed to make scones for now, but it's progress. As the unsupervised queen of the kitchen, I can take breaks when I'm tired of standing, and I can pick music.

I blast sappy Taylor Swift, dancing as I mix sticky dough.

I'm in the middle of belting the second verse of "You Belong with Me" when Daniel pokes his head in, serious as the grave. "Excuse me."

"Yes?"

"Can you keep it down?"

I'm feeling particularly magnanimous today. "Sure." I turn the volume down. "And I won't sing. I can admit that I'm not a great singer."

His lips quirk into a blink-and-you'll-miss-it smile. And then his entire demeanor turns back to perpetually serious. "Anyway, the thing I'm supposed to tell you is that the shipment of blueberries is delayed for the week."

As a loyal customer, I knew that normally all the fruit in the summer is fresh from local suppliers. No blueberries is not good news.

"But I'm in the middle of a batch of blueberry scones," I say uncomprehendingly.

"Right, and if you had checked the fridge, you'd have noticed that the blueberries weren't there."

I throw my hands up, tossing a cloud of flour. "Well, what am I supposed to do now?"

"My grandad's manning the front. I'm supposed to go buy them from the grocery store."

"Like an industrial amount of blueberries?"

"Correct." He looks extremely thrilled at the prospect.

"Okay," I say. "I guess I'll just hold until you're back then."

He doesn't move.

"Yes? Is there anything else you need from me?"

"I don't have a driver's license," he says crisply.

"Oh. You mean in America?"

"I mean anywhere," he says, sounding annoyed. "You can drive in America with a driver's license from the UK. I just happen not to have one." He shrugs. "No need to have a car in London. Yet another one of my mistakes in coming here."

I sigh. "Okay, why would you be assigned to go get the blueberries then?"

"Can you drive me?" He looks pained to even have to ask.

"Can't you just take a Lyft or something?"

"And do you think a Lyft driver will just let me fill his trunk with an industrial amount of blueberries on the way back?"

"Point taken."

Maybe the expression on my face is sufficiently distressed. He runs his fingers through his dark hair. "Look, I'm sorry."

"What?"

"I'm sorry for having been such a tosser the past few times

we've talked. It doesn't have to do with you. I was sort of just taking it out on everyone. I promise I'll be nicer if you drive me."

"Really?"

"Really."

I stick my hand out at him, and he shakes it, looking amused. "Deal. My car's out back. Let me wash my hands."

Somehow, the ten-minute drive to the store opens up the floodgates, and Daniel starts talking as if I'm timing and will cut him off if he goes on too long. We pile our grocery cart with, well, basically all the blueberries we can buy at the store.

He grimaces. "It's really my fault. I had this whole idea about coming to America and bonding with my grandad, sight unseen."

"You've never met your grandfather before?"

"No, we were estranged until last year. Not me, per se. My dad. He and my grandad—well, they never really saw eye to eye. Couldn't be two more completely different people. My dad gently suggested that it might not be the best idea to dive in headfirst as I didn't know him that well, and I had never spent any time out of the UK. But you know. In my mind, I thought my grandad and I would hit it off." He sighs.

"What happened between your dad and your grandpa?"

"Bakersfield Bakery has been here forever. My grandad started it when he was incredibly young. I guess he always thought my dad would want to take it over." He laughs. "Well, Dad hates baking. Is pretty shit at cooking generally, as I can attest to from personal experience. Never had any interest in running a small business. He did well in school and wanted to do international law and policy. I only know my grandad from the couple of weeks I've spent here so far, but I think he's barely even aware of things going on outside of this state. He couldn't ever wrap his mind around what Dad wanted to do. So anyway, it all came to blows eventually. Dad told him he wanted nothing to do with this business, eventually ended up working at an NGO in London, where he met my mum. And we've always lived in Europe."

"And your dad never said anything about your grandpa?"

"I mean, I always knew Dad was American. I suppose the two of them just stopped talking, and neither was big enough to reach out to the other."

"So who did the reaching out first?"

"Mum did, actually. After I decided I was going to come to the US for uni. She thought it had been long enough. Dad and my grandad would never have been the first to reach back out. I suppose they have that in common. An inability to be wrong. Amazing that my parents have managed to be married for so many years."

"Amazing," I echo, smiling. I can tell from the way he talks about them that his parents are really happy. I don't often think about my own father, partly because when he comes up, Mama's mouth gets thin and pressed, and Margaret just gets moody. But sometimes I do feel a pang of—what? A vacuum, maybe. Like being reminded that something you never noticed is gone. "And then?"

"And then I got this idea that instead of visiting for a weekend, like Labor Day or something after I'd already moved, I'd spend a summer with my grandad. You know, I thought I'd uncover this profound relationship with this long-lost relative and explore my American roots, like some heartwarming BBC special." His mouth twists sardonically.

"I take it that it's not going the way you expected?"

"Understatement." He grimaces. "He barely tolerates me. Goes about most of the day in silence. Except to tell me on occasion all about how Dad made the wrong choice thirty years ago, until I'm begging we go back to a place of silence. It doesn't seem to occur to him that if Dad had made the other choice, I wouldn't exist."

"Sorry."

"Honestly, I've been thinking maybe it's better to just call it and go back to London. But then I'd have to listen to Dad say, 'I told you so' a thousand times." He rubs the back of his head. "That's possibly worse than sitting through my grandad's righteous diatribes."

"Sounds like all the Bakersfield men are more similar than you'd think."

He glances at me wryly. "Mum said that to me too when I called to complain."

I laugh. "Well, I think it was pretty brave of you to come to America for the first time and hang out in this small town where you don't know anybody."

"Brave or silly. Neither of which I normally am."

We opt for the self-checkout, so we don't have to explain to the cashier why we're buying a million cartons of blueberries, when I notice a girl from my class. She makes eye contact with me, and her face morphs in slow motion from recognition to sympathy.

"Oh no," I mutter. "Hurry up, hurry up, hurry up. Scan faster."

"What's wrong?"

"Just do it!"

It's too late. Gemma Morgan comes up to us. There's nowhere I can hide. For a brief moment, I fantasize about sprinting out the front door and leaving Daniel to pay for twenty pounds of blueberries.

"Hi, so good to see you," Gemma says. A strange thing to say, considering that I think Gemma has only spoken to me twice in my life, and once was to borrow a pen in AP Lit. "I heard about your house."

She keeps scanning my face, as if she's waiting for me to cry or scream about the injustice or laugh it off like it was no big deal. But I don't know what the right reaction is. "Yeah," I say, feeling awkward.

Daniel keeps scanning blueberries without introducing himself, and I don't introduce him or say anything else. Gemma shifts from foot to foot. "So sorry," she says after too many seconds. The sound of the scanner beeping is loud in my ears. This would be comical, if it weren't so horrifying.

What next? Should I say thank you? Me too? I'm okay? All these things seem off, like saying *you too* when a waiter tells you to enjoy your meal. I imagine experiencing some version of this conversation a hundred times over on the first day of school again.

"Yep," I say after fumbling. "Um, anyway, gotta go. Big rush. Nice to see you. Have a great summer!"

I grab three bags and practically smash into the sliding automatic doors on the way out in an effort to escape to the parking lot.

We throw everything into the trunk, and I'm huffing and puffing as we collapse into our seats in the car.

"So," Daniel says as I'm catching my breath. "That was odd. Care to explain?"

I put the key in the ignition and exhale. "Not really, but here we are, I guess."

"This is going to be worth it," I tell him as we wait for the blueberry scones to bake. It's late in the afternoon now, hours after our grocery store excursion. After he helped unpack everything, it seemed unsporting not to let him try the end result.

"So you are actually half-Chinese?" is Daniel's first question after I tell him the story about the garage.

The question comes up whenever people find out. I always anticipate people telling me that I don't look it at all. When I was younger, it used to make me feel pleased, because people usually said it like a compliment. I only realized later that it wasn't really. "It's easier to tell with my sister. She takes after my mom." It's my standard answer to head off a cringey line of additional questioning.

He tilts his head. "Oh. Well, that's cool," he says simply.

His response surprises me in the best way.

"And still no idea who might have done it?" he continues.

"That's the police's job." I shrug. "And my sister's," I add, wrinkling my nose.

"Sounds like you don't exactly get along."

"You could say that. And this isn't helping things at all."

"Well, the vandalism is a disgusting thing to have happened. And I'm sorry about the difficulty it's causing with your family."

Somehow, coming from him, it's not as bad, although maybe it's the way he's looking at me, right in the eyes, earnest. I know he means it. "The vandalism is disgusting," I echo. "I just hope we can put this all behind us soon."

The oven beeps, and I pull out the trays. With gloves, I put one scone on a plate and slide it over to him. "Hot. Be careful."

I watch him expectantly.

He blows on it, delicately picks it up between his fingers, and takes a tentative bite. I can practically see his eyes roll back in his head. "Wo-ow," he says, and I glow. "These are incredible. You're a really good baker. My grandad should've had you as a grandchild instead of me."

"Thanks. I mean, I spent *a lot* of time baking scones last week because your grandad said they weren't up to snuff, so practice makes perfect. But the good news is, now he tolerates me."

"Teach me your ways," he says jokingly. "If I could bake like that, maybe my grandad would love me."

"He does love you."

"Not as much as he loves you if this is what you make." I blush.

We eat our scones in silence. "I think I should probably get back to the books. Thanks for driving me. To be honest, if I spent another day cooped up in the office without speaking to anybody, I'd probably go mad."

"I'll see you later, Daniel."

He pauses at the door. "Yes, you will."

It doesn't occur to me until much later, after I'm driving home, that he didn't actually need to come with me to buy blueberries. The thought makes me smile.

"I promised you I'd take you to something other than ice cream," Thom says.

We're downtown at dusk. The dark edges of the shadowed buildings cut sharp into the twinkly teal sky. It's my favorite time of day. And Thom and I just got dessert crepes at the local creperie. Now we're just walking along, peeking into the shop windows we pass. The air is cool and comfortable against my bare legs. Tonight feels like magic.

"It somehow seems that all our dates involve sweet things," I say as we go up the street.

"Sweet things for a sweet girl." He grins.

"Incredibly corny."

"But true." He slips his hand into mine. My heart flutters. I think about impressing everything about this night into my mind, so I can relive it and never forget. I want to remember the sweet summer smells. I want to remember the feeling of his fingers intertwined in mine. I'm sure this is the beginning of the rest of my life.

We pass by Bakersfield Bakery, and I can see Bakersfield inside, dimly lit against a single light behind the counter. He's sweeping up to close the shop.

"Oh, I got a new job there."

"At the bakery?"

"Yeah."

Thom raises his eyebrows. "You really are a dessert queen. Are you as good at baking as you are at scooping ice cream?"

"Better."

"Hard to believe. You were a vision back there with the ice cream scoop."

I try not to go completely red. If this were Victorian England, I'd need some smelling salts and a fainting couch.

He puts his arm around the small of my back, his hand wrapping around my waist.

The fountain at the center of downtown, diagonally across from the front of the bakery, is all lit up with the lamps underwater and with twinkle lights in the trees. The kissing park, they call it.

We settle on a bench. My head fits under his chin. I feel shaky and nervous but electric with anticipation. The water sparkles against the lights.

I swallow. I haven't told Thom, but I've never kissed anyone before, and I'm sure he has. What if I'm terrible? What if my mouth doesn't know how to move in the right way? How do people learn how to kiss anyway?

I think I'd rather die than be told I'm a bad kisser.

"Annalie?"

"Mm-hmm?" I try to calm down and not overanalyze, which is completely impossible. I can't look up at his face. It's too intense. I know he's looking down at me. He puts his hand beneath my chin and turns my face to his. Blood rushes to my head and I feel dizzy, but his grip around me is firm. He leans down.

The moment where he's coming toward me, his luminous golden skin inches away from mine, lasts both seconds and an entire lifetime. But then his lips are on mine and I can't think of anything. We're kissing.

We're kissing!

I'm frozen and terrified but also triumphant. His lips are firm against mine, and I feel the slight brush of his tongue against my lips. I can't even close my eyes because I'm so wound up, so I'm staring at him, inches away from his closed eyelids. Thank god he can't see me.

Finally, he comes up for air, and I am a new person.

"That was my first kiss," I blurt out, unable to help myself.

"Really?" he says, pausing. He seems to struggle slightly with what to say next. "Wow. That's cute." I feel relieved. He puts his hand in mine. "It was pretty good for a first kiss, huh?"

"I think so."

"I'm glad you came out with me tonight, A."

"Me too," I whisper. A lull. I clear my throat. "I, uh, better go home."

"Wait. Are you serious? Right now?" He sounds disappointed.

"Yeah."

I find myself standing up, my legs unstable. I don't know what's compelling me to say this. I don't want to go home. I want to stay out all night. I want to dance until the sun comes up. But I'm too pent-up with emotions, and I don't think I can handle holding together this cool version of myself in front of Thom for much longer. Maybe ten minutes. Maybe fifteen. It'll all come tumbling down after that.

I need to call Violet. Or jump on my bed. Or take five shots of espresso. But I can't be in this park with Thom.

This feels like perversely the wrong reaction to have to kissing a boy who allegedly may be my boyfriend (does kissing him automatically make him my boyfriend?)—this urge to spend *less* time with him at a pivotal moment instead of more. Still, I can't stop myself from making my escape. "Walk me to the parking lot?" I say over my shoulder.

"Sure, okay." He seems both taken aback and amused, but he catches up to me. "You're good at playing hard to get."

"Me?"

"I feel like you're always running out on me." He smirks. "Soon I'll have you for longer than just a short date."

"Soon," I say, feeling light-headed, giddy. "I have to keep the mystery alive."

As we walk closer to Bakersfield Bakery, I notice that a tall figure has been standing by the front entrance. I don't know when he appeared. He turns to lock up. It's dark now, and we're away from the lights. I can still recognize him, though.

It's Daniel. He sees me.

He doesn't say anything. He only adjusts his glasses, slips the keys into his pocket, and walks away in the other direction.

Ten

The poster board in the back seat of my car is huge. I wrestled it in, but I don't know how I'll get it out. I stare at it, shading my eyes from the strong glare of the bright, overcast sky.

"Hey!"

Rajiv strides over through the parking lot with a big grin. "You made it."

"Of course I did," I say primly.

"Oh no," he says as he gets closer. "Do you have a giant social justice poster board?" He peers into the back window. I spent last night putting it together with photos from our house, surrounded by facts and statistics on hate crimes against Asian Americans. I figure the subject can find a good audience at Taste of Asia.

"Don't act like you're surprised."

"I'm zero percent surprised." He doesn't look upset. In fact, he's got a face like a pleased puppy. He's so radiant that you can't help but be happy around him too. "I saved a spot for you by my aunt's booth."

"Is your aunt okay with this?"

"Yeah, of course. My aunt Amita. You met her once, maybe. She likes you."

I stop myself from saying, *That probably makes for just one person in your family.*

He pulls open the door. "Well, let's do this, I guess." It's not really that the poster board is heavy so much as it's bulky, and its dimensions make it hard for one person to carry. But he pops it under his arm easily.

Taste of Asia is in this old strip mall that has a bunch of vacant space. It's flat-roofed and ugly, but rent space is extremely cheap. Although this event could probably be outside in the summer, for some reason, it's always been indoors.

We go inside to the gentle waft of clammy artificial cold air, and the savory smells of sesame oil and spices. There's a main conference room where people are setting up rows and rows of booths, lined with big metallic lidded trays. The carpet is this dingy brownish red color with darker speckles. It bends stiffly beneath our feet as we cross the aisles, past the pho and banh mi, strips of spicy lamb skewers, egg rolls and fried rice, soup dumplings, naan and chana masala.

The food stations are interspersed with craft stations, where kids can make paper lanterns and get henna art on their hands.

All the food and activities are free with a fifteen-dollar entrance fee.

It's quite kitschy, especially the crafts—catered to be more fun than educational—but it's a good opportunity for local

Asian restaurants to get exposure.

Rajiv stops by an Indian food stand and sets the poster board on the carpet. "Hi, Auntie," he says, going to kiss a middle-aged woman on the cheek. She looks like his mom but with softer and rounder features, and she's got a great big smile on her face.

"There he is," she says. She looks over his shoulder at me and waves. "And Margaret. Haven't seen you in a while." She doesn't show a trace of discomfort. She comes right over to me and gives me a hug that completely catches me off guard. "I heard what happened to your family," she says, whispering in my ear. "I'm glad you came here to talk about it."

"Thanks," I say, touched. I met Amita Auntie once at a family picnic that Rajiv invited me to. While I didn't spend a ton of time there, she was exceedingly nice to me, and in a genuine way.

Rajiv pulls his aunt away for a second and says something to her in an undertone, and her eyebrows knit together. She nods. He pulls away and comes back over to me. "What was that?" I ask.

"Nothing. Don't worry about it."

He's hiding something, but what?

"Let's get this up, shall we?" he says, gesturing at the board. We prop it up on the table. He steps back to read it, and I watch him, trying not to get too distracted by the way his brow furrows and how beautiful his eyelashes are. "This is great. You should actually just reuse this for a group project in college."

We both smile, remembering our first one together.

"Hey, listen. I actually have a favor to ask of you," he says.

"Do you know a Professor Schierholtz?"

"Actually, yes, I do," I say, surprised. "History professor? She taught the Eastern history 100-level gen-ed requirement this past year. I loved her. I went to her office hours all the time, and I'm taking another class with her next year. Why?"

"That's her. She's actually focused on the history of dance. And, well, uh—" He flounders.

"Come on. Spit it out. What is it?"

He rubs his neck, looking away. "Look," he says, talking really fast like he wants to get it all out before I can say no. "I know this is a weird thing to ask, but I'm trying to get a scholarship to do some research work on the history of break dancing, and she's the preeminent scholar on it in the US. I want to work with her, but I don't go to NYU, and in order to get the scholarship, I need to confirm that I have a professor, either within the university or elsewhere, to supervise. And I need to lock one down in two weeks, to be able to meet the deadline for the scholarship, or else I'll need to come up with a totally different concept." He pauses to take a breath. "I know you're my ex, so it's kind of weird to ask you to put me in contact and say nice things about me, but—"

I put my hand up. "Stop it. Just shut up, right now. Of course I'll reach out to her and tell her to take you on. Don't be ridiculous. Just because we had bad horoscopes doesn't mean that I don't think you're brilliant."

"Really?"

"Obviously! I'll reach out to her in time to meet your deadline."

"No, I meant the part about where you tell me how you think I'm brilliant."

I shove his shoulder softly. "Let's not get carried away. Besides, I'm not going to tell her I'm recommending my ex-boyfriend. That would be weird. I'll say we're friends. We are, aren't we?"

"Sure, sure." He grins at me. "Thanks, Margaret. I mean it."

"I know. I'm very magnanimous."

I spend an hour and a half manning my booth and answering questions from passersby. It's sort of like being one of those persistent people on the streets who pass out flyers and watch as everyone who takes a flyer indiscreetly tosses it into the closest garbage can before they reach the next block. Rajiv helps out his aunt but occasionally looks over at me to give me a thumbs-up.

I get a mix of reactions. Some people are truly appalled and tell me what an important thing it is that I'm doing. Other people come in close out of curiosity, maybe thinking I'm doing some sort of local history presentation, and then I see them actively avert their eyes and try to walk away once they see what the poster board actually says.

But eventually, Rajiv coaxes me out of the booth to try some new foods. "You have to eat. Have you eaten since breakfast?"

"No, but—"

He grabs my hand and pulls me away. "Let's go. Defeating racism can wait." His hand in mine is warm and smooth. His skin on my skin is an immediate electric shock, but then it's back to being comfortable. It's so easy to slip back into where we used to be, once upon a time. Our hands still fit together. Maybe our bodies do too. I am so surprised that I'm unable to let him go.

He doesn't seem to notice at all, as we thread through the crowds. "I've been wanting to try these pork buns."

Wordlessly, I trail behind him, still linked. I think about the first time he told me he loved me, and how in that moment, I couldn't imagine a future without him. I think about how I could never have guessed at the beginning of the summer that I'd be back here with Rajiv, as if nothing had happened.

I wonder if he feels his heart beat fast the way mine is doing.

We split a haul of pork buns, a bowl of pho, garlic naan, and japchae, sitting on the curb outside, watching cars pull in and out of the parking lot, where there's room to spread out the food all around us.

I'm afraid of saying the wrong thing to break this spell or ruin the moment. His legs are next to mine, and I remember every dimple in his knees. I smile at him and try not to look like I'm falling for him again.

"Ever walk down memory lane?" he asks through a mouthful of noodles.

His question catches me by surprise, but I keep myself from revealing anything. Yes. Too many times. Not that I want him to know that. "What do you mean?" I give a half smile, unsure of myself. "Sure I do. I'm glad I didn't have to stay in Illinois, though."

He laughs. "Of course not. I wouldn't have expected you to."

I nudge him gently. "What about you?"

"Well, yeah." He quiets. "Things happen, and I still think about telling you first. Then I remember that you're not the first person I should tell anymore."

I feel that too. I feel it every time I read a stupid thread on Reddit and I want to send it to somebody. I feel it every time I watch a TV show that references a joke he's made to me, or hear a song that we listened to together, or read a new sci-fi book, a genre I never read until Rajiv got me into it. Sometimes the need to tell him about a new thing I'm dealing with is overwhelming. Because the thing is, we have a history, a very specific history, that gives significance to experiences in a way that I could never replicate with anyone else. But the longer it's been since we dated, the more different we become. The fewer memories we'll share with each other, and the closer we'll become to being strangers again.

I look at him, and it makes me unspeakably sad. The slow unwinding of him and me.

"I'm sure you will find somebody else to tell things to first. A guy like you must have a lot of options." I mean it as a quip, but it comes out flat and not funny. I think of the girl on his Instagram again. I'm not petty enough to ask about her.

I shouldn't care anyway. But I do.

"They're not like you," he says quietly.

My heart is pounding, but I'm staring at my lap because I'm afraid of what may happen if I meet his gaze. And while I know deep down there's magic here still, I don't know if I want us to be together the way we used to. Nothing is different this time around. What are second chances anyway except the ability to screw up a second time?

He takes his napkin and brings it over to the corner of my lips, tapping lightly. "You have hoisin sauce on your face." It's so intimate that my breath hitches.

Before we can do anything we regret, my phone starts ringing and snaps the moment to an end.

Nine times out of ten, it's just spam, but I always check.

Voilà, this is the tenth time. The caller ID identifies it as the police station.

I show Rajiv.

"Well, pick up!" he says.

I do. "Hello?"

"Hi, is this Margaret Flanagan?" It's a woman on the other end. I can hear typing in the background.

"This is she."

"This is the front desk of the police department. I'm calling you regarding the police report that you filed on Monday, May twenty-sixth."

"Yes?" My stomach tightens in anticipation. I guess I'm waiting for them to tell me that they caught the person, that somebody's been arrested or indicted.

"Right. Well, the case status is now suspended." She sounds crisp, but bored, like she makes twenty of these calls every day.

"Wait, I'm sorry, what?"

Rajiv is watching me, frowning.

"The case is suspended," the woman on the line says.

"No, I heard you the first time. What does that mean?"

I hear her sigh. "It means that there are no credible leads at this time, so the case is being put on hold until additional actionable evidence is uncovered."

"No credible leads? Did they talk to everybody? The neighbors? Did they look at recent crimes in the city to see if there are any similarities?" I'm practically shouting into the phone.

"I'm sorry. I don't have any answers for you. I just have the case number, the filer, and the status."

I can't get angry at this woman. She has nothing to do with this case. And she can't do anything to help me. "Thank you," I manage to get out. "Are you going to notify me if the status changes?"

"Yes, we will do that. You have a nice day, Ms. Flanagan." The call ends. I look at Rajiv. "They're suspending the case. No leads."

"Oh god, that's terrible. There's nothing else?"

"I don't believe it," I say staunchly. "I don't believe they've looked into everything. This just isn't a high enough priority." I stand up, furious, my fists clenched. "You can't count on anything these days except yourself." The anger from when I first came home, dulled and buried, springs to life again.

It makes my thoughts sharp again. It reminds me that I am not home for a summer romance with my ex-boyfriend. It shakes me out of my nostalgic, soft feelings and back into the world of hard facts.

"I have to get going," I tell him.

He looks disappointed but patiently gathers up our garbage

and tosses it into the can nearby. "Okay," he says. "Can I help you get your stuff back to the car?"

I nod. We head inside. We do not hold hands this time.

Taste of Asia is almost over, so people are filtering out. All my stuff is at the end of the row.

Amita Auntie sees us as we head toward her and rushes to us. "I don't know how it happened," she says. "I was only gone for five minutes."

"What happened?" Rajiv asks.

She points tremulously. We look over where she is pointing. My poster board is smeared with food, like somebody walked by and swabbed an entire container of brown sauce over it. I'm furious.

Amita Auntie took it and put it behind the table carefully. "I didn't see," she says. "Maybe they have security footage?"

Her kindness takes the edge off my anger. "It's okay," I tell her gently. "It's not your fault. I doubt they have any security cameras in this old building." But Amita Auntie's comment gives me an idea. It's obvious—so obvious, in fact, that I would've assumed the police would've followed up on it. I know they haven't. Of course they haven't.

I have to go home, right now.

"Do you still want to take it home?" Rajiv says about the poster.

His eyes shine. He once told me that when someone hurt me, he felt the hurt. All he wanted to do was keep me safe. I steel myself and harden my heart. My eyes are dry. The air-conditioning feels colder than before.

"No," I say. "Just toss it."

I pull into our cul-de-sac, and someone is outside unpacking her groceries.

Just the person I was hoping for. It's Mrs. Maples, the old lady who lives across the street from us.

She was always nice in a nosy neighbor kind of way. She brought us a mountain of cookies a couple of weeks after Dad skipped town. She said she was checking in on Mama, but honestly, it also seemed like she just wanted to confirm that my father had actually left. She's lived alone all the years she's been here but always told us to call her Mrs. Maples. I don't even know what her first name is. Sometimes I've seen a guy in his twenties come to her house and stay there for a few days, then leave again.

It occurs to me that even though Mrs. Maples has lived across the street from us for my entire life, I know nothing about her. As is true for the rest of the neighbors. I know even less about them. And I assume they don't know much about us either.

She unpacks the bags from the trunk, her white hair glistening in the warm afternoon sunlight.

Her driveway faces ours, almost exactly square on.

I jump out of the car and wave to her. "Hi, Mrs. Maples!"

She pauses as I run across the street. She squints at me.

"Margaret," I prompt her.

"Of course! Margaret. Come back from college?" She beams. "Where did you end up again?"

"New York."

"Ah, that's right. The big city. How are you doing, honey? I just came over a few weeks ago with some food. Your sister was home." She clucks sympathetically and whispers conspiratorially, "I heard what happened. Horrible, just horrible."

I manage a strained smile. My face feels all wrong. I've never been one to handle sympathy well. But even I have the awareness to recognize that I'm not going to convince this lady to let me into her house without a greater level of gracefulness than I'm usually able to muster. I hear Rajiv ringing in my head, the only time he ever told off a teacher, who had said that I was mouthy. *That's what's great about her*, he'd retorted.

"It was horrible," I echo.

"Have the police figured out who was responsible yet?"

I shake my head.

"I'm sorry, dear. I simply can't imagine what would possess someone to do that. That's just not the kind of place this is." Her voice lowers. "I've been worried about the crime in this town after that. Do you think it was gang related?"

"I don't think so." I try not to sound impatient. People are always too quick to attribute everything unpleasant broadly to "gang-related activities." I resist the urge to tell her that her comment is racist. I have to focus on getting her help.

Behind her, I scan the front of her house. Her porch, her garage door.

Bingo. There it is in the corner. I feel a surge of hope. This could be it.

"Well," she says, looking at me curiously, "I'm sure they will crack the case eventually. Don't you worry."

"Have the police contacted you, Mrs. Maples?" I blurt out finally.

She stiffens. "No, honey. Why would they contact me?" She looks uncomfortable. Well, it's like I expected. They just let the case sit for weeks and then closed it without bothering to do much of anything.

"I was—well, I was wondering if they might have asked if you'd seen anything."

"Ah, I see. They haven't reached out. But unfortunately, I didn't see anything. I must not have been home. And I'm sure it happened quite quickly."

"It must have happened in the afternoon," I press. "During the day. My sister came home before it was dark."

"Mm-hmm," she says. "If you say so. It sounds like you're over here looking for something."

I stand up a little straighter. "Actually, I am."

"Oh? What's that?"

"Do you have a home security system?"

"A home security system?" she repeats. "I do. My nephew installed one for me last year." She laughs and shakes her head. "Smart boy. He works at one of those Silicon Valley tech companies. I've never thought it necessary, but it was a Christmas gift." She shrugs. "Not sure I've ever made use of it. The alarm is supposed to go off if someone tries to break in. I guess you never know if it's working unless somebody actually does."

My heart pounds. "Do you have a security camera?" I point

at the little white knob with a black screen on the corner of her garage.

"That? Is that a security camera? I think you're right." Her voice wavers with slight embarrassment. "I have to admit, Margaret. I don't know how the dang thing works, and my nephew only comes over a few times a year. I never wanted to admit to him that I couldn't quite figure out the settings online. Locks have always been good enough for me."

There has to be some way to get into the footage. I don't know if the camera's field of vision extends to my house, but the way it's pointed—slightly elevated, facing directly ahead—makes me dizzy with excitement.

"Mrs. Maples," I say cautiously. "Can we check the footage? It might've captured something from that day."

"Of course. Come on in. I'm afraid you'll have to do a lot of the figuring out yourself."

"I can do that. Thank you."

We go in. I have never seen the inside of Mrs. Maples's house, not in all the years that we've lived across from each other. It's very pastel on the inside. Pastel blues, pastel yellows. And it smells vaguely of perfume. The ceilings are low, which gives the sensation of being cramped. She flips on the lights. "Okay," she says. "If I remember right, I think you manage everything on the computer, but I've never tried." We turn the corner into her dining room, which looks mostly unused as a dining room. The table is covered in papers and other miscellaneous items: a hairbrush, a tabby cat that meows loudly and leaps off, and a chonker of a laptop. All sprawled across a faded floral-patterned tablecloth.

The laptop is older, and it wheezes and whirs with protest when we boot it up, but it does turn on eventually. I wait while it gets through all the setup screens. She goes into the living room and brings back a bundle of papers. "All the manuals and sign-ins are in here somewhere. I'm sure you're laughing at me for having all this fancy equipment and not ever using it."

I'm just hoping that it's working, despite her never having checked. I flip through all the papers feverishly. It gives information about the website and how all the applications work. It turns out that Mrs. Maples's entire house is decked out in home security tech. She's got motion sensors in the house and door sensors for every entrance. "Do you never turn any of this stuff on?" I ask in amazement.

She chuckles. "I push the button on my key ring when I leave and push it again when I come back. That's all I really know. Does it work? Would it go off if some intruder tries to break in? I couldn't tell you that. The camera I've certainly never used."

There, on the last page of the manual, in neat script handwriting, are the username and password. I go on the website and log in. All of Mrs. Maples's installed features show up on the side of the page.

I click on *home security camera*. The video footage appears on the screen. The field of view is dead on. It shows Mrs. Maples's front yard, the driveway to the garage, and also a perfect shot of our garage door. It's farther out and not perfectly crisp imagery, but it's there. "Come on," I murmur to myself.

Right under the video window, small text: *Recorded footage available for previous thirty days.*

I glance over my shoulder at Mrs. Maples. "Can I run home and get a flash drive?"

Eleven

I stifle yawns as I flip on the lights in the bakery kitchen. The sky is gray, lined with a peek of pink. It's going to be a hot summer day, I can tell. The morning, usually bright and cool, has an edge of humidity to it. Which is a bad sign, as it's only five thirty.

I've never been an early riser, but the work of a baker is in the morning.

The mornings are mine alone now, and I savor them. Getting up earlier than everyone else has become my routine, and even though this is the earliest I've ever gotten up in my life, I'm surprised to find that I kind of like it. The roads are mostly empty. Everything is so quiet in the kitchen. I never realized how loud the world is all the time until I got these mornings to myself. It feels like peace.

The double doors leading to the storefront push open. I expect it to be Bakersfield, who drops by sometimes still. But it's not him. It's Daniel.

"Good morning," he says. He usually looks immaculate and

tidy, but his hair is a little rumpled now, as if he just crawled out of bed.

"Oh, you. What are you doing up so early?" I am surprised.

"Thought I might catch you here. And get some breakfast."

"Well, that part I can do." I pull out the coffee beans, grind them, and start a fresh pot going.

He clears his throat. "I also wanted to apologize."

"For what?"

His face flames, and I remember the last time I saw him. Outside the bakery in the evening, right after my first kiss with Thom. Then I'm blushing too, although I have nothing to be embarrassed about.

"So you did see me," I say finally.

"I didn't want to intrude. Sorry. I shouldn't have skulked around and said nothing."

"Now you've made it weirder," I point out. "You probably shouldn't have said anything."

He shakes his head and flushes again. "I think I should just leave now before I continue to make things worse." He's so mortified that I mostly forget about my own embarrassment and pivot to trying to ease his.

"No, don't do that," I protest. "I have coffee for you, at least. Stay."

I examine him as I start the KitchenAid for my first batch of dough in the morning. It's so weird that he's here in central Illinois, in the kitchen of this bakery. He definitely doesn't belong. He looks like he should be somewhere rainy and urban. His skin looks like it would burn after ten minutes in the midwestern summer sun.

"What are you thinking about?" he asks. "You're staring."

"Wondering how weird it must be for you here. Pretty different from London. How do you take your coffee?"

"With milk, no sugar. Milk, not half and half, just to be clear. I've learned I have to make that distinction."

We have both, so it doesn't matter. "Why not half and half?"

"Only Americans use half and half in their coffee. It's so thick and creamy."

"That's what makes it good! Don't you want a creamy coffee?"

"No, that's revolting. You might as well put butter in your coffee."

"That's a thing here too, you know. It's called bullet coffee," I say, and I laugh at the horrified expression on his face.

"Culture shock," he says.

"So I'm guessing you *don't* like it here."

"Not true. I'm treating it as an anthropological experiment. I'm logging all this information in my head."

"And writing a thesis about it?"

"Mentally." He grins. "Practice for uni."

"College. We say college here."

"Right."

"Is that what you're studying? Anthropology of the Midwest?"

"I haven't drilled down to that level of granularity, but maybe." He clears his throat, as if he's announcing something of extreme importance. "I'll be double majoring in economics and anthropology."

"Impressive. You should talk to my sister. You seem like you'd get along. She's studying economics and political science with a minor in gender studies at NYU. She's the smart one in our family."

"And what are you?" he asks inquisitively.

I shrug. "I don't really know which one in the family I am yet. The indecisive one? My mom is always telling me I have to be a better planner." I dust flour on the cool marble countertop. "The one thing I am good at is baking."

"You could start a bakery. Like my grandad."

I shake my head, smiling. "I don't think I could do that."

"Why not? I think you're a better baker than him."

"Yeah, you should not tell him you said that, ever. But I can't become a pastry chef. My mom would kill me."

"Why?"

"Um, she's Chinese. Isn't that self-explanatory? She wants me to be like my sister and be a doctor or lawyer or engineer. Or failing all those things, major in finance. Finance sounds prestigious but less hard. And I guess I'm not terrible at math. If I told her I wanted to go to culinary school, she'd freak."

"It sounds like you have the opposite problem my dad did."

"Yeah, maybe your grandad should adopt me, because then I could just inherit his bakery."

"It's a pretty good solution," Daniel says, chuckling.

"Just to be clear, I'm only half joking. My mom can have you. She's always wanted a son."

"Families are so strange."

"Agreed."

"Luckily, for all the dysfunctionality on my dad's side, my mum's side is super normal."

I have no idea if my dad's side is super normal or not.

My mother has never taken us back to China to meet any family on her side. She sometimes tells us stories about when she was a kid, mostly as parables about how we should work harder and eat more. She was always hungry. That's the main moral of every story.

As for my dad's family, I don't know anything about them. I don't know if we have living grandparents. If we do, I don't know if they know about me and Margaret. I have never asked because I don't want to upset Mama. Margaret has never cared about that, but she's never asked either. I think it's because she's afraid of the answer. It's easier to imagine than to know for sure. Your imagination is usually less depressing.

"Are your parents going to visit?" I ask, trying to steer the conversation away from taking a dark turn.

"Nah, I don't think so. For one, my dad still is not talking to my grandad. And two, my parents are coming to New York City in the fall to help me move in, and I think they're way more interested in spending time in New York than here."

"This is Real America, though," I joke. "Surely your dad tells you that?"

He laughs. "I think my dad tried really hard to get out of Real America, if I'm to be honest. I do call my mum every day to tell her about it. She finds it fascinating."

"That is really adorable."

"What?"

"The fact that you call your mom every day."

"Well I'm updating her on my anthropological experiment in the Midwest, and since she's never lived anywhere remotely similar. She grew up in Paris. She thinks it's interesting."

"Good save. I still think it's very sweet."

"Anyway, I'm running out of things to tell her, because this place isn't very big."

"You're not doing a great job on your thesis, then. And you're not trying hard enough. There are things to see here that you could never get in London or your fancy international travels."

"My dad always made it seem like a place not worth exploring."

"Well, he's wrong." Margaret, Daniel's father, Daniel: they're just people who can't feel the live beating heart of this town. Although the vandalism incident is a sour note, it doesn't change what I see when I go around. My home, and the place that shaped who I am. Rejecting it would feel like rejecting a part of myself. "I can show you all the highlights. You'll see."

I say it before really even thinking about it. I only think about Thom after it's already out, and then I feel guilty because it sure sounds like I'm asking Daniel to go on a date, even though I'm not.

But he smiles big, and it makes me happy anyway.

A sound at the door startles us, a jangle of the sticking doorknob. "What's going on back here?" It's Bakersfield. I step back guiltily, even though I've done nothing wrong.

"Are the croissants in the oven?"

"Yes!" I say quickly. "Almost ready to come out."

He sweeps across the kitchen, poking suspiciously at the oven and then turning to glare at Daniel. "This isn't supposed to be a gab session. She's on the job."

"I know that. I just came to apologize for something," Daniel says.

"Personal drama already." Bakersfield snorts. "Not while she's on the clock."

"Look," I say, "he wasn't bothering me. I was making coffee for breakfast anyway."

"I was just trying to be friendly," Daniel says, exasperated.

Bakersfield crosses his arms. "You're supposed to be helping with the books and getting a new accountant lined up. You aren't supposed to be underfoot. Your mother promised that before she sent you over here."

"Oh, my mistake. I thought I was supposed to be getting to know my grandfather, not merely be around as the hired help. Perhaps I should just head back to London, then, and you can just call up a new accountant? Leave out the middleman."

Bakersfield stiffens and then jerks his chin up. "Nobody's stopping you, kid. Sure it would make your dad happy."

Daniel storms past me and out of the kitchen. The door slaps closed behind him.

I'm frozen, feeling like I've witnessed something painfully private. I don't even dare make eye contact with Bakersfield, who seems rooted to his spot as well. I hear him sigh and shuffle around the counter.

I look up, and his shoulders seem more hutched than usual. "He wants to be here," I say gently, not sure if I am about to be fully ignored or told to mind my own business.

"I know he does," he replies. He pats me lightly on the shoulder as he slips out too, leaving me alone in the kitchen and wondering why it is so hard for each of us to say what we really feel to the people who matter.

Kissing Thom gives me this quiet thrill every time, like I still can't quite believe it's real, his freckled face in my hands, his silky hair between my fingers. We haven't done much else yet. But the kissing. That's happening everywhere.

"But what is he *like*, Annalie?" Violet says one day as we're eating bowls of chocolate mousse I made and watching the dessert show at her house. "You keep going on and on about how cute he is, but you're squirreling him away like some kind of secret. Are you going to introduce us at some point or what?" We're settled on the big squashy sectional in her living room and watching her baby brother, Benji, who's sleeping peacefully in his playpen, while Mrs. Faraon takes Violet's younger sister, Rose, to her piano lesson. We've made a wreck of the kitchen, of course.

"I don't know," I admit. "Is it too early? I don't want to scare him off. Right now, it feels like this amazing private thing between just the two of us."

I can tell Violet is hurt.

"I'm not trying to hide you!" I insist.

"Feels like you are. I get it. I'm not like the crowd he normally hangs out with." She tries to sound level, but her voice wavers slightly.

"I promise I will introduce you two. Soon," I say to placate her. "I'm just trying to feel out exactly what we are right now."

"You mean even after all this, you still haven't discussed whether he's your boyfriend?"

It is becoming weirder the longer this goes on. I guess I only ever imagined up to that first kiss and no further. After that, I assumed we'd just . . . be together. Turns out real life isn't so straightforward.

"We haven't put a label on it," I say finally, as if it's a mutual choice, and not me avoiding the issue.

Violet flaps her hands dismissively. "It's not that hard if it's right. Like with Abaeze, I knew." Her face glows with love. "He's literally in Nigeria right now, and we still talk every night."

"We can't all be as flawless as you and Abaeze admittedly."

"It's hard to achieve this level of perfection; it's true."

"Vom." I stick my finger in my mouth, but I'm smiling. It's impossible not to be charmed by how cute they are.

She pops her spoon into her mouth. "Look, all I'm saying is, if he isn't jumping at the chance to call you his girlfriend, then maybe he's not all that. Always remember that you're the prize," she says.

I feel a surge of affection for my friend, who genuinely sees me the way I've always wanted to see myself. "I know, I know."

She gives me a sidelong glance. "Okay." She makes a motion of zipping up her lips. "I've brought this up enough times. That's all I have to say."

"*Anyway*," I say pointedly, "how is it going now that Abaeze is in Nigeria?"

Violet looks down. "It's fine. I mean, I miss him. But it's probably good practice for when we go off to college and have to do real long distance."

"I don't understand why you can't just go to the same college."

"We're not going to go to the same college because we're so clingy we can't handle four years apart," she says crisply. "We're going to go to the best college for what we're doing. Or, we'll go wherever we get the best scholarships. But I've told you a million times, Abaeze is going to go somewhere amazing for art. And I'll probably have to go somewhere different with a good environmental science program." Her eyes go all dreamy. "Maybe Vermont."

"You're so practical."

"We have our whole lives to be together. What's the rush? Not going to make dumb decisions now to screw up our futures later."

Right then, Benji wakes up and starts bawling. Violet hands me her bowl and picks up an armful of screaming baby brother. She follows me into the kitchen as I start piling everything into the sink for washing.

"You're getting really good at desserts. This chocolate mousse was award-worthy. You should go on the Food Network show."

"Hah!" I lather up the sponge and start scrubbing. "I don't think they're taking high schoolers. But things at the bakery are going well. Bakersfield trusts me in the kitchen now. And even his grandson—the grumpy guy, remember?—he's come around too."

"Oh?" she says, eyebrows raised, bobbing Benji up and down in her arms. "Tell me more."

"He's not so bad. He doesn't know anybody here, and his relationship with Bakersfield is . . . complicated. I think he might be talking to me out of desperation."

She glances at me slyly.

"What?" I demand.

"Nothing! I said nothing." She grabs a dish towel with one hand and puts it on the counter next to me. "No Audrey, endless baked goods, a British guy? This job sounds way better than the last one."

"Daniel doesn't come with the job like some kind of accessory."

"Daniel," she repeats. "Okay. Hope Thom puts a label on you fast."

"Violet!"

"I'm just kidding," she says. "And I swear, that's the last time I'll bring this up. Last time."

I'm in the bakery kitchen, cataloging ingredients for banana bread. Daniel sips on a cup of tea in the corner while reading by the window.

He and Bakersfield seem to have reached a strained détente—a silent but mutual agreement not to criticize each other in exchange for continued harmony under this roof. I asked Daniel whether he was really going to go back to London. "No," he said curtly.

"Because you and your grandpa made up?"

"Because I can't admit to failure."

I'm glad he's decided to stay. I've gotten used to him sitting there quietly where the light is good. There's an office area in between the front of the bakery where the customers come in and the kitchen in the back. But the office is windowless and tight.

Sometimes we talk, but not always. It's nice just to have a person back here, and when Daniel is here, Bakersfield usually isn't.

I look over at him at the same time he looks up. Our eyes meet. He smiles.

"What are you reading?" I ask.

"A book about imperialism in the 1900s."

Okay. I already feel out of my depth. "For school?"

He laughs. "No, for fun. My mum recommended it. I figure if I am going to be here the entire summer, barely knowing anybody, I should at least do some reading. It's pretty interesting. Do you want to borrow it?"

"No, it's okay."

"Not your type of preferred reading?"

"That's really something my sister would probably like."

"And what do you like?"

I shrug. "Fiction. Fluffy books." He smiles slightly. "You think I'm not very smart."

"No," he says emphatically. "Just because you don't like

reading the same books I like reading? That doesn't make you not smart."

"It's fine. I *am* the average one in my family," I tell him, smiling.

"I very much doubt that." He pauses. "You talk about your sister a lot, as if she's better than you."

"Well, she is. Do you have any siblings?"

He shakes his head. "I always wanted a brother."

"My sister, Margaret, is older. I wonder what she would've wanted for a sibling. She's been around for my whole life, obviously, so I never really thought about what I would've wanted if I got the choice."

"Being an only child can be a lot of pressure," he says.

"But then there's nobody to compare you with, at least. It was hard to measure up to Margaret. Is hard." I exhale loudly. "I wish I hadn't asked her to come home."

Daniel crosses the space to the range and turns on the flame to reheat the remaining water in the kettle. "You don't like her."

"No, I love her. Of course I do," I say immediately. "We just have really different ideas about how we want to handle things."

"For example?"

I sit down on a stool and lean forward. "Okay. For example, she's two years older than me, right? So in high school, I was a freshman when she was a junior. Our high school mascot is the dragon, because, well"—I grimace—"back in the day, it used to be 'the Chinks.'"

He almost spits out his tea. "What?"

"I mean, like, way back in the day. In the seventies or whatever."

"That's not that long ago."

"You know what I mean."

"Why?"

"Why that was the mascot? I guess originally, there was a big fad around orientalism in this area, and they thought it was a cool idea. Who knows? I'll admit, our town doesn't have the most amazing track record on this kind of thing." I feel defensive just telling this story. "Anyway, they changed the name because eventually, everyone realized it was offensive. But then my freshman year, some people in my class took a photo at the homecoming football game with the dragon mascot, making peace signs and their eyes all squinty on purpose."

He winces.

"I know, it's not great. But basically, it was a bunch of dumb kids who probably dedicated less than two seconds of thought to that photo. It got posted on Instagram. Margaret was student body president at that point, and she *flipped out* when she saw. She wanted all those kids expelled. She had a full-on campaign for it, circulated petitions, had multiple meetings with administration, called in their parents. It went on for weeks, and there was even media coverage. Eventually, she agreed to drop it if she got a full public apology from the students involved."

At the time I thought it was tasteless but not that big of a deal. Now, seeing Daniel's facial expression makes me wonder if I didn't take it seriously enough.

I remember the way people looked at me, how people didn't want to sit with me at lunch because they thought I'd be too sensitive if they ever said anything off-color. I was so miserable. "Not saying those kids weren't wrong, but it was also my first year of high school. She's my sister and everyone knew it. You can imagine that little incident didn't make me a ton of friends. And I'm not convinced everyone walked away from that situation feeling like we had all learned something. Mostly, people just thought Margaret was a real bitch who couldn't take a joke." I look down. "I know this is horrible, but I was so glad when she graduated and left. And then *this* happened. God, I have no idea why I called her that day."

Daniel frowns. "You don't want to find out who vandalized your garage?"

"Sure I do. But mostly I wish this just hadn't happened at all. And now that it has, I wish I could just put it behind us. I know you think this place is an unsophisticated backwater compared to London, but it's my home, you know? I belong here. I like the town, and I like the people. And I don't want Margaret to make my life harder than it needs to be."

"It sounds like things are complicated."

"Yeah," I agree. "I guess my feelings are. I feel guilty for not being more up in arms about it. But what's the point, in the end? I would rather just let it go than dwell on it forever."

"I think people can have different opinions about the best way to confront problems."

I busy my hands with pouring a cup of tea for myself too and wrap my fingers around the warm cup. "Thanks," I say. "I didn't mean to use you for therapy."

"What else am I doing? Sitting in the corner, reading about imperialism in the 1900s," he replies wryly. "You were going to take me around town, weren't you? Show me what's great about this place."

"Oh yes." I had forgotten about that.

My phone buzzes. I check it. I grin—it's from Thom, and he wants to know if he can come see me in my "natural environment."

I peer at Daniel, who is watching me text. He can loiter back here because his grandpa owns the place, but I can't just let a random guy in the kitchen because he feels like it. That's probably a one-way ticket to getting fired, and I actually want to *keep* this job. Still. I think I can trust him to keep a secret. "Hey, do you think your grandpa is going to come back here?"

"Probably not," he says slowly. "Why?"

"The guy I'm dating"—I find myself blushing as I say it—"he wants to drop by real quick. Only for a minute. Don't tell."

He looks at me skeptically. "I don't think my grandad would love it if I just let a stranger back here. Scratch that, I can tell you: he will murder me."

"Please," I plead. "Pretty please. He just wants to see the giant kitchen I've been gushing about. You can go back to the office and pretend like you don't know anything. I swear, I'll pretend like you weren't involved."

He's got a reluctant expression, and I know that I've got him.

"All right, all right. Relax. I'm not a snitch."

"Thank you!" I feel mildly guilty for peer pressuring Daniel, but I text Thom to come over. Almost the minute I push send, I hear a knock on the back window.

"Ooh, that must be him," Daniel says dryly. "That was fast."

Clearly, Thom was waiting to get the go-ahead. I open the door. Standing on the stoop are Thom and the whole crew of Accidental Audio. "Surprise!" he says.

"Oh, hi," I say, flustered. I feel nervous bringing a whole crew in here, but I'm happy to see Thom. "This is a surprise."

Mike steps in first. "This was my idea. Thom is always raving about your baked goods."

Mike is definitely the ringleader of the group. Unlike the other boys, he's stockier and shorter, with dark brown hair and a snub nose. But I notice that the other boys listen to whatever he says. His dad is some executive at a big insurance company in town. I've never been there, but everyone says his house is incredible. A great place for boozy, wild parties, the kind that cops love to break up. The kind that I'd never be invited to, and even if I were, the kind Mama would murder me for if she ever found out I went to one.

I step aside slowly. "You can come in for a second, but then you have to go." I hate that I sound so uptight.

"Got it, babe," Thom says, winking at me mischievously. "We'll be out of here in no time."

They gather inside, and I notice Daniel standing a little ways behind me.

"Who's—"

"This is Daniel," I say, cutting him off. "Daniel is Mr. Bakersfield's grandson. He's visiting from Europe."

"Pleased to meet you, mate." Daniel offers his hand.

This is probably more formal of an introduction than Thom has probably ever gotten, but he takes Daniel's hand and shakes. It's kind of funny watching them, because even though Thom's not short, Daniel towers over him. I've never seen Thom look uncomfortable before, but he does right now.

"I have some chocolate cupcakes." I offer the boys a tray of them.

"These are delicious," Mike says, after biting into one. "Thom wasn't kidding. Professional."

"Thanks."

Daniel stands around for a couple more seconds before clearing his throat. "I'm going to, uh, head back into the office. Lots of accounting to do. Math. Boring stuff. See you around, Annalie."

"Bye," I say brightly, trying to ignore Thom staring at him. I watch the kitchen door swing closed behind him. I turn back, and Jones is poking at the KitchenAid. "Hey—maybe don't—" I sound sharper than I mean to. I soften. "This isn't my stuff."

"This kitchen is crazy," Jeremy says, marveling at all the open shelving. "Look—there's an entire shelf of coffee beans. Do you get free stuff as part of working here?"

"No, not really."

"Do you just eat all the time?"

I laugh. "No. Believe it or not, after you spend days in a row baking, stuffing your face loses some of its appeal. Just means I'll have to bake more." I look nervously over at the door, hoping and praying that Bakersfield doesn't decide to come back here and check on me. He normally doesn't, but if the guys stay and keep making a racket, he might hear. A horror flashes before my eyes, where I imagine Bakersfield seeing five grimy teenage guys poking around his prized kitchen, leaving fingerprints and germs on everything. Goodbye baking job.

My discomfort must show, because eventually they stop exploring. "So, I think we're going to head out, but I'm glad we caught you," Thom says, squeezing my hand. "You want to hang out later?"

I breathe a sigh of relief. "After my shift is over? Sure. What are you guys going to do?"

"Try not to get into too much trouble," Mike says, tossing me a grin. "Let's go."

They file out of the kitchen, laughing and whispering, and I'm alone in the kitchen again. I'm glad they're gone, but somehow, I'm still left with a sensation of being the awkward hanger-on, watching from the outside in.

Thom and I catch a movie after my shift is over. Without the guys, to my relief. It's a brainless action flick, but we get to do the thing where we make out in the back of the theater, which is honestly something I've dreamed about but never thought would happen to me. I'm extremely nervous the entire time that some-body is going to see us. I'm getting better at kissing. I think so, anyway. I have no idea what the movie is about.

After, we exit into the cool night air, his arm loosely wrapped around my waist. He walks me to my car. He leans me up against the door and kisses me, deep and slow. I get chills. Is this really happening? I imagine him kissing me like this by my locker, on the school steps.

"This is fun," he says when we come up for air.

"It is," I agree. I try to sound light about it, not too desperate. I can feel myself trying not to say it. *Don't do it*, I tell myself. *Don't say it.* "Does this mean I'm your girlfriend now?"

Too late. In the throes of the moment, I'm too scared to look at his face to see how he's reacting, so I stare at the collar of his shirt instead. An entire millennium passes while I wait for him to answer. I slowly die, hating myself for succumbing to my insecurity, my neediness.

He chuckles, and his hazel eyes wrinkle as he grins. "Sure. I guess it does."

This is happening. I feel like I have hiked to the top of a mountain and now I am looking down at the world. I am above it all. Thom Froggett is my boyfriend. *My* boyfriend.

It's funny how you never know when everything will change. How it will catch you off guard, and by the time you realize it's happened, you are standing there, wondering when you stepped into this new reality and wishing you could retrace your steps.

I come home to Margaret sitting in the yellow circle of overhead light in the kitchen, grimly looking at me with her laptop, her eyes shadowed.

I stop in my tracks.

"I found footage of the day the vandals painted our garage door," she says bluntly.

I blink. "How?"

"Mrs. Maples across the street. It turns out she has a security camera."

"Oh."

She turns the laptop toward me. "I think you should watch it," she says.

I take a step back instinctively, shrinking. "Do I have to?" slips out meekly before I can even think about it. It's what I used to say when Margaret would tell me what to do as a kid, and I didn't want to do it. I could never just say no.

She sighs. "Yes."

I don't know what I'm scared of. I approach the laptop. I nod, and she pushes play.

The video flashes across the screen in full color. It's from the afternoon, and the footage isn't fuzzy like you'd imagine security footage to be.

What I see:

Two dark-haired boys emerge from one edge of the screen onto our lawn and then onto our driveway. They spray-paint so fast, it's almost a blink-and-you'll-miss-it. The ugly word blooms on our garage door. Seeing it again makes me nauseous. You can't see the boys' faces, but you can see their backs.

One of them is wearing a soccer jersey, and the colors are familiar. The number is 69, and I bet if you zoomed in, you'd see that the name on the back is the Frog.

What I feel:

Like having the floor pulled out under you in a dream. That moment of falling before you wake up, where you don't know how far the ground is or if there's ground at all.

I am not looking at Margaret. I am sinking somewhere far away.

For the longest time, I was the only Chinese girl in my entire grade. You wouldn't have known I was Chinese. People never do. I never spoke it at school. I ate hot lunches instead of the food Mama would've packed for me, so no one would know I was different. I knew, instinctively, that fitting in was critical. I knew, the way sea turtles know to crawl to the ocean the moment they hatch.

In second grade, a Chinese girl from San Jose, California, moved to our town, and she joined my class.

She was very quiet. She had these severe bangs and a bowl haircut (which I'd had when I was three, but had blessedly grown out by the time I was going to real school). She was short for her age, and she did not like to talk. The teacher asked her to share her name with the class and she wouldn't. Instead, she handed the teacher a slip of paper with her name on it, also phonetically spelled out, because her name turned out to be Li Bin.

"Lee Beeeen," the teacher said, stretching out the *ee* sound in a question mark.

Li Bin didn't nod or shake her head, from what I could tell, so the teacher assumed she had it right.

"Please welcome your new classmate," the teacher instructed the class.

Her assigned seat wasn't next to mine, but I couldn't stop looking over there. I knew she was Chinese. I didn't know if she could tell that I was. I wouldn't meet Violet for another year, and even though I knew other girls like us from TV and Sunday Chinese school, it felt weird to have her in class.

After school, we all waited in line for the bus to come pick us up. There was basically no teacher supervision.

I don't remember how it started.

One minute we were all standing in line. The next minute, people were chanting, "BEAN, BEAN, BEAN" at Li Bin, and then one boy started pulling on the corners of his eyes and laughing. It was a strange feeling, watching it happen. Almost out-of-body. I was frozen, too afraid to move and be noticed. Too afraid to say anything.

I didn't know anything about Li Bin. I didn't know what flavor ice cream she liked or what made her family move to our corner of Illinois. I didn't know what her favorite color was. I barely even knew what she sounded like.

I watched her stand there. She didn't cry or react at all. She just stared straight ahead, but I didn't dare make eye contact with her.

All I knew was that she and I were the same, branches arching out from the same roots. Nobody could see it, but I knew. And all I could do was watch and say nothing, and know, deep down inside, that I was lucky. Lucky to only be the same on the inside, and not on the outside, where everybody could see.

* * *

Margaret studies my face. I wonder what she sees. My sight is not focused outward; I am looking within. I can hardly see the video anymore. I'm watching the swirl in my head. Scenes and colors. Lights and sounds. I think I am going to be sick right on the floor.

"Do you recognize them?" Her voice doesn't betray anything.

I close my eyes. I do. I can't see their faces, but I do, I do, I do.

What do I say, Margaret? What can I say? The next moment will change everything, no matter what happens.

My eyes snap open. "No," I hear myself say, going into hiding the way I do best.

Margaret's expression shutters, disappointed.

It's too late now.

Twelve

MARGARET

"Cheers," Rajiv says, clinking his milkshake against my root beer. "I'm impressed you found the video."

"Thank you. Your auntie gave me the idea, when she mentioned the security cameras at the strip mall." I take a sip of my drink, tasting of comfort and childhood. We're at the local Steak 'n Shake, where everyone used to go after football games. Something about it just feels like home. The part of it I miss, anyway. Rajiv convinced me to go for a quick celebration after work when I told him I turned the video footage over to the police, who reopened the case.

"Well, I'll have to tell her that. What did they look like?"

I shake my head. "I don't know what I expected. They look young. High schoolers, probably."

"Did you show Annalie?"

"Yes. She didn't recognize them. You can't see their faces." I remember her pinched, pale expression as she watched the video. I pressed her on it, insisted that she had to at least have a guess. She snapped that she didn't want to guess and was tired of constantly being reminded of something that was over. She went straight to bed after without another word.

"Well, chin up. It's great progress. And besides, they were wearing jerseys, right? Idiots. They must be school jerseys from around here."

I shrug. "I don't recognize them. Maybe they bought them somewhere. I spent three hours googling different retail stores for those designs, and there are a ton of custom ones, and the colors aren't that unique."

"They'll find the guys." The conviction behind his eyes is intense. I can't remember the last time somebody has looked at me the way he has. None of the guys I went on various dates with at NYU, each of them as forgettable as one of a thousand leaves on the same oak tree. "And then after, we'll celebrate again."

We sit silently, drinking our beverages. For all the ease we have around each other at work, it still feels like uncharted territory to go somewhere voluntary, just to be together.

"You know that for the longest time, I couldn't bear to come here." Rajiv says quietly.

"What? Steak 'n Shake?"

He nods.

"Why?"

He looks at me with an expression of surprise intermingled with frustration. "You don't remember."

He was always more sentimental than me.

"We were going to come here after prom. You wanted to do that, remember? Come here in your prom dress." He grimaces.

"Oh, right," I say, almost inaudibly. Somehow, in all the things that happened that night, this particular detail didn't stick in my mind, because to me, it seemed insignificant in the enormity of the wreckage. If I had remembered, I never would've agreed to come here. "Is this why you brought me here? So we could talk about it?"

"No. I mean, maybe some small part of me did." He exhales and gives a wry half smile that's more of a frown. "We never did talk about it."

Yes, we never did talk about it. After that day, we never talked again until this summer. There are some things that you can't come back from. I don't like to think about it, any of it, because uncovering those memories feels like standing on the edge of a well where I can't see the bottom. It's safe to be on the rim, but fatal to tip forward.

Yet here we are, where it all ended.

It was only a matter of time before the secret came out, so when Annalie broke our cover, it felt like our reprieve had ended. Before she knew about our relationship, I could still hope that when she found out, it wouldn't be a big deal.

I was wrong.

At home, Mama dropped her cutting comments into her soups and stir fries, tossed them in while she folded laundry, greeted me with them when I came home.

"You shouldn't date him," she'd say.

"Why?" I'd demand. "Because you don't like brown people?"

It's not about race, she'd say. It was about culture. It was about food. It was about how I was young and wasting my time. It was about her ability to converse with a son-in-law in Chinese.

We would go round and round, and I'd try to nail her down, expose her for her racism and hypocrisy. I'd fail because she'd never say it outright. But with my family, it was never about what you said out loud.

I lived with the tension because deep down, I believed that all it would take was time. Eventually, I'd wear her down. Eventually, she'd change her mind. She had the capacity to change for me. I believed that.

Rajiv fought his own fight at home with his mother. She didn't understand why he couldn't just date any of the Indian girls she introduced him to. He pleaded with her just to meet me, just get to know me. And finally, she agreed. I was supposed to come over before prom to have dinner with his family and take photos.

That was the plan.

It didn't turn out that way.

It started out so simply. A tear in my dress on prom night. An easy fix for my mother.

"Hold still," she said irritably. I was shifting from one foot to another, checking the time on my phone. "Such effort for a silly boy."

I was already jittery about meeting Mrs. Agarwal. "Why do you have to be like this?" I said, pulling away from her abruptly.

"Be like what?"

"Oh, stop. You hate Rajiv. Just say it. Just say what you really want to say. What are you going to do, never talk to me again? He's here to stay, okay?" My voice kept getting louder and louder until I was shouting.

"He's too different. You will regret if you stay with him." she insisted. "Listen. Listen to me." She grabbed my wrist. "It's not just me. You think his family will ever truly accept you as a daughter? Chinese and Indian—it will never work. I fought my ma and ba, I didn't listen to them, and for what? Your father left me alone here anyway. He could never understand me, and I could never understand him. It will be the same for you. You'll always be outside."

"That's not true," I said.

She dropped her arms. "I thought you were a smart girl," she said quietly, her face impassive but for a tiny quiver in her lip. "I didn't raise you to be stupid."

Her words cut deep.

"This isn't stupid," I said. I was daring her, provoking her to say the thing that would hurt the most. It felt dangerous, but also, like a huge relief. I wanted to feel the pain now, rather than later. "Tell me," I said sharply. "What are you going to do if it works and we get married one day? You're just going to keep being like this? What will you do, Mama?"

The silence was deadly. I knew I had gone too far. "Mei liang xin." Ungrateful. Cruel. "You would choose him over your own mother? I don't need a daughter like that. If you stay with him, you'll no longer be mine." The needle was still in my dress. She didn't take it out. I could see a tear sparkling in her eye, but it didn't fall. Mama never cried. She left me alone.

I forced her to draw a line in the sand, and so she did. Who else did I have to blame but myself?

I always believed that Mama could come around, because I was her daughter, and she loved me like no one else.

She spent late nights sewing until her vision blurred to pay our mortgage so we could stay in our house after Dad left. She paid for the art classes, the piano lessons, the tennis coaching. She cried when she was able to take us to Toys "R" Us for the first time to buy whatever toy we wanted. She told us repeatedly that no matter what happened to her, as long as we could make it in this life, everything she had suffered would be worth it. Her sacrifices were real. She loved me. I never questioned it.

I knew that deep down, she was afraid, but for the first time, I could feel fear too. The fear of losing her for good, when my father left, and my grandparents were long gone. My mother, my root. No matter how wrong she was, I couldn't imagine cutting her off one day. There was an old Chinese lullaby—a child without a mother is like a single blade of grass. Turning your back on your mother was the worst crime imaginable.

Some things could be mended. A dress, a fight. Some things couldn't.

I didn't go to prom.

Rajiv broke up with me the next day.

Now we're here, and Rajiv is quiet and motionless, waiting for me to say something. I feel the space between us, while the world all around, oblivious, continues to clatter about.

"I'm sorry," I say, meaning it more than I've meant anything but knowing it can't ever be enough.

"You just left me. On prom night. My mom hired a photographer, prepared the house, made a million dishes for you so you would feel welcome. I called you eleven times." He pauses. "I finally changed out of my tux at ten o'clock."

His words crack me open. I don't say anything. There's nothing I can say now that would make up for it.

"How could you do that?" he asks. He doesn't sound angry. Just sad. He simply wants to know. Rajiv, my beautiful, funny Rajiv. He could never hide anything when he talked, and now, even now, his voice bleeds with emotion. I hurt him, and I feel every bit of that hurt, still.

I look down at my lap. Shame chokes my throat. "I know it doesn't fix things or change what happened, but I am so, so sorry. I think back to that night all the time. I thought after so long, I'd stop missing you, but I don't, I can't—"

It's too close now, dangerously close—what I'd never wanted to admit to myself, even in the emptiness of my dorm room, the cavernous hallways full of strange faces I didn't know.

I had put our love in a box and tucked it away, but it's tumbled open and the contents are winding, climbing, everywhere, everywhere. There's no place left to hide it away. I can't stop myself, and right now, I don't even want to. I am the metal filings, and he's a magnet at full blast.

"I never got over you," I tell him. It's the truth. And now, it's too late to take it back.

His expression when I say that is stripped away, full of wanting, and I know that there's only one direction for us to go from here.

"My parents are at my Amita Auntie's for the afternoon," is all he has to say, and then we're out of the diner and driving across town at full speed. It's incredible that we don't get pulled over. It is both the longest and shortest drive of my life. I can barely remember the trip, and before I know what's happened, we are in his bedroom. He's pushing the door shut and we are alone. His mouth and body are on mine, and we are back to who we were.

It was so tiring to constantly remind myself of all the bad things, but here we are, at last, and I am ready to let it go. I feel enormous, overwhelming relief. To love, simply.

I am so used to this angle of his room; I have seen it a million times. The sunlight slants through his window as if this is any other day, but it isn't.

I missed this, and this, and this. Time passes, and it doesn't.

This is happening.

We tumble backward onto his bed, and I feel like I can see the smoothness of his skin out to the flares on the surface of the sun and maybe even all the stars blinking in the far reaches of the universe.

It's the sensation of the first day of summer, of being wholly awake to every molecule, of letting you know, we are alive.

Afterward, we lie in his bed, entangled and silent with euphoria. I wish we could stay there forever. I close my eyes and pretend like this is our apartment. We are in our own bed, and there is nothing to do for the rest of the day other than feel the sheets against our skin, hearing our breathing sync up like we are sharing a single pair of lungs.

But eventually, my anxiety at getting caught seeps into my fingertips. I reach for my phone and my clothes. "I'm going to go. Your parents are going to lose their minds if they see my car in your driveway."

"So what?" He pulls me in for a kiss before I can roll away. "Stay," he says.

"Yeah, well. I don't know if I'm quite ready for that confrontation yet. You better bury that condom in your garbage can." I get dressed as he watches me wordlessly.

I pause at the door, marveling at how easy it all is when it's just the two of us, but how quickly it becomes complicated when the rest of the world inevitably intrudes after the fact. I'm already beginning to feel the edges of uneasiness being with Rajiv. We were careless. *I* was careless. We've gone through this before.

My gaze settles on him, draped in a sheet. I don't want to go. When I leave this room, I don't know what will happen to us.

"What's wrong?" Rajiv asks as I linger.

I shake my head and cross the room for a kiss goodbye. "Nothing," I lie.

He smiles. "Okay."

I could stay here. I could choose to keep living in this moment, for just a little bit longer.

"I'll see you at work," I tell him, and turn away.

I leave his door open so he can watch me disappear.

* * *

I come home to a quiet house. Annalie isn't here. I know she has a summer job at the bakery, but I also suspect that she's deliberately finding reasons not to be at home to avoid crossing paths with me.

Mama is in the kitchen by herself, and I immediately feel a surge of guilt. "You hungry?" she asks by way of greeting. "I'm making bing for church this week."

I watch her roll out the dough that she let rise earlier. She dusts the rolling pin. Flattens the dough and turns it in small increments until it forms a perfect flat circle, a millimeter thin. She rubs the top surface with a glistening layer of vegetable oil, scatters a handful of thinly sliced scallions on top, and dusts it with salt. I always loved how she cuts them on the diagonal, so they peep out from the bing like pretty green ribbons.

She rolls up the dough so that it forms a cigar, with all the oil, salt, and scallions wrapped up inside, coils the roll around and around in a spiral, and flattens it slightly.

Even though I'm not hungry, my mouth waters in anticipation of the savory golden crunch and tender doughy inside once it's cooked and sliced.

While I know there's no way Mama can know where I'm coming from, the paranoia still grips me. Can she smell him on me? Can she see it in my face? Annalie always said that I was good at hiding what I was thinking, but it seemed to me that the one thing I could never hide was how I felt about Rajiv. I shift on my feet uncomfortably.

"I dropped off the video at the police station," I tell her to fill the empty space.

"Okay." She dusts the flour off her hands. "I hope this will be over now. You are too worried about this."

Her comment slaps me in the face. Mama is an expert at getting under my skin in the fastest way. She doesn't waste words. "What do you mean?" I demand.

"Aiya, sheng yin xiao yi dia'er," she says, annoyed. Make your voice quieter. "I just think you are too involved. Let the police figure it out."

"The police are failing at their job, Ma."

"It doesn't always have to be your problem. You have too much to do already. And we are fine now. These things happen." She sighs and shakes her head, sounding disappointed. "Wo zhe ge nu er, lao zhao shi." This daughter of mine, she always looks for trouble.

Always looking for trouble. That's how Mama has labeled me since childhood. The older daughter who couldn't behave as an older daughter should.

Annalie, the good one, who put on an extra layer in the winter when asked, who never raised her voice and dutifully signed up for all the classes Mama told her to. My grades were better, but that was the only thing I ever had going for me.

Listen to me, Mama's mantra, an admonishment that I got so used to because she'd say it so often. In her mind, I listened to too much of myself, and I was just a silly girl who didn't know what was good for me.

Swallowing hard, I turn to go upstairs, my earlier happiness fully squashed, but Mama isn't done talking yet.

"Sometimes you must listen to what other people tell you," she says. She slaps the dough harder than she needs to, her voice agitated. "When I came to America, your lao lao and lao ye were worried. They did not want me to come here with a wai guo ren, a foreigner, but I was so determined to come to this country. I did not listen to them. And then this man, he leaves me here in the middle of nowhere with two girls and no money. I was too afraid to go back to tell lao lao and lao ye what happened, so I stayed. And now they are gone. Too late."

I am quiet. Mama almost never talks about my father.

I sweep a glance across the room, where there are pictures of Mama in black and white when she was young, and me and Annalie growing up. My father must have been there for some pictures, early trips we took, but there are none of him. No pictures of him and Mama.

In my head, I have this image of him, but I don't remember what he looks like, not really. Memories can be tricky. I wonder what our family would've been like if he had stayed. I don't have the language to ask my mother. I know better than that.

Mama continues. "But I am here, a Chinese woman, wai guo ren everywhere. No husband. Bad English. I learn to chi ku, eat bitterness, learn how to belong where nobody want me." Her face is red. If I didn't know any better, I'd say her eyes were glassy. But Mama does not cry. I almost never see her cry.

"Do you wish you never came here?"

"Of course not," she says shortly. "I want to be here. But I wish I came here with someone else." She pauses for a moment.

"I learn to be a part of this community alone." The edges of her voice take a tint of hard pride. She lifts her chin and looks me right in the eye. "But I don't learn to be part of this community by complaining."

I am torn apart. What can I say in response to that, Ma?

She wipes her eyes furtively with the back of her hand and turns to the stove.

This is my mother, who raised me and my sister by herself, who is the reason we are in this country and not somewhere else.

I wish I could talk to her the way I want to. I wish I could make her understand my heart, or that I could understand hers, but between us, there is an entire ocean that we will never be able to cross.

Mama slips the bing out of the pan and onto the cutting board. She cuts it like a pie into six wedges. She puts a piece on a plate and slides it in front of me. I blow on it and gingerly take a bite. My teeth crunch through the crisp outer layer into the pillowy inner layers, ringing around like an onion. It tastes salty and delicious, but I've lost my enjoyment of food.

"How is your internship?" she asks me.

"Good," I say tonelessly. "It's fine."

She wipes down the counter with a wet cloth, vigorously scrubbing at a stained spot in the corner.

"Rajiv says hi. He hopes you are doing well," I say, pushing myself. I am anxious and raw. I am tight with hope and nauseous with fear.

She stops cleaning abruptly. "Oh yes. You are working with him. Is it okay?"

"It's okay, Mama." Feeling dizzy, I want to tell her every-thing. *You try at everything, so don't tell me that you just can't,* he had said to me before. I have to tell her everything, in order for Rajiv and me to have a chance.

"He went to U of I, hah?"

"Yes."

She resumes cleaning, rewetting her cloth in the sink. "You are so far away during the year. Very far." She says it like she's reminding herself, rather than making conversation with me.

"Yes," I whisper, and I feel a cold pit in the bottom of my stomach.

"It's good that you broke up with him," she says crisply. "You were both so young. Better to focus on school, find someone more like you."

Her words are loaded with a warning, at least that's how it sounds to me.

I wish I could shout at her. I wish I could blame her for my unhappiness. I look at her pinched, withdrawn expression—older than before, but still as immovable. The weight of her opposition and my fear of losing her settle on me once again. All the things she said to me right before the end come back. My desire to fight dissipates, a receding wave that sinks flatly back into the ocean at night.

Humiliated, I push the plate away. "I'm going to go take a shower."

I escape upstairs and retreat into the bathroom. I shed my clothes. I turn on the water and wait for it to get so hot that it steams up the mirrors. I wash away my guilt.

Thirteen

ANNALIE

When I told Margaret that I didn't know who was in the video, it was true. I didn't know for sure. But I knew that in all likelihood it was Thom or one of his friends. I mean, I had seen the custom jerseys! What were the chances that it was somebody else, who happened to be around the same age, happened to be wearing the same clothes, and also happened to have picked my particular house?

There must be some explanation, I told myself. Thom and his friends had nothing against me. Surely they could explain what really happened. Or maybe it wasn't them. I could believe that, if Thom told it to me, right to my face.

But as I went to bed to get away from Margaret, who I was sure could tell that I was lying, I sat in bed with the lights off for hours. It dawned on me that I had committed to this lie, maybe forever. And I had to keep lying, to my sister and probably to Thom. I couldn't imagine asking him something like this. How could I?

I wanted so badly for him to tell me it wasn't him, that he and his friends couldn't have had anything to do with this.

Yet I had a greater fear that I couldn't say or even think. It kept trying to come into my mind, sneak into my dreams, and I kept pushing it out. What if they *were* involved? I couldn't know the answer to that question, but I also didn't know how I could see Thom again without him seeing it written all over my face.

I lay awake in bed the entire night, tossing and turning, unable to stop seeing the bloom of red paint on our garage door, the flash of colors on the jerseys.

The next morning, Margaret is in the kitchen when I go downstairs. Her expression is so determined that she may as well have just stayed up all night, trying to will the answer out of the computer screen.

She's replaying the video over and over, her teeth clenched so hard I'm afraid she is going to give herself lockjaw.

"You have to stop," I say lightly, trying to sweep over my deep-seated anxiety.

"I just keep watching to see if there are any clues," she mutters. "These people picked our house because they know we live here. They must be local. They probably go to our high school."

"Well, you have to be careful with unfounded accusations. We don't have any proof of that."

"It doesn't bother you that somebody you're going to school with could do this to your house?" she asks.

"I don't know that it was anybody from school," I snap,

turning away so my hair covers my face. I take a sweet bun from a bamboo basket next to the stove. "And right now, you don't either." I march out of the kitchen.

I am a terrible liar.

"Buckle up," I say. "Get ready."

Daniel is sitting in the front passenger seat of my tiny two-door. *Wedged* is probably the more accurate description. He's so tall, his legs are practically crumpled at a forty-five-degree angle.

"That looks comfortable," I tell him, trying not to laugh.

He gives me a reproachful look. "I should learn how to drive while I'm here. I don't know what I was thinking."

"Why don't you get a learner's permit and get your grandfather to teach you?"

He laughs. "There's literally no way he would consent to spending that much time in the car with only me."

"That bad?"

"I should really just go home, but I can't give my dad that satisfaction, and my mum is so thrilled about this whole family bonding situation. She thinks I'm good for breaking the family embargo. I can't admit defeat."

"Why don't you guys do some bonding activities or something?"

"Like what?"

"What does he like to do?"

"Baking?"

"We can all bake together!"

Daniel grimaces. "Sounds terrible. I can't cook worth shite."

"Baking is different. It's more science than art. Anybody can follow instructions."

"I am good at science," he admits, "but when I bake, it's like the laws of physics and nature bend to throw a wrench in things. Honest. That is what happens every time."

"And how many times have you tried?"

"Like, three."

I crack up.

"Three is enough times for the universe to tell me that I did not inherit my grandad's genes on that front."

"Okay," I say. "Something else. You can figure out something to do with him. Movies? TV?"

"He doesn't consume media other than books. He thinks Netflix is still a DVD trade-in program."

"You just have to meet him where he's at. Give it a try."

"Right. Hey, maybe you should come to dinner or something. He'd have enough to talk to you about."

"Mm-hmm," I say noncommittally. "Maybe."

We're driving down the main street of town. I roll down the windows to get a breeze.

"No air-conditioning?"

"Windows down is better." I turn on the radio and flip to the right station.

Daniel looks thunderstruck. "Country music?"

I shoot a glance at him with a grin. "Soak it in. Today is supposed to be an educational experience, remember?"

He sighs, trying to slump back, but unsuccessfully. The top of his head grazes the roof of the car. He looks ridiculous.

I wonder how Thom would feel about me having dinner with the Bakersfield family, along with all the things we're doing together already.

Then again, I have been avoiding him for going on four days now, so I don't know how he'd feel. I've made excuses about my weird bakery shifts and having various "family" activities. He isn't suspicious. Yet. But I can't just ghost him until I go to college. He is my boyfriend. I will have to see him eventually.

I don't know what will happen when I do.

I haven't told a single person. Not even Violet. I feel like if I don't say anything, if it's locked away in my head, maybe it will go away. And who would it be hurting if it went away? The garage is clean. Nothing else has happened. Margaret will go back to college. I will keep dating Thom. It all will have been one bad nightmare that we've woken up from, never to be repeated. What's to be gained from saying something?

What if it really was Mike? Worse, what if it was Thom? How can I bear to know the answer?

"Where are you taking me?" Daniel says.

"Are you afraid?"

He raises an eyebrow. "Should I be?"

"Trust me. You'll love it."

"I haven't loved anything so far, so I'm skeptical." He scans the skies. "Is it going to be outside? I think it's supposed to thunderstorm later." Right now, a fluffy cumulus floats lazily on the horizon, but the sun is otherwise happily undisturbed. The air is thick with heat, so the breeze through the windows is welcome.

I shrug. "The weather here is unpredictable. Anything could happen in five minutes." I pull my hair off my neck. "I hope it rains. With this humidity, we could really use it."

"Carpe diem then, I say."

"That's the spirit."

I'm driving down the main street and toward the outskirts of the city. We pull to a stop at a red light, and I glance over at him, still uncomfortably jammed into the passenger seat. Despite having spent half the summer here already, it doesn't look like he's picked up a whisper of a tan. His nose is slightly red. "Did you burn?"

"Hmm?"

"On your nose, I mean. The sun is pretty strong here."

"Oh right. Yes, I'm used to that weak sun and misty, wet weather. My skin doesn't so much darken as it roasts like a lobster."

I laugh. "Charming."

"I can't help it!"

"I meant, you are rather charming when you want to be. Like, not in the beginning, when you were a total curmudgeon to me."

"Of course," he shoots back, ignoring my last dig. "Brits are always charming. It's a core feature."

"Did all that charm get put to good use back home? Leaving a trail of broken hearts behind you?"

I can't believe I said that. It almost sounds like I'm flirting with him or trying to find out if he has a girlfriend. Which I am not! On both counts. Obviously. Because I've already got a boyfriend, who I—well, if I don't exactly *love* him yet, I'm getting there.

Daniel raises an eyebrow at me, and I swear he can hear my entire internal monologue. "Why, are you interested?" I'm blushing so madly that I might as well be the one roasting like a lobster.

"I'm taken," I say coolly, way more coolly than I actually feel inside at the moment.

"Don't get too excited. I wasn't offering." He grins, though, like he *was*. "And I know I can't compete with your superstar boyfriend." He pauses and repositions himself in his seat. "I dated one girl in secondary school for three years."

"That's a pretty long time. Dat-*ed*, though?"

"We broke up before I came over."

"Why? Because of the long distance?"

"She is going to Oxford."

I feel immediately inferior. "She sounds supersmart. Power couple."

"She *is* supersmart. But no, we didn't break up because of the long distance." He shrugs. "I guess I was way more excited by the idea of taking macroeconomics than scheduling time to go back to the UK and see my girlfriend. And that's when it became reasonably clear that maybe it's not normal to not find it exciting to see your girlfriend."

"That's sad."

"It would've been sadder to have kept dating after that realization."

"How did she feel?"

He props his right hand at the top of the window opening. "She wasn't too torn up about it either. Which confirmed that it was the right decision. In high school, it's so easy to date people just because they happen to be nearby. But then you realize there's an entire world out there, and there might just be someone that you feel actually amazing about."

I catch his eyes for an instant, and then I stare fixedly ahead at the road.

"Anyway, how are things going with Tad?"

"Thom."

"Right."

"You met him."

"I did."

"Thoughts?"

"You really trust a random person to give you feedback about your boyfriend? Isn't that strange?"

"You're not a random person." I pause. Because is he a friend? I barely know him. "You're at least a good acquaintance now."

He bursts out laughing. "At least a good acquaintance. That's a really good descriptor. I am honored."

"Well," I sputter, "what did you want me to say? My BFF?"

"I'm certainly not your 'BFF,'" he says with air quotes. "I can settle for 'at least a good acquaintance.' My professional opinion is, though, that you shouldn't be taking feedback on your boyfriend from 'at least a good acquaintance.' So we have to bring that intimacy level up a little more, to at least 'a casual friend.'"

"Is casual friend above good acquaintance?"

"I'd say so."

"Okay, I think we can do that. You are in my car right now," I point out.

"Still good acquaintance territory, Annalie."

"Working on it, Daniel!"

"Okay, we should get back to this issue, but before that, can I ask—and I mean this with the utmost respect—where in the bloody hell are you taking me?"

We are fully out of town now and surrounded by nothing but miles of cornfield. I turn onto a side dirt road and head into the field. In the distance, tall white windmills rise out of the green and whirl lazily round and round. The wheels from the car kick up a cloud of brown dust around us. The air has that golden-green summer smell, earthy and alive.

"I think this is where people take victims to get murdered."

"In broad daylight on a weekend afternoon? Are you seriously concerned that I am going to overpower you?" I roll my eyes, grinning. "We're almost there."

"Almost *where*? This is the middle of nowhere."

"Look around you."

He does. "Yeah, there is corn. Corn and"—he glances over expectantly—"windmills?"

"It's a windmill farm!" I beam. "One of the biggest in the country." He doesn't look impressed. "Hold your judgment, okay? It's cool. Let's check it out." I turn onto an even smaller road than we were on, heading deeper into the fields. The corn lines our car on either side, an emerald city. The road leads to a clearing. Windmills line the side. They look like little toothpicks from far away, but close up, they tower above our heads. From the car, all we can see are the thick white trunks, like metal trees growing out of the ground.

I park along the side of the clearing. We hop out of the car. Daniel dusts off his pants. I stand, squinting in the sun. "Don't you love the summer out here?"

He considers. "It's hot. Much hotter than back home."

"I love the heat. Everything just feels so much more *vivid*, you know? Does that sound weird?" Sometimes when I'm alone, I talk to myself, and it sounds exactly like this babbling that I'm doing right now, but I don't do it in front of other people. I would never spew this kind of nonsense in front of Thom.

Daniel leans against the car. "No." He smiles. "I don't think you sound weird. I think you just sound a lot like someone who loves where you're from, which is nice."

I lead him to the base of the windmill. "Okay, now lie down."

"Excuse me?"

"Trust me. On your back."

"*Now* you sound weird."

I sit down and pat the area next to me. The ground is dusty and bare in a five-foot radius around the windmill before it gives way to cool, short grass. Aside from the path we drove up on, we're surrounded by corn. A wall of solid green, dappled with honey-yellow tassels, as far as the eye can see.

Daniel sits down delicately next to me. "Okay, now what?"

I lie back on the ground with my head to the base of the windmill, so that I'm looking straight up.

"I'm going to get dirt in my hair!" he says.

"'I'm going to get dirt in my hair,'" I whine back at him. "Stop being a baby and just do it."

He grumbles and lies down.

From this vantage point, I can see the trunk of the windmill rising up toward the bottomless sky. The blades rotate slowly above us, slicing through the air and then down toward us in a thrilling turn, so close, impossibly close. It's dizzying. It feels like I'm stuck to the roof of the world and that any second, I am going to go plunging into space, falling forever. It feels like I am heart-to-heart with the earth, its pulse, its vast and secure solidness. I am anchored to this place, a tiny piece of an unimaginable, infinite universe. It's hard to describe the feeling, except to be there and feel it for yourself.

And when I turn on my cheek to look over at Daniel and he turns to meet me, I know that he feels it too.

For a minute, we just lie there looking upward, squinting against that whitewashed blue you can only get from the center of the summer sky, refusing to break the silence. This is my favorite thing in the whole world. I could stay here for hours and watch the windmills spin. When I close my eyes, I hear the soft swish of the blades and the chirp of unidentified insects mingled with occasional birdsong. It feels like we could be in a completely different place, or a completely different time. Tomorrow, or a hundred years ago.

Daniel shifts slightly beside me and his arm brushes against mine. This brings me from floating dreamily in the ether solidly back into my body. My skin tingles. I'm wondering if this was perhaps not my best idea. If we both turned on our sides, our lips would be a whisper away from each other.

If our lips *were* a whisper away from each other, my body could take that story in a million unwanted directions.

I cough and scoot away slightly, breaking the spell of silence. "What'd you think?" I say. It sounds incredibly loud in my own ears.

"This is cool." For the first time, he sounds extremely earnest and in awe, his voice stripped of his normal cynicism.

He props himself up on his elbow. "Hey."

"Hey."

"Honestly, thanks for being my good acquaintance this summer. It was really kind of a dud before you decided to talk to me."

"You're welcome. And I officially upgrade you to casual friend."

"Amazing. I'm honored again." He heaves a big sigh and looks up. "Even if this family summer thing didn't turn out the way I thought it would, I'm still glad I came to America early."

"You excited to go to New York?"

"Intensely excited. Two more months to go."

That's right. Two months, and then Daniel will be in glitzy New York City with Margaret and back to the UK on breaks, and so on. He'll never come back here. He is brilliant and kind, and his future is endless. He is the type of person I could easily imagine doing some fancy high-powered job at the UN one day. I am a blip in his life. Someone he'll look back on and think, *Oh yes, I remember that one girl who I talked to for lack of options that one summer.* If I ever even crossed his mind again.

It makes me feel small and sad, to be a footnote in his story.

Daniel turns to me and asks a question about American pop culture, and time lurches forward again. I don't mean to lock eyes with him, but I do, and it's startling. I have to look away immediately, which is maybe the surest sign that I am completely, utterly screwed in the love department.

We lie back on the ground again, looking upward so we don't have to make eye contact as we're talking. I don't know about him, but it feels a lot safer to me for some reason.

It's silly to have brought him here, in light of all this, to this place that I treasure but haven't even shared with my own boyfriend. My boyfriend who I haven't spoken to in almost a week. I feel guilty. It's not like we've *done* anything, but somehow, being in this spliced field of man-made and natural wonder seems grossly intimate in a way kissing Thom has never been. As if I'm sharing something of my heart with someone I'm not supposed to.

But here we are, anyway, in a trap of my own making.

If future-me could look back in time and figure out the exact moment I screwed up, the top one would probably be when I let him come with me to buy blueberries, and this right here would be second.

An hour later, I drop Daniel off at the bakery. "You want to come in for a coffee?" he asks, hand pausing on the car door.

I hesitate.

"It's free," he says with a grin.

I think I should leave it for the day. My heart is feeling shaky, and I need some time to think. Some time with Thom. I'll feel better if I text him. Maybe. But I'm already pulling over into a parking spot. "Okay," I say. "I could use some coffee." And then it's too late to walk the words back.

We go in from the back. I am super careful to keep a respectful distance, as though if I'm standing far enough away from him, it'll make me feel less guilty for making eyes at him in a cornfield. I mean, we didn't *do anything*. So why do I feel like I got caught with my hand in a cookie jar?

Bakersfield is in the kitchen, which catches me off guard because there isn't anything new to make today, no reason for him to be back here. "Oh."

He swivels to look at us. "You two," he says, mirroring my surprise. "What were you up to?"

"She was just showing me around town," Daniel replies. "Seeing some of the sights."

"The sights?" Bakersfield says incredulously. "You?"

Daniel looks like he's about to bite out something insulting. I put a hand on his arm and shoot him an insistent stare. "Come on," I whisper. "Remember what I said?"

He lowers his chin and sighs. "Yeah, it was nice. What have you been doing all afternoon?"

"Trying to get ahold of the accountant that you put me in touch with. He's asking for a bunch more documentation that I can't make heads or tails of."

"Oh, I can do that," Daniel says. "Just leave it to me. You don't have to figure it out yourself."

"Well, I had nothing else to do anyway." He glances around wistfully. "Having two extra people around leaves me with more free time than I'm used to."

"Maybe you can pick up a hobby," Daniel suggests.

"Feel a bit old for that. But you know, I used to like fishing, back when I had more time."

This is good! I don't want to make any sudden movements in case I disturb a fragile détente.

"That seems like it could be okay," Daniel says. "Where would you go?"

"There are some lakes nearby that are well stocked. But ah," Bakersfield says, "it was a long time ago."

"Is that something you used to do with Dad?" Daniel asks softly.

Bakersfield pauses for a long time, his face unreadable. I wonder if Daniel has touched a nerve he shouldn't. "When he was younger," Bakersfield says eventually. "It's hard to remember, but everything was easier when he was younger. He used to like it." His mouth scrunches up, and I can't tell if he's about to grumble or cry. "I don't know much of what he likes now." His hand clenches and releases on the counter.

I don't dare look at him—the moment feels too tender. I wait to see if Daniel will go to him, but maybe he feels the same, because he stays where he is.

Bakersfield coughs. "Don't leave the kitchen a mess. I'm going to the grocery store to get stuff for dinner." We watch him turn and leave.

"You should go with him," I say gently to Daniel.

He shakes his head. "I just remind him of things he doesn't want to think about."

"I don't—"

"Thank you for taking me out today. Really," he says. "I'm going to the office. You can just let yourself out after you've had a coffee, yeah?"

And then I'm by myself.

I can't avoid Thom for the rest of time. He texts me every day, pushing to see me again, so eventually I relent.

His parents are going to a dinner party, so when they leave at three in the afternoon, they tell him in advance that they'll be gone until ten o'clock. He invites me over for dinner and Netflix while they're out.

Don't blow it, I tell myself a million times before I go over. *Don't blurt it out without a plan.*

I go back and forth about whether I'm going to say anything, all the way up until I'm at the front door. I've almost convinced myself that I will drum up the courage to ask him about the video, but when he opens the door and grins at me, I'm back to square one. All I see is my boyfriend, who I've spent my entire life trying to get to like me, standing in front of me like a dream come true.

Dinner turns out to be spaghetti out of a box and jarred tomato sauce, but he did add some fresh basil from the garden, which was honestly pretty impressive from a teenage boy. Certainly, I've never had one cook for me before.

"Do your parents know that I'm here?" I ask as we eat in his cavernous dining room. I insisted on putting plastic down on over the tablecloth, even though Thom said his parents wouldn't care. But the idea of splattering red sauce on a clearly expensive lace tablecloth was too much for my nerves. I didn't want them to hate me before even meeting me.

"Sure. My parents are cool about this kind of thing. That's why they tell me when they're going to be out. They trust me."

"That must be nice," I say.

"Your mom doesn't trust you?"

I crack a laugh. "She's strict. I don't think she's that supportive of dating in high school."

"Bummer. My parents are sorry they're missing you tonight. They want to meet you."

Hold on. "Your parents want to meet me?"

"Yeah, of course. They've heard about you, and they want to know what you're like. When you're ready. My parents are pretty cool. They're not scary." He glances over sidelong, twirling his fork on his plate. "Guessing your mom doesn't want to invite me over."

Umm, well.

When I don't respond, he asks, "Have you told your mom about me?"

"Not exactly."

"It's cool. You don't have to. I mean, we're casual, right?"

"Right," I say immediately without thinking. And then I sit back in my seat. Right? One second he's inviting me to meet his parents, and another, he's confirming that we're casual? What does being casual even mean? I want to ask, but I don't want to come off as clingy or insecure. There's nothing more unappealing to guys than incessantly trying to define someone's level of commitment. Just thinking about it is making me feel progressively less sexy about myself.

At the same time, *I* don't know what I want us to be anymore. Which wasn't a problem until recently. Can you be desperate for both more commitment and less commitment? I can't stop thinking about the video and the jerseys, and I have this intense desire to break into his dressers and rifle through his clothes so I can find his shirt and compare.

Margaret would, if I told her. But I can't tell her. At least not until I know for sure. I can't just subject Thom and his friends to her exceptionally high level of scrutiny. She could be completely wrong. Who's to say? Maybe the jerseys are more common than I think.

All this is swirling in my head as we clean up the dishes and settle into the den to put on some streaming show.

I've come over to Thom's house twice before. His mom's an interior designer, and it shows. The house is, first of all, twice the footprint of my house. Our house is cute, but this house is wild. It has twice as many bathrooms as people. I've never really understood why people are so obsessed with having a million bathrooms, but it does feel pretty luxe to know that everyone in the house could be doing number two at the same time at totally different ends of the house.

Thom has come over to my house exactly once, when I was

super positively sure Mama and Margaret would be out. Even then, I was freaked the entire time that one of them would barge in and catch us.

I try to remember if he seemed guilty when he drove up. Did he have a weird reaction? Did he act like he recognized the place? I've gone over and over it in my head since. Mentally restudied every twitch of his eyebrow and downturn of his lips. There's no detail I've left undisturbed. But none of it tells me anything.

Thom slides his arm around me as if this is our most natural pose. "You seem quiet. Everything okay?"

"Mm," I say, leaning deeper into him, trying to overcome my own uncertainty. I want to enjoy spending time alone with my boyfriend without overthinking it. I want to savor the moment without getting distracted by something that's already over. I want to kiss Thom without wondering in the back of my mind what it would be like if he were Daniel instead.

Especially that last part.

We've put on a movie. It's pretty bad, though we're not really paying attention. Before I know it, we're kissing, and it's with an urgency I haven't experienced before. His mouth is crushing mine. He's the leader, I'm just following. At first, we're sitting up, but he craftily maneuvers me down until he's pressing me into the couch. I can feel his hips grinding against mine, and there it is. It should be exciting, but I am mildly terrified.

Suddenly, the possibility of—well, not being a virgin—is more imminent than it has ever been in my entire life. I am not prepared. Of course, I've thought about what *it* would be like when the time came. And sure, I've thought about it with Thom. But it's different when you're thinking about it happening, versus when you've got a boy on top of you and it could actually happen.

Thom's hands have started moving from my face farther down my body, below the waist. I shift uncomfortably, shocks going up my spine. I can barely believe myself right now, but I don't want this. Everything feels wrong. This moment. The logistics of having sex. My mental lack of readiness. I should want to do this, but it scares me more than I have ever been scared before in my life. Nobody in all my sex ed classes, awkwardly fumbling about the consequences of sex-having, has ever mentioned how intimate it is, how nerve-racking. I have never seen a penis before in real life. What if it hurts? What if I bleed everywhere?

I break the kiss, and he moans. His hands are fumbling at the button of my jeans. "Annalie," he whispers.

"Hey," I say. I grab his hands. "What if your parents come home early?"

"They won't. I promise."

I struggle to sit up. "Come on," he coaxes. "I have condoms in the drawer." He runs a thumb along my lips. "I want you." He reaches for me again.

"I'm not—I'm not ready, okay?"

"What's wrong?"

I can't tell him I'm a virgin. I feel embarrassed. My mouth has inexplicably lost all its words. I couldn't describe it even if I wanted to. "Nothing. Just, not today," I say lamely.

He flops back and sighs. All the tension in the room has

deflated. I know you should never feel guilty about not wanting to have sex, for any reason, but I feel guilty anyway. So guilty that I'm about to suggest we go for it and I'll just power through it, but he turns to me and gives me a lazy smile.

"Soon, I hope? You drive me crazy."

"Soon," I tell him, though I don't know what that means. Next week? In a month? In an hour? Will I be ready then? When will I be ready?

What if I have sex with him and then I find out that he was involved in spray-painting our house?

Why? *Why?* Thom has never given me any indication that he has racist tendencies or thoughts.

The dizziness of the questions swirling all around force me to close my eyes and reorient myself. I can't go forward without finding out the truth. It makes me sick to think about being an unknowing victim in this. But if I ask, it will change everything. There will be no going back to before. The accusation, no matter how I word it, will blow a hole in our relationship. The only uncertainty is the size of the blast radius.

Thom startles me by touching my shoulder. "Hey, you know I really like you, right? I'm not just trying to get in your pants."

And then I feel guilty all over again. I should be able to give him the benefit of the doubt. If I were a good girlfriend, I wouldn't need to ask him. I'd just trust that he is a good person.

"I *like* spending time with you. You are beautiful *and* adorable. It feels so *easy* with you, especially compared to my ex." I blush. He continues. "Hey, actually, my parents are going out of town for a whole week after the Fourth of July." He looks at me a little hopefully. When I don't respond right away, he goes on. "Maybe you could stay over?"

The implication is clear. This is when *soon* is. Soon is two weeks.

In a flash, it's clear to me that I can't not know. "Thom, I have to ask you something."

"Okay?" He looks confused.

"And when I ask you, I don't want you to get mad. I'm not accusing you. I just need to know."

He raises his eyebrows, but he is silent. And so is the room. The episode has ended and it's waiting for us to click forward. We are on a knife edge.

"Do you remember when that thing happened at my house? When somebody spray-painted 'Chink' onto the garage?"

His entire body is still. He nods barely, imperceptibly.

"My sister got video from the neighbors." I try not to tremble. "The jerseys," I whisper. "They look like yours." The next question takes an eternity to get out. Or maybe it only takes a second. I don't know. Later, it will be impossible to remember exactly how I managed to say it, the moment is blacked out in my mind. "Did you do it?"

I hope against hope, with everything I have, that he will turn to me and laugh. He'll brush it off, kiss me, and call me silly. He'll tell me that he's sorry it happened, and that he'd punch any person who would do such a thing.

Or he'll get angry and order to me to leave. Insist he would never in a million years do such a thing and be so insulted that I asked.

Either of those responses would've been better.

Instead, he doesn't look at me. I watch him swallow once, twice. I think, *Maybe the universe will end before he responds and spare us.* When he looks up at me, his eyes are all splintered in different colors from the lamplight. "It wasn't me," he says, his voice hollow. For the first time in the whole time I've known him, Thom Froggett looks extremely unsure of himself.

I would let out a sigh of relief, but the tone isn't right. It's not done. He hasn't told me everything yet.

"It was Mike," he bursts out in a quiet rush. "Mike and Brayden."

I am shocked. Before I can even react in any way, Thom grabs my hands. "Don't tell anyone. Please," he begs.

Never could I have imagined this. I stare at him wordlessly. My body doesn't know how to feel. It pulses hot and cold. My hands, still locked in a desperate grasp with his, begin sweating. "Annalie," he says urgently. "Please."

I should leave. I should call Margaret. Oh god, I should do anything but continue to sit here like a coward. All I manage to do is open my mouth and say timidly, "But why?"

"Because it was a onetime thing, and we're all applying for college next year, and it would really ruin their lives," he says hurriedly. "Nobody got hurt. It was a dick thing, we can all agree, and they shouldn't have done it. But think about how it would seriously mess things up, okay? They could get prosecuted. They could lose scholarships. And Mike's dad would legit kill him." He's talking so fast that it's somewhat disjointed, like he can't get it out fast enough.

He's answering a *why* I wasn't asking. The question isn't why I should cover for them. I know all those reasons. The question is why they would do it in the first place. Did they know I lived there? They must—our high school is not that big. But still, I barely even knew them. I've had maybe two conversations with them in my whole life. We were two classes below my sister, so they did know *of* her, but I doubt they ever talked to her either.

Why would they use that word? I remember what I said to Margaret only a few days ago, that the perpetrators probably never thought about it again after they did it. Thom is repeating the same words I said to her then: *nobody got hurt, nobody got hurt, nobody got hurt*. It was a flippant comment then, and now I feel stupid.

I feel so, so stupid.

Thom is looking at me, searching my face. I can't tell what my expression is right now. Betrayal? Rage? Numbness? Confusion? I want to be able to tell him it's no big deal. Be the cool girl I keep trying to be.

"Why would they do that?" I say finally.

He sighs. "They're idiots. It was a prank. Who knows? They were probably kind of drunk because we had the day off from soccer practice." He shrugs helplessly.

I want a better answer than that. I need a better answer than that. But I think this is the only answer that I will ever get.

"It was dumb. It *is* dumb. They know it was wrong, and they won't ever do it again. Just, don't ruin their lives for something that's already over. I'm sorry, Annalie. You know we're not like that, right? We're not racist. They're not racist. I would never be friends with racists."

He's earnest, absolutely insistent and unwavering in his conviction. He squeezes my hands again. "How could I date you if I was racist? I like you. Please. I'm only telling you because I trust you. You're my girlfriend, and I want us to be together."

I couldn't live with myself if I didn't know the truth. Now I know the truth. I wish I didn't. How can I face my sister? Or my mother? If they ever found out I kept this to myself, they would never speak to me again. *If* they ever found out.

I want to be brave. But I imagine everyone's reaction at school in the fall if I ratted like a baby, and the police really went after Mike and Brayden. Their futures, marred. That would be my burden, wouldn't it? How could I live with that?

People make mistakes.

Don't they?

Is this really a hate crime? Or is it just a prank that a couple of teenagers pulled on a bad day? I know what Margaret would think. What do I think?

I don't know.

"Please," Thom says.

"Okay," I finally tell him.

Fourteen

MARGARET

"We're going to see fireworks together. For July Fourth," Mama says to Annalie and me abruptly one night.

"Why?" I ask.

"Because," Mama says, shooting a sharp glance at me. "You've been home this summer. All you two do is fight or not talk to each other. Not like a family here. Not like sisters."

I resist the urge to roll my eyes. Mama's always had such a strong idea of what sisterhood should look like and chastised us for not matching it.

"We have not much time this summer," she continues. "Let's put aside our disagreements for the holiday, okay?"

"Only if she wants to spend *that* much time with me," I say sarcastically.

I expect Annalie to protest, tell Mama she already has plans lined up, but she seems distracted. "Sure, sounds good," she says. I know that something has to be wrong, because she's never said "sounds good" to hanging out with me.

Mama looks satisfied, even though Annalie excuses herself

immediately and goes up to her room. "Something's up with her," I say.

"You are da jie, older sister," Mama says. "Can you be nicer to her? You've made this summer very hard."

I bristle. I've heard this speech a million times from my mother. The responsibility of being older. The elder child is supposed to have restraint, patience, grace. All the traits I never had. And even now, still placing the blame for any tension on me, not Annalie.

"Why is everything my fault?" I burst out.

"I never said that," Mama says. "One day when I am gone, your sister will be your only family. Don't forget that. You must choose your family."

As if I could ever forget.

The next day at work, Rajiv is blooming. I can barely look at him, so I pretend to be extremely busy with a new batch of assignments.

I keep thinking about the last time we saw each other. In the harsh light of the next day, the hazy romance feels far away. I already feel like I'm ruining everything at home. Why, exactly, did I decide to reintroduce another source of ruin for myself?

That's what this is, after all. A devastating ruin. An exquisite mistake. I can see the heartbreak coming in slow motion.

Rajiv interrupts my thoughts to ask if I want to come over to his house for a barbecue for the Fourth of July. "Sorry for the late notice."

"With your family?" I ask, startled.

He looks at me shyly. "Yeah."

"Do they know you're inviting me?"

"Well, I was going to gauge your reaction first, and then tell them. No need to get them all hyped up for your appearance before I know." He pauses. "Margaret. It's okay this time. Really. You should come."

I wish I could just dive in. I wish I could move forward without fearing the past catching up to us.

"Bummer," I say, staring stiffly at my computer screen. "Mama wants us to do Fourth of July together. Sorry." It's true, but somehow, it feels like a lie to protect myself anyway.

"Oh, I see." He sounds crestfallen.

"I really wish I could."

"It's okay. Don't worry about it." He doesn't push me, but he's quieter than normal for the rest of the morning.

I think of Mama's comment about him being far away during the year, and the last thing she said to me on prom night. I dare to glance sidelong at Rajiv, typing away. I feel myself shrinking into nothing.

Mama, Annalie, and I bring lawn chairs and a basket of pork baos for snacking to the park where you can watch fireworks. We settle at the crest of a hill, looking down on a smoothly descending grassy slope of people milling around who are trying to secure their spots before the fireworks start in half an hour. The sky is dusky. The air is warm and smoky with the lingering smell of grilling.

We sit in our chairs and silently watch the park fill with other families laughing, children waving around glow sticks. Mama munches on her bao. "Remember we did this when you were young?" she says to us wistfully.

Annalie is scrolling aimlessly on her phone. She looks over to Mama and not me, nodding. I tamp down the urge to say something snarky—it's been years since we saw fireworks together. I stare at my lap instead.

It's amazing how the loneliest I have ever felt is sitting with my own family.

I don't even know why Mama bothered to do this. When I was younger, I used to wonder if she could get her human need for love fulfilled simply by being physically near someone, instead of sharing her feelings out loud, since we never did that. I thought if I just pushed myself hard enough, I could do it too— grasp for love in silence.

Families surround us. It's hard for me not to imagine, fleetingly, what it would be like if my father had stuck around, and we were here, the four of us. But some things are hard to envision. If my father were here, everything would be different. We'd be completely different people. Maybe we wouldn't even be living here. Would we be happier and closer? Or is that just a fantasy too?

I close my eyes and listen to the sounds around me. The hum of human activity, the chirps of crickets on the ground, and the whining buzz of cicadas in the looming tops of trees.

"Hey," Annalie says to my left. Her voice surprises me and jolts me out of my zen. I look over and she's scooted her chair closer to me, where we had previously been sitting with a foot and a half between us as if we were allergic to breaking one another's personal bubbles.

"What's up?"

"How are things going with Rajiv?"

"What?" My tone must come out sharp with shock. For a second, my brain doesn't catch up with the situation, and I think she somehow knows that we hooked up.

"At work? Aren't you guys working together?" Her eyebrows knit together. She sits back in her chair. "Okay, sorry. I thought we could have, like, a one-day truce over everything rather than sit here and not talk to each other for an entire hour."

"No, I'm sorry. I thought—never mind." I look over at Mama, who isn't paying attention at all.

"What?" Understanding dawns on her face. "Are you guys dating again or something?"

"Shhhh!"

She grins. "Oh my god, a backslide."

"I don't want to talk about this."

"Okay, fine," she says, putting up her hands. "We don't have to talk about it." She pats my arm. "I always liked him, you know." She pauses. "I'm sorry I spilled the beans the first time to Mama. Is that why you hate me?" She says it with a light sarcasm, but with Annalie, you can always tell when she is joking to cover up her real feelings.

"I don't hate you," I say firmly. "It wasn't anybody's fault. She was bound to find out eventually. But yeah, maybe don't talk so loud right now. I don't know what we're doing." I do hate how I can't keep my face from breaking out into a smile anyway.

"You're glowing," she teases.

"You seem particularly chipper too. Any possibility you'll do something that will finally take the heat off me for once? You owe me."

"Hah. Maybe." She shrugs, her expression flattening out again. "You know I don't always listen to exactly what Mama says. I just don't antagonize her the way you do. But sure, I guess I can tell you that I have a boyfriend. Or something."

"Oh? Or something?" I'm intrigued.

"We're dating. I don't know how exactly I feel about it yet. He's on the soccer team."

"White?"

"Yeah," she says, her gaze sliding away as if she's guilty. She needn't be. I wouldn't want her to have the same fights with Mama I did anyway.

"Popular?"

She laughs. "Yeah, very popular."

"So you're going to be homecoming queen this year?"

"I know you're making fun of me, but you don't have to do that, because I definitely won't be," she says darkly. My sister's profile against the glow of the evening sky is exquisite. She's like the subject of all those crooning boy-band pop songs, where the subject of the song is pretty but coyly acts like she isn't.

"We'll see," I say, feeling a slice of annoyance. Even though that popularity isn't what I wanted in high school, it still hurts a little knowing that everyone thinks Annalie is more charming than me. And there's nothing more familiar to me than the resentment that comes with competing against your younger sister.

"Why do you always act like everything I care about is stupid?"

"What?"

She crosses her arms. "I can tell that you think homecoming court is shallow. And sure, it probably is. But it's not like I'm running a campaign for it, and it's not horrible to want to be liked by your classmates. You talk about stuff as if you're patronizing me. I'm not a baby."

I'm genuinely startled. "I don't think everything you care about is stupid."

She rolls her eyes. "Okay, sure."

"I don't! Why would you think that?"

"Oh, I don't know. You never trust me to do anything. You feel like you have to take over everything because I won't do it good enough. You think I'm not 'serious' like you because my grades aren't as good and I don't want to be a lawyer. So you disregard my opinions because they're not valuable to you." She ticks the reasons off on her fingers.

"I don't think those things." I'm abashed.

"I can hear it in your voice," she scoffs.

"Come on," I say defensively. "You're being unfair. Every time we ever fought about anything, Mama took your side because you were younger. She has always liked you better, and you're the golden child. She's always mad at me."

"So you're taking it out on me?" she retorts.

She catches me at the truth, and it leaves me speechless for a second, mouth open without a response. I sigh. "Why are we fighting about this right now?"

"I don't know. I don't remember ever not fighting with you. Is it any wonder why I don't also want to fight with Mama?"

Annalie may not be a star debater, but somehow she is able to get under my skin in a way nobody else can.

"Besides," she continues, "you act like I'm some robot that just does whatever Mama wants all the time. I'm my own person. I just know how to pick my battles. You pick every battle."

"I literally cannot think of a time you've ever not done what Mama wanted. You two always gang up on me. If Mama told you that you couldn't wear purple for the rest of next year, you'd do it." I'm being petty and cruel, but I can't stop myself.

"Well, I think I'm going to become a pastry chef one day. Mama isn't going to like that," she says shortly.

Whatever I was going to say goes back into my throat. "What? A pastry chef?"

"I know, you think it's not ambitious or whatever and a one-way ticket to being poor." She waves her hand, her face reddening.

"No! I just . . . I didn't know that."

"You've never asked," she says brutally. She turns away.

I think back to nights when I was still in high school and Annalie was home with nothing to do. She was usually in the kitchen, banging around, filling the house with the smell of baking. I guess, if I'm to be honest, I never thought about what Annalie wanted to be when she grew up. In my mind, she was so much younger than me, years away from growing up and having to do things like choose a career.

"You could just tell me," I say. It feels small and pitiful, an offering that has come too late.

"I'm afraid to tell you things."

"I'm your sister. I can keep secrets. You can tell me everything."

Her mouth twists with a knowing smirk I don't entirely understand. "Not everything."

I stare at Annalie, feeling suddenly that she seems like a complete stranger to me. It's only been a year since I've left home, and yet.

There's a crackle behind the trees and then a loud boom. The first firework launched into the night sky. Mama sits up, alert. "Look, look," she says, as if we could miss it, the sparks trailing down above us.

The fireworks start at a slower pace, sporadic little pops and bursts, before building to a steady stream of color. Kids are shouting and pointing. I remember how, when we were little, Annalie was so afraid of the sound. Mama used to try and calm her down, but Annalie would always cling to me when the show got going.

Now, her upturned face is bathed a blue and red glow from the changing lights overhead. She glances over and meets my eyes. For a moment, we both smile.

The car ride home is quiet, but nice. In some ways, it feels like we've finally experienced something great together, even though it's just a silly fireworks show.

We walk through the front door. I flip the light. Nothing happens. I flip it back and forth.

"Ugh, power outage, it looks like."

Annalie peeks out the blinds in the front window. "The neighborhood is dark," she confirms.

It's pitch black inside. "Do we have any candles or flashlights somewhere?" I've been gone long enough that I don't remember where these miscellaneous things are stored. Postage stamps. Spare batteries.

Mama slips off her shoes, and they clatter to the ground, missing the rug. "I think there are some in the sewing room. One of the drawers." She starts walking and stubs her toe against the corner of the stair. "Ah!"

"Stop," I tell her, putting out my arm. "Just wait here. I'll look."

In the hallway, I turn on my phone light to beam a small lit circle to guide my path. The house creaks as I creep slowly across the floor over to the basement. I hold the railing as I go down each step gingerly. The basement is almost inky black, except for the slim window edging the ceiling, letting in a thin rectangle of moonlight on the floor.

I step gingerly across the carpet and into the corner room where Mama does her sewing for her business. There's a big, broad wooden desk with a sewing machine tucked neatly in the corner. It gleams dimly white. Mama has an entire cabinet on the other side of the wall with three rows of drawers. She keeps her threads and fabrics and other miscellaneous sewing equipment in this cabinet.

Annalie and I never go into this room. We knew, even as kids, that this was Mama's private working room. Usually, when she's inside, she shuts the door. You'd be able to hear the even buzz of the sewing machine at work.

I open a bottom drawer and shine my phone inside. It's full of spools of thread. Another one has different bolts of cotton fabric. Another drawer has a tin box, and when I shake it, I hear the clatter of buttons. I work my way up. Finally, I get to a drawer with squat white tea lights and matches. One flashlight rolls around.

I try the drawer above it to see if there are more flashlights or candles in there. One of the drawers is full of paper. No, not paper. Photos. I peer inside. The illuminated pictures are faded and the corners worn. I take out the stack. I stare without comprehension. The one on the top is Mama holding a baby, with a tall redheaded man standing next to her, beaming at the camera. Mama is wearing an old-fashioned white button-down blouse and a long denim skirt. I flip the photo over. It's dated the year I was born. The baby is me. The man, of course, is my father.

Trembling, I flip through the pile.

There are early pictures of my mother and father, before they had either of us. Pictures from right after Annalie was born. Pictures of me, Annalie, and my father at the beach, grinning, laughing. I run my finger over the images lightly, afraid the paper will crumble in my hands. I run my hands across the bottom of the drawer again, but it's empty except for the dust.

Annalie calls from the top of the stairs. "The power is back! We don't need the candles anymore!"

I sit there for a moment, unable to stand up, the photos in my stiffening hands. Should I put them back? I keep staring at my father. He looks different than I remember, but I don't remember much.

Slowly, I shut the drawer, without returning the pictures. My heart lurches.

A memory in broad brushstrokes—

I am in a park with Mama, Dad, and baby Annalie. It's a warm summer day, but Mama's biggest fear for her children is them catching a chill, so Annalie is wrapped up so tight that all you can see is her little circle of a face, a tuft of pale hair peeking out the top. She had such pale hair as a baby, sweet blue eyes; she looked like a little Caucasian child. People always thought Mama was the nanny. She sits on a blanket with Annalie, who is being fussy.

I am barely three, and I am tired of sitting with Mama and the baby, so Dad takes me to the edge of the pond. Everything is fuzzy, painted with swaths of sensations, sounds, and colors. But oh, the colors. The mottled blue of the pond, inverse of the cerulean sky, the splatters of red and purple mums, white and yellow wild daisies, and the green, endless verdant, hunter, kelly, emerald green, spilling past the canvas of my field of vision.

The surface of the pond is dotted with lily pads and pink lily flowers. "Lily," Dad says, pointing out over the water. "That kind of flower is called a lily."

I see round, well-fed ducks waddling on the bank at the far edge of the pond. "Ducks!" I shout, and I run toward them, running on my sturdy, short toddler legs. I am at the age of security, where I cannot imagine being more than ten feet away from someone who loves me and is watching me. I run run run run—

I hear my father's laughter receding behind me.

Before I can get there, the ducks start squawking and flapping their wings. They scatter. Feathers fly. The bank is slippery with mud. My little foot slides into the goop, and I fall.

In the split second before I hit the water, I glance backward in a panic. I see a flash of Dad's red hair glinting in the sun, but he isn't facing me, and he hasn't followed me. He is walking the other way, toward Mama and Annalie. He is not looking at me.

I hit the pond water, inhaling liquid. Too startled to make a sound.

The important part is that I cannot see his face. And no matter how hard I try, I cannot conjure it from my imperfect memory, because he is turned away.

In my mind, I am screaming, *Why didn't you follow me, Dad? Why didn't you see?*

But the three-year-old me, locked in a frozen past, just keeps falling silently every time.

I head upstairs. The yellow kitchen light shines bright in my eyes, and I blink. Mama is sitting at the table, clutching a cup of tea. Annalie is inspecting the snack cabinet.

I lay the pictures gently on the table in front of Mama. I don't say anything.

"What's this?" she asks.

"Dad," I say.

Annalie drops the bag of chips she's holding. It hits the ground with a crackle. "What?"

"Pictures of Dad." I'm still staring at Mama, who isn't responding. She tucks a strand of hair behind her ear. She pinches her mouth. I'm staring so hard that I wouldn't be surprised if my eyes turned into lasers and burned her forehead.

Annalie steps over to the table tentatively and starts flipping through the photos. Mama doesn't stop her, but she also doesn't move.

"Why didn't you show these to us?" I demand. "I thought you had gotten rid of all the pictures. You kept them, and never told us?"

"He's not in our life," she says simply. "He is gone."

"He is part of us!" I yell, enraged. "You can't just make these decisions for us. Do you know where he is? What else are you not telling us?"

Mama stands up. "He's not coming back," she says. "No use in screaming and shouting." She walks out of the room without another word.

Annalie is silent. She puts the pictures down and shakes her head.

"And you?" I say.

She shoots a look at me. "You're not angry at me." She leaves too. The pictures are still on the table.

I think about how nobody in this family wants to talk about anything. I think about how my decisions are always colored by Mama's opinions, but Mama's decisions can never be colored by mine. I am itchy with anger.

My dark circles must be overwhelming my face on Monday at work. My concealer feels greasy on my face. I sip my coffee, feeling slightly queasy from my lack of sleep the night before. I wish I didn't have to be here.

Rajiv comes in thirty minutes late, which is unusual for him. He looks tired too. "Good morning," he says.

"Hi. You look terrible," I say lightly.

"Immediately charming on the morning after a holiday weekend." He says it with a sharper bite than he normally would.

He sits down at his computer, aggressively flipping through the planner on his desk. "Barbecue at my house was nice."

I am annoyed, and I can't help it. My nerves are strung tight. I wanted to yell the night of the Fourth, but instead, I had to swallow my words and go upstairs with the pictures, which I stuffed into the back of my closet so Mama couldn't reclaim them. I tossed and turned in my bed, seeing the images of my father flashing before my eyelids.

I only asked Mama whether she knew where he was to irritate her. I knew she didn't. I knew he wasn't coming back, and that a man who really wanted to be with his family would've found some way back to us. My father deliberately left us, and Mama was trying to protect us. But he wasn't around to be angry at, so she was the next best thing.

And now the next best thing is Rajiv.

He's sitting next to me, and I can tell he's in a bad mood. Rajiv is rarely in a bad mood, but when he is, he expresses it via stony silence. He hates being confronted, likes to sulk. I'm the opposite. I would shout and demand that we resolve whatever I was mad at immediately. The most explosive fights we ever had were when I forced him out of his cold-shouldering when he didn't want it. I know how to push all those buttons.

"Why did you invite me to your house?" I burst out. "Is this some kind of weird way to get back at me for prom night?"

He looks shocked and then erases it with a frown. "Well, a normal person would think it's a nice thing, an invitation to a family barbecue. Honestly, I think even allowing you to come over is more than generous from my mom, all things considered."

I have that queasy, sticky satisfaction of getting a rise out of somebody to serve as a foil to my own frustration. "What exactly do you think we're doing right now?" I demand. "The two of us, I mean."

"I don't know. But I'm sure you're about to tell me."

I wish I could tell him about my father's pictures. I wish I could say that I'm scared of us making the same mistakes again. I'm afraid of feeling our family's disapproval, and deciding that I'm still not brave enough to go against them. I don't think I can handle it, the feeling of my heart breaking a second time. I don't say any of those things, because if there's anything that's the same between then and now, it's that I still don't know how to say the things I want to say.

Should I have fought harder? Believed that if we just stayed together, things would change for Mama? Are we older? Wiser? My mind is spinning in this déjà vu.

"This is all happening really fast. I didn't expect this. I always do irrational things when I'm around you," I say finally, turning away.

"Is being with me irrational for you?" His voice is hard. "*You* were the one who told me you never got over me. *You* came over to my house. *You* came back into my bed. You're going to sit here and act like I lured you back into my clutches as part of some master plan. I got this job before you, okay? You just showed up back in my life and you never even—" He stops and exhales, shaking his head. "Forget it. Just forget it."

"What?"

"Nothing."

"Say it."

"You just have to make everything about you all the time."

That strikes me hard, like a slap, because it sounds like something Annalie would say when she's trying to hurt me. I sit up straighter. "You're being mean for no reason."

"Oh yeah? Did you remember my scholarship deadline?"

"What?"

"Professor Schierholtz? You were going to email her? My deadline is today."

It feels like cold water poured down my spine. I did forget. With all that was on my mind with the video of the vandalism, and then finding my father's pictures, I lost track of everything else. "I'm sorry. But you didn't remind me," I say weakly.

"Somehow everything that I ask you to do for me requires a reminder, but when did you ever have to remind me to do something for you? You never need reminders to do anything else on your to-do list." He glares at me. "I was going to remind you last week when I asked about the barbecue, but then after you said no, I didn't really want to have you do me any favors. Don't worry about it. I figured out something else. I wouldn't want to owe you anything anyway."

The last part stings the most. "I'm so sorry," I say. "I really am. I forgot. I didn't mean to."

He scoffs.

"It was just a barbecue," I say gently. I'm suddenly scrabbling down the sides of a hole that I dug for myself, and I'm scared that I won't be able to climb back out.

He looks so furious, scowling at me. "I meant to tell you. I was going to tell you before you went to the barbecue. I finally felt like it was time, because there was never any good time to say it before I knew what exactly we were. I thought I knew, but I guess I was wrong."

"What are you talking about?"

He takes a deep breath. "My mom had a brain tumor, and she had to get surgery to take it out a couple of months ago. That's what I've been doing this summer, helping take care of her post-op. She's okay now, but it was a bad weekend because she was really dizzy and sick." His words drop like heavy stones into my lap.

I'm speechless. Everything is upside down. "Oh my god."

"Yeah, we found out in April. It all happened fast. Like I said, she's okay now. Or at least, she's cancer-free, but she's just dealing with the side effects from the surgery."

I don't have the right words. I can't help it, but I reach out to him and give him a hug. He holds me tight for a second the way he used to, but he lets go too soon.

"So you can rest assured," he says, "I didn't go into this summer with some plan to win you back."

"Rajiv—"

He waves me off.

I try again. "Why didn't you tell me?"

"I don't know, Margaret." He sounds resigned. With him, the anger runs fast and hot but disappears just as quickly, leaving nothing but disappointment. "You never tell me everything. Why would I trust you with something like that when you've given me no reason to?"

I close my eyes.

"You asked me, what exactly did I think we're doing. The truth is, I loved you—maybe I even love you. But you're constantly pushing me away, and I'm done trying to pull you closer. You win. Like you always do."

I can't be here. I can't stay without crying, and I can't cry in front of Rajiv. I stand up abruptly and stuff everything into my purse. "I have to go. Tell them I'm taking a personal day."

He nods. "I'm sorry," I hear him say as I run out.

Fifteen

ANNALIE

When Margaret and Rajiv started dating, I understood without needing to be told that it was a secret, not to be shared with Mama. Margaret and I had grown up together under the same roof, with the same unfathomable gap where our father was, and the same solid presence of a mother whose authority could never be questioned. We were as different as anything, but for some things, we knew without words.

I kept that secret, until I didn't, and then everything fell apart. If Margaret and I weren't very close before, the spilling of that secret widened the gulf between us.

To be honest, I've never been the best secret keeper. I was just one of those people who couldn't resist the deliciousness of sharing a secret. The momentary thrill of bringing someone into your circle. Violet always rolled her eyes at my inability to keep my mouth shut about the inconsequential things she'd tell me. "I might as well be shouting it in public," she used to say.

But this secret about Thom—this is something of a different magnitude. I can't stop thinking about it. It echoes in my head before I go to sleep. When I wake up in the morning, it rises to the top of my consciousness, ringing like a bell.

If I tell, he and the boys will know it was me. If I don't tell, how can I live with myself? I hate Thom for burdening me with this unwanted knowledge. I hate him for changing everything between us, polluting our relationship. I can't look at him the same. I can't think of him the same.

When we see each other, he searches my face for a sign. And I feel like I'm not only keeping this secret from the world, but keeping my own emotions a secret from Thom. We don't discuss it. We never speak of it again. But it's at the center of our every interaction. Every time he grabs my hand. Every time he kisses me. The weight of his expectation.

What if I tell someone?

What if I never tell anyone?

The two questions ping-pong back and forth in my head, every day, every night.

Racked with guilt, I begin making excuses not to see him. The last time we were alone at his house, we were getting more intimate, and the idea of having sex with him now seems unimaginable.

He starts texting me more and more about where I am, what I'm doing. I say I have been taking on extra hours at the bakery. The pauses between our text messages are loaded with more meaning than the messages themselves. It doesn't matter if he believes me, only that it forestalls any face-to-face conversation for a little bit longer.

I wonder if we will break up. I don't want to. Do I? Haven't I wanted this since all my life? But then. But then. What do I do with this information?

If we're together, I have an ironclad reason for keeping this to myself. Do I still have that reason, if we become past tense? And I agonize, of course, about what kind of person I would be to release this kind of explosive secret after a breakup. Like blackmail, almost. The secret ties us to each other, a web between us that can't be seen, more substantial than our feelings.

I wonder if everything between us will eventually get whittled away, and the only thing left will be this secret, swallowing our relationship whole until we are this secret and this secret is us.

But for now, I'm not ready, and I can't tell anybody. The hardest part is when I'm with Daniel and Violet, pretending like nothing is wrong.

"A burger, fries, and a mint chocolate chip milkshake," I tell the waitress, before turning to Daniel. "You have to order a milkshake too. They're known for them here."

"Okay, ah, same as her, I suppose. Except instead of mint chocolate chip, I'll have"—Daniel squints at the shiny laminated menu—"Oreo cookie." He turns to me. "I didn't eat dinner today, and I'm starving, so this better be worth it."

"Oh, trust me," Violet says. "It's worth it. We can't let you leave for New York or England or whatever without having eaten here first."

"We'll have an extra order of fries," I add for good measure before our waitress turns back to the kitchen. "They're shoestring fries," I explain. "They'll be gone before you know it."

It's nine p.m., and we're at a Steak 'n Shake for Daniel's inaugural experience at this midwestern diner. Me, Daniel, and Violet, which if you asked me two months ago, I would've said was the most unexpected combination I could think of for my Saturday night.

This is their first time meeting each other. I was afraid it would be weird, but I guess I underestimated how easily Violet could smooth over every social situation. She fills the gaps in conversation. Her family went to Europe last year, including Abaeze (a level of relationship seriousness I couldn't fathom with my own family). She knows exactly how to get a conversation going. And then it turns out they're both into the same HBO drama (which I could never be interested in watching) and reading all the online theories about it, and all of a sudden, they might as well have known each other forever.

Daniel lights up talking to her, his face wide and open, and I smile. He looks happy—the polar opposite of how he looked when I first saw him lurking around the bakery. He meets my eyes. His grin widens.

"I'm so glad that I finally get to meet you," Violet says. "I know my Annalie has been spending a lot of time at that bakery with you."

"Violet," I warn. "You're being a mom right now."

"No, no," Daniel says solemnly. "It's true. It's important that we meet. Annalie talks about you all the time. And I should get to know the friends of my friends."

"Friends?" I ask with a cocked eyebrow.

"That's right. We get to drop the 'casual' label."

"Wow, serious. No longer casual, huh?" I'm teasing him, and it feels dangerous. The innuendo, his willingness to play along.

Violet looks between the two of us. "Whew," she says. "Should I leave, and like, give you guys a minute?"

"Stop," I say. But I feel the radioactive heat glowing on my cheeks. And across the table, Daniel lifts his water glass and drinks like a man who's been rescued from the desert after ten days.

By the time the food comes, we've moved on to other topics, thankfully, and Daniel and I aren't trying to make too much eye contact or too little eye contact. It somehow feels like a tough thing to balance. He takes a bite of his burger, chewing carefully. We watch him grab some fries to accompany it, and then finally a sip of his milkshake. We await his verdict.

"This is very satisfying," he pronounces at last. "I approve of this experience. And of your twenty texts after five p.m. reminding me not to eat."

"And now you can say I did good."

"You did good."

"Sorry," Violet says. "My shift at Target ended late today. But in my defense, diner food honestly tastes better at night. That's when you go to diners, right?"

"Definitely," I say.

"Enjoy it," she says. "Maybe you can get it in New York, but it's just not the same as having it here."

I laugh. "How would you know, Violet? You've never even been to New York!"

"I stand by what I said. Anyway, Daniel can come back here next summer and tell us if I was right or not."

He shrugs noncommittally.

"You're going to come back, right?" she asks. "I mean, your grandpa is here. And you're all made up and stuff."

"Honestly, I don't know," he says. "He surely doesn't seem so eager to have me back. We will see, I suppose."

This makes me sad, even though it shouldn't. After all, a year from now, he'll be a nice memory.

"So we should keep coming to this place, as I don't know if I'll get to experience it much after. But it's not all bad—I could've spent the summer with a worse crowd."

"You really don't think your dad and your grandad will make up after this?"

He shakes his head. "It's hard to say. They're both quite stubborn, and they've kept it up for over twenty years, after all. They might not even remember the genesis of their feud, but it's become so entrenched that it's practically religion now."

"Well that doesn't make any sense," Violet announces. "I mean, I yell at my mother daily. And I mean daily. And my mother calls my grandmother in the Philippines once a week, every Sunday, and half the time they are yelling at each other. And she calls my aunt who lives in Houston every Monday night. But five minutes after we've finished yelling, we've already forgotten. Women in my family, maybe. My dad never yells anyway. Somehow, I can't imagine anyone in my family keeping up a grudge for that long."

Violet's family is huge—the opposite of mine. "I guess I can understand. My parents evidently had a feud so massive that my dad walked out, and he's still gone."

They both stare at me.

"Jeez, way to kill the vibe," Violet says with a chuckle, but she pats my arm. She never talks about it with me, but her family has always known, and we always get extra food from them and invites to dinners around the holidays because of it.

"I didn't know that," Daniel says, stricken.

"Yeah, my dad walked out when I was three." I shrug, trying to seem light about it. I am, honestly. It's hard to feel deprived of something you've never experienced. Whenever it comes up, though, it still feels strange. Like I accidentally pressed against a long-forgotten bruise. "I don't remember him at all, obviously."

He whistles. "And you've never heard from him again?"

"Nope. No idea whether he's alive or dead or has another family." I wonder if Mama knows. My mother's thoughts on this are a mystery to me. She has opinions about everything except my father. When it comes to him, she is a black, silent ocean. Sometimes, I can see her in Margaret. The way Margaret closes down her emotions rather than display weakness. I am the opposite. It's easy to see everything I'm thinking right on my face. It's partly why I've been avoiding Thom. I don't quite know what my face would show around him. I'm afraid to find out.

This is the reason I haven't told Violet either. The other being that Violet would be marching down to the police station no more than five seconds after the words left my mouth.

"My mom's all about moving forward. She never talks about it. And we turned out fine," I say.

"Mostly," Violet jokes.

"If you ever found out your dad was still around and living in Florida or something, wouldn't you want to make contact?" Daniel asks.

I think about it. "Honestly? I don't know."

"Why not?"

I shift in my chair uncomfortably. "I don't know if I'd want to upend my life that way. I'd rather just pretend he didn't exist. At this point, what would it even change?"

"Annalie is a pragmatist," Violet says.

"That's not such a bad thing," Daniel replies.

"She just needs a push sometimes to do what scares her." Violet is looking between me and Daniel, her eyes glittering. I'm sensing that she's about to do or say something that will make me want to die, but that's "for my own good," so I jump quickly into a different topic.

I tell them about the downtown fair that's coming up. It'll involve a bunch of contests, including one for baking. Usually the local downtown restaurants and shops have booths set up, with dishes to sell for the fairgoers.

Bakersfield doesn't usually attend. He doesn't like the crowds and "the drunk people," he says. While it's a family-friendly affair, there is plenty of beer to go around, and a very light touch on carding.

I want to convince Bakersfield to register for a booth and

let me run it. "It's just an idea." I shrug. But I can feel my heart pounding. The idea of putting myself in a contest is both exhilarating and terrifying. I've never baked with my name really attached to anything before.

"You should absolutely do it," Violet says, pounding the table. "I've always thought that you should be a professional baker. For real. Even if you think your mom will kill you."

"She would. Mama only believes in three professions: lawyer, doctor, engineer. I have to survive to graduation at least."

"But you can at least do this baking contest," Daniel says. "How can she be mad at that?"

He and Violet exchange looks. "We're aligned on this," she says.

"Okay, okay, I will," I say, smiling. "Daniel, you have to convince your grandad."

"Done," he says decisively. "But I don't think he'll need any convincing from me. He gets to sell pastries and he doesn't even have to interact with anyone? He'll be so pleased. It'll be the one good suggestion I've had for him all summer."

We move on to talking about Daniel's major, and his planned curriculum, and what it was like to live in Geneva for two years.

"Hold on, hold on," Violet says, pulling a ringing phone out of her purse. "Abaeze is calling on FaceTime. Want to say hi?"

"Definitely," Daniel says.

Abaeze's face swims into view on the screen. "Hello, babe. Oh! A crowd," he says, surprised.

Violet waves her fingers in front of the camera. "Hi. It's late for you!" She turns to us. "It's six hours ahead in Nigeria," she tells us by way of explanation.

I lean into the frame. "Hi, Abaeze! We're at Steak 'n Shake."

"Mm," he says. "I miss that. Please get a peanut butter cup milkshake for me."

"I will," Violet says assertively, and we laugh.

"Are you going to introduce me to the new guy? Where's Thom?"

"That's Daniel," I say too quickly, glossing over the second question. "He's my coworker at the bakery. Bakersfield's grandson."

"Nice to meet you," Daniel says. "I've heard a lot about you."

"Only good things, I hope?"

"What else would I say?" Violet exclaims in mock indignation.

"We wish you were here," I tell him.

"Me too. It'll be the end of the summer before you know it," he says. The line is true, both promising and full of dread.

We chat with Abaeze for a while. I'm so content to be part of the circle, laughing at Abaeze's stories about his grandmother and not feeling exhausted about my mental war. This group feels right, and I wish I could just stay forever and pretend like the world outside, with all its problems, doesn't exist.

After we've been there about an hour, Violet says she needs to leave because she promised her mom she'd be home by ten thirty. For all her strictness, Mama has never cared about curfews, but Violet's parents definitely do. "I'll leave you guys," she says, giving me a super-obvious wink that I pray to god Daniel doesn't notice. "You're giving Daniel a ride home, right?"

"Mm-hmm," I say.

Violet gives us both hugs—she has to stand on her tiptoes to get Daniel on account of her being so short and him so tall—and then she breezes out the door.

And then there were two. Even though I gave Daniel a ride here, and it was totally normal, somehow, nighttime and dinner, plus Violet's not-so-subtle digs, have transformed the situation into one that's distinctly more uncomfortable than it was before. The car ride to his house, really only ten minutes, feels like it could be an unfathomably long one. *Anything* could happen with two people alone in a car at night. I mean, what are we supposed to do when I let him out?

At that very moment, I hear a familiar voice coming through the door, and I freeze.

"I'm starving," one of the boys in a group says.

I should run, hide, or jump out of the bathroom window, but I'm anchored in my chair, facing the entrance. Before I can cover my face or duck, they spot me in a moment.

"Annalie!" Jeremy shouts across the restaurant. Behind him, Thom emerges, his sandy hair looking more disheveled than usual. The expression on Thom's face tightens for a split second. I imagine all the texts deferring our meetups running through his head. And then he strides over.

The exact moment Daniel turns around, a flicker of recognition flashes across Thom's face. Thom looks from Daniel to me, and then from me back to Daniel.

"Hi, friends," he says. "Fancy seeing you here."

I swallow. "Hi, Thom." His eyes flash furiously, but he doesn't show it outside of that, except maybe a thinning of his lips. The three of them crowd around us.

"Daniel, right?" Mike says. "We met you at the bakery. You're the baker's grandson." He sounds bright, relaxed.

"What are you both doing here?" Thom asks.

"Violet just left," I say. I sound guilty, and I hate it. It's very apparent that Thom doesn't believe me.

"Right." Thom keeps looking between us, his expression uncertain. He glances at Mike. For a second, I think that he might be nervous, and then it dawns on me. He thinks I might have told Daniel. He's worried about it. I can't tell whether Mike knows that I know. He's casual, doesn't betray anything. It's clear he's a far better liar than Thom is, though. If Thom hadn't told me anything, I never in a million years would've guessed that Mike was the vandal.

I guess you can never tell what people do when no one's watching.

There is a long pause. Daniel doesn't interject, seemingly unbothered by the fact that we're surrounded.

"It's good to see you," Thom says finally. "Are you around this weekend?"

There's no way I can blow him off in front of everybody. I *don't* have anything this weekend, and in this split second, I can't come up with a convincing enough lie. His eyes are soft and beseeching again, his voice tentative. I can't deny him. "I'm free."

He smiles, relieved. "Okay, good. I'll be seeing you then."

"Yes."

He leans in to kiss me, and I only realize when he's already inches away from my face. It startles me. I flinch ever so slightly. Not enough to prevent his lips from making contact, but enough for him to notice and his expression to catch. As he pulls away, I see everyone watching. I remember how when Thom looked at me on our first date in front of everyone while he was singing, I felt like I was glowing. Now, I just feel small.

The boys start to turn away to find their seats. Mike lags just a couple of seconds behind the others and says, "I'm having a party at my place next week. My parents are out of town. You should come." He glances magnanimously at Daniel. "You too. You're both welcome." He pauses for a second and then gives a cheeky wink. "Don't want to toot my own horn or anything, but it's going to be pretty baller. Maybe the party of the summer, if I do say so myself." He gives a little wave and heads off without waiting for an answer.

I watch him go, knowing that he doesn't need an answer because in Mike's world, nobody would turn down a direct invite to his parties. Sure, they weren't totally exclusive. You could bring along friends and nobody would turn you away at the door. But it's different being a hanger-on who just shows up at one of Mike's parties versus someone who Mike himself personally invited. And I have never been invited before.

Three months ago, hell, even three weeks ago, I would've been ecstatic. Now, I am uneasy.

Daniel and I sit at the table, now radically uncomfortable, as we try to wave down a waitress to get the check. It's taking forever when all I want to do is get out of there. I'm wondering if he's going to ask me about why I'm being so weird, but thankfully he doesn't.

Finally, we get the check, and he figures out how much to tip. Almost home free.

Then I see Thom come back over to our table, and my stomach clenches. His face is tight and scared. I know something has happened.

"Hey," he says. "Can we talk for a second?" His eyes flick over to Daniel. "Alone?"

"Sure. What's going on?" I reply, but I'm already standing up and following him out the front door.

"I'll be right back," I mouth to Daniel. His brows are furrowed with concern, but he stays seated.

We step outside and turn the corner so people can't see us.

"What's up, Thom?" I try not to let my voice sound so strained.

He unlocks his phone and sticks the screen under my face. "This went up on Twitter a couple of hours ago. I just saw it because the tag is trending and people at school are retweeting it. Did you know about this?"

I take his phone. It's Margaret's Twitter handle, and the post is a video clip. Right away, I know what she has done. The bottom falls out for me.

"God, they were so stupid," Thom says, shaking his head.

"The shirts." He looks at me. "You could tell right away."

"Okay, sure I could, because I saw them before and asked about them. They look like generic soccer jerseys," I say desperately. I want to believe what I'm saying too, even as some part of me wonders why *I'm* trying to make *him* feel better about this. "You can't read the back, and you can't see their faces. How would anybody be able to narrow it down to them?"

"This is all over the internet. Someone will be able to tell." His voice rises. "Shit. Goddamn it."

"I didn't know she did this. Swear to god, I had no idea. I know she turned it over to the police, but not that she posted it online." I should've guessed, though. Of course she would.

"We have to get it down," he says.

I'm expecting him to say it. I know what he's implying. That I should try to convince Margaret to take the video down. Fat chance of that, if he knew anything about my sister. But I feel a mountain of disappointment.

I know this is what I wanted in the first place, to keep it quiet, to keep the secret. I swore to him I would. Yet some part of me feels betrayed that Thom isn't even acknowledging that this is my house, me, that his friends called a *Chink*. That it's still all about protecting Mike and Brayden.

Thom must catch a glimpse of my inner conflict, because his face changes immediately to guilt. "I'm sorry. You know I think this is terrible. I'm not implying that it isn't. We talked about this, though, and why we have to keep it quiet." He groans. "I wish you hadn't been dragged into this."

"Well, I got dragged in because Mike and Brayden targeted me," I say curtly.

"It wasn't like that."

"What was it like, then? Why don't you tell me? Because I still don't know. Why do they hate me?"

He grabs my hands. "Annalie. Annalie. They don't hate you. Let's not fight about this, okay? I wish we could go back in time, and I could tell them that they were being assholes before they did it." His eyes are pleading. "Please help us. I don't know what to do."

"I don't know if I can . . . keep doing this."

"Please, Annalie."

I don't want to look at him, but my hands are still in his, so I do. He is scared. Really frightened in a way that I've never seen before. Despite myself, I feel sorry for him. In my mix of emotions, the strongest one that overshadows the others: a need for this to be over, to stop letting it continue to fester.

"Okay," I say. "I mean, you can just start reporting the video. Spam, offensive, whatever. It has a racial slur in it. I'm sure if enough people flag it, it'll get taken down."

He squeezes my fingers. He's waiting for more, like wringing the final drop of juice from a lemon.

"I won't tell Margaret." It feels like yet another piece of myself that I'm giving away. But I've already lied to my sister once. Doing it again doesn't even count as a new lie.

He exhales in apparent relief. "Thank you."

I am tired. I want to go home. And anyway, I don't think I

can keep talking to him, keep promising him more and more.

He lets go. "This will all go back to normal," he promises. "And we can just be the way we were. You and me again." His words are delusional. I know, deep down, that nothing can make us normal again, but for this moment at least, I choose to believe him, because if I don't, then I'm not sure how we can go on.

Sixteen

MARGARET

The door slams so hard downstairs I can hear it from my room. Mama is out at a nighttime church potluck and Bible study. She wouldn't shut the door like that.

"Margaret!" my sister yells from the parlor. I hear her pounding up the stairs like she used to do when she was eight and she was mad that I had ditched her at home to play in the neighborhood with my friends.

She pushes my door open, filling the doorway with her rage.

"Hi," I say. I am calm and empty. I have no more tears from earlier today after I left work. I exhausted them in the car. I came home, heavy with the kind of hopelessness that makes you do reckless things.

I knew what I had to do. I posted the video and watched the retweets and likes mount.

I didn't feel a thing.

"Why did you do that?" Her face is red and teary.

"I found the video. I can do whatever I want with it."

"Really? That's all you have to say for yourself."

"Yeah, it is."

"What is your problem?" she demands. "Why do you have to be this way?"

"I don't know what you're talking about." I started out cool, but I can feel my blood heating up as Annalie screams at me. "I'm confused as to what your problem is with this entire thing."

"We've had this conversation a million times."

"I agree. And I'm tired of your inability to have a single ounce of backbone about anything. I'm sorry if this ruins your chance at being homecoming queen."

She recoils as if I've stung her. "You're a real bitch sometimes."

I turn away from her. "Surprised that it's only just occurred to you now."

She disappears down the hallway into her room and shuts the door. Her light stays on deep into the night, but she doesn't come back out.

When I go to work the next morning, I'm dreading seeing Rajiv. I'm not sure how to get through the rest of the summer.

But he isn't there when I show up. I sit down with my coffee, feeling the silence of our office without him in it. I tell myself I can be cordial for a few weeks. We can do our work without being friends. People do it all the time.

Still, the idea of sitting next to Rajiv and pretending like we are strangers makes me unspeakably sad.

I finish my entire cup of coffee and make another. I open up my monitor and check my emails. There's an email from the Twitter abuse team. I click on it. It says:

Hello,

We have received a complaint regarding your account for the following content:
Tweet ID—234892388493

Your tweet contained a video that was reported for containing hateful imagery, which is a violation of Twitter rules. We have investigated and verified the complaint and accordingly, we have removed the video.

Sincerely,
Twitter

I log in to my Twitter account immediately. I have twenty-three DMs. The tweet with the video has a message showing that it has been removed for violating Twitter's policies. But even without any content to show, the tweet has been retweeted over a hundred thousand times. I click on some of the replies. Some of them are people I knew from high school, but others are from people I don't recognize at all.

Everyone seems to agree that the perpetrators look like they're from high school too, or at least around that age. Carol, someone I went to high school with, tweets that it's disgusting that people would do that to our house. But other messages are flooding in.

Ones from people who are rolling their eyes, accusing me of trying to prolong my five minutes of fame after the newspaper article stopped getting me the attention I wanted, and why couldn't I just go to the police with this video.

People saying that this happened seven weeks ago by now, and why do I still care.

People saying that I have a proven vindictive streak, and it's obvious from the video that it's a stupid prank. *Of all the things happening in the world today*, one tweet says.

I keep scrolling, and it's more and more people saying that I'm out to ruin some kids' lives, with another guy from high school saying, *That's what she always does—remember the mascot photo?*

I check my DMs, and they're universally worse than all the retweets. Much, much worse.

I can't read them anymore. I want to vomit.

I can hear Annalie saying, *What did you think was going to happen?*

Rajiv still isn't here. I can't take another personal day. I close out of the browser and take some deep breaths. I go over to the window and open it, letting in fresh air. I sit in the corner chair, the big comfortable one, and try to compose myself. I can't let him see me like this when he comes in. First, because I don't know whether I can handle it if he wants to comfort me, and second, because I don't know whether I can handle it if he doesn't want to comfort me. Either is unbearable.

Slowly, I work my way back to my desk and start going through my work emails, opening up the documents I'm supposed to be cite-checking for today. It's almost ten, and Rajiv still isn't here. I have his number. I think about texting him, but I can't. It's ironic that I told Annalie that I wished she'd have an ounce of backbone. I might as well have said it about myself.

A knock on the door. Jack Fisher pokes his head in. "Hey there," he says.

"Good morning. What's going on?"

He steps inside and gently closes the door. "I just wanted to let you know that Rajiv gave his notice of resignation yesterday, so he won't be coming back."

I feel a wave of guilt. "What? Are you serious?"

"Unfortunately, yes. He offered to give two weeks of time before he left, but I told him it was unnecessary if he didn't want to."

"Did he say why? Was it because of me?" I say, unable to stop myself.

Jack gives me a strange look. "You? Heavens, no. Of course not. He told me it was personal circumstances with his family. You can understand that I won't share the specifics."

"Sure, I get it," I murmur, embarrassed.

"Anyway, I thought you should know, if he hadn't told you, since you'll be on your own here until the end of the summer. We'll try not to double your workload." He grins.

"Okay. Got it." I feel hollow.

He leaves, and I sit back. Rajiv, gone for the rest of the summer? It dawns on me that the last time he was in the office might be the last time I ever see him. What other excuses do I have to cross his path?

I guess it's the ultimate irony that he finally gets to do to me what I did to him first.

Seventeen

ANNALIE

I tip my head back on Violet's couch when we hit a commercial break during the baking competition show. I'm at her house instead of mine, because I need any excuse not to be home with my sister. Everyone has seen the video now, but nobody has brought forth any tips.

When I can't sleep, I catch myself hoping that someone else will recognize them, and they will turn the boys in. Then it wouldn't be up to me, and my boyfriend and I could escape unscathed.

But what does "unscathed" even mean now? Could we ever be that?

"I've been thinking about the video," I say to Violet after the episode ends. There is no need to say what video I'm talking about. She knows instantly.

Her head swivels in my direction. "Yeah?"

"What if Margaret is right? What if it *is* someone we know?"

"I always said she was probably right. Did she get any new info?"

I shake my head. My mouth is dry.

"I keep rewatching it to see if there are any details I recognize," she says thoughtfully. "I wish I knew."

"You do?"

"Of course." She turns to me. "Why?"

"Wouldn't it be worse if you did recognize them and it was someone we knew?" I try to say it in as detached a tone as possible.

"Would you rather hang around someone who could do this to you and not know anything?"

"If you knew, would you report them? Even if it was someone you liked?"

"What kind of question is that?" she asks. "It was a crime, Annalie. I wouldn't like them anymore if they did this. Of course I would."

She looks at me expectantly.

I turn away. I wish I could crawl into the shadows. The guilt gnaws. "Me too," I lie to the wall.

There is a news van outside our house, blocking our driveway. "Margaret!" I yell where I know she's holed up upstairs. "Your groupies are here! I have to go to work this weekend. Can you make them go away?"

I wait for a moment, but I don't hear anything. She's the worst.

The past few days have been hell. The video online, even though it was only up for about twelve hours, has increased interest again. This is way worse than the prom dresses or the mascot photo. It's the only thing anyone in town is talking about. I locked down all my accounts to be private, except for followers.

But I'm still getting messages, the worst messages.

And then the reporters started showing up. Not just the local *Gazette*, but national press, because now that it's hit Twitter, we're getting phone calls from BuzzFeed and CNN. I can't believe everyone is so interested in this. Articles about what constitutes a hate crime state by state. Think pieces about increased racial animus against Asian Americans. And all the while, Margaret, the one who lit the match, is unwilling to deal with any of it.

It's uncharacteristic of her. I thought she'd be outside, doing every interview like it's her job, but she's mostly been nowhere to be found. She goes to work and comes home and doesn't talk to anybody. Mama is mad at the attention, but she just shakes her head whenever Margaret comes home, like she doesn't know this daughter of hers at all. It gives me some measure of gross satisfaction to feel Mama's disappointment like a layer of dust all over Margaret. But I can't feel too smug about it, because Margaret seems sad and not herself. Except, of course, that Margaret can never apologize for anything, so I'm not holding my breath on that.

Meanwhile, my relationship with Thom is like a guitar string that's on the edge of snapping. I haven't seen him since the video went up. He hasn't texted me either, not that I want to talk to him at this point. I wonder if it's because he's afraid of having any written messages about this.

I wonder if he's afraid to break up with me because he thinks I'll spill the secret. Something I will never be brave enough to ask.

My car is parked in the driveway. I step outside, and immediately, someone is walking up to me with a notepad.

"You want my sister, Margaret," I say by way of introduction. "She's inside." I don't care about throwing her under the bus.

"You're Annalie?" the woman, who is wearing dark skinny jeans and has a tight ballerina bun, asks.

"Yeah." I shake out my keys, feeling annoyed about even confirming my name.

"Nobody in your household is responding to calls or messages."

"Maybe the lack of response is the message." I step past her and unlock my car. "Can you move the van? I have somewhere to go."

"Sure," she says. "So you don't have any comment on the vandalism? The video?"

"I didn't post the video."

"Right. But you saw it."

I nod curtly.

"Do you think it was a racially motivated hate crime or a prank gone wrong, like some people are saying?"

I pause, halfway in the car. A fire blooms inside my chest. Thom has said as much, but I have never asked Mike and Brayden. Even if I did and they told me, I don't know that the "why" even matters to me at this point. The real question is why people keep asking me, as if I know the answer. As if the answer makes any sort of difference at all.

The woman is still waiting for an answer.

For a second, I want to just tell her who it was. I could do it now. It's what I should do. It's what Violet and Margaret, and maybe anyone with an ounce of courage, would do. I glance at the garage and remember the red lettering, the ugliness I felt when I looked at it.

The blood rushes to my head; the words rush to my lips.

But I'm still afraid.

Not now, I tell myself. Now is not the time for rushed decisions.

The woman stares at me.

I think of Thom, the pleading in his face. The momentum slips away, and I feel carved empty and exhausted. "I would never prank anybody with a racial slur," I say finally. "Maybe I just don't get the joke." I slide into the front seat and slam the door shut.

I pull out of the driveway and watch from the rearview mirror to check that they don't follow me. My heart pounds hard. For the first time, I don't want to live here anymore. I want to keep driving until I leave the borders of this town behind. Until nobody can find me.

"Strawberry shortcakes, vanilla lemon tarts, pecan and toffee bites, chocolate almond cake with amaretto cream, and blueberry eclairs. Is that what we're working on today?" Bakersfield asks. He ties his apron back and cracks his knuckles. We are narrowing down our final recipes for entering into the baking competition.

Being in the kitchen, among my favorite sights and smells,

is the only place I feel safe now, where the outside world can't intrude.

Bakersfield wasn't too hot on the idea of entering the competition at first, but Daniel and I talked him into it. I came armed with the emotional appeal, and Daniel came with the calculations of how much profit we could make by participating, based on revenue reports from other small businesses that participated in the fair in previous years. Once Bakersfield saw the numbers, I could see that he was going to cave.

The *Closed* sign is up on the storefront. The kitchen has transformed into an assembly line of battle stations for different activities. We have to get through a batch of each recipe by the end of the day so we can sample each and make a final call. This is the best kind of workday.

"Well, let's get started, shall we?" he says, clapping his hands together.

I go to the fridge to pull out butter for thawing when the door to the kitchen opens.

"Hi," Daniel says nervously. As much as he's back here when Bakersfield isn't here—reading, chatting, grabbing a coffee—it's been a long time since the three of us have been in the same room. It feels immediately like too many.

"Do you need something?" Bakersfield asks.

"Um, no," Daniel replies. "I thought I could . . . help?" It's kind of funny how intimidated he looks by his grandad. I give him an encouraging smile.

"You don't know anything about baking," Bakersfield says.

"I know that. I meant I could just help with other things, you know. The menial tasks. Whatever you tell me to do."

Bakersfield stares at him, as if trying to decide whether this is a joke or not.

"I'm trying," Daniel says softly. "I know my dad thought this shop was a waste of time, but I don't think that. That's why I'm here. I'm trying really hard."

I watch as Bakersfield swallows, his throat bobbing. "Okay," he says, sounding gruffer than normal even, but I think he's trying to keep his voice steady. "Okay, fine. You listen to Annalie, though. And don't get in the way."

"I can do that," Daniel says. The thaw in the air is real. He glances over at me and gives me a hidden thumbs-up. I grin and turn back to the stand mixer.

Six hours later, we're gathered around the central counter with an array of different desserts for final tasting. We've gone through iterations of each with different ingredients and amounts in the past week. This is the distillation of the best. My taste buds are in heaven.

My joints are creaky from standing all day. I could really use a long nap. I would expect Bakersfield to be wiped, but he seems even more animated than when we started out.

Daniel, who wasn't wearing an apron like his grandfather and I were, has a shirt covered in flour, but he isn't bothered. He's beaming.

We line up in a row, surveying the remains after having done the taste test. "So?" I ask. "What do you think?" I have an opinion, but I keep it to myself.

"They're all great," Daniel says. "You could go with any of these."

"But which one was your favorite?"

He shrugs. "They're all good!"

"You're not helpful," I say. I look to Bakersfield.

"The vanilla lemon tarts," he pronounces. "That's the one."

I can't help but smile. "Those are my favorite too. It's the vanilla, I think."

"Great job," he says, a rare compliment from him that sends me glowing. "This is going to be fun." He claps a hand across Daniel's shoulders.

Daniel flinches at first, before relaxing. "Yes, fun."

"You know what else is fun?" Bakersfield says. "Calling it a day early and leaving the cleaning to the folks with better knees."

"Oh, come on!" I protest. "That's not fair!"

"That's the fairest way to go about it when you're my age. I let you use my kitchen; you get to clean up," he says, chuckling. He lingers by the door for a minute. "Have a nice night."

We wait until the door closes.

"Hey! That wasn't so bad!" I say. "You didn't get in a fight the entire time!"

Daniel shakes his head and laughs. "Unbelievable. I guess the kitchen was the way to his heart all along. I could hug you. Couldn't have done it without you here."

I go to the sink to wash my hands. "You could thank me by letting me sleep here so I don't have to go home and deal with all the attention on my family."

"Is it that terrible?"

"Have you looked online?"

"I try to stay away from all that. I'm a little old-fashioned."

"Well, I'd recommend keeping it up. The internet is a cesspit. Do you think I can transfer schools for my final year and go to some boarding school or something?" I'm half joking, but really only trying to lighten the mood for myself.

"It'll be okay by then."

He doesn't know what I know. Which is that, assuming Thom and friends will still be at school and haven't magically disappeared, it won't be okay. The thought fills me with anxiety. I can't imagine a year of this tension.

"Besides," he says, "we would never let you sleep on the floor of the bakery. Grandad would let you have the spare bed in our place, and I'd take the couch. Order of importance, you know." He smiles.

"You're kidding, but I'm fifty-fifty on taking the offer."

"I'm absolutely not joking. Except that I don't know if Thom would like it," he says lightly.

I blush, turning away so he can't see. I shouldn't be spending so much time with Daniel when things with Thom are so . . . messy. But this is really the best place to go, since being at home is also unbearable. And being around Daniel makes me happy in a temporary, uncomplicated way. A good distraction that'll go away once he leaves for New York.

"Let's not talk about this stuff," I say. "Let's talk about nicer things. Tell me something good."

"Soon you'll graduate and be able to go wherever you want."

"Soon is a year away," I remind him. "And I don't know

about 'wherever I want.' I'm not a genius like you or Margaret."

His expression softens. "Stop saying that. You're very smart. Where do you want to go? There's an entire world out there."

"I don't know. We don't travel that much as a family, to be honest. I've never been to Europe. I've never even been to New York. We went to California once when I was really young. Disneyland. I don't remember it much." I shrug. I turn away from him to wipe down the oven. "It's hard to imagine being away from here. Aren't you nervous about being away from home and going somewhere new where you don't know anybody?"

"No. I think it's exciting."

"I guess that was obvious. You came out here, after all. That's pretty different."

"It is."

"And what's your verdict?"

He smiles. "It's better than I expected. Mind you, my expectations were very low."

"You'd come back?"

"Well, I don't know if I'd go that far," he says. I make a noise of protest and push his shoulder. He laughs. "I'm glad I came out for the summer. And possibly, even one day, my dad will come out here. That might be a bar too far, but anything is possible."

"I hope that's true."

"And I'm glad that I met you."

My eyes flick up. I swallow. I feel out of control of my body. He is close, and I want him to be both closer and farther away. I know if he comes closer, I am lost. I take a step backward and go to the fridge. I don't dare look at him. I open the door and the cool air blasts against my face. It brings me back to reality.

He doesn't say anything, and neither do I. The tension stretches between us, taut like a rubber band. I'm waiting for it to snap.

Daniel isn't anything to me. He's just some guy who is easy to talk to and who will be nothing to me a year from now. I repeat this silently, but I know it isn't true. The truth isn't so easy. And what do I know about truth now anyway?

I keep thinking about Thom and his pleading face when he asked me to keep a secret. In the moment, it felt like there was nothing else I could say. That I was powerless against his request. I didn't think ahead. I didn't think about how difficult it would be day in and day out to look at his face and know what I know, and say nothing to anybody.

I thought I could do it. Hold this secret all by myself. But I feel incredibly lonely—the kind of loneliness that envelops a person and distances them from the entire world.

In the darkness, a memory floats up from nowhere, one that I didn't even know I had. I am thinking about Mama's futile attempts to teach written Chinese to Margaret and me when we were little. She started after our father left, maybe because she thought it would strengthen us, fill the gap that he had left. Flower, car, family, horse. She would make us write the characters over and over again. Ten words a day, ten times a day. I hadn't even learned how to write English words yet before Mama was teaching me Chinese. She persisted up until I was eight, when it became clear that without anyone to practice with except her, we would never learn enough. Teaching us Chinese was like filling a sieve with water.

I can't read most words. A few. Every third word in a children's book. But I do remember the word for "secret": *mi mi*. Two characters, pronounced the same, with the same tones, but written differently. The two characters, though, both have the character for "heart" embedded in them. A secret is two hearts.

It seems silly to be thinking about this ancient history here in the present warmth of the kitchen, alone except for a boy who isn't supposed to mean anything to me.

But there's no one I can tell who will keep it to themselves—not Margaret, not Mama, not even Violet.

So I tell Daniel.

Eighteen

MARGARET

When I first moved to New York City, I thought that I'd finally found my place. I could be whoever I wanted, I could find my group of people; I could find the elusive feeling of belonging that I never had in high school. I reveled in going to cafés and watching the bustle of people around me, feeling part of a larger tapestry. But it turned out that I had just moved from one place to another. Moving to New York didn't magically grant me a better ability to make friends or be a different person. It was the same me in a new place, but surrounded by enough people to remind me of being alone.

Now that familiar feeling is creeping up. My in-box is full of press inquiries. My social media accounts are full of messages that I don't want to read. My workdays are full of loading up on assignments from the lawyers at the firm. But I've driven every-one I care about away.

I texted Rajiv to see if he was okay, and he didn't respond. I deserve it, I guess.

I mostly stay in my room when I'm home, reading and trying to avoid the internet except for when I can't. A Chicago news station wants to do an interview. I respond that I'll do it, because there isn't much else for me to do at this point. I don't want to, but I feel like I should see this through to the end.

Annalie has stopped trying to fight me and only ignores me now. Mama looks at me as if she wishes I had never come back for the summer.

I wish I had never come back.

But it's almost over. I've booked my ticket to return to school. I am ready to leave this behind again. I can trade one loneliness for another—a change in situation makes it a little easier to bear.

My sister is waiting for me downstairs. The only thing we have discussed is getting a birthday present for Mama. We're normally not a family that gives gifts, but the one thing we can agree on is that Mama's had a tough year with all of this. She deserves a present, and for her daughters not to kill each other.

As to be expected, it's Annalie's idea. I am embarrassed not to have thought of it myself, but she's the one who is always thinking about how to do the right thing for other people.

I grab my stuff and go with her to the garage. We get into the car wordlessly, her on the driver's side. She turns up the radio on country music, which she knows I hate, but I don't say anything. I'm just hoping we can do this as quickly as possible and go home.

We cruise down the main street with the windows cranked down, heading toward the mall. I look out the open window and breathe in the grassy summer air. I glance over. Annalie's skin glistens in the light. Her sunglasses are balanced perfectly on her face.

We pull into the parking lot at the mall and circle around three times before we get a spot.

It would've been better if just one of us had gone to pick up a gift, of course. But buying gifts for Mama isn't so simple. She isn't like most gift recipients who appreciate that it's the thought that counts. You have to get her something that she'll use, or else buying her something is worse than useless. No, Annalie and I have to go together to see what's there and pick out the exact right thing. Something that Mama will actually like.

I love the sensation of cold air-conditioning on your face on a hot day. We push through the doors and go to one of the department stores. We head straight for the home goods section. I'm thinking some nicer kitchen pots to replace the grimy, scuffed ones that Mama has. "I'll go browse the linen section," Annalie says.

I can't remember a time when my sister and I used to be close or do things together. Movies about sisters seemed so foreign to me because I couldn't imagine a relationship where Annalie was my best friend and we'd gossip about life and boys. When we were younger, she was an annoying sidekick that I kept trying to ditch, and then one day, she stopped wanting to follow along because it turned out, she wasn't anything like me.

You can tell me everything, I told her on the Fourth of July. But that wasn't true, not even as I said it. The day I graduated from fifth grade, when a boy told me he didn't like me, the times I felt insecure in high school when people talked shit about me behind my back, even what colleges I got rejected from. I never told Annalie; I never even let her see me cry. Why would she tell me anything?

My sister is the person in this life who has the most in common with me, blood and experience and hopes and fears, but the main thing I remember about our childhood is me pushing her away until a wall grew up between us. Now it is so high and so broad that I don't know how we would begin to bring it down. It seems too late.

Now we can't even go to the store to pick out a present for our mother without a lingering stale awkwardness.

I run my fingers over a brand-new wok, smooth and black, with a lacquered wooden handle. I wish I could fix this, but I know the best we can hope for is to get this shopping trip over with as soon as possible.

I head over to the linens section to find Annalie. I comb through several aisles before I see her in the section where they have a hotel collection of fine-threaded sheets. She's talking to several high school girls, and at first, I think she must've run into a group of her friends. They look like they fit in with her, Daisy Dukes, tanned legs, perfectly wavy summer beach hair. Their expressions are too tight to be a friendly reunion, though. None of them look over at me.

I hear one of the girls say, "You have to admit that she's blowing it out of proportion, just like she always does. She doesn't even live here anymore."

I duck behind the end of the aisle before they can spot me, my heart pounding hard. I prepare myself for the knife's

283

blow—Annalie agreeing, because that's what she thinks too. But her voice comes through, annoyed and sharp. "No, Alexa, I don't have to admit that. Are you telling me you're okay with what happened?"

"No, of course not! But she's milking it. You know she is. I think she enjoys the fame more than she hates the fact that it happened."

"So we should just get over it?" Annalie says. "Why would you even say this to me?"

"Jeez, take it easy. She's out here doing all these interviews, acting like we're all a bunch of racists, and screaming at people on Twitter. Nobody got hurt. Why are you so mad? We know you're the rational one."

"Well, you thought wrong. Maybe I agree with her. Maybe I think she should be making a big deal of it until somebody takes it seriously. Obviously you don't."

"Whoa, Annalie. Clearly we caught you on a bad day," one of the girls says. "We'll see you at Mike's, I guess. We were going to ask if you wanted to grab dinner ahead of time and come with us, but sounds like it's better if we don't. Not sure if we might accidentally offend you." Her frostiness is bright and rings louder than her words. "Come on, let's go."

I step into the aisle, thinking that they're walking in the other direction, but I find myself right in front of them.

Their faces morph from momentary surprise to lofty contempt. "Oh, speak of the devil," says one of the girls. I don't recognize them, but if they're in the same class as Annalie, then they must know me from when I was in high school. They sweep past me without another word. All my snappy comebacks are trapped in my throat.

They leave me and Annalie alone. I'm frozen. Her eyes are red.

"Who were they?" I manage to ask.

She shakes her head. "I don't need your help. Just stay out of it." She brushes past me too. I stare at the pale blue bedsheets lined up in a row on the shelf. I can't move.

I catch up to her silently in the kitchen section after I'm able to regroup, but I'm shaken. The rest of the time in the store feels like a blur. We buy a new set of woks, checking out without a word to each other. The entire drive home feels like a country-music-fueled nightmare. I feel cold despite the temperature outside reading above ninety. We're home before I even know it. I can barely look at Annalie.

"I'll wrap it later, when Mama is out this weekend," she says after we've gotten home. "There's wrapping paper in the basement."

"Are you sure? I can do it. I'm . . . not doing much," I offer. It feels weak. I should do it. I should apologize to her. I can't stop picturing her face, angry and wounded after those girls said they were afraid to accidentally offend her. I wish she had just thrown me under the bus. It would be easier if Annalie hadn't stood up for me, so I could tell her that I forgive her for not taking my side. But she's not the one who is in need of forgiveness. It's me. I need forgiveness from her. From Mama. From Rajiv.

There are so many things I should say, but I don't have the right words, and I don't know how to open up the right conversation to her after so many years of failing to do so.

"No," she says. "You're doing enough." She pauses, fiddling with her keys in her purse and tightening her fingers around the handles of the gift bag. "I'll see you later."

I wake up to a rare rainy day. Usually in the summer, it's clear with a passing thunderstorm in the afternoon, but it's evident that today will be saturated with soft gray rain.

I'm numb and morose. I regret agreeing to do an interview next week. I don't want to do anything except lie in bed until it's time to go back to New York.

But today we're celebrating duan wu jie—the Dragon Boat Festival. There is work to do.

Mama never explained to us the significance of the holiday or anything about boats, dragon or otherwise. We only know it as the holiday where we eat zongzi, a sticky rice lump, savory or sweet depending on your preferred add-ins, wrapped in bamboo leaves and steamed.

I go downstairs without brushing my teeth, my hair sticking up and sleep in my eyes. Mama is already in the kitchen prepping. It's hard for me to think of a time when Mama wasn't already in the kitchen when I wake up.

I can smell the cooking rice and the sweet dates boiling.

Annalie isn't here today; she had an early morning at the bakery. Normally, she's the one who makes zongzi with Mama. I'm not much of a cook. I burn most things I try.

"Good morning, sleepy," Mama says, more brightly than anything she's said to me in the last two weeks. I plop into the chair at the counter, rubbing my temples. I feel like I have a hangover, but I haven't been drinking. "You want to help me today?"

"Okay," I tell her. I don't have anything else to do anyway.

What I really want to do is talk to Rajiv. I think about calling him. I think about writing him a letter. I think about doing it even just to hear him yell at me. Then I remind myself: Rajiv resigned from the job to get away from me. I don't think he wants to hear from me, and it would be cruel to push myself on him.

The truth is, I loved you—maybe I even love you. But I don't like you very much right now.

His words echo. I want to wipe them clean.

I tie up my hair and roll up my sleeves to my elbows. Mama pushes over a bowl of fragrant sticky rice and a pile of damp bamboo leaves. She comes and sits next to me. She seems very pliant and soft.

"Did you book your flight back to New York?"

"Yes."

"Okay." She nods. "Summer is almost over. Fast."

"Mm-hmm." I blink hard, feeling a stone of regret in my stomach. I've been here all summer, and what do I have to show for it? All of a sudden, I'm sorry for not spending more time with my mother. I notice that her hair is slightly grayer than it was when I left for college. The summers stretching long and endless in my future, filled with internships and jobs, fewer and fewer of them ones where I can afford to come home. I am vulnerable, terrified to grow up and be forced to leave this home. But I have already left.

"You are going back soon. It's hard to say goodbye again." It's as if she can hear what I am thinking. She gives me a sad smile.

She is struggling to tell me something, but she doesn't know how to say it. "I used to make these with your grandparents," she says, folding the bamboo leaves around the lump of rice until it's cone-shaped. "They were my favorite."

"Did you ever make them with Dad?"

She pauses. I'm afraid that I've made her angry and that I'll have ruined this too. It seems I only know how to make Mama unhappy these days. "I did," she says finally. "He wasn't very good at them. He would break the leaves." Her mouth curves in a half smile, as if remembering a nice thing.

I am amazed. It feels as if she has opened the door a small crack on my past. I can't see inside, but there is a sliver of hope.

"Which ones did he like best?" I have to move slowly, gingerly, so that I don't break this moment.

"The ones with sausage."

"Those are my favorite too."

"I know." Her eyes flick over at me. "You are like him in many ways. More like him than mei mei."

I don't dare breathe or swallow or move.

"It was harder for me to understand you. Jingling was so easy, even as a baby. You always seemed to want to run away. When I said to hold my hand for crossing the street, you would let go and not look back. I had to chase you."

It seems as if Mama is asking me to apologize for something I don't even remember. But she continues. "You were mad at me when your father left." She says it matter-of-factly.

That part, I can remember. I was five, but even so, I felt this hot resentment toward my mother. Maybe only because she was the one around to be resented, because I couldn't direct my outrage toward the person I wanted to come back.

"You hated me so much. I could see it."

"I was a kid," I say. "I didn't know any better. How could you hold that against me?"

She sighs. "I didn't blame you. I just wanted my daughter not to be so angry all the time. I put away the pictures because I thought it would help you forget. Why should you remember anyway? You were so young. He was never coming back."

I'm silent. The aching in my heart expands to fill the entire space. I say the thing that I have never been able to say out loud, but has plagued me my entire life. "I thought you didn't like me because I was like him." It is small—tiny—when it comes out of my mouth.

"You are like him," she says, her expression delicate and tender. "But you are your own person. I always knew that." She pats my shoulder.

I think about all the times that I wished I could get my mother to say sorry to me. Sorry for when she pushed me to do things I didn't want. Sorry for when she would take Annalie's side automatically in every fight, just because Annalie was younger, and in Chinese culture, the older sibling should always give way to the younger. Sorry for when she said all those things about Rajiv and why we shouldn't be together.

Mama will never say sorry. Not today, not on her deathbed. I know this.

Still, we lock eyes, and I can see her asking for forgiveness, for leaving me so alone, for keeping me away from my history. The other half of me. The things I could never know without her help. My throat is thick with emotion.

"I should have told you about him," she says.

"It's not too late," I tell her.

She nods.

Something inside me unclenches. And I feel lighter.

It is never too late for a change. And there are things we should talk about. Things we should've talked about a long time ago. I look at the zongzi in my hands, warm and aromatic. "I have to tell you something."

"What is it?"

"It's Rajiv's mom. She's been sick."

Mama's eyebrows knit. "Sick? How do you know this?"

"He told me at work. She's recovering from her cancer treatments."

"I am glad she's okay." She pauses, heavy with significance. "How is he?"

I stare at her. I'm not sure if I dare to push it further. But I steel myself, and I do. "He's having a tough time. He came home for the summer to take care of her. He's a good guy."

She turns her face away. "You still like him?"

"Yes, Mama," I whisper.

She doesn't reply for a few moments. "You're unhappy. You blame me," she says flatly, acknowledging the tinder between us, waiting to be lit.

"How could I not blame you? You *hated* him."

"I didn't hate him. Why would I hate him? I don't know him."

"You always wanted us to break up."

"Aiya," she says, sounding irritated, all our goodwill evaporating. "You decided to break up. I didn't make you do anything."

I refuse to be gaslighted, like Mama always does when things are not going her way. "You told me all the time how if we stayed together, our kids would be 'dark,' how we would be disadvantaged. You said all that!" I point a finger at her. "You said you would never talk to me again if we stayed together."

"I was trying to protect you."

"You were being racist."

She sighs. "I don't want to talk to you when you're yelling like this."

I am hot under my clothes, steaming from my ears. Normally, this is when I would storm out, refusing to hear another word from her. But something keeps me from bailing. I need to stay. I need to do the work. I need to fight where it counts. "You were wrong." I think about how she yelled at me on prom night, calling me ungrateful for choosing him over her, as if that were some kind of choice. "I shouldn't have listened to you. You made me weak."

I watch her, expecting her to scream at me and tell me what a silly, disobedient child I am. But she just takes a sip from her water, like she's unsure of what exactly to say next. She looks more tired than anything. She finally shakes her head. "You are still so angry at me, even now. You don't believe me, but I was trying to help you do what was best, what would make you happy in the end. But I don't know what's right and wrong these days. My parents taught me to listen to my elders, but I didn't listen to them when I came to America. Now I am old, and I don't feel wiser, like I thought I would."

She closes her fist on the top of the counter, pausing. "I shouldn't have said that I would never talk to you again. You know that no matter what happens, I would not leave you."

The lump in my throat rises. I say nothing.

"You have left this house. Zhang da la, grown up. You will make your own mistakes too. And I can't stop you."

"Rajiv wasn't a mistake, Mama," I say softly. And I believe it intensely. I will always believe it. No matter what may happen from here on out.

Now Mama is silent.

"Mama, I didn't tell you."

"Tell me what?"

"Do you remember prom? When we had the big fight?"

She gives a jerky little nod, like she doesn't want to remember it either.

"I was supposed to go to Rajiv's because his mom really wanted to invite me over for dinner. She wanted to get to know me better, and I didn't end up going." Even though it's just the two of us, I'm shaky with embarrassment. I think about Rajiv calling me over and over again. If I were his mom, I wouldn't like me either. And it was Rajiv's last straw. "I didn't go. That's why we broke up."

"She invited you?" she asks, sounding surprised.

I nod.

Mama's eyes flicker, and she looks away.

Her hands start working again after a long pause, and I think that she has moved on, but then she speaks up again. "Let's finish these zongzi and give to Rajiv's family," she says, picking up the bowl of rice. "For his mama. Would they like sweet or sausage?"

I can't believe it. Two miracles in one day. It feels impossible. Yet impossible things happen every day.

I don't think she is blessing anything yet, but this is as much of a victory as I could've hoped for right now. I'm sure the discussion isn't over. But for once, I'm glad it's not over. The important thing is that it seems, at least, there's room to grow.

"Sweet," I say finally. "That's a good idea."

We work quietly and quickly after that until we have an entire pile. Mama gets them into the steamer. The two of us clean up. We survey the kitchen, the smell of steaming food.

The rain falls steadily outside in a gentle hum against the windows and rooftops. We don't talk, but we don't need to anymore. It feels like we can hear each other without words.

I'm counting on the change in the air. For Mama and for me.

As I pick up the keys to leave, she taps me on the shoulder. "You aren't weak," she says. "You're strong. Stronger than me." Mama's fingers are warm, and what she says settles in my bones. After you have been clenching on to something for so long, you can go numb, forget that it hurts. And as she watches me leave, the guilt that crouched constantly on my shoulders disappears; I didn't know how heavy it was until it is gone.

I drive up to Rajiv's house with a basket packed full of fresh zongzi. It's afternoon, and his house is quiet in the rain. I don't see anybody in the windows or cars in the driveway. The last time I was here, I couldn't remember the details from the outside. I was too preoccupied with getting inside to his bedroom.

They have relandscaped the front since high school. A new strip of garden edges the garage door to the front of the house. Bright petunias cluster against the brown vinyl. The baby Japanese maple that we planted in the strip between the sidewalk and the road has filled out. Its dark red leaves stretch toward the sky.

I used to come here all the time when his family was out. So much so that it was almost a second home. We used to do our homework in the basement on the squashy pale couch in front of the TV. His family's orange-and-white cat, Mishi, loved scooting over to my lap. She liked me more than Rajiv even. Maybe more than anybody. I wonder if Mishi is still there. She was an old cat. Another thing that saddens me.

Before I came over, I thought about all the different things I could write on the note to go with the food. There were many things I wanted to say: regrets, pleas for forgiveness, an entire accounting of our relationship that we never got to have. I want to call Rajiv and spend hours on the line until the early light of the morning until we've run out of things to say and then stay on past that. If I let myself, I could write pages and pages—the story of us from beginning to end.

In the end, I don't write any of that.

In the end, all I write is *I'm sorry*.

Rajiv always said I had enough words for three people. But he also said that he could always tell what was in my heart, no matter what I said.

Nineteen

My Lyft drops me off in front of Mike's house. While I've never seen it before, I have driven by the neighborhood and I had a good idea of what I was going to be getting into. It's massive, beigey-tan all around, and looks like three houses meshed into one. There are wings jutting out from all sides. It's ugly, but it sure does scream wealth.

I hate going to parties alone.

Violet is on vacation with her family.

Daniel told me I shouldn't go, but I have to.

I need to see Thom. He's been texting me nonstop since the video came down, and we've barely had time to talk. I'm chaotic inside, and I need to see him. If only to know how I feel about us. If there's anywhere for us to go from here. I hope there is. In the beginning, there was something that was brilliant and golden about being with Thom that made all the other stuff go away.

I want to know if it's still there.

Besides, nobody's ever turned down an invite to Mike's house, and I'm not going to be the first.

It smells like beer when I step inside, like somebody has

already spilled something onto the carpet. Is it possible that Mike's parents don't know that he throws ragers when they're gone, or do they just not care? What kind of life would I be living if my mother didn't care whether I used our house for beer-soaked social events?

There are probably already around forty people here, milling about in the kitchen, hanging over the railing on the second floor, which opens into the foyer.

I don't see Thom or Mike or the other guys. Nor do I see Alexa, Joy, and Christine, who were ever so pleasant when they ran into me at the mall earlier this week. I always thought they were generally pretty cool people. Nice to me in classes. We weren't friends, but I also didn't have anything against them. They ran in Thom's circle of friends.

It's incredible what comes out of people when you're not expecting it. They came up to me to say hi at first, but the video came up right away, and then.

Well. When you peel a layer of the onion back, the real sharpness comes out.

I wondered for a moment there whether they knew, but I could tell they didn't. The boys hadn't told anybody else. For once, they were smart enough to keep their mouths shut.

I am the only one who knows. Me and Daniel, anyway.

The kitchen is all chrome fixtures and pristine white Shaker cabinets. There's a cooler full of beer and a glass fishbowl with a bright red drink. "Has vodka in it. It's pretty good," a girl from my AP Lit class says by way of greeting. Her name is Katarina. "I never see you at these."

I grab a Solo cup from a stack on the counter and ladle myself a cupful, just so I have something to hold. My hands otherwise have a habit of losing track of what to do and just flutter around awkwardly. "Have you seen Thom?" I ask.

She shrugs. "I think he's upstairs. You guys are together now, right?"

"Yeah."

"How did that happen?"

There must be something in my face, because she cuts in quickly, "I didn't mean anything by that—it's just I've never seen you together at school."

Now it's my turn to shrug. "My first summer job. Saw him a lot there."

Speaking of summer jobs, somebody I haven't seen in months turns the corner and makes eye contact. Audrey. She's wearing a black velvet skirt and a floral top, and her golden-red hair is swept in a messy but studied bun perched on the back of her head.

I hate it, but I do wish I could make my hair texture look half as good as hers. My hair is too flat in front and not fine enough to do a beachy look.

She's already spotted me. Too late to avoid her now. Her eyebrows jump in surprise before she manages to hide it. "Oh, it's you," she says. "I wondered where you disappeared to." She pauses, slightly awkward. "How are you doing?"

"Fine, I guess."

"I hear you're dating Thom, so that's exciting, but not unexpected. I guess that's why you're here?"

"Maybe I'm here because I'm cool and not just Thom's girl-friend," I say. It comes out sharper than I mean.

Katarina's eyes widen. She looks down into her cup, then turns away to escape the circle of conversation, like *yeeeesh*.

Audrey puts her hands up. "Whoa."

"Sorry," I reply, abashed. "Kind of aggressive."

"Kind of? Damn. I just meant that it makes sense you're here."

"Well," I say, trying to save this conversation, which might be a lost cause, "at least I'm out of your way at the Sprinkle Shoppe now."

She stares at me. "Do you think I hate you or something?"

"Do you not? I mean, at least you didn't seem to love me when we worked together."

"Yeah, because you were bad at everything, which made *my* life harder, but I assume you're decent at other things." She sighs. "The other girl who replaced you is worse anyway."

I laugh, surprised. "Sorry, that was my bad. I jumped to con-clusions." It occurs to me that part of the reason I didn't like her was because I thought she was competing with me for Thom. And maybe at the time, she was. But seeing her here, leaning against the counter and relaxed, I think maybe I misjudged her.

"Any chance you want to come back?"

"I don't think the manager would hire me back, but in any case, I work at Bakersfield downtown now."

"Really?"

"Yeah. You should come by sometime. Believe it or not, I am actually a much better baker than an ice cream scooper."

Audrey grins. "I'll believe that."

I can't believe Audrey and I are getting along. Of all people. Another thing I would never have guessed at the beginning of the summer.

"I've never been to one of these parties," I confess to her.

"They're not that great. I tend to come for the first hour and a half and then bail before it gets too sloppy or before the cops inevitably get called for violation of noise ordinances."

"Really?"

"Yeah. Applying to colleges this fall. Can't get in trouble."

Mike finally comes in the back door, hauling a giant aluminum beer keg over his shoulder. Seeing him for the first time since the diner makes me uncomfortable again, like I am somewhere I don't belong. He sees me and flashes a smile, perfectly innocuous. "Hi, Annalie! Glad you were able to make it! Thom's bringing some stuff inside."

He's never been anything but nice to me. It makes me doubt myself. I shake my head.

Audrey looks at me curiously. "Hey," she says awkwardly.

I pull myself out of my thoughts. "Mm-hmm?"

"I'm sorry about the thing that happened earlier this summer. When you quit."

For a second, I actually have no idea what she's talking about, and I have to swim through my memory to remind myself of my last day at the Sprinkle Shoppe. Oh, right. I take a big gulp of the drink in my hand. It's deceptively bright red and pretty-looking. It tastes sweet and bitter at the same time.

"Do they have any suspects? From the video, I mean? I saw that your sister posted it."

I twist my lips. "No."

She shakes her head. "That's terrible. I'm really sorry."

"It's okay," I grunt.

"I just can't believe it would happen *here*."

"Probably just some dumb kids." The lie feels slimy coming out of my mouth, like it sticks all over my tongue.

"Probably. I just can't imagine it was anybody we know."

I nod, feeling ill. I drink more jungle juice. That feeling of wanting to escape this town comes over me again. It must be so freeing to be somewhere where nobody knows you.

Finally, Thom rounds the corner and spots me. He strides right over, puts his arm around my waist, and gives me a kiss. His expression is warm and happy, no sign of the apprehension from when we saw each other last. "Hi, A! Glad you were able to make it."

He smiles at me lazily—and he still has the most perfect teeth I've ever seen. He looks over my head to the others. "This girl is amazing." His praise warms me. I realize that if I thought seeing him would in some way inspire a snap decision one way or the other, I was wildly wrong.

The crowd that always seems to gather around Thom wherever he is glows in our direction.

"You've never been here before, right?"

I shake my head.

"Let's give you the tour." He steers me out of the kitchen and back into the foyer. I glance over my shoulder back at Audrey, who gives me a wink and thumbs-up. Mike and the other guys are in the foyer, setting up a beer pong table and filling cups.

They wave at us. "Come on," Thom says. He leads me to the back. There's a piano room (a room dedicated entirely to a piano), a formal dining room with a crystal chandelier and a white wooden china cabinet (seems entirely too fragile to be twenty feet away from a major keg operation), a living room, and a "den," which I think is just a fancy word for a living room when you already have another living room.

The backyard is fenced and pristine. We go upstairs, where there are a few people lingering in the hallways. His hand is touching the small of my back. "This house is huge," I say.

"It's pretty nice. There's a home movie theater downstairs too—you'll have to come back when there are fewer people. Mike has us over to watch movies sometimes."

We peer into Mike's room. "Are you sure we're supposed to be up here?"

Thom grins. "Yeah, sure." He flips on the light.

To my surprise, Mike's room is immaculate. I don't know what I expected, exactly, but Thom's room has the vibe of a teenage boy: a bit messy, undone bedspread, clothes on the floor. Mike's room has none of that. Thom has band posters on his wall that I don't recognize because I'm not cool. Mike has framed paintings of nature. On his bookshelf, Harry Potter and the Hunger Games, and lopsided clay sculptures clearly formed in elementary school and painted with a young kid's hand. Some old, well-loved stuffed animals line an artfully distressed sideboard. His room is kind of . . . sweet.

"I know. Mike's room is decorated like an old lady featured in *House and Garden*."

I choke back an unexpected laugh. "I promise not to make fun of him later. I'll try, anyway."

"You don't have to try," Thom says confidently. "We all don't."

"We all have our faults. My room looks like if a hoarder really liked both rabbits and the color blue and only those things."

"Rabbits?" He quirks an eyebrow. He has never been in my room because he has never been inside my house.

"Not real ones."

"Okay, because I was imagining a bunch of rabbits just hopping around your room."

"I always wanted a pet rabbit when I was a kid, and my mom never let us have any pets. So I just have a lot of stuffed bunny toys."

"Adorable."

"I probably should get rid of them now. My room makes it look like I'm five." It doesn't really matter, because the only people who see my room are me, Margaret, Mama, and Violet.

"Don't, I want to see it. It's cute." He leans in. "You're cute."

My heart flutters a little. I can't stop it. He kisses me, slow and sweet. His hand is against the doorframe, over my shoulder, and he's leaning forward. My resolve melts. I think about our sun-drenched afternoons before I found out the horrible truth, the thrum in my heart when we are together. My fingers snake up and seize the fabric of his shirt. I pull him closer.

"We're okay, right?" he whispers to me, so quiet, a universe of space surrounding us. "I just want to make sure we're okay. Please be okay with me." His grip tightens on my arms.

Yes, I want to say. *We're okay. Let's leave this party and be together. Let's forget you ever said anything.* I want our relationship to be smooth and happy. I want it so badly that if I could drink enough tonight to black out and forget the last month, I would do that.

"Why do you like me?" It leaks out, and I can't stop it.

"You're beautiful," he says. "I don't know why nobody has ever told you before, but I want to tell you all the time. You don't even know how pretty you are. You're funny, even though you don't know it. I don't know. I like you. I always have. What do you want me to say?"

I kiss him again, blocking out a vague disappointment. *This is what you want*, I tell myself. I'm not sure I'm convincing myself, but it's insidiously easy to give in to Thom. Insidiously easy to let myself forget the bad stuff.

Downstairs, the party really kicks up when the rest of the soccer team shows up lugging more drinks. I don't know where these people get alcohol from, truly. I wouldn't know the first thing about going to the store to buy booze; are you just supposed to loiter around and ask somebody older? Are you supposed to get a fake ID? Where do you get a fake ID from?

Thom corrals me into playing beer pong, with me on his team. "Are you sure? I'm not very good."

He slides his arm around me. "The point of beer pong is not winning or losing. It's that you drink no matter what. Don't worry, though. I'm great."

We play Mike and Katarina, who trounce us, and I drink half my body weight in beer. It's so unpleasant. But halfway through the third game, I'm feeling buzzy and light, like I'm being propelled gently on a cloud. My cheeks are warm, and I keep touching them. I have never drunk this much before. The beer even starts tasting less bad.

This is okay, I think. This is what it could be like for me, to really be part of the popular crowd. It's . . . so easy.

In fact, I'm feeling great. Confident. I'm laughing at people's jokes and not feeling self-conscious about the way my bottom teeth are slightly crooked when I smile too big or if I snort when I laugh. At some point, I see Alexa and her friends come in and shoot me a look, but I sidle right on over and start chattering like we've been pals our entire lives. I stop thinking about whether people find me charming. *I* find me charming.

And I'm radiating that charm all the way up until the front door swings open and Daniel fills the frame.

He looks around the room tentatively, full of screaming drunken Americans. His presence is so incongruous here that it doesn't feel real. I am either so drunk that I'm hallucinating or it's one of those dreams where you are watching a movie and then all of a sudden, you are in the movie. Am I in the movie? Or is Daniel in the movie?

He notices me a split second before Thom notices him. He's tall enough that the crowd effectively parts for him to go through.

"Hi."

"How did you get here?"

"I have apps on my phone."

"Oh, right."

Daniel never looks uncertain no matter where he is, but I've found that Thom does. After a moment, though, Thom manages to recover from his surprise. "I'm glad you were able to make it."

"Thanks, mate. Me too." I waver a little, wondering if I'm supposed to be the middleman between the two of them, passing messages along because it's just a little too weird for them to speak directly to each other. They come off as if they are from entirely different worlds, too vastly divergent to even interact. And I guess, in some ways, they do.

Daniel is relaxed but alert. Thom is a little drunk at this point, as am I. "Do you want to play?" I ask Daniel.

"I really want to talk to you."

I push him toward the table, which is kind of like pushing a brick wall, but he complies. "Play first."

"With you?"

"With Thom." I'm feeling daring. Thom shrugs and hands him a Ping-Pong ball. I stand off to the side and watch, sipping out of a bottle. Mike comes over from wherever he was and joins me on the side. His face is a little red and his eyes glassy.

It turns out Daniel has great hand-eye coordination. It might be helped by the fact that the other participants in the game are drunk, and he is sober as the grave. He and Thom win handily, which Thom seems less than excited about, but I give Daniel a high five.

"Okay, can I steal you for a minute?" he asks.

"One more, one more!" I say. "I want to play!"

"I think I'm good."

"Come on," Mike says, cutting in from the sidelines. "You

305

can't just steal A away just like that."

"Yeah," I add belligerently. Only Thom calls me A. It sounds strange coming from Mike. But I pause only for a second. "One more."

Daniel glances back and forth between the three of us, his expression hovering between helpless and annoyed. He sighs. "All right, fine."

I whoop, probably much louder than I intend to. I grab his arm. "You're on my team."

Thom shuffles over to the other side of the table with Mike. Even through the warm bath of my fuzziness, I can feel a whiff of chilliness in the air from all parties. Swimming somewhere in the back of my brain, I think, *This will be bad in the cold light of the morning.* But there's nothing to do but muscle through this now.

I take a big gulp of my drink and look over at Daniel. "Ready?"

He nods.

Thom and Mike are good. And I am so terrible I might as well have no depth perception at all. But Daniel is so dominant that it doesn't matter how bad I am. He makes all his shots, except one, coolly, with barely a shift in expression. He's almost surgical in his precision and aim.

We win, and it's a short game, even with me heavily holding us back.

"Ugh, okay, this guy's really good. Next up," Mike calls from the other side of the table.

"No," Daniel says firmly, definitely having gotten his fill of unwanted games of beer pong. "Someone else can take over."

"We won, though," I protest.

Thom comes over from the other side. "That was fun," he says, sounding very forced. He edges closer to me and grabs my arm.

"Right, yes. Fun," Daniel says crisply. "Can I borrow Annalie for a second?"

"I'm not an object to be borrowed," I interject. I am literally standing between the two of them.

"For what?" Thom asks.

"It's about the baking contest. It's private."

"The baking contest?" Thom looks confused. I realize that I never told him about it, not even a passing mention. What does that say about us?

Daniel clearly realizes this at the same time. His face glows with a smugness that makes me feel guilty. "He doesn't know about it?" he says to me.

"It's not that important," I mutter.

Thom lets go of me. His mouth tenses. "Fine, whatever." Without another word, he turns and strides away.

"Your boyfriend doesn't like me," Daniel remarks after Thom has left the room.

"That's not true."

He laughs. People around the room are starting to notice him. Well—more like notice him and me. I seize Daniel's arm. "Let's step outside. Get some air."

He follows me wordlessly out the front door. The neighborhood is twinkly and quiet. It's a newer neighborhood; the trees lining the sidewalks are saplings. The fireflies flicker in and out above the lawns in flashes of green and yellow. Even after dark, without the air-conditioning in a humid July, my shirt already starts sticking to my skin.

I loved these summer nights when I was a kid. Margaret and I used to play nighttime hide-and-seek tag outside with the neighborhood kids, running wild around the subdivision without any supervision, crawling through people's brambly bushes, smearing mud on our cheeks to hide, coming home with burrs in our hair. All those kids eventually moved away before junior high, and we transitioned to spending our evenings inside. Somehow less magical all the time. I am gripped with a fierce nostalgia for simpler times. I inhale deeply, full of freshly mown grass smell and summer smoke.

Standing outside, just the two of us, I suddenly feel exposed in my tank top and shorts and a great deal more sober.

I put my hands on my hips to ground myself and seem more intimidating. "So what did you really drag me out here for?"

Daniel shuffles his feet and puts his hands in his pockets. "It's not about the baking contest," he confesses.

Now that we are alone, I feel the anger welling up about the whole exchange. Him being here. Deliberately trying to make it seem like he is closer to me than Thom. "Oh, so you just wanted to bring it up so I would look bad in front of my boyfriend?"

"How is this my fault?" he says. "You were the one who didn't tell him. And if it's not that important, then what's the big deal?"

He's right, but I'm mad and I just want to lash out at someone. And I can't lash out at Thom.

"You did this on purpose."

"I didn't!" He pauses. "Annalie, why can't you talk to him about things that are important to you?"

The question feels like a slap in the face. I don't know the answer, so I avoid it. "Why are you even here?"

"I wanted to make sure you were okay."

"Why wouldn't I be okay? You just showed up. You could've texted."

"*I did.* You didn't answer. Check your phone."

I haven't looked at it all night. "Whatever, fine. I was too busy having a good time. What's wrong with that?"

He gives me a significant look. "Are you *really* having a good time?"

"I shouldn't have told you about who did the vandalism," I say. "It was a moment of weakness. Forget I said anything and uninvolve yourself."

"You shouldn't have told me? You should be telling everyone. You should be going to the police. He and his friends, they're not good guys."

I flush and steady myself. "It's complicated, okay?" The truth is, I agree with him, but it's hard to speak up when I'm around them. It's one thing to recognize that what they did was a horrible thing, but another to be the only person in the position to turn them in. Still, either the guilt or the alcohol is sitting badly in my gut. Maybe both.

"Look, I know it's hard, but it's the right thing to do."

"Ugh, I knew it was a mistake to tell you. I thought you'd be able to understand and just listen to me, instead of being another pain in my ass like Margaret."

His face immediately contracts with pain, and I feel guilty for being so cruel. But the alcohol is making me bold and reckless. I am tired of being told what to do by everyone all the time. Margaret. Alexa and her crew. Daniel, making me feel like a coward.

"Why are you here anyway?" I demand. "Just to make me feel shitty about myself? Because you get to hang around me all the time at the bakery, you can start tagging along to my real life?"

He takes a step. "I'm here because I thought you needed a friend."

"I have plenty of friends," I say nastily. I know I'm hurting him, but I can't take in his words right now. He's saying things I don't want to hear, and I want him to stop.

I dare to look up at him defiantly, and then it becomes obvious to me why he's here. And it's not because he's my friend. It shines out of his liquid brown eyes behind his glasses, big and clear, and full of concern for me.

Oh.

His intentions are unmistakable. How could I have let it go for so long?

I don't say anything. We are statues.

"Annalie," he says, and his voice lays it all bare. "Fuck." He looks furious at himself.

The turmoil inside me falls to silence, so soundless, it's like a nighttime snowfall. I imagine Daniel's arms around me, strong and safe, and his laugh, so clear. I catch myself dreaming in the stratosphere, flying far away, dizzy with possibility.

Before I am dragged back to the ground with the stoniness of the fear that always brings me back to earth. Fear is solid. Fear is more substantial than flighty wishes and fairy dreams.

I'm afraid that this is going to change everything, in a summer where there has already been too much change.

I wish I could just take his hand, and we could run away together. But there's nowhere to go. We are trapped here, in this mess. Everything about the two of us is intertwined in the debris of me and Thom, our relationship, the vandalism. . . . Daniel leaving at the end of the summer. I can't introduce another complication to my life right now.

I shake my head.

He reaches for me, and I back away.

"Please stop before you say something that we can't come back from. You should go home." I am trembling. "Please go home."

His expression crumples, and his shoulders fall. For the first time, he seems fragile to me, something too precious to hurt, and yet I have done it anyway. My head aches. My ears ring.

"I'm sorry," he says. "I'll leave."

He does, and I'm alone. I sink to the ground, my tears blurring the grass. I wanted him to go, but it feels like the wrong decision. Everything I do feels wrong.

* * *

A silver Camry pulls up to the curb where I'm waiting. I peek in the side window.

"Get in," Margaret says.

I slide in the front passenger seat, deeply grateful.

She wrinkles her nose. "You reek of booze. You better hope Mama is asleep already." The clock on the dashboard shows one a.m.

I fumble slightly with the seat belt but eventually click it in. "Thanks for picking me up." My face is blotchy. I didn't want to cry all the way home in a Lyft with a stranger. But I'm feeling steadier.

Margaret is in her polka-dotted pajama pants, a tank top, and bright pink Old Navy flip-flops. She taps her mouth with her fingers to shield a yawn. "I'm glad I was awake to get your call. What happened?"

We drive away. I look out the window toward the house as it shrinks behind us, still lit up, the faint sound of music pounding from the inside. I didn't say goodbye to Thom. I just left. Is he wondering where I went? My phone is dark and silent. My stomach is roiling, and it's hard to tell if it's from the alcohol or the emotional earthquake.

"You know, the usual. I was with my boyfriend. Another boy showed up to confess his love. I didn't really know how to deal with it." I sound very wry and casual. I even manage a small giggle.

"Your face is glowing," she answers. So there's definitely some part of the alcohol. "Like, bright red. I guess in that way, you got Mama's genes. See? There's the Asian in you." Mama lights up like Rudolph's nose when she drinks a glass of wine. Even though Margaret has made these types of comments before, faulting me for not caring about things as much as she does because I don't look Asian the way she does, I feel unexpectedly stung by it. Just because I don't react to things exactly as she does, doesn't mean I'm not Asian too. I turn toward the window and fall silent.

Margaret's gaze flicks to me sideways as she drives along the empty streets at night, the pavement dotted periodically with spots of yellow lamplight. "Anyway, so did they duel over your hand or something?"

I don't look at her. "Not exactly. I told the confessing one to go away. And he did. And then I called you before I went in to say goodbye to anybody. God, I'm such a mess. I've screwed everything up."

"How? Because you didn't pick anybody?" She is incredulous. "I know that not dating you is a major tragedy, but I think that these practically grown men can handle it. You don't *have* to pick a man, you know."

I sigh. "You're always so sympathetic."

"Who else will give you the tough love you need?"

"Mama? Violet? Literally everyone in my life. Where's the soft love? I need somebody to give me some of that."

"I still don't see what the problem is. Do you want to pick one of them? Do you want to pick neither? Both of these are options."

"I don't want to hurt anybody. I just want to make the right decision." I slide down the seat and moan.

"Okay, please don't vomit in my car. We're almost home."

"It's my car now," I mumble. "You don't live here anymore."

We pull up into the driveway. The house is dark. As I sit up, I look right at the garage door, now pristine and white, whiter even than when we first moved in. They did a really good job cleaning it. All the grime with the paint.

Before I go inside, I can't take my eyes off it. You would never know that anybody had vandalized it, just by looking.

Margaret tucks me into bed like I'm five, after getting me up the stairs (in the dark) without me falling or waking anybody up.

"I'm drunk," I tell her.

"Here." She hands me a glass of water. "I'll fill it up after you're done and leave it on your nightstand in case you get thirsty later." She also brings over the garbage can from the corner and puts it right next to my bed.

I drink out of the glass slowly. I feel hazy but not sleepy at all. Margaret sits on the edge of my bed and glances around. "You really need to clean your room."

"I like it this way."

She snorts and moves a stuffed bunny away from her foot. She shifts in her spot. "You sure you're okay?"

We used to share a room when we were little. We had bunk beds. I think it was one of those small things Mama did that acknowledged that we'd lost a parent. Dad left us; we got bunk beds. I suddenly remember that even though we both wanted the top bunk, Margaret let me have it. She moved out into her own room right before she started junior high. I was eight, and that first night was the loneliest I had ever been.

"Will you stay here for the night?" I say. I sound like a scared little girl, and right now, I'm not convinced that I'm not one.

There is a long pause, which makes me think she is going to tell me to stop being a baby, but then she holds out her hand for my half-full glass and sets it down on the nightstand. "Promise me that you won't puke on me."

"I promise!"

"Fine. Scoot over."

She swings her legs into bed and I slide over onto the far edge. She settles under the comforter. My full-size mattress, years old and unaccustomed to the weight of two people instead of one, sinks into a gentle sag with a light whine of protest. Margaret's breathing is even and soft. I hadn't realized how silent, deathly silent it is when I normally go to sleep. Hearing her breathe is so natural that it's hard to believe it's possible to sleep without it in the background.

I'm beginning to feel the fuzzy blackness claim the edges of my consciousness when she breaks the pattern of her breathing with a whisper. "Why'd you make me come take you away from the party? What are you so afraid of?"

What am I afraid of? The list is long and constantly growing. I used to believe that as you got older, you'd stop being scared of stuff, like one day you'd become a card-carrying adult and boom, you'd magically gain a critical dose of wisdom and fortitude, understand the silliness of all your fears, and go forth, able to live your life with confidence and serenity. It's a devastating day when you realize that none of it is true.

Maybe, actually, that's the day when you do become an adult. The day it dawns on you that adulthood is just the same, except you know for sure that there's no end to your fears, and some of your fears have no solution.

I'm scared of spiders, public speaking, clusters of small holes (which I learned on the internet is called trypophobia and not just something I made up). Those are the things that you can avoid, if you're really dedicated about it.

Then there are the fears that aren't so avoidable. Like loneliness, being unloved, and other dark, unnameable things that you're afraid even to say out loud because in some paranoid way, they might come true. Wu ya zui, Mama would say as a warning when we talked about bad things, scary things. It directly translates to "crow's mouth," but it means that saying bad things might bring them into being.

"I don't know, Margaret," I whisper back at her finally. "I think I'm scared of doing the wrong thing. Picking the wrong person. Making the wrong choice. And then I've screwed it up forever."

"Usually your choices aren't so permanent. You're very unlikely to have screwed it up *forever.*"

"Or I pick something, and it's the wrong decision, and I can't take it back. And I spend all my time regretting it." I turn toward her so that I'm facing her profile. Her eyes are open and looking up at the ceiling. "I feel totally paralyzed sometimes. So then I just don't decide anything."

Margaret blinks slowly and doesn't speak.

"I wish somebody could just tell me what to do. Help me do the exact right thing, always."

"It's too bad that doesn't exist," she says softly.

I laugh. "Yeah, thanks for the reality check." I see her quirk a smile. "What are *you* afraid of?" I ask curiously. To be honest, Margaret never seemed to me like she was scared of anything. I half expect her to say she has no fears. But she answers right away, precise and small.

"That I might be a bad person. A hypocrite."

Her answer catches me by surprise. "How could you of all people be a bad person? You're always trying to do the right thing."

"You told me that I was a bitch, like, a week ago," she says wryly.

I'm abashed. "You know I didn't mean that."

"I get it. I don't spend enough time thinking about other people's feelings. I hurt people," she whispers.

I think about our old bunk beds, and her giving me the top bunk. She always cared about what mattered to me. I look at the outline of her profile, edged by the ambient silver light outside. My sister, smaller than I remember, in the dark. It seems to me, for a fleeting second, that our fears aren't true, or at least, they are never as true as we make them out to be.

During the school year, I go weeks without talking to her, without even exchanging a text. But when I called at the beginning of the summer and told her we needed her, she came back home that very day. And when I called her at the party, she showed up fifteen minutes later, not a second longer.

For whatever happens between us, I know that Margaret will always be there for me if I really need her.

"You're a good person," I say. "I know you. No matter how far away you go."

There is a long pause. I wonder if she will argue back or disagree. She rustles the sheets and sighs. "Thanks," she says, and turns on her side. "I wish I were more like you."

I'm too stunned to respond. Me? I'm cowardly and mediocre at everything that matters. I'm not even the hero of my own story. I've spent most of my life wishing I were more like Margaret—more successful, more secure in myself. I don't think what she says is quite right. "Do you ever think, if we were just one person, we'd be, like, the perfect person?" I blurt out.

That breaks the moment. She bursts out laughing, which makes me kind of embarrassed and offended, but I can't help but begrudgingly grin. "I do," she says, wiping the tears from her eyes. "I do."

Eventually, I doze off, Margaret's warmth next to me, and I fall asleep smiling.

"They picked the hottest day of the year. I almost wish it rained, and this got bumped a week," Bakersfield mumbles as he pats at his forehead with a handkerchief from his pocket. For some reason, old people always have handkerchiefs on hand, and I briefly imagine a drawer in his closet of just white, embroidered handkerchiefs that he swaps into his pocket every day.

"At least they're selling iced coffee in the stall next to us," I say. "That was smart stall placement by whoever organized this." I fan myself with a flyer for the fair. The plastic cup of iced coffee I bought earlier this morning is sweating and slick already. It's not so much "iced" as "warmish."

Our baked goods are neatly wrapped and stacked at the table, with trays in the back of the tent. Almost all of them are my output, which I'm proud of. I spent all of yesterday baking and boxing up the goods for transport after they'd cooled. The bakery smelled incredible all day. I kept the door to the back open deliberately, half hoping that the scent would lure Daniel in, but I never saw him.

"Where's your grandson?" I ask Bakersfield, casually as I can, as if he could be in Tanzania for all I care.

He shoots a piercing glance at me. "At home. He'll drop by later. Why? Can't you text him yourself?"

"Just asking," I say, shrugging, but mentally, I'm already trying to figure out when he might pop up and scanning the crowds. For obvious reasons, I haven't spoken to Daniel since the party at Mike's. I'm not sure he ever wants to speak to me again, and I guess that would be fair. I don't deserve to see him again, but it still feels painful to me, the idea of him leaving at the end of this summer, with the finality of a period.

Violet is back from vacation, and she'll be here too. I'm nervous to see her. There's so much I haven't told her yet, but anything I tell her, I have to do in person. And I don't know if this is the right place. She'll be here to see which desserts win the contest.

I entered the vanilla lemon tarts, which Bakersfield believes are the best thing I've made. I believe it too. There are a couple of other stalls with baked goods—a cupcake shop and a pie shop among them—and I'm planning on sampling the lot. But I feel good about my entry.

Even with the heat, the fair is bustling with attendees. Tents line the main street downtown, most of them generic rented white tents, a few fancier jewel-toned ones dotting the way. Ours too is white and nondescript. A live band is playing at the end of the street, set up on a stage. It's been rotating genres. Right now, it's a bluegrass band, the banjo twanging cheerily through the crowd.

Accidental Audio played earlier, but I didn't go watch. I couldn't bear to see the boys and hear their casual banter, and act like everything was okay. Thom has been texting me to ask why I left without a word, and I haven't responded. I know I can't just ghost out of this relationship, and the eventual confrontation will just be worse. But what can I say? I'm not ready to have the conversation yet. And with all the mess going on with Daniel, I'm not equipped to craft the right breakup for Thom.

Bakersfield collapses into a chair behind me, loudly gulping an iced bottle of water. He's grumbling about regretting being talked into this, but we've sold a weekend's worth of baked goods in the course of a morning, so he can't be that miffed.

"Hey," comes a voice from behind. It's Daniel.

"Oh," I say hastily. "Hello."

Bakersfield grunts his greeting. There's a silence.

This is the first time I've seen him since the party. It feels weird to see him in the light of day, with my last memory of him, crestfallen and embarrassed, shrinking into the night. My chest seizes a little at the sight of him.

Daniel betrays nothing. He's way better at a poker face than me.

"I'm going to do a lap and see if there's anything good for lunch," I say to cut the silence. I'm not hungry at all. "Do you want me to get you anything? Can you cover for me?"

It must be so obvious that I'm trying to escape, but Daniel just nods. "Sure. Take your time. The empanada stall is good. I already grabbed some food before I got here."

"Okay. I'll be back soon." I slip into the crowd quickly, fighting the temptation to look back. I wonder if he is going to be there all afternoon. I thread through the crowds aimlessly, just trying to put more distance between me and the Bakersfield stall. Even though I know it's not possible for him to see me anymore, I feel Daniel's eyes boring into my back.

I turn onto a side street that's less crowded. It's cheaper to get tents here. There are some jewelry vendors and local beer brewers.

I stumble on Thom and the whole crew. They're laughing and shouting. They spot me and wave me over before I can escape. A flicker of contrition flashes across Brayden's face before he recovers. They're all holding cups of beer. I can smell the rankness of the cheap alcohol and salty sweat from their performance this morning.

"Hey, there you are," Thom says. He hands me his cup and puts his arm around my waist, a little too tightly. "Been looking all over for you." He doesn't ask me why I haven't texted him back. I realize in an instant that this is a performance for his friends. We're not going to fight in front of them. We're going to be in love.

Okay, I can do this. After all, we've been pretending like nothing is wrong for so long already. It dawns on me that I've always been putting on a show for him, the entire time we've been together. The girl who is cool, who doesn't make a fuss, who's supportive without asking for anything back. It's sad. I don't even know who I am around him.

But it's just one more day. I'll find private time to talk to him, after all this. I'll do it tomorrow.

"Want to try out some different stalls with us? We were just about to grab some food, and then maybe bounce to a bowling alley or something."

"Sure. Food. Let's do that," I say.

I trail them out of the side streets and to food stands, hoping we'll avoid running into Daniel. We go past the wafting smells of grilled meat and buttery corn. Smoke from grills rises, wispy, into the clear blue air.

Thom bends over to me. "What do you want?"

"I heard the empanadas are good."

"Works for me." We go over to that stand, and the other boys grab burgers two vendors over, giving us some privacy. I order a chicken one and a corn one, and I fish in my pockets for the loose dollars I had.

"I got it." Thom hands over a twenty and orders two beef empanadas for himself.

"Thanks. You didn't have to."

"You're my girlfriend. I want to." There's an edge to his voice under the surface breeziness, as if he is emphasizing it to me. That I am his. That I should stop forgetting that.

I take a bite of the empanada, bursting with sweet corn and cheese, attempting to brush off Thom's possessiveness.

Somebody taps my shoulder. I turn around. "Hmm?"

"There you are." It's Violet.

"Hi! Oh, sorry. My face is covered in cheese." I hug her with my hands carefully curled so I don't get any grease or crumbs on her clothes. She's tanner than before she went on vacation, her hair in two braids. She's wearing an amazing orange eye shadow that I remind myself I need to ask her about later. I missed her.

"Hi, Thom," she says around me. "About time we met, huh?" She shoots me a look, and I feel guilty all over again. "I've been waiting all this time."

I'm wincing because I don't really want Violet to meet Thom. Not after all this. But she reads my expression wrong, which is fair, because she's been begging to meet him all summer, and I've been hiding him away like a dirty secret. "I can go if you want."

"No, it's not that," I say. "It really isn't. I have to talk to you about something later."

Thom raises his eyebrow. "Something later? What do you girls talk about anyway?"

"This doesn't have to do with you," I tell him firmly. "It's not the thing you're worried about."

His face transforms at once when he understands what I mean.

"Um, what are you both talking about?" Violet asks.

"Nothing," we say in unison. I close my eyes against the lie.

I'm sick of lying. I don't want to lie to my best friend. Keeping the secret for Thom is poisoning my life. This is not how I wanted everything to go down.

There's an awkward silence as the three of us trying to figure out what goes next.

"What's your name again?" Thom blurts out.

Jesus help me.

She takes a step backward, her face crumpling, realizing at the same time as me that I have never once mentioned her to my boyfriend, never intended to introduce them. "Her name is Violet," I say. There are only a hundred and fifty people in our class. I would recognize any one of them by name, even if we have never spoken before. I put my hand out to reach for her. "Hey—" I start out, but it's too late.

She shakes her head. "No, no worries at all. Don't bother. I get it." She's already backing away.

The other guys start crowding up around us, hands packed with food. "What's going on?" Mike asks with his mouth full.

"I don't belong here," Violet says, her eyes shiny. "I'll find you later, okay?" And then she's disappeared in the crowd before I can blink.

"Shit," I mutter. I feel like a garbage person. "I have to go."

"Wait, don't," Thom says. "Why do you keep bailing on me like this? Am I not important to you anymore?"

I stare at him, his beautiful face that I know so well now, furrowed in confusion and frustration. I try to remember all the things I like about him. All the years that I pined. All the time I spent daydreaming about being Thom's girlfriend. And yet here

I am, exactly where I wanted to be, and all I want to do is get away.

I can't pretend like I don't know what kind of person he is. A coward. A person who brushes away my pain to protect his friends.

I can be that person, too. Or I can choose to be myself, choose the parts of me that hid away so that I could be the kind of girl someone like Thom would want to be with.

"I don't want to do this anymore." The words I never thought I'd say drop out like stones into a smooth pond.

There's a pause. "What?" he says.

"You can go," I say softly. "I don't want to make a scene in front of everyone." The boys are trying not to look like they're listening in. What a nightmare.

"Hey, let's not do this here, okay?" He looks around nervously. "Come on. Let's get some privacy." He grabs my hand, and although I don't want to go anywhere with him, I don't pull away. We thread behind a few stalls and into a bricked alley. I wonder how the Bakersfield stall is doing. I have to get back soon.

The light breeze from earlier this morning is completely gone. The dead heat of midday sits perfectly still and heavy on our shoulders. A sliver of blue shows overhead between the two buildings. The noise of the fair is muffled here. It's just the two of us.

"This really feels like it's coming out of nowhere, A," he whispers to me urgently. "You can't just do this out of the blue. I want to talk about it." It seems weird that he feels like it's coming out of nowhere, but I guess it's been so constantly on my mind that it's an old and worn thought to me. He's so close to me. I feel claustrophobic. His hands are slick and desperate on mine.

"I'm sorry," I say. "I just don't think that we're good for each other. You know, after everything that's happened. What I know."

Thom grabs my hand, and I try to pull away. He doesn't let me. His grip is like iron, like I am a life preserver and he is drowning.

Out of the corner of my eye, I can see Mike entering the alley. He's followed us here. The other boys are nowhere to be found.

"I have to go. Thom—Thom—let *go*!" He does, and I stumble back.

"Okay, okay," he says. "I'm so sorry. I didn't mean that. I'm sorry. Let's not do anything ridiculous. Why don't you go back, and we'll leave you, and you can call me tonight. Okay?"

I've never seen him this desperate. I almost pity him. I won't call him tonight. I won't call him ever again.

After a moment, my silence appears to settle on him.

He exchanges looks with Mike. They seem to come to some kind of understanding, between the two of them.

Mike steps forward. "A," he says seriously. "We have to talk."

"We? Why we?"

He speaks slowly, like he wants me to understand. The way people talk to Mama when they think she can't understand their English because she is Chinese. "Thom told me that he told you.

About your garage." Beside him, Thom winces and gives me an imploring look.

His words hit me in slow motion. At first, I'm only seeing his mouth move, only hearing what he's saying like a string of sounds, nonsensical. It takes a second for the meaning to catch up, as if the words are traveling at the speed of light, but the significance is traveling at the speed of sound.

"You shouldn't have told her, man," Mike says. "I told you not to."

"I didn't want to lie to my girlfriend," Thom snaps. He turns to me. "I didn't mean for it to be like this."

I shake my head, trembling. I want to make sense of it all, but there is no way to make sense of this. "Did you date me because you thought it was the only way to keep my mouth shut?"

"No! Of course not!"

"Why then?"

Thom throws his hands up. "Because I liked you! This isn't some giant conspiracy. I dated you because I liked you. I like you. You found out, and it fucked everything up, but that's not what we meant to happen."

I'm trembling. I'm not sure if it's from rage or sadness. The emotions are too wound up to pick apart. I only feel them as one giant wave, crashing over me, again and again. "I didn't fuck it up by finding out. You fucked it up by doing it." I look over at Mike, furrowing his brow. "Why did you do it?" I ask him.

His face is impassive, except for a quirk of his mouth, a feature I now realize that I hate. "It was a mistake, Annalie. We were drunk. I can admit it. You know we get stupid when we get drunk." Thom is nodding along silently.

We were drunk, we were drunk. I picture the spray paint on our garage door, garishly red, the paint splatter in the corner, like the person who did the spraying pushed too hard on the trigger to start. The animosity behind that trigger. Where does it come from? The alcohol? Is it always buried deep inside and the alcohol lays it bare? Can you really blame the booze?

Mike is still talking, his voice is calm and measured. He sounds logical. Believable. A good guy. The kind of guy the public looks at and thinks, *Don't ruin his life. Don't ruin this scholarship athlete's life with this slur.* ". . . happened to be in the neighborhood . . . wasn't about you."

That part sticks out to me. The rest of it feels like it's on bad audio, because his reasoning is beyond meaningless, and nothing he says can make what he did understandable. "Hold on," I say sharply. "What do you mean it *wasn't about me*? How could it not be about me?"

"We were thinking about Margaret and all her high school shit," he says apologetically. "I know you live there and everything, but you're different."

"How am I different?"

"You don't even look Asian. You know? You don't have to be offended."

People have said that to me over and over again. Mrs. Maples. Bakersfield thinking that I'm white while recognizing Violet as Asian. I think about all the times strangers thought Mama was my babysitter, the way I never spoke up when the kids taunted

Li Bin. I brushed it off—sometimes even hid behind it. Margaret always acted like I couldn't feel her pain.

I've heard it all my life, but Mike saying it now, as though it's a blessing rather than an insult, hurts me deeply. Turns me inside out. It makes me feel invisible under my own skin.

And I don't want that any longer. I want to be seen.

"I am Asian," I say, but he isn't listening or looking at me anymore.

He's simply reciting his entire speech of what he was always planning on saying. "It happened months ago. We just—want you to be rational about this situation. You want to break up with Thom, which is not my business, you know? But don't, like, lash out in the wrong way."

"Don't lash out in the wrong way?"

"Look." He rubs the back of his neck reproachfully. "This is a tough situation. And I don't want to get in the middle of it. But you get me, right? How I might be worried about what you might do? I wouldn't have brought it up otherwise. I know this is between you and Thom."

The ridiculousness of the statement. Between me and Thom. This is clearly an issue for the four of us. And not even just that. It includes Margaret. It includes Mama. It includes Daniel. It includes every Chinese person in this town, maybe even every Asian person. Really, it includes anyone in this town who is perceived to be different from everyone else.

Thom stands off to the side, like he wishes he could be in the periphery of this frame—like he wishes he could be out of this frame entirely.

"You want me not to tell anybody." The words are sour on my tongue.

"I'm not trying to tell you what to do or not do," Mike says. "It's just about not acting irrationally. Not that I'm saying you're irrational. Only that emotions can make us do things we don't mean. Don't do anything you don't mean."

"But you don't want me to tell anybody. About the thing that you did. You and Brayden." My voice rises. Anger thrums inside me with alarming sharpness. It is hard to breathe. There's a stone lodged underneath my ribs, and I can't remove it. "It's a hate crime, you know," I say with a deadly casualness.

Mike's gaze flattens. His lips purse. I notice for the first time how thin his lips are, how easily they rest into a pout when he isn't getting his way. "I don't think you know what you're talking about."

"I think you and I both know what I'm talking about." For the first time, I am afraid of how enraged I am. It's the kind of rage I didn't know I could feel. It's so deep that I fear it will stain me like a tattoo. I begin to understand why Margaret clung on to her quest. I begin to feel a quarter of her unrelenting anger.

I know what it means to hate someone.

"You know us, A," Mike says quietly. "You know what kind of people we are. We're not racist."

Thom said the same thing to me. They're not racist. Nobody claims to be racist these days. I don't know how to distinguish between people who are racist and people who use racial slurs while they're drunk. If there's a difference, then maybe I'm mis-understanding what the word *racist* means.

Even the word *racist* makes me cringe. It's so stark, so accusatory. But Mike and Brayden—they didn't shy away from using the word *Chink*. They sprayed it on my garage door. And I can't even think about using the word *racist*.

How absurd.

"Okay, Mike. Sure." I laugh in sharp splinters. "You tell yourself what you want. And I'll do what I want."

"Let's go, dude. This has nothing to do with the breakup. Just let it be," Thom says to Mike. "Annalie, we can talk about this later. I'm sorry. I didn't mean to make it this big thing."

Mike doesn't move, though. His eyes narrow. "I can't tell you what to do. I'm only telling you how I think this is all going to come off. You breaking up with Thom. You leveling a bunch of accusations right after a breakup. You think people will believe you?"

"I have proof."

"You don't have anything. And my dad's got a million lawyer friends. Everybody in school is going to hate you. And *nobody* is going to believe you. I can promise you that. Your word against mine."

"You're a racist asshole."

"And you're a dumb cunt." I would recoil, except nothing from Mike surprises me anymore. I am cold all over, even though the temperature out here simmers.

"Mike!" Thom shouts.

Mike is glaring at me. He starts moving toward me, out of Thom's reach. I don't know what he is going to do. I back away, but he doesn't slow a beat. I don't know what's going to happen.

Fear floods me. *Get away*, my brain is screaming. But I can't. My body won't process the neuroelectric signals to move.

Somebody appears in the alley behind Mike.

"What's going on?"

Daniel is here. He's looking back and forth between me on one side, and Mike and Thom on the other. Mike's body language, his neck pushing forward aggressively, chin up. I'm sure Daniel sees the expression on my face. I can't hide anything. The worst poker face in the world.

How did he find us?

I see Mike size him up for a moment, all six foot something of Daniel. Mike's mouth is in a snarl, but he doesn't move any closer. His shoulders relax. "Daniel, right?" he says. He's struggling to sound calm. It takes him a few seconds, but he gets there. There isn't a hair out of place on his head. I look borderline hysterical. And then I begin to realize how right Mike is about who people will believe.

"Good to see you, *mate*," he says with a mocking emphasis. "Enjoy the fair, the two of you. Remember what I said, A. Don't think we haven't noticed what's up between you and your new boyfriend here. So convenient that he's here to save the day, huh?"

His implication is clear. I'm a cheating whore who's out to get Thom and his friends.

Daniel and I watch them leave. Thom doesn't look at me, not even once. We stand there until they are out of sight and gone.

"Violet told me to come find you," Daniel says.

I am exhausted. And scared. And furious. And sad. And the

entire color spectrum of feelings in between. I am feeling lost and sorry and betrayed. I hate that Mike and his friends—and yes, Thom—have taken away the safety I had in my home. I always thought I belonged here, but now I'll never stop wondering which people think I don't.

I want to shout at Daniel that I don't need a man to come save me, and he's not my knight in shining armor because I'm a feminist and I don't need one, and I didn't ask for one, and why does he think I want to see him right now anyway?

I want to tell Daniel that I hate him for being here, because there's some fleeting part of me that wished Mike would punch me so I'd have real proof of something, or so I could see if Thom would defend me instead of his racist friend when it really came down to it. Some small part of me still holds out hope that Thom would choose me. Choose to do the right thing, even though it would be hard. But Thom did choose, in the end. He didn't choose me.

More importantly, I didn't choose him.

But I also want to tell Daniel that I'm sorry and that I do like him and that I wish I hadn't wasted my time on Thom, and I wish I could tell him a fraction of the things that are coursing through me. But I don't know what to say, and sometimes when you don't know what to say, it's okay.

Maybe one day we will find the right words, but at the moment, he just stands with me in this alley, shielded from the sun. Dark, but not alone.

Twenty

MARGARET

I'm sitting in the backyard under the shade of Mama's tallest rosebush, reading a book, when Annalie comes running through the back door. Her hair is wild around her face. Her eyes are liquid, as if she's been teary.

I stand up immediately. "What's wrong?" I know she was at the downtown fair and that she had entered the baking contest. "How did the competition go?"

She looks momentarily surprised, and then waves her hand dismissively. "Oh. Yes, that. I won."

"That's great!"

"It's not about the competition." She flushes. "I have to tell you something."

"Annalie," I say slowly, afraid of her expression. "What happened?"

She rocks on the balls of her feet. She hugs herself and blinks.

"Are you okay?"

"I know who spray-painted our house," she whispers. She takes a big breath. "I've known for a long time. I'm sorry."

I don't know what I was expecting, but it isn't that. I don't respond. She makes her way over to where I am and sits on the grass like a supplicant.

"It's someone I know," she says bitterly. "Guys from high school. My boyfriend's friends." She pauses. "Ex-boyfriend, I guess." She lets out a sardonic laugh.

"I'm sorry." She isn't showing any sign of regret, but it must be her first breakup. What a way for it to end. "How did you find out?"

"I knew when I saw their jerseys on the video. And then I asked. I didn't really want to know, but Thom confessed right away that it was his friends. He asked me not to say anything. I told him I wouldn't."

She isn't looking at me.

I close my eyes. I knew it. I knew it wasn't a random stranger.

I thought I would feel a sense of triumph when we finally figured out who did it. It means a path to justice. But I don't feel victorious. It was just a bunch of high school kids, after all. I feel disappointed and vaguely sad that Annalie knows them. Stupid boys who will grow up to be stupid men. A dime a dozen, and I've met boys just like them. The guys who get drunk and make a pass at you, and then toss a racial slur at you for not wanting to sleep with them, because it's the first insult that comes to mind.

"Why are you telling me now?"

She shrugs. "I don't know, I thought you should know. In case you want to turn them in or whatever."

"I don't know them. I can't turn them in. I heard it from you."

I lean over to her. "It's up to you if you want to say something."

She shakes her head. "I thought you'd be upset. I thought you'd be halfway to the police station by now."

"Me too," I say. "But you're right. I barely live here now. This is your house. Your fight. And you said you wouldn't tell."

She snorts. "Well, that part I don't care about anymore. It turns out he was afraid of me breaking up with him because I would tell."

"Wow. What a dick."

"But I kept defending him and hiding the secret until the end. So it's my fault too." Her eyes are wet. She blinks and falls silent for a moment. "It's going to sound pretty vindictive if I bring up the accusation right after the breakup, huh?"

"Maybe. But it's the truth."

"Do you think people will hate me?" she asks timidly, shifting in her spot.

I feel a surge of protective sympathy for her. High school is hard. I forget sometimes because I spent all my time thinking about life after, about getting away. Annalie isn't like that. She has always lived in the present. I weigh my words. "Yes, some people might. If you say something."

She gives me a long stare that's part resentful and part amused. "God, I wish you would just lie sometimes."

"Sorry."

"Hey, one of the guys who did it said something that I can't stop thinking about."

"What did he say?"

"He said that he spray-painted our house because of you, but I shouldn't be mad because I don't even look Asian." The pain shines out from the stiff set of her expression. "It made me think about how you couldn't ever hide from the hate like me. I'm sorry if I ever didn't stand up for you or see things your way. I'm so sorry, Margaret."

I'm shaking my head. "No. Stop. Don't say that. I'm sorry that I ever made you feel like you weren't Asian enough. We are the same, you and I. But please remember that you're allowed to have different opinions than me."

She's crying now, so I do something I can't remember having done in a long time. I grab her and hold her to me as tight as I can. I spent so much of my life pushing her away, but for once, I wish I could keep her here.

Eventually I let go, after Annalie's sniffling quiets and subsides. There seems to be nothing else to say after that. We sit there for a while. I don't know what she will do, but I can guess by her somber expression. Maybe she is imagining her last few days of peace before she blows it up. I think about returning to school soon and leaving her behind.

I am sorry for it. I wish I had come back for a better reason. I wonder if some part of her is enjoying being an only child without me. I was never that great of an older sister.

"You should come visit me in New York," I say, breaking the silence finally. It feels strange to say. I have never invited my sister to come do anything with me, not even to see a movie, just the two of us. Imagine the hours of awkward silence that would fill a multiple-day visit. What would we say to each other? What would we do? I expect her to laugh it off, maybe let me down gently.

Instead, she says, "Really? You'd want me to come?" Her voice ripples with hope.

"Yeah. Of course I would."

"That would be nice," she says shyly. "I'll visit. I promise."

The thing that surprises me the most—the swell of gladness inside me, bubbles in a bottle of sparkling water, a rising sun.

I am fidgeting in my chair as the reporter looks over her notes and the cameraman readies for shooting a short segment on the vandalism at our house. The reporter is from a TV station in Chicago who's come down here. We've cleared out our living room for a ten-minute feature video that'll be posted on the website. We'll also go out in front so they can get shots of the garage door where it all happened.

I am leaving for New York in two weeks. I know who is responsible. But the police don't. Not yet.

The reporter's name is Jenna Miles. Her hair is glossy and blown out. Her lips are swiped with a matte blossom pink.

My hair isn't sitting right today; there's a lopsided kink on one side of my part. I am convinced I have a sty developing on my left eyelid. You can't tell for now, but I can feel it emerging from under my skin.

I'm ready, though. I have planned what I'm going to say. It will be my last interview, and my sister can decide if she wants to do any more follow-up. This summer has felt both like a quick minute and a hundred years. For the first time, I'm a little reluctant about leaving this place.

It's been more than a week since I dropped off zongzi at Rajiv's house. I haven't heard anything at all, and I can't ask anybody at work. I don't text him about it. I'm not begging him to get together with me; he doesn't owe me forgiveness. The point of the apology note was, no strings attached. And there aren't any strings, except for the one from him to my heart. It's just one that I'll have to sever at last before I return to New York. If seven hundred miles doesn't do it, then I don't know what will.

Jenna tucks her hair behind her ear and nods at the cameraman. "Are you ready?"

I twist my fingers in my lap. "As ready as ever."

The cameraman counts us down and starts rolling. Jenna gives the introduction and starts asking me questions. And I start talking.

I tell her about how it feels to be part of a community, only to be rudely told that you are "other" out of nowhere. What it's like for something racist to happen to *you*, only to have to defend whether it's racist *enough* to count, and whether I've considered the feelings of everyone else about my own harm. I talk about how being Asian means that people only like you when you're trying to assimilate, but you're the first to be scapegoated when somebody needs a scapegoat. How easy it is for you to forget for even a moment that you are still not one of them, how easy it can be to turn away from other people of color when it matters. You're standing with a foot inside the door of whiteness, but you'll never step all the way in.

I keep talking and Jenna lets me. I keep going until I hear my phone start vibrating on the table in front of me.

I'm furious with myself for not putting it on silent until I notice the caller on the front.

It's Rajiv.

My mouth snaps shut. My brain is wiped clean. I watch it ring.

"You there?" Jenna asks. "Don't worry, we can edit this out."

My hand shoots out to grab my phone. "I'm sorry," I tell her. "I have to take this." I hit accept and run out of the room while I hear rustling and squawks of protest behind me.

"Hello?" I sound vaguely out of breath, hiding in the bathroom, clutching my phone like it's a lifeline.

"Margaret?" I hear his soft voice on the other end, a little shell-shocked, as if he didn't expect me to pick up.

"It's me. I'm here."

"I don't know why I called." He's choked up. "I, um, I guess I just wanted to talk to somebody and you were still the first person I thought of."

"Hey. Hey. Is everything okay?"

He coughs. "Yeah. It's fine. My mom—she had a seizure, and we're in the hospital, but she's okay now. Just a weird side effect we weren't expecting. She's okay. It was just scary."

"Do you want me to come down there?" I'm ready to jump in my car and leave Jenna in my house.

"No. Of course not. What do you want to do, give her another seizure? After all the family events you blew off, she'll probably think she's in an alternate universe if she sees you at the hospital." He laughs, his voice sounding more stable.

Despite myself, I grin into my phone.

"Thanks for the food, though. It was gone in a day. I should've texted you. Am I interrupting something?"

"No," I say. "Not at all."

"Look, I have to go, but will you meet me at the park in an hour? We're getting discharged soon. I just want to say goodbye. A proper one."

All my hopes, quashed in a devastating moment. Still. I close my eyes. "I'll be there."

Stevenson Park is a sprawling ten and a half acres with a pool, tennis courts, and sand volleyball. Gracious old oak trees with pale warm leaves and dark branches curve over grassy knolls with grills and picnic tables. It smells beautiful—a comfortable loamy smell that reminds me of home.

The park has a play set that is almost always abandoned. It's old and falling apart. A hazard for kids. Particularly because it's made of unfinished wood, gray and splintering. The city has always intended to bulldoze it down and turn it into something colorful, plastic, and less likely to lead to lawsuits, but it keeps not getting around to it.

But now there are big signs at the perimeter of the mulch, letting people know that the playground is scheduled for demolition in several weeks. They are finally doing it. I climb up the metal bar ladder and sit on the edge of the platform, looking out. Waiting.

Rajiv and I used to spend a ton of time here when the weather was good. A Dairy Queen abutting the eastern border made this place perfect. Ice cream at the park. It was a regular date for us the way other people go to dinner and a movie.

We saw this park in all seasons.

I wait past six, which is normal because while I am always punctual, Rajiv is always late. I watch a blue jay bounce around on one of the maples. I try to steady my breathing. I have to allow us to do this with dignity, even though I'm not ready to let him go. I need to at least accomplish that much.

Finally, a figure emerges from a grove of trees. He's walking slowly with his hands in his pockets. I wave self-consciously for a few beats. I don't know if I'm supposed to be happy or sad for this conversation. He stops in front of me. Me with my legs dangling down on the platform, him standing before me—we're at almost exactly eye level. He's frowning.

"Hi," I say. My mouth is dry. "I'm sorry about your mom."

His expression softens. "Thank you. And thanks for picking up. I meant to call you before we both left. I just—that wasn't the moment I thought I'd do it."

"You were going to call?"

"Yeah." He grins. "You thought I was going to ghost you like prom night? One of us is the more mature one in this relationship."

"Very funny."

"I'm also the funnier one."

He makes me laugh, like he always does, so I can't argue with him.

"See?"

I shake my head, smiling. He looks hesitant, then puts his hands on the platform next to mine. I scoot over, and he jumps up and settles down next to me.

"I guess I screwed it all up, huh?" I say lightly, probing for a response, hoping he replies in a different way than I expect.

He glances at me sidelong. "Yeah, I guess so. But to be fair, we should've known. From the horoscopes. We're star-crossed. Always doomed to fail."

He says it as a joke, but it crushes me nonetheless. I won't let it show, though.

"Anyway, you're leaving. I'm going back to school in a couple of weeks. I didn't want to leave it where we left it. You know."

I do know. "It was worse than when we broke up."

"I don't know. It was pretty bad when we broke up. But yeah, I didn't want to leave it at that. We did have over three good years. I assumed we'd probably never talk again, but then you showed up at Fisher, Johnson, and I swear, I thought the universe was punking me in the meanest way possible, but I also thought—" He rubs his forehead. "I thought maybe the universe was trying to do me a favor. There was no way that we would end up back home the same summer—you, especially—and we'd somehow find ourselves working together as interns at the same place. Just no way it could be a meaningless accident of fate."

"You thought we'd get back together?"

"I don't know," he says fervently. "Didn't you?"

It's the first time our eyes make contact while we're sitting next to each other on this platform that's so familiar to us from the past, I wonder if its wood remembers our legs. Rajiv's ink-dark eyes are deep, like the richest cup of black tea. "Yes," I whisper.

"I'm not going to pretend like I never stopped loving you or anything. I did. Stop loving you, I mean. I had a really good freshman year. I made friends with people. I went out with other girls. I thought about you *a lot*, but I wasn't going to pine after you forever. I was fully over you. The kind of over you, where I thought we'd see each other at our high school reunion one day, talk about our spouses and our kids, and be like, 'Wasn't that great?' in a nostalgic, nice way, not in a life-ruining way."

Tears leak out of my eyes and slide silently down my face. I can't wipe them without bringing attention to my pathetic state. I hate crying, and now it seems it's the main thing I can do. As if the first time this summer, I broke some kind of emotional dam, and as a result, my body is making up for my years of forced suppression by releasing unwanted liquids from my face whenever inconvenient.

"But then I saw you on the first day, and it's like I rewound to senior year of high school immediately. The minute I saw you, I wanted you again. And I loved you again so fast, I couldn't remember why we had broken up."

"But then you remembered."

"But then I remembered," he agrees. He isn't looking at me, so if I stay quiet, he probably can't tell that I'm crying.

"I'm sorry," I say, to his face this time. "I didn't mean to come back and ruin your summer."

"You didn't ruin my summer. I just thought we had a chance,

you know? I thought maybe you believed in starting over. We had so much baggage, before."

"There's no such thing as starting over."

He brushes his hair out of his face. "Why couldn't you just talk to me about your mom? You couldn't ever even talk to me about it. I didn't expect you to broker a nuclear arms deal. I didn't expect a miracle with your mom. But instead you pushed me away, and I'm supposed to be the person you can trust above everyone else. We could've been a united front."

He's right, of course. I thought I was protecting him from Mama, and Mama from him. But I was just using Mama's logic and dodging the hard conversations.

I know I can't undo the past, but I do the next best thing. I tell him what Mama really said on prom night.

"She told me to choose," I say. "Between you and her." I draw my knees to my chest like a little girl. "I was afraid of losing her. It was hard. But I was wrong to just drop you like that. Not fair to you or to Mama."

He shakes his head. "I was ready to fight for us," he says. "But you just let me go. The funny thing is, I loved you because you were brilliant and tough and I knew that one day you were probably going to be a senator or something because you set your mind and heart on everything you wanted to do. I loved your ambition and drive. I loved how you never backed down from anything, and I thought that would extend to me too. I believed it, all the way to the end."

"I know. If I could go back in time and do it again, I would've chosen differently. I would've put on my shoes and walked out the door. I would've gone to your house for prom, spent time with your mom. Had dinner. Taken pictures. Tried to make her like me. I would've gone to prom with you. I would've held your hand, brought you home, introduced you to Mama instead of hiding you. I wish I could've."

You can't go back in time, though. You can't just start over. You can only push someone away so many times before they never come back.

"I'm really, really sorry," I say again. "But you don't have to forgive me. I just wanted you to know."

He looks at me with a probing intensity, like he's trying to decide something. I can't read his expression. "Well, thank you for saying that. I wish things could've been different too."

I feel a sliding disappointment that I hide away. This is what I expected, after all.

He taps my shoe with his. "I'm glad we got to have this conversation. I was so mad the morning after that I couldn't handle it. This . . . helps."

"I'm glad."

"And anyway, I thought I'd come out here and give you one final giant emotional dump. You always loved that. Me dumping my feelings while you sat there like the rational one, trying to fix things. At least I got a feelings dump from you this time too."

I laugh and wipe the tears away from my face. "Yes, that's a good way to do a send-off."

The air settles cool on my skin. I am drained, but also, strangely, peaceful. All the tension has leaked out of us, and it's just Rajiv and me, like in the beginning. Next to each other. Feeling our slow breathing sync up. Measuring the final drips of summer before we have to leave this in-between place and go back to our new lives. The late orange sunlight has never been more beautiful in Stevenson Park.

"It's pretty here," I say.

"Yeah, it is."

"This is how I'm going to remember us. The good stuff."

He turns to me. "I keep thinking, when we were dating, that was the good stuff."

"It was nice, huh? Worth it?"

"It was. For instance, I didn't mind it when we'd spend hours at Barnes and Noble, inhaling coffee drinks and doing crosswords at the café, all while we got the stink eye from the staff for being there for five hours at a time every Saturday."

I'm smiling.

"Or when you'd sneak over to my house when my parents were out and fall asleep in my bed while doing homework. You snored."

"Did not!"

"Did too." His hand is creeping close to mine. I pretend not to notice, but I feel the painful germination of hope in me, the sprout cracking through the hard husk of my heart.

"I liked how you would relax with me, even your posture. Your shoulders would slouch when nobody else was around, and I got to see that." His fingertips reach mine.

"I like that you never change in the best ways, but you can still surprise me, even after all this time," he whispers.

I'm silent. Past tense starts to make me spin. Present tense makes me fly.

"I like how you can make me love you in fifteen minutes flat, even when I haven't seen you in three weeks. Even when I haven't seen you in a whole year. I think you could make me love you even after an entire lifetime. I just want you to choose me, okay?"

"Okay."

And now there is no more time, no more space between us. He is reaching over to me, and I'm falling into his arms, his lips on mine, his hands in my hair and on my cheek, his scent overwhelming, and in the brief coherent moment when I can still formulate any thoughts at all, I'm thinking—yes to this, and yes to us, and yes yes yes.

This is the end of our end.

This is the beginning of our beginning.

And this time, we make our own choices.

Twenty-one

ANNALIE

In the end, I go through the pieces one by one.

I make amends with Violet.

We sit under a tree in her backyard to escape the chaos of her house for a minute. "I can't believe you didn't tell me," she says.

"I'm sorry. I should've. I knew that if I saw you, I would tell you. And I couldn't face that yet. The whole thing made me such a bad friend. But I was scared."

"Scared of what?"

"That you would judge me for knowing and not doing anything. Or for dating Thom." I should've known from how I was acting around Violet that something was really wrong with my relationship. If I felt confident in it, I wouldn't have wanted to hide him from my best friend. It seems so clear now.

"Well, I am judging you for that, just to be clear," she says, smirking. "Can't believe you pined after him for so long when he's actually a huge d-bag."

I poke her shoulder.

"I wouldn't judge you for not wanting to report him, though."

"Really?" I ask, raising my eyebrow.

"Okay, maybe a little bit. Just because if you don't say anything, these guys are going to continue living their life with no consequences." She sighs. "That'll probably happen anyway. You have to at least try, though, right?"

"I'm going to."

She perks up. "You are?"

"I have to talk about it with my family, but yeah. I want to." Saying it out loud still freaks me out a little bit. I should get used to it.

"Good for you," Violet says. "I'm glad."

"Will you still be friends with me after everyone turns on me?"

She makes an outraged noise. "I'm your ride or die. Obviously I'll be with you, no matter what. Even if you had decided to do nothing." She grins. "Although, again, I would've secretly judged you a little. Secretly! On the inside. As a friend."

I break out into a smile.

"So you forgive me? I wasn't trying to hide Thom from you because I was ashamed of you. I was ashamed of him."

She gives me a hug. "There's nothing to forgive," she says.

The breeze through the leaves today is cool. It has a kiss of autumn. The light is getting soft. Soon—too soon—we will be going back to school. Margaret will be gone. Daniel will be gone. But I'll always have Violet.

I say goodbye to Daniel.

He leaves early. His parents are going to meet him in Maine for a pre-college vacation.

His grandfather and I see him off at the train station to Chicago for his flight. Bakersfield says he's going to get a coffee while the train is delayed.

This is probably our last chance to be alone. We stand there, two awkward people, not knowing how to say the awkward things. If this were a movie, it would be just him and me, and I'd confess my feelings before he leaves, and we'd kiss at the last moment and swear that we'd make this long-distance work. But it's not a movie. And I don't know what we are.

We should've talked about what we meant to each other, but everything at the fair passed in such a blur, and then—

Well, we ran out of time.

"Have a good trip," I say. "I've heard Maine is beautiful."

"Maybe true," he says. "Funnily enough, I think it's quite nice here too. I've learned to have an open mind. But I feel fairly certain it won't measure up."

"It sounds like my summer project was successful," I joke. "But why the skepticism about Maine?"

His eyes search mine. "Because you won't be there."

I've swallowed a helium balloon.

I memorize the way he looks right now. Slightly messy hair for the early morning train. Long-sleeved stone-colored linen shirt with the top button unbuttoned. The light burn on the bridge of his nose from being out in the midwestern sun for the fair. His square jaw and wide forehead.

"I want—" I start out.

The bell rings, signaling that the train is pulling into the station.

"Time to go," Bakersfield says from behind me. I drop my hand, suspended halfway to his face. Disappointment sinks me. The moment is past.

Daniel takes another helpless look at me. I shake my head ever so slightly. *Don't go*, I want to say. *Stay with me.*

"I'll see you later," he says like a promise as he backs toward the exit. "I will."

He disappears. Leaves me heartsore, a thing I now know to be real.

I tell Mama the truth.

Before Margaret leaves for school again, our small family of three sits around the dinner table so I can tell Mama what I know.

"I'm going to report them to the police," I tell her. The dim circle of light from the overhead fixture envelops us. The mirror across the room shows our reflection. Sitting together like this, our family resemblance is clearer than ever before. Mama and Margaret always looked like a pair, but their face is my face too.

Mama sighs. I wait for her to tell me not to. To reiterate her list of reasons why we should just keep on going, as we always do. Her mantra. I wait for her to be disappointed. But she just says, "Are you sure?" I feel a cracking sliver of bright surprise.

"I'm sure."

Her eyes are scared, darting back and forth between me and my sister. And I'm heating with anger again, feeling protective over her. The sheer unfairness of my mother having to be afraid in her own home. I look toward Margaret, and we understand each other.

"I won't if you don't want me to," I add firmly. Some things are more important.

She puts her hand on mine. "Your decision," she says. "I support you." She switches to Chinese. "My daughters, both grown up. I can't tell you what to do now." Her voice rings with a different kind of pride than I've heard from her before.

"I mean, I'm sure you'll still try," Margaret says dryly.

We laugh together, a sound that ripples through the house. I store away this moment with the three of us. The things I want to keep forever.

I report Mike and Brayden.

Although Margaret offers to come with me, I decide to go by myself. The police station is squat and rectangular, constructed entirely of concrete. Small windows are cut into the facade like peepholes. Even as I'm walking up the steps, the voice in my head says, *You can turn back. Turn back now.*

But I don't.

I push open the heavy glass double doors, and my legs carry me forward. I feel like a third-person passenger in my body, watching myself go through the motions. I wish I could skip to the part where this is over. And then I realize, by telling the police, this will never be over. At least, not for a very long time.

The front desk woman gives me a form to fill out and asks me to wait after I'm done. I sit, like in a doctor's office, nervously tapping my nails against the metal armrests of my chair.

You can still leave, even now.

I see a police officer approach me. I close my eyes. In my dreams, I see the spray paint on our garage. I hear Thom's voice begging me not to tell.

I take a deep breath. And then I start talking.

After that, I go on as best as I can. Whatever that means. Because ultimately, I have to.

School is both better and worse than I imagined.

The prosecutor actually does decide to bring charges: for criminal damage to property as the underlying crime, conspiracy, and a hate crime as a separate charge. If convicted, Mike and Brayden are facing felonies, with fines of up to $25,000, and potentially one to three years in jail. Those guidelines never seem real to me, but the prospect of people I know in real life going up against them make them seem significantly more sobering. I even feel bad about it, which I know is ridiculous, because I'm just reporting—it's not like *I* did the crime. Still, I can't fully separate out the vague feeling of guilt that lingers.

The first couple of days, it's mostly the staring, which I expected. People are terrible at pretending like they're not staring, is the main thing.

Some people do come up to me, people I've never spoken to before, and tell me that they can't believe Mike and Brayden would vandalize our garage like that, and it was definitely racist, and I'm amazing for figuring it out and reporting them.

But it's not as if Mike and Brayden are shunned.

The first time I see the group and they see me, we all freeze.

I steel myself. There's an endless moment where I'm looking at Mike, and his face reddens, and I can see all the furious insults running through his head. But he just narrows his eyes and says something to the group that I don't hear. They all laugh and turn away, even Thom. I don't know if he said something about me or not. It doesn't matter, I suppose. It still stings.

Plenty of people continue to hang out with them, even with the pending charges.

I get the sense, mainly from Violet, that even of the people who believe that Mike and Brayden did what I'm claiming, the consequences for spray-painting a word on someone's property isn't deserving of jail time or a $25,000 fine, or even the stigma of being labeled racist. And some people definitely think, like Mike predicted, that I'm just being vindictive for making such a big deal about it. That I'm just mad because Thom dumped me.

There are days I wake up and think that I did the wrong thing. People whisper about me at lunch. I overheard one girl say to her friend that I was being "overdramatic."

Thom and I cross paths often. He's in my senior AP Calculus class. We mostly avoid eye contact. Usually I grab my things and hightail it out of there when the period ends. Once, I stay behind for a bit to ask the teacher a question. When I'm done, I realize he and I are the last two people in the room packing up.

He seems startled and embarrassed. He has to walk past my desk to get to the door. He approaches in a rush. My heart speeds up, preparing for a confrontation of some sort—an apology? an insult?—but he hustles past me without saying a word.

I'm vaguely disappointed. I thought I would get closure from this incident, but I don't think I ever will.

Sometimes, I imagine a world where the vandalism didn't happen at all, and there was no secret between me and Thom. We start the summer the same way, meeting at the ice cream shop, and Margaret doesn't come home. We're happy. Maybe we keep dating through senior year. I imagine a senior year so much different than the one I'm having. I'm popular, and I get a viral video worthy promposal from Thom. Would we have stayed together?

It's easy to daydream about another outcome. So easy that I can become choked with envy for this other me, the one who got everything I want. But the vision never lasts. I think about how Thom treated me—like an idea of a girlfriend instead of an actual person—how I made myself small for him, and I know better. Thom and I, we were broken from the start.

I wonder what kind of person he will become. Does he have any lingering guilt about how our relationship ended? About who he decided to side with? Will he learn from this? I have so many questions, and no answers.

Maybe one day, he'll realize that he was in the wrong. I hope he does.

All I know is that wherever Thom's story takes him, I won't be a part of it. It's not my responsibility to make him a better man.

I go to school, keep my head down and do my extracurriculars, go home, and hang out with Violet. Rinse and repeat. I try to get through things without thinking about them too hard. Eventually, things die down.

It's hard to believe that at the beginning of the summer, the thing I wanted the most was to be Thom's girlfriend, to finally be part of the in-crowd my senior year.

Now I'm just spending time applying to colleges, and thinking about what I'll be doing next year. I put in some applications in New York and California, but also in-state. I've talked to Rajiv about the University of Illinois, which is big enough that if I went, nobody would know who I am, which means I can be whoever I want to be.

He and Margaret are back together, which makes me happy.

As for me, Daniel's number in my phone sits there unused for weeks. I want to text him and ask how school is going, how his vacation was, but I can't. The longer that time goes on, the more our summer together feels like a faraway memory. Did I imagine my feelings? It's hard to know if my brain is tricking me now that he's been gone for so long.

"Why don't you just text him first?" Violet asks. "What's the big deal? You don't have to declare your love."

"He's probably forgotten all about me."

"And maybe he's staring at his phone just like you, waiting for the other person to go first." She clucks her tongue. "You're both ridiculous. Want me to text him?"

"No!"

"Okay, fine. I offered."

If I could ask his grandfather about how he's doing, I would. But Bakersfield decides to retire for good and do some traveling for the first time in his life. During a rainstorm, I drive by the bakery, its windows dark and empty, with the for-sale sign propped up in one corner. I remember the three of us in the kitchen. The warmth from the oven filling the room.

I think about how nothing lasts.

Then one day, I come home from school and pull out my phone. There it is, my screen lighting up with an unread text from Daniel, as though no time has passed at all.

And there it is, the spark I had buried deep, lighting up too.

The leaves turn, shrivel, and blow away in the wind, leaving our town drab and gray. I somehow make it through almost an entire semester.

Margaret and I don't talk on the phone, but we text each other pretty regularly, and I'm surprised at how much I like it. I book tickets to visit her (and although I can't think about it too much—Daniel too) over winter break. I imagine a future of us doing sister trips, going to Italy and eating gelato. Maybe one day we'll even go back to China, where Mama is from, where we've never gone. There's no one I'd rather go with than her. And I know one day, if I have to fight Mama on becoming a pastry chef—a discussion I'm not ready to have just yet—Margaret will be in my corner.

I skip the homecoming dance, even after weeks of Violet and Abaeze cajoling me to go with them. I'm not in the mood to have people watching me for signs that I'm having a good time, that I'm not psychologically scarred by what happened over the summer.

The thing is, most of the time, I am fine. I am happy.

What I really hate is that no matter how much time passes,

when I think back to this summer, I will always associate it with this. And it feels unfair that I have to carry this burden, when I'm the one who's been wronged.

The memory is a bit like the sun—it illuminates everything for me, but when I look directly at it for too long, it stings. I still feel the bottomless shock of seeing the word for the first time, in writing, and on my house. I will never forget it.

I tell my sister this, because she is the only one who can understand how I feel. "It sucks," she agrees. "Burn it all down."

I don't want to burn it all down. It's a grim responsibility for me, one that I'm committed to seeing through to the end, but I don't get any pleasure from it. I wonder if I will have greater perspective after I leave for college and come back, because I don't know what lesson I was supposed to get from this.

For Margaret, her eyes always on the horizon for bigger and brighter things, I think that she feels a sense of joy at leaving this place behind. Rising above, like a phoenix, or something poetic like that.

For me? I don't know. I can't be unmoored like her, always looking forward. I need an anchor, and I can't just leave this place behind. It's a part of me, part of who I am. Although I'm half-Chinese, China is just an idea to me. When people ask me where I'm from, I'll forever tell them that I'm from here.

Mike and Brayden tried to transform me, turn me into something foreign, and strange, worthy of being singled out and stared at. They tried to transform this place too.

But I know there is more to it than just the ugly thing they did. I have to believe there is more.

As I go around, living my life, the small transactions and moments with my friends, the support of teachers, the smiles of strangers, I tell myself repeatedly that there are good people. People can be bad, but they can be good too. I don't want to forget that. I don't want to look at every person who lives here and fear what they're thinking about me.

The winter sunsets creep in, fanning out oranges and purples into the sky against the endless stripped fields, dotted with tangled golden debris from the fall harvest. At night, the windmills that Daniel and I lay beneath blink red in unison against a night sky so cold that you can feel the depth of space, millions of miles away.

I feel tender as I watch Mama raking up the dead leaves on the rosebushes in the backyard and carefully mulching their bases, planning for spring. The branches are bare and thorny now, but in a few months, they'll be loaded with fat buds splitting with color.

One day, these events will have faded like an old sunburn. When I pack my bags to move away and become the person I'm meant to be, I can choose what matters to me about my home. I can choose the good parts, because to let Mike and the others take that away from me would be a greater victory than they deserve.

I can look out the rearview mirror as the future awaits me, another summer melting into another fall. I can allow myself to think that this place is still beautiful, just before I drive away.

ACKNOWLEDGMENTS

First and foremost, enormous thanks to my agent, Wendi Gu, for your unwavering faith and tireless efforts on this book and my career generally. Your genuine passion for my writing allows me to believe in myself when I'm feeling discouraged. You are an unparalleled professional champion, and I am immensely delighted to have you in my corner. Thank you for taking my messages over email, text, and Instagram simultaneously. Of course, I also cannot forget all the support from the whole agency at Sanford J. Greenburger, especially Stefanie Diaz, my wonderful foreign rights agent.

To my editor, Alessandra Balzer, I am so grateful that you saw something special in my book and wanted to work with me. It has been such a pleasure. I'm continuously amazed by your thoughtful editorial suggestions. Sending my most heartfelt gratitude that you are the person at the helm of bringing this book to market.

A huge thank-you to everyone at Balzer + Bray and HarperCollins who worked on this book to make it beautiful on the inside and out: Jessie Gang, my cover designer, who set forth a stunning vision and brought in Robin Har, whose art I adore, to bring the cover to life; Valerie Shea, Rosanne Lauer, and Alexandra Rakaczki, my copyeditor, proofreader, and production editor, whose detail-oriented notes were amazing and much appreciated; Anna Bernard, Caitlin Johnson, Audrey Diestelkamp, Shannon Cox, Patty Rosati, Katie Dutton, Mimi Rankin, Andrea Pappenheimer, Kerry Moynagh, Kathy Faber, who all worked on getting this book in the hands of readers.

I owe much to Joan Claudine Quiba, Eleanor Glewwe, and Yesha Naik, for approaching the story and characters with great care and providing their insightful thoughts while reading.

I am deeply grateful to my entire UK team at Penguin Random House, especially Asmaa Isse, who originally acquired the book, and Naomi Colthurst, my editor, for developing this book for readers across the pond.

Thanks to my film agent, Mary Pender, for working to push this book into a new medium, something I never even thought about as a meaningful possibility while writing this story.

There are also so many people who have supported me in one way or another throughout my life to make my writing possible over the years, even if I never talked about my writing very much (or at all)! To all my friends and coworkers generally, without you, this book could not exist.

I have to specifically thank Angela Kim and Andy Chon, not only because I promised to, but because you were my first real readers and believers in this book. But also, I especially appreciate the years of daily group chat therapy for my legal career and for my life in general. I don't know how I would p-counsel anything or buy the right baby stroller on my own.

I almost cannot find the right words for Jessica Kokesh, my writing friend of thirteen years and critique partner for the earliest drafts of *This Place Is Still Beautiful*. Our friendship is now old enough to be a YA reader! My life was forever changed when the Percy Jackson fandom brought us together, and I'm incredibly happy our friendship has endured over all these years even though we've never lived remotely near each other. I could not have written this book (or any of the numerous fan fiction pieces and unpublished books over the past decade) without your moral support and editorial suggestions.

Thank you to the Citro and Drago families for welcoming me joyously into the big New York Italian family I have always wanted, and for cheering on my writing career with great enthusiasm.

All of the gratitude, always, to my family in China and the United States. In particular, thanks to my cousin, Jane Liu, for her translation help, my brother, John, for being my best hype man, and my grandfather Zhihou Liu, for my lifetime love of language.

Thank you to my parents for making my life here in the United States possible and choosing all the hardship so that I wouldn't have to. I feel lucky ten times a day.

And finally, to Chris: writing love stories is nothing compared to living a love story with you. Thank you for being my husband.